Maggie's Turn

PAM COVERT

Copyright © 2013 Pam Covert

All rights reserved.

ISBN-10:1492152455
ISBN-13: 978-1492152453

Dedicated to

Lisa Hall

February 11, 1961 – January 5, 2013

You may have left this world but the sound of your laughter

(usually at me and not with me)

will ring in my ears forever.

We helped each other shake the crazy out many times

through the years we spent together raising our kids.

I'm grateful to have had a friend like you for it all, and I appreciate

that you supported my writing even through my Stephen King phase.

(And thanks for volunteering your kids for the fear factor testing)

You will always, always be remembered.

Miss you my friend.

CONTENTS

Acknowledgments	i
Chapter One	1
Chapter Two	35
Chapter Three	75
Chapter Four	99
Chapter Five	131
Chapter Six	151
Chapter Seven	183
Chapter Eight	207
Chapter Nine	233
Chapter Ten	245
Chapter Eleven	269
Chapter Twelve	283

ACKNOWLEDGMENTS

Special thanks to:

Debbie D.
Karissa S.
Laura P.
Tess K.

CHAPTER ONE

"BOYS! Let's go! You cannot miss the bus on the first day of school! Move it!"
Everywhere in the state, maybe even the nation, mothers were sniffling into tissues, blinking back tears, holding their hands over their hearts with their heads tilted as they gazed at their growing children. Maggie felt a prickling of guilt at the edge of her mind. She leaned against the counter, closed her eyes and brought up random memories of the boys as babies, as toddlers, as little boys with their arms around her neck clutching her in a tight bear hug. She opened her eyes. Nope. Nothing.

"D.J.! Derek! Dylan! Daniel! Todd! Move it! Let's go!"

Freedom was just five bologna and cheese sandwiches away, this was the moment all of the other moments had led up to. The baby was going to kindergarten.

Maggie Conners dropped the sandwiches into Ziploc baggies and did a three step happy dance from counter to table where she dropped the baggies into two brown paper bags, one New York Mets lunchbox, one LL Bean lunchbox, and one Superman lunchbox.

"Come on! Now!"

The boys flew into the kitchen sounding like a stampede of wild animals and looking like the aftermath of a collision of back to school clothing commercials.

"Give me that it's mine!"

"I don't want bologna and cheese."

"I'm gonna rock it this year!"

"You are such a loser, you'll only rock it if you never open your mouth again."

"Mommy? I think I have to poop."

The bus!

"No you don't! You can poop at school how great would that be huh?" She grabbed the lunches and handed them out one by one as she herded them toward the front door.

"Love you. Have a good day. It's going to be great you'll see. You'll rock it for sure. Love you." She stood in the doorway kissing heads as they went by and hoped they didn't detect the slight shove as she moved them along.

She watched as they climbed aboard the bus. She raised her hand for the obligatory wave while grinning the proud-of-you-gonna-miss-you smile and then...the grinding of the gears...the forward movement of the bus...and...sweet freedom!

Maggie stepped backwards into the house and closed the door to seven hours of absolute peace and quiet, seven whole hours to do anything or nothing. She twirled to the kitchen, waited for the dizziness to pass, and then poured a cup of coffee. Her first achievement would be to finish an entire cup of coffee uninterrupted and then she would start the process of reconstructing herself.

An involuntary smile stretched across her face, for as long as she could remember she'd anticipated this moment as the defining moment, the moment that divided before and after. That moment was finally here.

Before, she was a young girl with hopes and dreams and a wide open future. At seventeen, a high school senior, a prom queen, a girl with extravagant dreams, Maggie's promising future slammed shut. At eighteen Maggie Kennedy became Maggie Kennedy Conners, wife and mother.

After, at thirty two she didn't expect to pick up where she left off nearly fifteen years ago but she was determined to resurrect a piece of who she used to be.

Maggie put her coffee on the table and sat down. The question was, how?

What could she do with seven hours five days a week? She'd built this moment up to be THE MOMENT in her mind but she hadn't figured out what she would do. A terrifying thought planted itself in her mind. What if there is no Maggie? What if she hadn't emerged in the midst of all those years not because she was too busy taking care of everyone else's needs but because she no longer exists? What if after all those years the person she thought was put on hold was permanently disconnected?

She dug through her memory for an image of herself at seventeen. The image that emerged was of her and her best friend Jillian shopping for prom shoes. She shook it away and tried again. She and Jillian riding their bikes. She closed her eyes and tried again. She and Jillian filling out college applications. She tried to zoom in on herself but her mind refused to isolate the two. When she opened her eyes the image that remained was of two carefree teenagers with an abundance of confidence in who they were and a naive expectation of who they would be. Never in her wildest dreams would she ever have guessed she would wind up a mother of five. And never in her wildest *wildest* dreams would she ever have guessed she would look and act like a mother of five. That's what she would undo first.

Maggie glanced at the clock and was devastated to see that twenty five minutes of her freedom were already gone. She got up and poured her cold coffee down the sink, grabbed one of Dylan's power drinks from the fridge and went upstairs to change for a quick trip to the mall to get what she needed. It was a start. And she had to start somewhere. She would begin by getting back to the 25 pound ago Maggie that she left in high school. If she didn't start somewhere, if she didn't start today she was afraid there never would be a Maggie Conners.

An hour later Maggie sat in the car in the parking lot of a sporting goods store re-reading the string of texts.

Jillian I'm sitting in front of a sporting goods store eating a yogurt parfait.

It's 8:55 in the morning Maggie.

I know, they don't open until 9:00.

Okay, why are you telling me this?

Because it's 8:55 in the morning and I'm sitting in front of a sporting goods store eating a yogurt parfait.

I get it. It's not 10:55 and you're not in front of a mall eating a Big Mac. Something's wrong?

No, something's right. I'm going to start running, get back in shape and all that, that's why I'm here. I need running shoes but here's my problem, their website shows walking shoes and jogging shoes and running shoes.

And?

And I don't know which to get. So what do I get?

Uggs.

Huh?

Maggie? Are you really going to start walking? Jogging? Running? Or is this about something else? Meet me at the diner in Colton at noon, we'll talk.

But I ate a yogurt parfait.

Maggie hit the back button and then the home button and immediately picked up on the irony.

At eleven fifty eight Maggie pulled into the diner's parking lot on Higley Road. On a map Higley Road was actually on the opposite side of the Raquette River but as kids they always referred to Gulf Road as Higley Road. Maybe Higley was more fun to say, who knows, for whatever reason for Maggie and Jillian and many others it would forever be Higley Road. That was the thing about small towns, when you leave you can never go back but when you stay nothing changes no matter how much it changes.

Maggie pulled up to park next to a big black Suburban. Along the lower left portion of the back window was a stick family story…Tall Dad in shorts, Shorter Mom in a dress, Little Boy with baseball bat, Baby Girl with pig tails.

Jillian Francis, her best friend, who moved to New Jersey almost four years ago had, apparently, lost her mind. She was becoming radically suburbanized, in more ways than one. The stick family was just one more sign in a long list of signs that Jillian was disappearing into the abyss of suburb mania. She had to convince her to move back before it was too late.

Maggie opened the diner door which rattled the bell causing every head to turn her way. She saw Jillian immediately, which wasn't difficult as the diner consisted of one open room with less than a dozen tables. But it was quaint, it was cute, the food was great, the prices reasonable and it was a quintessential small town diner which she would take any day over a chain restaurant.

Jillian stood to greet her and they hugged as if they didn't text multiple times every single day.

"You never listen to me do you?"

Maggie followed Jillian's eyes down to her new sneakers. "Nope!" She lifted a foot and held out one New Balance Breast Cancer Awareness Pink Ribbon Stability Running Shoe. "I'm supporting the cause and making a fashion statement! What do you think?"

"I think you left out supportive arch, breathable mesh, dependable traction..."

"Ah yeah, that too. I'm gonna do it you just watch. I started running today as a matter of fact."

"You did not!"

"Well not yet but I'm going to. I'll probably be ready for a 5k in a month."

"You can't use the past tense until it's past. And I'll be back next month, sign us up I'll run with you."

"Whoa whoa, let's not get crazy." Maggie heard a snicker from a table nearby but she couldn't tell which one, in a room that size they were all nearby. They sat down and lowered their voices.

"You look different." Jillian cocked her head, "What's different?"

Other than her new running shoes nothing was different. Her hair was the same color blonde and the same length it had been since she was sixteen. She was still five foot six, she hadn't gotten any taller or shorter and Jillian had seen her many times in the last couple years since she'd gotten wider.

Her Ralph Lauren jeans (her favorites as they hid the extra 25 pounds the best) and her Nantucket T-shirt (a gift from a neighbor who actually took vacations) were both a couple of years old.

"Nothing is different. I look the same as I always do. Why will you be back next month?" Maggie asked. "Not that I'm complaining but what excuse did Louise use this time? Is it Frank or her? I bet it's her isn't it?"

Frank and Louise were Jillian's almost in-laws. Four years ago Peter, their son and Jillian's live in boyfriend, was killed in a car accident just days before Jillian discovered she was pregnant. They pulled her through the most difficult time of her life.

"You know I love them and I owe them everything but I'm telling you Maggie, it's getting ridiculous. She is constantly coming up with some pathetic excuse to get us to come home. First she told me she needed help rotating the dishes in the cupboards which apparently she does every fall. I swear she's not quite right." Jillian pointed at her head. "Anyway I didn't offer to come help so then she blurted out that Frank was having surgery on his corns and she needs me to help *tend* to him."

Maggie burst out laughing. "Come on! You have to drive from New Jersey to Potsdam to *tend* to Frank's corns?!"

Jillian glared at her over the top of her menu.

"Jillian, come on that's crazy. She's taking advantage of you."

"Well what am I supposed to do? They're Pete's Grandparents. They have no one else. You want to do it?"

"Whoa whoa whoa." Maggie pulled her menu up and hid behind it.

Maggie's right shoulder began to itch and, speaking of not

quite right, she imagined a little angel sitting on it whispering 'help Frank and Louise…do the right thing'. But she wasn't going to do the right thing. She brushed her shoulder off. She was just today getting some freedom of her own and she wasn't about to start raising two seniors citizens. She should. She and Jillian were more like sisters than best friends. They lived each other's lives as if what was happening to one was happening to the other. Maggie was even at least partially responsible for Jillian's marriage to her husband George who she disliked more than she liked. She felt Jillian's burden of having to travel back and forth from New Jersey with a three year old and a 9 months old. Truth be told, she even loved Frank and Louise nearly as much as Jillian did. But she wasn't going to do it. She brushed at her shoulder again and was grateful to see the waitress heading toward their table.

Jillian ordered a salad, hold the cheese and croutons, dressing on the side.

Maggie rolled her eyes. "So Hoboken." She ordered a bacon blue cheeseburger with fries.

"What about the yogurt?"

"I know! Who eats that stuff anyway? You know they try to make it look like ice cream, you know that right? I don't care what fruit or nut or candy you put on it, it's still yogurt. That's my biggest regret of the day so far. I could have had an Egg McMuffin."

Jillian lowered her voice to a whisper. "That's so sad."

"I know!" Maggie clapped her hands together. "You can't make yogurt into ice cream. Jillian you used to be the biggest junk food junkie I knew. Come back. You have to die of something. Eat a cheeseburger!"

"I mean it's so sad you measure your days in regrets."

Maggie visibly shrunk into her seat. "Way to stick a pin in

the balloon."

"Sorry." Jillian took a sip of her water.

"Forgiven. So," Maggie sat back up, "since we're already there I guess we might as well get it over with. Fix me. I need help. Here's the thing, I don't want to just be a Mom anymore, I'm finally getting time to do something I want to do but, I don't know what I want to do. I've already lost almost fifteen years. I don't want to end up being eighty and still not know what to do. I don't know what to do. So what do I do?"

"What do you want to do?"

"I don't know!" Maggie put her elbows on the table and cupped her face in her hands. "Were you not listening?!"

"Okay, okay, calm down. We'll figure it out, but you have to realize everything is different now Maggie, you're not the same person you were. You're not seventeen with a wide open future in front of you. You're a wife and mother."

"So what are you saying? I should still spend my seven hours a day wearing an apron?"

"You wear an apron?"

"Are you going to help me or not?"

"I'm trying but it doesn't help when you throw images out there like that."

"Focus. I don't wear an apron, it's a figure of speech."

"No it's not."

"Jillian!"

"Okay, okay. I guess start by thinking about what you want to do. Do you want to work? Do you want hobbies? Do you want to belong to something, maybe an organization or be on a committee?"

"Hobbies? A committee? You're not helping. You want me to start knitting and purling between taking the minutes at the Rod and Gun Club meetings? That's not helpful." Maggie scowled at Jillian. "That's actually hurtful. I thought you were my friend."

"I meant more like running, or going to the gym, or photography, but if knitting is your thing..."

Maggie thought for a minute. "I've already started running." She lifted one new sneaker as if that proved it. "But I want to do something that will feel like I've actually done something. I want an accomplishment. I don't want to just run for fun, which is kind of an oxymoron isn't it?"

"So train and run a 5k. You used to be really athletic, it probably wouldn't be that hard for you."

"That was a million years ago." Maggie sighed, "I could do anything then, remember how I used to want to be in the financial world? I still think if D.J. didn't come along I would be on Wall Street right now. How do I get from a memory that doesn't exist to a new memory that also doesn't exist?"

"I remember." Maggie always wanted to be a career woman even way back when they were playing with Barbie's. "Remember our first day of kindergarten? All the girls wore shiny black patent leathers and had a character backpack and you wore high heels and had a briefcase!"

Maggie laughed. "I wish I had a daughter, at least then I'd have someone to live vicariously through since my chance is gone."

"Why is your chance gone? It's not like you're in the nursing home yet. Maybe you should sign up for some classes at the college. You could start with one class just to get back in the swing of things."

"By the time I finished I'd be in the nursing home."

"That's just an excuse. Maybe you won't run the financial world but you can still have a career."

Maggie sighed heavily. "Doubtful. I'm still married to the

man that thinks women should stay home, barefoot and pregnant."

Jillian laughed. "He's not that bad! At least when he's not drinking."

Maggie shrugged. "Okay. Hobby. 5k. College. Any other ideas?"

"Frank. Louise. Corns."

Maggie smiled at her and shook her head. "Not happening. You know you have to move back Jillian. First, Hoboken is so wrong for you. Second, Frank and Louise need you. Third, I need you. Leave George and come home to us. Jillian, seriously, think about Frank's corns."

Jillian looked at her watch. "Speaking of, eat faster, I need to go soon, I don't want Frank and Louise to think I'm taking advantage of their babysitting services."

"Real food takes longer to eat than rabbit food and Frank and Louise would gladly take custody of them in a heartbeat. So what about moving back? Are you still thinking about it?"

Jillian ran her hands through her curly black hair. It wasn't as black or as curly as it used to be thanks to two hundred dollar New York City beauty salons appointments but Maggie had gotten used to it. Just like she'd gotten used to Jillian in designer clothes and make up and heels, all the things Maggie always loved and Jillian always mocked.

"Tell me you're still thinking about it." Maggie begged.

"We're still thinking about it. George even talked to someone who said all he had to do was to put a proposal in front of the board and if they approve it he could work from home as long as he went back for certain meetings and things. He said there are a few people that already do that, one lives in Pennsylvania and one lives in Connecticut. I think he said there were a few others too."

"So why hasn't he done it?! Jillian! Come home!"

Jillian smiled.

Maggie sat up straight and grinned from ear to ear. "He did it? He did it? You're coming home?!"

Jillian held her hand up. "Not yet. But he is putting a proposal together." She smiled.

"Yes! I knew it! I knew I loved that man!"

"Loved him? You never even liked him!"

"But I will. I will love him if he goes through with it!"

"Well then you better start loving him because he's going through with it. We're moving back! Not yet, but hopefully soon!"

Hopefully soon. It was in the forefront of Maggie's mind all afternoon, if Jillian moved back she felt that her derailed life would automatically click on track and move in a direction she wanted it to. She started a fresh pot of coffee and sat at the kitchen table while it brewed. It was one thirty, she had exactly two hours until the boys came traipsing in from their first day of school. She wondered how Todd and D.J. were doing. They were the two she worried about the most, the oldest and the youngest. Of the two, she probably worried most about D.J.

D.J. was at such a crucial age and it wasn't going well. He had left the boy he was behind but hadn't yet discovered the man he would be. He had always been determined and strong willed which made him a little difficult but the year he turned thirteen he became in touch with his inner 'Goth'. It had gone straight downhill ever since. He would be fifteen in three weeks. She had hoped he would be out of it by now. Dark was the only word that described him. He was withdrawn and quiet and angry most of the time. He wore a black hooded sweatshirt every single day, the hood always up and shrouding his face. She never found any sign of drug use but her fear was that either he hid it extremely well or it was the next obstacle right around the corner. She and various school personnel were on a first name basis due to D.J.'s behavior issues. She hoped and prayed that this year would be different.

Dylan was so wrapped up in athletics that he kept himself on the right track. Not sports, he hated organized sports, but athletics. He constantly worked out with weights and ran and always had a football or baseball or some sports item in his possession, but he adamantly refused to join any team. Different coaches had approached him and even gone as far as to call her and ask her to encourage him to join a team but Dylan refused. He played every sport there was outside of school with his friends and was constantly pushing himself to do better, be better, beat his last accomplishment, but participating on a team sports was not an option as far as he was concerned. She had to respect his determination, if he was able to be so true to himself at thirteen she had no doubt he always would be.

Derek kept himself pretty much in line with his natural inquisitiveness. That kid spent every waking moment taking something apart to find out how it worked. There were boxes in the basement to prove it, putting things back together was not part of his psychological need. Take it apart, figure it out, move on to the next thing. Everyone in the family had, at some point or other, lost a valued possession to Derek's inquisitiveness. And they'd all learned a couple of lessons, if you want it to remain in one piece…hide it, and if it smells funny or starts smoking…run. Which was the reason Derek had a room to himself while the older two and the younger two shared. No one wanted to share a room with the Mad Scientist.

Daniel and Todd were well suited as roommates, even though they were almost four years apart. She initially thought putting an eight year old and a four year old together was a recipe for disaster but it actually worked perfectly. Daniel was sweet and considerate and the only one that possessed the quality of compassion. He liked the role of being Todd's guardian angel and Todd, being the baby, loved that at least one of his older brothers paid attention to him.

Maggie poured a cup of the fresh brewed coffee. The school hadn't called and no news was good news. The thought to start a load of laundry prickled at the corner of her mind but she ignored it, it was still *her* time.

On the way home from the diner earlier she stopped and bought a newspaper at the corner Mini Mart. Hobby? Career? College? She browsed the paper looking for something to pop out at her but nothing did. There was no advertisement stating, 'looking for housewife with sudden hours of availability to make lots of money and achieve instant gratification, no experience, education or skills needed'.

She started again. This time through she tried to widen her scope and scanned for not just jobs but clubs, meetings, and groups but by the time she was on the last page she still had no idea what there was, only what there wasn't. There was no place for Maggie Conners outside of this house. She had no particular skills, no particular talents, and no particular interests. The only thing she did have was one more hour of freedom. She shuffled the papers together and whisked them into a haphazard pile and threw them in the garbage. A load of laundry and a dust cloth filled the remainder of Maggie's first day of freedom.

At three thirty two when the boys came through the door they were a mix of adrenalin and exhaustion. Dinner was a comic display of bursts of conversation followed by long spaces of silence. Todd fell asleep on the couch before she even finished the dinner dishes and the other boys retreated to their rooms with the exception of Dylan who went to the basement for a weight lifting session. Donnie was in his recliner with the remote in his hand surfing from station to station. Normally she would have been grateful for the unusually quiet evening but tonight it felt like it was mocking her.

Today hadn't gone at all like she'd expected even though she didn't know what she'd expected, she just knew it didn't go that way. She'd even already put her sneakers back in the shoebox they came in. She folded herself onto the couch in the little space Todd wasn't sprawled across. For lack of anything else to do she watched Donnie flipping stations.

For some unknown and annoying reason he refused to use the guide channel and instead hit the up arrow pausing for a few seconds at each channel. Every now and then he would pause long enough that she would just begin to get interested in the show and then he'd hit the up button again. In twenty minutes they watched specs of seventeen different channels. On the eighteenth channel, The Outdoor Channel, he put the remote down. She would never understand what it was about camouflage that grabbed a man's attention.

"Donnie? Are you happy?" She had no idea why that question popped out then and there but it was irrelevant anyway, he didn't answer, he grunted.

"Donnie?"

"What?" He picked up the remote and hit the volume. Up.

"Jillian and George might move back."

"Mm."

"I'm thinking that now that the boys are all in school I might," she shrugged like the idea was just occurring to her, not that he was watching, "I don't know maybe get a job or something."

"You are not getting a job." He shook his head back and forth. Like his words weren't clear enough?

"Not? Or can't?"

"You can't so you're not."

"Why not? Maybe I could find something while the boys are in school, like part-time, like from nine to three or something."

"No."

"Can you look at me please? Why not?"

He made a big effort of turning toward her. "Cause I said so."

How many times had she said that to the boys over the years? That sentence belonged in a parent repertoire not a spouse's repertoire. "Donnie I'm your wife not your kid. You don't dictate to me what I can and cannot do. I'm telling you so we can discuss it, you know, like grownups."

"Maggie you're not getting a job. There's nothing to discuss. I make enough money. Your place is here. I don't get it, you should be happy that you don't have to work. Just drop it." He turned back toward the television and hit the volume again. Up.

Maggie opened her mouth but what was the point? He was right, he didn't get it, and he wouldn't get it. Donnie was Donnie and he had long ago clamped and cut his umbilical cord to reality. Donnie lived in Donnie's world. He'd been an on again off again alcoholic for years. According to what she'd read there was no such thing as an on again off again alcoholic but she begged to differ. Donnie was capable of going for months drinking on a daily basis, often heavily, but then he would stop and the Donnie she originally fell in love with would emerge. They would get along okay for months and then the drinking would start again. Either way, drinking or not drinking, he thought life was always going exactly as it should. Donnie didn't live according to circumstances, he lived and the circumstances gelled outside of his existence.

There was no sense trying to talk to him. The end result would be that she would get angry and frustrated, things would be said that couldn't be taken back and at the end of it all she would lie awake all night feeling miserable and he would forget the entire thing and sleep like a baby. Some part of it would embed itself in her brain and remain there forever festering and oozing and he would walk away unscathed. It wasn't worth it.

Other women might not put up with it but she balanced the good with the bad and justified the relationship. He did work and support them sufficiently, he never laid a hand on any of them, and when he was not drinking he was usually kind and compassionate and funny. When he was drinking a little creative thinking helped. She couldn't count the number of times she used his alcohol induced lack of memory to alter reality. She ended up with a brand new state of the art washer and dryer set after convincing him he had agreed to it when he was so drunk he couldn't even say washer and dryer. It wasn't the healthiest of relationships but it was her relationship and it was healthy enough. You make the best of a situation and it isn't as bad as it might otherwise seem.

It didn't do any good arguing about getting a job anyway when the newspapers clearly proved there was nothing she was qualified to do.

She picked Todd up and carried him to his room, he was still sound asleep and at this point it was a given he would sleep straight through till morning. Daniel was lying on his bed reading and she slinked in next to him. "Whatcha reading?" He showed her the cover of a Goosebumps book and curled in tighter to her before he went back to reading. She laid next to him for a few minutes just taking in his natural peace and tranquility. This was a habit she'd developed with him way back when he was just a baby. They shared many silent moments together. He was her stabilizer and she hoped he was getting something equally valuable from it too.

After a few minutes she left the room, feeling calmer. She walked by Derek's room, the door was closed but there was no smell or smoke so she moved on to the older boy's room. Their door was closed too and she stood outside it a moment deciding if she should try to talk to D.J. The very thought exhausted her, talking to D.J. would annihilate the calmness she had just stolen from Daniel. She walked past and went to her own room, opened the shoebox and took out her new running shoes.

Dylan was still in the basement lifting weights. He threw a questioning glance her way as she stepped into his space but he didn't stop or speak.

"Dylan?"

He replaced the weights, "What?"

"Will you show me something?"

"What?"

"How to lift weights?"

He looked at her like she had told him she had fourteen toes.

"Say again?"

"Show me how to lift weights. Please? I have new shoes."

He looked down at her feet. "You don't lift weights with your feet."

She fake smiled at him. "Funny guy. Seriously Dylan, I want to learn. I want to get back in shape. I ate yogurt for breakfast."

He sat down on a weight bench and stared at her. She waited him out.

"Is this one of those mid life things?"

"What do you know about mid life things? Are you going to help me or not? And before you answer remember that I own these weights and if I decided to take them to the donation center tomorrow morning I could do that."

"You'd have to be able to lift them."

"No, I just have to be able to lift my phone, they'll come get them."

"Fine."

But it wasn't fine. How did she not know Dylan was such a monster? Her legs ached and she could barely raise her arms by the time she finally called it quits. Ten minutes later.

"Mom?!" Dylan laughed, "Don't quit! You just started! No pain no gain."

"Forget it! You know what makes more sense than no pain no gain? No pain no pain." She pointed to her shoes, "I'll stick to jogging."

"You jog?"

"Not yet, but starting tomorrow yes I jog."

She could still hear him laughing as she shut the basement door.

The second day of school started much the same as the first with one exception, muscles she didn't even know she had screamed in pain as she tried to conduct even the simplest tasks. Dylan was the first to join her in the kitchen and from the look on his face she suspected he knew exactly what he was doing in those ten minutes to create the most lingering pain and secure the basement all to himself. She didn't have a chance to call him on it though because the rest of the boys followed almost immediately and truth be told, she had no intention of ever stepping foot near those weights again.

Once the lunches were made and the whirlwind of chaos became the bus driver's problem Maggie poured a cup of coffee and sat on the couch watching the news. Maybe other people's lives were filled with careers and unending efforts to improve themselves but maybe hers was meant to be unveiled via a string of Today shows. She could live with that.

She was barely through the first half of the show when her phone dinged and Jillian's name and an incoming text message scrolled across the face of her cell phone. It surprised her how quickly and effortlessly she could have fallen into an abyss of nothingness and how instantaneous one simple communication with the outside world woke her out of that abyss. She felt like she had been sleep walking and the ding of the phone brought her back to the waking world.

She picked up the phone and opened the text.

Well???

Her thumbs did a speedy dance across the keyboard. As she typed it occurred to her what great shape her thumbs were in.

Well what???
Did you run?

Did she run? Of everything they talked about *that* was what she took away from the conversation?

Just getting ready now.
Nice! Let me know how it goes. Text me when you're done.

Shit. Note to self, never tell anyone your plans, accountability is bad.

She turned the television off and went upstairs to get ready for her first run. She took five steps into her bedroom and stopped. Should she shower first? In case she ran into someone she knew? Should she wait until after when she would be gross and sweaty? But what if she waited and she did run into someone she knew? What if she fell down and broke an ankle and had to be taken to the emergency room by ambulance with yesterday's underwear and this morning's bed head? Should she shower before *and* after?

She showered. She did her hair and dressed in her new pink sweat pants and t-shirt and put on her new pink running shoes. She looked in the mirror and admired herself. She looked like a runner, well, a runner who hadn't quite met her ideal weight goal yet.

She went downstairs inspired by her new look and ready to hit the road. She made it as far as the kitchen and stopped. Should she carry a bottle of water with her? Where would she carry it? Should she stretch? Should she stretch inside or outside? Should she take her phone with her? Where would she carry it? What about music? Should she listen to music while she ran?

She stuck her phone in her sock and passed on the water, the music and the stretching. She stepped outside and stopped. Should she walk first to warm up? Should she start right off jogging before she was too worn out? Should she run on the road or on the side of the road? Should she start timing herself now or wait until she was out of the driveway and at the road? She pulled out her cell and texted Jillian.

Jogging is a lot harder than I thought it would be.

She waited a minute but there was no response so she put

the phone back in her sock and walked to the edge of the road. Okay. Ready. Maybe Jillian responded by now. She leaned over and pulled her cell out again, no response. She glanced at the time, put it back in her sock, made a mental note to buy new jogging pants with pockets and began jogging. She instantly felt a wave of satisfaction soar through her and even though her muscles already ached from last night she felt like she was on top of the world. It was amazing. She was actually doing something for herself and it felt so good. Until it didn't. About forty steps later.

She was huffing and puffing and her calves were screaming in pain. She slowed to a walk and even that didn't help. She stopped and bent over until she caught her breath and felt like she wasn't going to die right then and there. How did she let herself get so out of shape? She used to be so athletic back when she was in school, she played all the sports, basketball, volleyball, soccer, softball, cheerleading, and she was good too. How did this happen?

She decided to push on. She walked another forty steps but her calves screamed and her toes pinched in the stupid new shoes. She sat down on the side of the road and untied her shoes, took them off one by one and threw them as hard as she could into the woods. She walked home, slowly, sock footed.

She took another shower and did her hair again then she got back in bed and indulged in feeling sorry for herself. She thought about where her life went off track. It was easy to pinpoint the exact moment. She was a senior in high school, on top of the world, had everything going for her. She was a good student, not great but good, she was pretty, popular, won all kinds of sports awards, and then she began dating Donnie and on February sixteenth she took a pregnancy test. That was the day her life went off track.

The rest of her senior year was a mess. To Donnie's credit he was incredibly supportive. He stood by her side from the moment she told him. Together they told her parents, and then they told his parents. They vowed to finish high school and they began planning a future with the same enthusiasm as if they had wanted it this way. She missed a lot of school but Donnie and Jillian pulled her through. They brought her homework to her and more often than not Donnie did it for her. When she did attend school the two of them made certain that no one made her feel uncomfortable and if they did, they never did it again. They graduated and Donnie and Maggie moved into Donnie's parent's basement and he got a job in construction. D.J. was born and barely a year later Dylan was born. By the time Derek was born they had saved some money and Donnie's parents helped them with the down payment on the house they still lived in on Pleasant Street. All in all she supposed it wasn't a terrible life. But it wasn't the life she'd imagined.

And now here she was, her first opportunity to reclaim the life she'd imagined and she was failing miserably. It would be so easy to fall into a pattern of nothing. She could watch the Today show and drink coffee and fill the rest of the day with laundry and cleaning and all of the household responsibilities and let one day slide into the next. For some people that was enough, and it wasn't such a bad thing really. But for Maggie it would never be enough.

She didn't regret her life, on some levels she even liked her life, love might have been a bit of a strong description but she knew if she had to do it all over again she probably wouldn't change a thing. For reasons she couldn't pinpoint she loved Donnie and although he and the boys could drive her absolutely insane at times she couldn't imagine a life without any one of them. She didn't regret the past but she knew she would regret the future if she let it attach to the past without change.

And that change was a career.

When it came right down to it *that* was what her life was leading up to. She jumped out of bed. The muscles in her body and Donnie's voice in her head screamed at her. The muscles were an easy fix, that's why pain medication was invented. But what would fix the sound of Donnie's screaming voice in her head? She sat on the side of the bed and played out scenario after scenario but no matter what spin she put on it it kept coming back to the same ending. He would flip out. So be it. She walked gingerly down the stairs and grabbed her purse and keys and bolted out the door to begin a day of job hunting.

She drove to the Mini Mart, bought a newspaper and a bag of miniature Snickers and took it to her minivan. In a world so bent on extravagance there seemed to be an awful lot of mini in her life.

She opened the newspaper and turned to the Help Wanted ads. She started with the full time ads and then scoured the part time ads. They were the same types of jobs that were in the paper yesterday. She glanced through them again. They were the same jobs that were in the paper yesterday. She turned back to the front and checked the date. It was yesterday's paper.

She opened the bag of Snickers and thought about what to do. She considered going back in and asking for an application but after four Snickers she decided she would keep the Mini Mart as a last resort. She drove north on Route 56 to the furthest end of Potsdam and began working her way back through town. She stopped at every place of business she could see herself working at. She filled out application after application. Then she drove to the furthest end of Canton on Route 68 and worked her way back to Colton doing the same thing.

By the time she returned home she had completed and turned in fourteen applications, had seven more applications on the passenger seat of her car and one actual appointment for 10:00 tomorrow when the owner would be back in town. She was exhausted. Work couldn't be any more tiring than finding work. She searched for her phone from the bottom of the pile of applications on the passenger seat. There were four texts from Jillian.

Sorry, was out job hunting.
Job hunting?? How did it go?
Not sure, one interview tomorrow.
Good for you! Where?
Not telling.
Come on!
Tell you tomorrow if it goes well!
Fine! Did you jog?
Kind of. You on your way back to NJ?
Kind of? Yes, heading back.
Are you texting and driving?
Maybe.
Stop! Goodbye.

For one of the smartest people she knew Jillian was also one of the most spontaneous people she knew, which often made her not so smart. Since Pete was born, or maybe it was George with his annoying compulsion for rules and neatness and organization, Jillian had lost a lot of her old traits, including spontaneity. Still, some habits were hard to break and the old spontaneous not so smart Jillian seeped through now and then. As dangerous as texting and driving were and as much as she didn't want Jillian doing something that stupid she loved when she caught traces of the old Jillian. She would never get used to Jillian the 'yuppie'. It was one of the reasons she wanted her to move back home to Colton, if she didn't catch it soon Hoboken would be a syndrome rather than a place.

Maggie took the applications in the house and hid them and then changed into sweats and took advantage of the last few minutes of freedom to sit at the kitchen table and sip a cup of coffee. Now that it was done she was already beginning to second guess herself. She tried not to think about the consequences if today's efforts miraculously resulted in a job. She just sat, sipped and stared.

The thought of what would happen if she did get a job was replaced with the much less lofty thought that for as much time as she spent in her kitchen it should have been embedded in her memory detail for detail, but it wasn't. She recognized every single detail but had she ever really *looked* at her kitchen like this before? The little Maytag emblem on her fridge, would she have known her fridge was a Maytag if someone had asked? Fourteen cabinet doors, did she know she had fourteen cabinets in her kitchen? How many times had she seen, used and cleaned them and yet never *really* looked at them?

Was it possible that life was like that? Was it possible that details about her very own life were overlooked in the day to day chaos? Certainly Donnie and the boys failed to see the details of her life but was she overlooking them herself?

The boys trampled into the house vaporizing her thoughts along with the peace and quiet. She watched dumbfounded as they pushed and shoved and grabbed boxes and bags and poured drinks. She made a mental note to hit the grocery store tomorrow. The boys ate like horses and yet they were all thin, another reason they annoyed her. She watched as they tripped over each other but not a single one of them acknowledged that they saw her sitting there.

She was invisible.

This is my life, she thought, I'm the detail no one notices. Her eyes moistened and she blinked back the threat of tears. That's really what it was all about. That's all she ever wanted. It's even what her whole career drive had always been about. She just wanted to be noticed.

Out of the corner of her eye she saw Dylan shoved Derek. Derek's orange juice spilled over the rim of the glass and a circle of juice splattered to the floor. He turned and tried to kick Dylan but Dylan was already out of reach and left the kitchen without even knowing he was being assaulted.

"Mom! Didn't you see that?! Do something!" Derek glared at her.

As a mother this was one of those moments where there was a right thing to do and a wrong thing to do. She could do the right thing and call Dylan back and make him apologize to Derek and clean it up. Or she could do the wrong thing and make Derek clean it up. Or she could take the third choice, the easy way out, she could clean it herself. "See what?"

"Mom! How could you not see that? *You're sitting right there!*"

How nice of you to notice.

"See what Derek?"

He didn't bother answering, or cleaning the spill. She got up and cleaned it. She could have sat back down when she was done but she had responsibilities to take care of. No one would notice her taking care of them but everyone would notice if she didn't. Between breaking up arguments and sorting school papers and supervising homework and eyeing D.J. the few times he graced them with a fleeting appearance, she didn't have a chance to think again.

Donnie walked in at five thirty, saw dinner just starting to be prepared, turned and went straight to the living room. In about five seconds Todd would come into the kitchen crying because Donnie changed the channel and he didn't get to finish his cartoon. Life was so predictable. She waited.

No crying. No Todd. Curiosity got the best of her, she put the potato peeler down and stepped to the doorway. Todd was sitting on Donnie's lap. They were watching cartoons together. Huh.

She couldn't remember the last time she saw Todd sitting on Donnie's lap. He would be too old to do that soon, there would be no more little boys to sit on anyone's lap. Her mood softened and she couldn't look away. She stood in the doorway staring. It was so rare these days for Donnie to put someone else first.

She was still watching them when D.J. tromped down the stairs and stood next to Donnie.

"Dad? I need twenty bucks."

Donnie looked up at D.J. in his black cargo's and his black t-shirt and his black sweatshirt with the hood shrouding his face.

"For what?"

"Some school thing."

"What school thing?"

"I don't know. They just said we needed twenty bucks."

Maggie would never have handed D.J. twenty dollars without a better explanation than that but she waited to see what Donnie would do. She already knew what she would say but for once he hadn't come to her so she decided to watch and see how it played out.

"Tell you what," Donnie scooted Todd to the side and pulled his wallet out of his back pocket and placed a twenty on the end table next to the couch, "Sit down and watch cartoons with us until dinner is ready and then you can have it."

What?

"What?! That's stupid."

Donnie reached to take the twenty back.

"Okay. It's stupid but whatever."

Donnie pulled his hand back and D.J. plopped in the recliner. She couldn't see the expression on D.J.'s face but she imagined it was equivalent to the expression of a fence post. Donnie, on the other hand, was still smirking when she turned and went back to fixing dinner.

Maggie shook her head and smiled. "What up with dat?" She was still trying to figure it out when dinner was ready and she called everyone to the kitchen. Instantly everything and everyone went back to normal. Everyone, except D.J., talked at once and no one, including D.J., listened. In a quarter of the time it took to prepare dinner it was either eaten or spilled, and then it was over and she was standing alone at the kitchen counter loading the dishwasher.

She made her usual rounds checking that the three youngest were finished with homework, had their clothes ready for the next day and that their backpacks were cleaned out and repacked. She checked to make sure Derek was not doing anything that would put the family in danger, then she went to the basement. Dylan was lifting weights as usual. She sat on one of the weight benches and watched him.

"What?" He asked after a couple minutes, "You back for more?"

"Not tonight. You want to make ten dollars?"

He stopped lifting and put the weight back in its holder, "How?"

"It's top secret." She looked behind her and then back at him.

"So top secret you can't tell me?"

"Do you want ten bucks or not?"

"Yeah."

"Okay, I need you to go outside, walk to the end of the driveway, turn left, take eighty steps, turn left again and then walk straight in the woods until you find my sneakers. Bring them back to me and I'll give you ten dollars."

His mouth moved like he was going to say something but he just started laughing.

"Oh, and you can't tell anyone, just say you're going for a walk and put the sneakers in the garage before you come back in."

He laughed harder.

"Well? Will you?"

"Twenty."

"No! That's robbery!"

He shrugged and reached for the weight.

"Fine!"

On Friday, the third day of school, the last day of the first week of school, life had already formed into a routine. Donnie was up and left for work before anyone else was awake. Maggie woke at six and then made her first round trying to wake the boys. She went downstairs, started a pot of coffee, put breakfast foods out on the table and went back upstairs for her second round at trying to wake the boys. She went back downstairs, fixed lunches, hollered to the boys and then stood back holding a cup of coffee securely with both hands. The boys barged into the kitchen and consumed a full box of cereal, a quart of milk, a full bottle of orange juice and a bowl of fruit. The next couple of minutes were a visual blur while the boys grabbed lunch boxes and backpacks and pushed and shoved and ran outside to the bus.

The last two days had been practice. They had reached the perfected choreographed chaos that would occur every day for the rest of the school year. Even though she recognized that, Maggie still felt that today was unique. With any luck today would be the day that divided Before and After.

Her interview was at ten o'clock. It would only take her ten minutes to get from Colton to Potsdam but she began getting ready as soon as the boys were on the bus. By nine o'clock she was wishing she had lingered over coffee longer and avoided the nerve wracking space of time between being ready and time to go.

She had never been to an interview before and had no idea what to expect. She turned the computer on and typed 'what to expect at an interview' in the search engine, picked the link 'ten questions to expect at an interview' and began reading. It scared her to death. 'Why are you a good match for this job?' 'What are your greatest strengths and weaknesses?' 'What techniques do you use to deal with difficult situations?' Seriously?

She shouldn't even bother going. There were probably tons of qualified people looking for jobs that had the answers to those questions. She was unprepared, unskilled, uneducated, un everything.

Jillian I can't go to the interview.
Why not??

Because I'm un. I have no strengths just weaknesses. I have no techniques. I'm un.

Un? Maggie knock it off. Go to the interview.

I've never been to an interview I'm scared.

Look at it as a learning experience, if it doesn't work out you'll be more prepared for the next one. GO!

Maggie?

Maggie! Don't ignore me! You're going to go right?

Maggie?

Jillian was right. She should go. She had to follow through, if she didn't, then what? Saturday, Sunday and back to Monday. She would send the kids on the bus and start this all over again. Everyday would be Day One which was the same thing as not having a Day One.

She couldn't sit and think about it anymore, it was torture. She left at eight thirty. The closer she got to FastTech Software in Potsdam the worse her hands shook and the harder her heart pounded. It had been a long time since anything made her this nervous. She couldn't even remember ever being this nervous. Why oh why did she bother filling out an application there yesterday? But she knew why, she was driving by and just happened to see the sign in the window. It sounded so simple and easy. Apply Within. So she had.

It was time for some self-talk. If you expect the worst you won't be disappointed. Okay, that was counterproductive. She sang Amazing Grace as loud as she could so her mind couldn't keep thinking. She pulled into the parking lot, put the minivan in park, took a deep breath, and turned the van off. She took another deep breath, got out of the car, walked to the door and expected the worst.

The building was a one story, three office, brick building. Facing the building Fast Tech was on the left, the two offices on the right were vacant. In the Fast Tech section there were two large windows on either side of the door that was centered under a small sign. The window on the left was empty other than a generic business hours sticker with the days of the week listed but no hours written in the spaces next to the days of the week. The window on the right was practically covered with a huge poster board sign with the words 'Help Wanted Apply Within' stenciled in black block letters.

Maggie opened the door and was greeted by the same girl she talked to yesterday. The girl looked to be D.J.'s age. She was sitting at a desk against the furthest wall behind a counter, the only desk behind the counter. The girl was wearing jeans which were fashionably ripped just above the knees and at the thigh and at the thigh and at the thigh again. Her ample top was barely covered by a body fitting tank. Both arms were tattooed. Her short dark hair was gelled into a spiky haphazard not quite style.

"Can I help you? Oh! You're the lady for the interview aren't you?" Just like yesterday Maggie was shocked at the unexpected tone of professionalism in her voice. She would have expected "What up?"

"Yeah. Yes. That's me." Maggie cringed at her own lack of professionalism.

"Have a seat. Someone will be with you in just a moment." The girl pointed toward the area next to the door where there were two seats. She was just about seated when the girl yelled, "Interview lady is here! I gotta pee so come get her yourself!" She then turned back to Maggie and pleasantly said, "Someone will be right with you Ma'am."

Did the girl not know that Maggie could hear her even if she wasn't talking directly to her? And did she just call her Mom??

The girl disappeared leaving her by herself.

Okay, she thought, think! Strengths. She had strengths, every mother had strengths or they would never make it past the first month. But how do you describe those kinds of strengths at an interview?

She heard footsteps from somewhere behind the doorway the receptionist had left through. They were not the same sound the receptionists sandals made and they were getting louder, coming her way. Not the click click of high heels, a man then. Her interviewer would be a man. That wasn't good. She would feel more comfortable with a woman, someone with kids' maybe, someone that understood someone with kids', someone that felt sorry for someone with kids'.

The thud thud of the steps got closer. Maggie's heart pounded in her chest. She took a deep breath and tried to relax. The steps got closer. A man came through the doorway.

He was looking down and typing into a cell phone. He took a couple more slow hesitant steps, the kind a person takes when they don't trust themselves to walk and type at the same time. Maggie took in as much as she could quickly, average to tall height, neatly trimmed dark hair, casual attire, quick thumb typist. So far so good, she didn't see anything Charles Mansony or Donald Trumpy, a good non-intimidating middle ground.

He stopped about ten feet from Maggie, his fingers did a fast final type and he slipped his phone in his pocket and looked up at Maggie.

He gasped at exactly the same time she said "Oh. Shit."

He recovered quicker than she did. "Maggie Kennedy. Damn. It's been a long time."

She wasn't going to get the job.

CHAPTER TWO

Maggie sat in her car in the McDonald's parking lot holding a cup of Café Mocha. She had walked out of her very first interview, not exactly the fast track way to a career but she did what she had to do. Mike Jensen was Donnie's worst enemy. Deal breaker. Even though they hadn't spoken since high school, even though to this day she had no idea what the dispute was about, even though it was over fifteen years ago, she couldn't take a job Donnie didn't want her to have working for a man Donnie despised.

Maggie?
Maggie??!!
Maggie!! Respond to this text or I will call the police!
She wouldn't call the police.

Something happened between Donnie and Mike during their senior year. Colton was small and everyone knew everyone but Donnie was a jock and Mike was a computer geek and they never said two words to each other. They didn't even exist as far as the other was concerned. Then one day about three weeks before graduation something happened between them.

If it weren't for the incident between Mike and Donnie she would never have recognized Mike. In high school he was a short skinny kid with dark brown hair that may have been clean but never came in contact with a comb. Those were his only defining traits, there was nothing memorable about him, he blended into the background wherever he was. In the years since he was just a name on a string. When he stepped into that room she shouldn't have recognized him. But she did. Immediately. He was taller, filled out and fit like someone that spends time at a gym. His hair was short and neatly combed.

But it wasn't *him* she recognized as much as the *feeling* of him. He could easily have been any nameless businessman in the world if not for the familiar anonymity that pierced her mind the second their eyes met.

She took a sip of her Café Mocha and leaned her head against the seat and closed her eyes. She was absent the day it happened. That she remembered clearly. The last couple months of her senior year were spent lying in bed secretly trying not to be pregnant. Most days she stayed in bed waiting for Donnie to come over after school. She'd cried, slept, tried to believe she was as happy as she pretended to be in front of everyone. That day, when Donnie didn't come over after school she called him. His mother said he refused to come to the phone, that he was irate and wouldn't tell her why. Maggie grudgingly pulled herself out of bed, borrowed her mother's car and drove to his house.

Donnie refused to come out of his room but he didn't stop her from coming in. He paced the small space next to the bed, back and forth, back and forth, mumbling incoherent words of anger peppered with loud clear profanities. He stopped pacing only once and that was in the midst of an outburst when he punched a hole in the wall. That was the one time she understood what he said, he was going to kill that little bastard Mike Jensen.

He refused to talk to her. She took her homework home and crawled back in bed preferring the silence of her parent's denial of the pregnancy to the silence of Donnie's anger. She called everyone she knew but no one knew what happened. Whatever it was, it was just between Donnie and Mike.

Graduation came and went and Mike Jensen moved away. Whatever it was that happened was over, except it never really was. Donnie refused to speak about Mike or what happened no matter how many times she asked him. She eventually stopped asking.

Not kidding Maggie!

She was kidding.

And now, more than fifteen years later Mike Jensen stepped into Maggie's day presenting her memory with a new image and her mind with a renewed curiosity for answers.

The faint sound of a siren in the distance caught Maggie's attention.

Holy hell, she called the police!

The siren grew louder and louder. A police car sped past the McDonald's parking lot. Maggie picked up her phone and opened it.

Didn't go well.

Oh no! I'm sorry, you ok? What happened?

Mike Jensen happened.

WHAT?! The one from high school? Donnie's Mike Jensen?? What do you mean happened??

Yup. I thought he moved to Texas or somewhere? Apparently he owns some computer place in Potsdam called FastTech. Can you believe I was going to apply for a job working for Mike Jensen?!

Wow!! Million questions…

I know, me too. Are you sure you don't know what happened between those two?

Maggie don't you think I would have told you? No idea. Does he know you married Donnie? Did he say anything?

Nothing. It was so weird. He came out, recognized me, called me Maggie Kennedy and before he could say anything else I turned around and left.

You didn't say anything?

Nope.

Holy crap shoot!! What are the odds!! Of all the people in the world! Mike Jensen!!

A zillion to one.

Now what?

Now I start over.

Are you going to tell Donnie?

No! He doesn't even know I went for an interview. Crap. Phone's beeping, it's the school, double crap, gotta go.

Maggie knew it was a case of shooting the messenger but she hated the school, hated the teacher, hated the principal. She paid her taxes every year on time, they should take her children in at seven thirty in the morning and returning them home at three thirty in the afternoon new and improved. These people had college educations for crying out loud, they should know how to fix her kids.

She put her coffee in the cup holder. It wasn't even eleven o'clock and her day was ruined. She would drive to the school and walk in to the principal's office, she would listen to him tell her all about whatever it was D.J. did and she would feel just as guilty as if she did it. She would apologize for him and assure the principal D.J. would be dealt with properly. Then she would take him home and deal with him.

She would probably yell at him, dole out an appropriate punishment after which he would retreat to his room where he would most likely sleep the rest of the day away and she would be left alone second guessing her parenting skills. And she already knew how that would go. The self interrogation would begin. No matter what she did the outcome would be the same. She would know she did the wrong thing. Parenting sucked.

Traffic was unfortunately light. Why was it little old granny in her 1985 Cadillac going twenty one miles an hour was never in front of you when you wanted to be held up? Hannawa Falls was supposed to be much further from Potsdam than it was today. If nothing prolonged her drive she would be at the school in five minutes. Her Mocha would still be steaming hot.

What did she do wrong with D.J. anyway? Her other kids weren't angels but they weren't outright rebellious and reclusive. How was it even possible to be rebellious and reclusive? He was a walking anomaly. They should be thanking her for giving them the experience of D.J. If they really cared anything at all about children they should study him and write a book for future educators instead of calling her every time he did something outside of normal.

Hannawa was in her rear view mirror already. Seriously? Not one Grandpa driving a tractor? Logging truck? Anything?

The closer she got to the school the angrier she became. Why didn't they call Donnie? His number was on file too.

She let up on the accelerator and slowed from forty to thirty five. What if? What if she just didn't pick him up? They would probably call Donnie and he would leave work and pick

D.J. up. He would bombard her phone with calls but she wouldn't answer them. She would drive right past the school, drive right through South Colton, drive to Tupper Lake, Saranac Lake, she would keep going until she got tired of driving and found some idyllic little town to disappear in.

It always worked out well in books and movies. It would be so easy. Just don't turn. Just don't stop. Just never look back.

She slowed and turned her blinker on. She pulled into the school parking lot and found a spot. She got out of her car and looked around. All these cars and not one person could deal with D.J.?

By the time she and D.J. returned to the car she was steaming mad and completely humiliated. She didn't drive more than twenty five miles an hour for fear she was going to have a coronary and swerve into a tree killing them both. Then she would never get the chance to kill D.J. herself.

"What were you thinking??!!"

Maggie didn't really expect an answer and she wasn't disappointed. D.J. sat in the passenger seat in total silence, his hood covering his head and hiding his face. She hoped it was a face full of remorse but she doubted it.

"You obviously weren't thinking at all!" She continued, "I don't know what is wrong with you! What am I supposed to do now?! I'm... I'm out..." a speck of spit flew from her mouth and made no apologies, "and I get a phone call from the principal! I can't believe you said that to a teacher! You don't EVEN SPEAK!!"

"Chill out Mom."

Chill? Out? Mom? Maggie yanked the car to the side of the road, slammed the brake to the floor and shoved the shifter into park.

"Look at me D.J.! Now!"

The hood moved but she could barely see his face.

"TAKE THE HOOD OFF! TAKE THE WHOLE SHIRT OFF!! THROW IT OUT THE DOOR!!!"

He slid the hood down and looked at her.

"NOW!! THROW! IT! OUT!"

She was well aware that she was out of control. She had no idea how she was going to get herself back in control before she said something she would regret but when D.J. closed the door after throwing his hoodie out she saw D.J. The real D.J. The D.J. that wasn't shrouded in a black hood and wasn't a symbol of darkness and doom. Control slowly began to seep in. D.J. sat still, his head stooped, his eyes staring at the floor. She wasn't stupid enough to think it was a posture of repentance, it was the normal posture of her almost fifteen year old son in his current attitude of life, still, he looked smaller and younger and slightly more lovable.

She took a deep breath and let out a long sigh. She wasn't in control yet. Words were incapable of forming into sentences that wouldn't do permanent damage. She wanted to scream some more, she wanted to grab him by his ear and make him look at her.

She wanted a cigarette but had quit that habit years ago. She should have waited until the boys were done being teenagers.

She put the shifter back into drive and pulled back onto the road. D.J. turned and looked at his hoodie lying on the side of the road as she pulled away but he was smart enough not to say anything. They rode home in silence. Exited the car in silence. Entered the house in silence. Only one word was spoken. That one word was 'sit' which Maggie said as she pointed at the couch.

Ten minutes passed. She sat on the edge of the recliner facing D.J. She couldn't figure out where to go from here. How could she love and not love her own child at the same time? This was D.J., her first born son who, no matter how much he tested her, she knew she would always love. And, this was D.J., her teenage son who shrouded himself in black and barely spoke and did nothing much other than to take up space and cause grief to everyone. How could she love and not love her own child at the same time?

Another ten minutes went by and she was still afraid to speak because once she did the tone would be set. She couldn't decide what tone she wanted to set. Should she talk to D.J. the firstborn son or should she talk to D.J. the figure in black? The very first word, the very first intonation would set the scene. Should her voice be soft and open and try to appeal to and root for the D.J. that she truly believed was somewhere deep within? Or should her voice be firm and deal with the D.J. at hand? Should she allow him the right to tell his side of the story? When you tell a teacher to do something to himself, something vulgar and physically impossible, do you even have a side?

"Hand me your backpack." She kept her tone completely neutral retaining the power to set it later.

His backpack was on the couch next to him. He picked it up and handed it to her. His eyes skimmed hers but never quite made contact.

She stood up with the backpack. "Do. Not. Move. If I see that you've moved even one inch when I come back this will not have any chance of ending well. Do you understand?"

He nodded.

She took the backpack to the kitchen out of his sight. She stood with the backpack in her hand. She had never searched any of the boy's backpacks other than to find homework or lunch bags or something completely innocent. This was her first seize and search.

She opened the backpack and found the usual crumpled papers, a notebook, a textbook, a couple pens and a pencil. She searched the notebook and the textbook, nothing unusual. She searched the inside pockets of the backpack and found nothing but a calculator. She opened the zippered pocket on the front and found a pack of Marlboros and a lighter. No illegal drugs, no guns, no knives, no notes, nothing to help her figure out her son. She put everything back where it was except the Marlboros and lighter.

She took a couple of steps back so she could see into the living room. D.J. had not moved an inch. She took the Marlboros and lighter and quietly went through the kitchen door and out to the patio. She could drop them in the garbage or she could break them and shred them. She did neither.

She sat in the wicker chair, opened the pack, took one out and lit it. She didn't care if D.J. saw her or smelled it. Technically they were hers. He was underage. He had no money to buy them which meant they were paid for from either lunch money, the money Donnie gave him last night or money stolen from one or the other of them. Technically he didn't have the right to so much as speak to her about the cigarettes or anything else at the moment. So she smoked it. And she enjoyed it.

By the time she returned to the living room she had decided how she was going to handle D.J. She sat back down in the recliner. He hadn't moved an inch.

She spoke calmly and non-threatening, "D.J. you have two choices. You can sulk and remain silent or you can speak to me in a tone that I approve of and we can discuss this. If you chose to speak I will listen. Either way you are grounded. For the weekend you will not leave this couch except to eat, go to the bathroom and go to your bedroom to sleep at night. What happens after that will depend on your attitude and your behavior over the weekend. There is NO negotiating this. Do you understand?"

He nodded.

"I will be in touch with the school when you go back next week. If I hear even one single utterance that you have not been an exemplary student you will remain grounded indefinitely. Is that understood?"

He nodded.

"Okay. Make your choice. I'll wait."

Eight long minutes of silence passed.

"D.J. have you made the choice to sulk and remain silent?"

"No."

"Then speak."

"Do you love me?"

"Yes."

"You don't get me. You don't know me. How can you love me if you don't even know me?"

"D.J. don't play me. I'm not nearly as stupid as you think I am."

Silence.

"D.J.? Do you want to talk or not?"

"Not. But can I say just one thing?"

She nodded.

"I'm not nearly as stupid as you think I am either."

Maggie wasn't sure what to make of the talk. She felt like something happened. She just wasn't sure what and she wasn't sure if it fell in the positive or negative side of things. At least the talk was over. All she could do now was to go on from here, which by the next day turned out to be much harder than she expected.

"Maggie you need to do something with D.J. he's, he's just, there. He's like a pile of blankets taking up space."

"What do you want me to do with him Donnie? He's a person. I can't exactly pick him up and put him in the closet." Maggie explained everything last night when Donnie came home from work, he didn't have a lot to say but he nodded and agreed when she told him the punishment she'd chosen. "You'll just have to deal with it. He's part of the couch for the weekend, we can't change his punishment now."

In hindsight it probably wasn't the ideal punishment. It started out the way she planned but it backfired on her quickly. D.J. wasn't allowed to touch the remote but since he was sentenced to the living room if someone else was watching television he could watch what was on. The other boys watched cartoons on Saturday mornings. Seeing D.J. sitting with his brothers she could almost believe he was a normal kid. He didn't say a lot but he interacted with his brothers more in that one morning than he had in months. By afternoon though, the other boys were off playing and D.J. sat on the couch with no television and no one around him. He dozed on and off and stared at the wall when he was awake. She brought him some books hoping he would be bored enough to pick something up and read. He didn't.

"Look at him. He's just sitting there."

"If he wasn't sitting there he'd be sitting in his room. I had to think of something and this is what I came up with. I thought immersing him into the family would be a good idea. It was the best I could come up with at the time."

"But, it bugs me."

"Well you bug me but I can't do anything about you

either."

"Can't he clean the garage or something?"

She had to admit, it bugged her too. Every time one of the boys walked by him they stopped and stared at him like he was a freak show at the fair. No one could quite figure out how to deal with D.J.'s presence, it made everyone uncomfortable. Maybe sending him to the garage wasn't such a bad idea.

"Fine."

Donnie made the mistake of offering D.J. the choice. D.J. chose to remain on the couch over cleaning the garage. By the time the weekend was over everyone was relieved.

At seven thirty five Monday morning after the boys left for school Maggie sighed in relief and poured herself a cup of coffee. She thought about what she would need to do to bring D.J. around. For the life of her she couldn't figure out what that would be.

She thought about the moment he was born. It was three months after she turned eighteen and graduated high school. While all her classmates were settling in to college routines or working she was, at forty weeks pregnant, living with Donnie in the basement of his parent's home. She had failed at trying to make peace with her own parents. They couldn't accept that their only child made an egregious mistake, they used words like egregious, unspeakable, unforgivable. When they stopped speaking to her about her egregious mistake they stopped speaking to her completely.

Donnie's parents were the polar opposite, they couldn't wait to welcome a grandchild into the world, they used words like gift, precious, blessing. The day she went into labor Donnie was at work at his construction job and his mother took her to the hospital. Donnie's father picked Donnie up and brought him to her.

MAGGIE'S TURN

She remembered it as if it were yesterday. She was scared to death, lying in the hospital bed with that light blue checkered gown and Donnie next to her holding her hand and promising her everything would be okay. His mother stood next to Donnie, his father paced the tiny space at the foot of the bed, but when they finally took her to the delivery room she was alone. And when they finally placed the bundled little baby boy in her arms it was surreal. She remembered touching his little nose and fingers and wondering who he would be and a second later when he started making noise she realized she had no idea what to do with him.

Almost fifteen years later she still wondered who he would be. She didn't know what to do with him any more now than she did the day he was born. But she knew, even in the moments she didn't like him, she knew she loved him and she would never ever do to him what her parents did to her. She might fail him but he would never fail her.

She freshened her cup of coffee. She was stuck. Her mind wouldn't reveal anything useful. She was stuck leaning against the kitchen counter looking at a room she'd spent countless hours in.

There was a time when this very kitchen excited her. Twice actually. The first time, she walked in the house with Donnie, his father, and the realtor, took one look at the kitchen and fell in love with it. It would be her space, the first thing she would have control over that wasn't owned by her parents or by his parents. She was so excited to have a space of her own that she didn't recognize the flaws. She saw a huge room without thinking about how a table would shrink the space. She saw a long counter but didn't see the faded red marbled Formica countertop. She saw a window over a sink but not the view of the shed or the chipped ceramic.

Before their first anniversary of owning the house she saw everything in opposite. Donnie and his father began the long and arduous task of remodeling the kitchen to fit their growing family. They gutted the kitchen and a mud room and combined the two to make the kitchen larger. They rebuilt it from scratch. The house was a mess for three months but when they finished it was spacious, updated and beautiful. She chose a pale blue for the walls, a pine table with seating for eight, a marbled countertop with shades of blue, gray and black, a black fridge, dishwasher and oven, and slate gray linoleum for the floor. That was the second time her kitchen excited her.

Maggie unglued herself from the counter and took her coffee cup with her. She moseyed from the kitchen to the hallway. The hallway led from the front door to the stairs with the kitchen wall on the left and the living room on the right. Soon after they moved in they replaced the downstairs carpet and found a beautiful hardwood floor that ran the span from the door to the stairs. She straightened the throw rug with her toe, something that had been done so many times she did it without realizing it.

Maggie stood in the hallway and sipped her coffee. The living room was not large but not small. There was a door on the far side that led to the garage. For the first few years she cursed the builder on a daily basis. Attaching a garage to a carpeted living room was the most senseless thing she could think of when it came to designing a home. The designer of this home took senseless one step further by putting the washer and dryer in the garage. But it was the kind of thing that when you live with it long enough you get used to it and forget to hate it.

She would have liked a larger living room but they managed to arrange the couch, loveseat, and recliner so that it didn't appear too overstuffed with furniture. With the television, a couple of end tables and a couple of bean bag chairs there was no other way to arrange it. Although she tired of it long ago she learned to live with it. There was one spot in front of the couch that was void of furniture and it was where the boys always managed to land in a wrestling match. She often thought about filling the spot with a coffee table but every time she thought about it the thought concluded with an image of taking someone to the hospital for stitches. Coffee tables and wrestling boys were a bad combination.

Maggie turned and climbed the stairs. The stairway ended at a hallway. To the right were three bedrooms, Daniel and Todd's, Derek's, and at the end of the hall hers and Donnie's. To the left was the room D.J. and Dylan shared, a large storage closet and a good sized bathroom.

She strolled to the bathroom and surveyed the damage from the morning. Clothes were strewn on the floor all around the hamper and she knew, without a doubt, if she went in and opened the hamper it would be empty. The rest of the bathroom was still in decent shape, the clothes could wait. She lingered at D.J. and Dylan's door but decided not to open it. Some things were better left unknown.

Derek's room required at least a glance. He was forbidden from conducting experiments in his bedroom but she occasionally found the debris of something he dissected, forbidden didn't mean it never happened. She stuck her head in for a quick reconnaissance, nothing smoked, nothing smelled.

She took her coffee and went into Daniel and Todd's room. They were old enough to be expected to pick up after themselves. The beds were made Daniel and Todd style. The comforters were pulled up over stuffed animals, toys, books and clothes. Good enough. She felt around Daniel's bed for a flat spot and sat down. She had no idea why. It was as good a place as any and she didn't know what to do next so she sat.

She wondered what it would be like at the end of 'boys at home' but the vision was blank. She supposed she would be right where she was now, the only difference being that instead of a space of time each day she would have all day every day to fill.

Not an option.

Her train of thought went back in years. She traveled back as far back as she could remember. She tried to picture who Maggie was when she was just Maggie. What filled her mind before her life was influenced by people and circumstances? She traveled to before 'boys at home' when she had a life to fill without expectations.

She wanted a career.

She wanted the executive desk and the nine to five plus. She wanted papers and notes and files piled and scattered everywhere. She wanted the click click of her heels in the hallway as she hurried to the boardroom. She wanted business suits and all expense paid trips to far away meetings.

She knew what she had to do. She had to make a decision between what Donnie wanted and what she wanted.

Maggie left the boy's room with a new sense of determination. She was going to Fast Tech to ask Mike Jensen what happened all those years ago and then she was going to decide if it was enough to stop her from asking for another chance for an interview.

MAGGIE'S TURN

The receptionist jumped at the sound of the bell when Maggie opened the door. Her low cut vibrant pink tank top made it impossible for Maggie to look at her face. The cleavage demanded attention so to be safe Maggie picked a spot on the girl's tattoo on her right arm and zeroed in on the center of the dragon.

"Oh you! You're back. Are you feeling better?"

"Feeling better?"

"Yeah, Mike told me how you suddenly got so sick you couldn't even stay for the interview."

"Oh, right. Yes, I'm feeling much better. Is he available?"

"Is he expecting you?"

"Not exactly."

"No problem. I'll get him."

Maggie looked to the seats by the door and back at the receptionist. "Should I?" She pointed to the seats.

"Sure."

Maggie's stomach was in knots, should she be doing this? It was so random, if trying to find out something she wondered about for fifteen years could be considered random. She took a deep breath and tried to calm her nerves. She'd been over this in her mind a million times, what could possibly have happened between them? Was she about to tug on a thread better left alone?

"Mike! Someone's here!" The receptionist yelled into the air and then turned and smiled at Maggie. "He'll be right with you."

He wasn't. Maggie fiddled with her watch and then her rings and then she opened her purse and pulled her cell phone out. No missed calls, no new texts. She put the cell phone back and fiddled with her watch and then with her rings some more.

"MIKE!!" The receptionist hollered again.

Maggie jumped and smiled nervously at the receptionist. She looked down at her lap and stared at her purse. She started to reach in her purse to check her cell phone again when she heard the sound of footsteps getting closer, a second later Mike stepped around the corner. He looked at the receptionist and she pointed in Maggie's general direction.

Maggie watched as his expression went from annoyed to startled to confused. Good. She had hoped to catch him off guard and by the expression on his face she succeeded.

He looked from Maggie to the receptionist and back, "I didn't realize you had an appointment today."

"I didn't. Do you have a minute?"

"Umm." He shifted his weight from one leg to the other. "I'm actually a little busy."

"With what?" The receptionist threw her arms in the air, "Live body Mike! Interview her!"

Maggie let the misunderstanding slide. She just needed a couple of minutes to talk to him. She didn't care what pretense it took to get those couple of minutes.

Mike glared at the receptionist but said, "Come on back to my office."

He led her around the corner. There was a small hallway, a set of two doors to the left and one at the end of the hall on the right. She followed him through the door on the right. It was a large office, executive large, but it was filled with tables overflowing with computers and keyboards and laptops and parts of computers in one big unorganized mess. He walked to the back of a big wooden desk that was the only neat spot in the room and gestured for her to take the only seat on the other side.

"So," he smiled, he seemed a bit more relaxed sitting

behind his desk but she could still see the worry lines around his eyes. Good. "So, you decided you want the job anyway? I have to say I'm a bit surprised."

She opened her mouth but not a single word traveled from her mind to her mouth. She closed her mouth quickly but not quick enough. Like an animal sizing up its prey he spotted her weakness and sat up straighter, she wasn't sure but she thought she even saw the corners of his mouth tighten in a smirk.

"I really didn't expect you to come back but since you did I guess we could discuss it. Awkward but you apparently want a job and I definitely need someone."

She cleared her throat and found her voice. "I just have a couple of questions."

"It's an easy job," he tilted his head toward the wall and rolled his eyes, "you've met Mandy, for Mandy it's difficult, for anyone else it would be a piece of cake." He smiled conspiratorially. "She gave me her notice a month ago, she's dying to get out of here, and well, I'm dying for her to get out of here. I need someone capable of answering the phone, making appointments, some filing, some computer entry, things like that."

"Actually that's not why I'm here. I'm not interested in the job, well that's not exactly true but before I can even think about it I need to ask …"

"Coffee?"

Before she could answer Mike stood up and went to a table littered with piles of computer parts. She didn't noticed the coffee maker wedged between a hard drive and the wall until he pulled the carafe out. He poured two cups and brought them to the desk along with a container of creamers and sugars.

"So," he poured creamer into his cup and took a sip

without stirring, "What's happened in the life of Maggie Kennedy since graduation? As I recall you and Don Conners were about to become parents."

"Donnie. Everyone calls him Donnie, now, and then actually, but you two didn't really hang out or anything did you?" It was a question but she didn't offer a chance for him to answer. "But yes, Donnie and I had a baby."

"That's great. Not to be rude but are you Maggie Conners then?"

"I am."

"Congratulations. Well, fifteen years late. You and Don still married, wow, not a lot of marriages last that long, especially starting the way yours, well, you know what I mean. Did you have any other kids?"

"We did." She took another deep breath, "Back in our senior year something happened between you and Donnie."

Mike sat up straighter and visibly stiffened. He didn't answer, but then, she hadn't asked a question either.

She continued, "I had no idea that you owned this place and when you came out for the interview the other day it startled me. It brought back memories, you know?" Mike held eye contact but didn't say anything. Maggie continued, "It shocked me, seeing you, last I heard you were in Texas or somewhere. Something about top secret computer projects for the government."

Mike smiled and waved his hand through the air, "Nothing as important as that. Just computer grunt work."

"You were voted most likely to hack the national security files. When we heard you were working for the government we believed it, so it wasn't true?"

Mike raised his eyebrows, "Is that what you wanted to ask me about?"

She paused to organize her thoughts, "No. What I wanted to ask you…well…I know it's been a lot of years but I want to know your side of what happened between you and Donnie." She thought Mike flinched but it was so fleeting that she wasn't sure if he did or if she imagined it.

"That was a long time ago, old outdated history, we were just kids. Kids being kids. I'm sure my side of the story is no different than what Don has told you."

Maggie managed to smile and nod, she wasn't quite sure how to continue. Was it old history? Was it possible that Donnie was just holding an incredibly long unreasonable grudge about something that was just kids being kids? Doubtful.

"That's probably true, but still, I don't see how I could apply for a job working for you without putting it to rest in my mind. I'd just like to hear your side to balance the scale."

"Why don't you tell me Don's side and I'll tell you if there's more to it. If I can even remember. It was so long ago."

If she tried to make something up he would know she was lying. She was cornered. It must have shown on her face because Mike stopped smiling and started shaking his head.

"He never told you what happened between us did he? It must be kind of hard to compare sides when you don't know *either* side . You know what you need to do Maggie? Let it go. He probably doesn't remember and neither do I. Don't take this personally but you women tend to dwell on things until they grow way out of proportion. I can barely remember much of it myself, and if your husband hasn't mentioned it in fifteen years then it's not really my place to go down that road. It sounds like it's more of a family thing, more of a Don not telling you thing. That's between you two."

Maggie stared at him. Mike cocked his head and templed

his fingers. He was thinking about what had happened she was sure of it, she could practically see the past replaying in his mind. It wasn't old forgotten history. He was replaying it detail for detail and she knew it. Donnie remembered exactly what happened. Mike remembered exactly what happened. She would be damned if she was going to let this go on one day longer. Someone was going to tell her what the hell happened and she'd rather have it out with a virtual stranger she would never have to see again than with the man she has to live with.

"Okay Mike you win. I don't know what happened. Donnie refuses to tell me and for fifteen years I've never come one bit closer to finding out what happened between you two but listen up Mike." Maggie felt her temper travel into dangerous territory but she couldn't rein it back in. "I am NOT leaving until I know exactly what happened. Start from the beginning. Do not leave anything out and DO NOT try to bullshit me because I swear Mike I will not leave this seat until I think you have told me everything there is to tell."

Mike leaned forward, opened his mouth, and then leaned back. His eyes slid above and behind her. She turned around. Mandy stood behind her, her mouth opened wide in shock and yet there was a hint of amusement in her eyes.

The phone rang startling all three of them. Mike flinched but made no move to pick up the receiver sitting six inches away from his hand. Mandy tentatively stepped around Maggie's chair and went to the side of the desk, stared at the phone but didn't reach out to answer it. It rang again. Mandy's eyes darted between Mike and Maggie. Maggie's eyes darted between Mike and Mandy. The phone stopped. And rang again.

The ringing grated on Maggie's already exposed nerves, she

jumped out of her chair and grabbed the receiver.

"Fast Tech!" Her voice was loud, abrupt and angry. She glared at Mandy while she listened to an arrogant jerk yelling at her about a computer program scheduling discrepancy. As far as she was concerned it was not only impossible to understand him but unimportant as well. He was just another man demanding what he wanted when he wanted it. She interrupted the caller, her glare sliding from Mandy to Mike, "Your name?" She snapped as she watched Mike stare dumbfounded, "Mr. Robert McKinley I hope your day has been wonderful up until now because it's about to change!" Mike's eyes widened and he visibly tensed. She ignored him. "You are one little fish in a gigantic ocean and if you think your loud arrogant demands are going to get you what you want you can just think again because I will not be bullied by some narcissistic suit coat sitting behind an executive desk thinking the world revolves around him. If you can't live with that than I suggest you take your business elsewhere!" She slammed the phone down.

No one moved. All eyes were glued to the receiver. No one so much as breathed. Mike's cell phone rang and they all jumped. He reached to his side and pulled it from the clip, looked at the caller ID, glared at Maggie, hit speaker and placed the phone on the desk. "Mike Jensen."

"Mike?! Mike listen, just got off the phone with your receptionist, wow, new girl? Anyway, she misunderstood me, got a little jumpy, probably that time of the month eh?! I have to take another call but just ignore whatever she tells you, the scheduling is good, perfect, couldn't be better, alright then, I need to take this call."

They heard the click of Mr. Robert McKinley ending his one sided conversation. Mike reached out and hit the end button on his phone. Mandy lifted her hands and started clapping. "You're hired." She laughed. "I'm outta here." She turned around and before Mike or Maggie could stop her she was gone.

Maggie looked desperately at Mike who was either too stunned to speak or didn't want to call Mandy back, possibly both. She fell back into the chair.

"What just happened? I know that was a little unorthodox" she pointed at the phone, "and I'm sorry, but" she pointed toward the door, "that? Mandy? What just happened?"

Mike closed his eyes and inhaled a deep breath of air through his nose then exhaled loudly through his mouth. He opened his eyes. "I think Mandy just hired you. And quit. In that order."

Maggie shook her head. "No. No no." She wagged her finger back and forth. "Not hired. Undo…undo it." She stopped wagging her finger and pointed toward the door. "Get her. Go get her!"

Mike put his elbows on his desk and dropped his head into his hands.

"Mike?!"

"Shh, thinking."

"Mike I…"

"Shh!"

She should leave. She should leave quickly. She started to get up from her chair.

"Sit." Mike raised his head. "Okay, that wasn't ideal. We'd have to work on your phone skills. You working here wouldn't be ideal either, under the circumstances, but I think we can work that out. How about ten dollars an hour?"

"What?! No, I can't…"

"Yes. You can. McKinley's been a pain in my ass since the

day I signed that contract, I doubt he will be anymore, thanks to you. But regardless, my receptionist just walked out, also thanks to you, so the way I see it you just got yourself a job. You owe me."

Maggie shook her head from side to side. "Oh no. No. No. I can't work for you. I'm sorry about your receptionist but I can't work for you. I'm not here for the job I'm here for information."

"Forget that Maggie, seriously it was fifteen years ago. Everyone else has moved on from high school, don't you think it's about time you did too? You came in here the other day looking for a job. Are you seriously going to let something from high school stop you? What time does Don get home?"

"What?"

"Tonight? What time does he get home from work?"

"Why?"

"Because I guarantee you when he gets home tonight, at five or six or whatever time he gets home, and you tell him you took a job working for me he won't care one bit. Guarantee it."

"You don't know Donnie, and it's Donnie not Don. He doesn't want me to get a job at all forget about a job working for you. He'll blow a gasket."

Mike sighed. "I need a receptionist. At the very least you owe it to me to ask him. I run a professional business here and I don't have the time to deal with this. Seeing how it's your fault Mandy just walked out the least you can do is ask him."

Again with a man thinking he should get whatever he wants just because he wants it. Maggie's blood began to boil, she shook her head. "I owe you nothing. Absolutely nothing. And professional business my ass, I met Mandy remember?!"

Mike stared at her. "You're right," he sighed, "I'm sorry.

I'm not thinking straight, not having a receptionist is a disaster for this kind of business. Mandy was far from even adequate but at least she took the calls and passed along the messages. I travel a lot. I need someone here."

Maggie let her head fall back against the chair. "I'm sorry about that."

Mike's eyes widened. "Sorry enough to think about it?"

"Did you even look at my application?"

He shook his head.

"I have no experience. No references. No skills."

Mike wrinkled his forehead. "Did you not meet Mandy?"

Maggie felt a small rush of excitement trickling through her mind, she could have a job, not the ideal job, but it was still a job. "Twenty."

"Twenty? Dollars? An hour?" He shook his head.

She got up and turned to walk out.

"Fifteen."

She stopped. "Really?"

"Against my better judgment."

She turned around. "Monday through Friday nine to three, ten to two during summer vacation, holidays off."

"You've got to be kidding me."

She turned around and took another step toward the door.

"No more talk about the past, nine to three all year and holidays off."

"I'll let you know."

"You'll…"

"Let you know. By the end of the week."

How could you let that happen? You CANNOT take that job! I know! Of course I'm not going to. I just got caught up in the moment.

Maggie?!

I'm not stupid Jillian! I know I can't take it. But I wish I could.

YOU CAN'T!

I know! Stop it! Just listen. I won't but I wish I could. It's the best case scenario.

Arrggghhh! How so?

I AM going to get a job, why not this one? The hours are perfect, the pay is good, and it's something I know I can do, if you met Mandy you'd understand. At the very least it's experience and something to put on a resume.

Donnie would kill you, divorce you at the very least. He'll flip.

Maybe not.

Are you crazy?

Probably. But I AM going to get a job and no one else is going to hire me with my lack of experience, it's this or flipping burgers or cleaning toilets. At least I'll get some computer experience.

Don't take this personally but why would he even want you?

Oh thanks!

No, I mean the whole high school thing.

Maybe it was just kids being kids like he said. Maybe because I straightened his client out? And maybe because his last receptionist was a douche bag, he's desperate.

You did not just say that.

Desperate?

Forget it, you're not going to listen to me anyway.

So you think I should take it?

No! I don't! I want to go on the record as being AGAINST it.

So you think I should take it?

Maggie stop! This isn't funny.

I know. What do I do?

Don't take the job!

Maggie? Talk to me!
Maggie??!!

"Mom?! Answer me!"

She ignored the first three 'mom's' but he wasn't going away. "What?"

"Derek dissected the remote."

Maggie continued loading dishes into the dishwasher.

"MOM?!"

"Dylan! WHAT?"

"Answer me!"

"It wasn't a question!"

"Fine! Can I kill Derek because he dissected the remote???"

She felt a bubble of hysteria start and before she knew it she was laughing and then she was sitting at the table and wiping tears from her eyes. She was mentally exhausted. She was terrified. She was elated. She was completely torn on what to do about the job, and Donnie. All she wanted to do was drag herself to her bedroom, crawl in bed and pull the covers over her head.

"Mom?" Dylan pulled a chair out but didn't sit down.

She wiped her eyes. "Sorry." A second wave of hysteria bubbled up and she tried desperately to contain it.

"Are you laughing or crying?"

"I don't…" she felt the wave catch in her throat and a sound like a hiccup came out, she cleared her throat. "I don't know." And then it started again, first laughter followed by tears.

"Should I get…?" Dylan was going to say Dad but Dad wasn't home yet. "D.J.?"

Maggie started laughing harder, even Dylan realized the ridiculousness of it and couldn't help but to snicker. He sat in the chair and giggled. It started feeding off one another, as soon as one thought they had control the other would giggle and it would start all over again.

When they were finally able to stop Maggie got up and poured them both a glass of milk. She brought them to the table and handed one to Dylan. "Sorry Dylan. I don't know what came over me. I guess I'm just pretty tired."

Dylan looked uncomfortable, he gulped his milk and put the glass down, he fumbled for words and finally ended up saying, "You want to lift?"

"Lift?"

"Weights?" He fidgeted in the chair. "I know you're tired but sometimes it helps when you're messed up."

She almost started laughing again but the sweetness of his offer stopped her and the truth of what he said saddened her. She was messed up.

She was tempted to accept his offer but she would have to lift weights and she was truly exhausted and what would their conversation be like? Dylan fidgeted as he waited for her answer. It was obvious he regretted the offer already.

"Thanks Dylan but I think I'm going to check on the boys and head to bed. Maybe another time?"

He nodded, relief clearly written all over his face. "Okay. But you know it's only eight thirty right?"

She got up and put their glasses in the dishwasher. "Yeah, I'll probably read for a while, till your Dad comes home."

Dylan got up and walked to the doorway and paused, "Okay, so, you need to buy a new remote tomorrow."

She smiled at him. "Good night Dylan."

She checked on the boys and then did exactly as she said

she was going to, except she didn't read and she didn't wait up for Donnie.

When the alarm went off at six o'clock she was shocked to find that not only the evening had disappeared but the entire night too. While she slept Donnie had come home, slept, and returned back to work. He was oblivious to everything that happened in her life over the past hours, well, that wasn't quite correct, over the past years. The realization made her want to pull the covers over her head and stay in bed. But she couldn't. She had responsibilities to take care of even though they didn't include her.

After the boys got on the bus Maggie put her jogging shoes on. Maybe Todd beginning kindergarten was not the monumental turning point she thought it was going to be. Maybe expectations don't really move a person forward in their journey but are a mirage that causes them to miss the journey. She went outside and then stopped and looked back at the house. She was barely out of her driveway but she didn't remember walking it, not in the sense of seeing anything as she was walking other than what was ahead of her, beyond her, where she wanted to go.

She looked at her driveway and yard, the grass needed mowing, there was a bicycle left on its side in the yard, there were footprints in the dirt on the edge of the driveway, there were still yellow daylilies in the flower bed next to the house. She hasn't seen any of it. Because she was looking ahead where she wanted to be instead of looking at where she was.

But that's normal, she thought, everyone does that. She started walking again trying to be aware of the spot she was in, where each foot landed or what was next to her on the side of the road. Before long she realized she was looking ahead again, picking a spot and when she reached it, picking the next spot.

She stopped and pulled her cell phone out of her sock.

When someone gets where they want to be do they know it or do they only see the mirage of the next expectation?

She waited a minute but Jillian didn't respond so she put the phone back in her sock and took a few more steps. Her calves were beginning to ache so she picked a huge rock in the near, very near, distance and stopped to sit and massage the pain from her calves. Even though it was September the sun felt warm and the air hinted of fall. Maggie thought about how that was a blessing, how in the Adirondacks September could feel like any one of the four seasons. The pain in her calves abated but she wasn't ready to start walking again. She was being aware. Of the birds. Of the sun. But not of the bug with multiple legs that slither walked up the rock and onto her arm. She jumped off the rock, slapped her arm and screamed all at the same time.

When her heart started again and she could walk she turned back toward home. Walking was for people without cars. From now on any exercise she decided to do would be done inside the house. She would buy a treadmill. She tried to think if there was enough room in the basement for a treadmill and decided if not she would put it in the bedroom. And then she thought about how she didn't even hear Donnie come in last night or leave this morning.

Marriage and family life definitely seemed to benefit him more than it did her. Donnie lived on the edge of their life. He didn't get involved with the daily monotony. He didn't get involved with the boy's schedules or personality conflicts or moods or fights or behaviors or discipline. He didn't get involved with the monotony of maintaining the home, with the groceries or meal planning or cleaning or laundry. He didn't think about his actions or words or the effect they might have on any of the rest of them. They were Saturn and he was the circle around them, a part of but not really a part of.

Was he happy? She doubted it. People don't drown their happiness in alcohol, they drown their sorrows or worries or they use alcohol as a means to escape something. So which was it for Donnie? What did he have to be unhappy about? He certainly wasn't burdened with the responsibilities of marriage or parenting.

Maggie's cell phone rang interrupting her thoughts. She pulled it from her pocket and glanced at it, the school. Crap crap crap. This was exactly what she was thinking about, Donnie didn't have to deal with any of this. Whatever it was that D.J. did this time she would have to deal with it. At some point later in the evening it would brush past Donnie barely even touching the molecules in the air around him.

She could pretend she didn't hear it or she could take the phone and pitch it into the woods and not have to deal with anything today. But then she wouldn't be able to stop worrying about whatever they were calling about. And she'd have to pay Dylan another twenty bucks to retrieve it.

"Hello?"

"Mrs. Conners it's Patsy Hawkins. I'm calling because Todd mentioned that you were interested in being one of our volunteer reading parents?"

Volunteer reading parents?

"We started this program years ago, you probably remember it from one of your other boys, although I don't think you actually participated. But anyway, we have a parent come in every morning from nine to nine fifteen to read to the kids. Todd wanted me to call and schedule you so I was wondering if we could count on you for Wednesdays."

Volunteer reading parents?

"We provide the reading material. All you need to do is show up and read to the kids. It only takes about fifteen minutes and we try to recruit the parents that, uh, don't work. The kids love it. So? So can we count on you?"

Nooooo! "Sure. Love to."

"Fantastic, we'll see you this Wednesday then? At nine."

Fantastic.

She thought again about pitching the phone in the woods but noticed a missed call from Jillian and three text messages.

Maggie?

Where are you?

I need a favor, it's important. Where are you?!

She opened the phone and started typing.

Sup?

Jillian responded immediately.

Louise. That's what's up. She locked her keys in her car and can't get a hold of Frank. She's frantic.

And she called you? In New Jersey?

She didn't know what to do. She's at the hair dresser, on Market Street, next to the bank. Can you?

Get her?

Please??? She just had her hair done. She's worried about the rain coming.

Maggie looked up at the clear blue sky. Rain?

Why doesn't she just go back inside the hairdressers?

She's embarrassed, doesn't want them to know.

Call the police to unlock her car?

Embarrassed. Maggie please? I'll owe you big.

Damn right you will. Tell her I'll be there in a half hour.

Okay, thank you thank you!!

A half hour later Maggie pulled into the parking lot the hairdresser shared with a few other merchants. She drove up one row and down the next, up the next and down the next. No Louise. She pulled out of the parking lot and drove in front again. No Louise. She went around the block and scanned the sides of the road and all the parking spaces. No Louise.

Maggie found a spot and parked the van. Jillian would owe her big for this. This particular hair salon catered to the elderly and elderly people loved to talk. Just what she needed.

"Can I help you?"

Flo? From that old show that was in reruns before she was even born? What was it called? "I'm looking for Louise. Louise Harper?"

"Louise?" Flo snapped her gum. "She left about an hour ago. She said she was taking some things to the donation drop box at the church and then meeting the pastor about something."

Maggie looked at the clock on the wall. "An hour ago? Did you happen to see her drive away?"

"I did. She was parked right out front. That Louise! She's so sweet. And funny! Do you know she comes early and drives around and around until a front spot opens? And when she's beautiful again and ready to leave she runs to her car with her hands over her head so her hair doesn't get messed up!"

Sweet. And funny. Maggie thanked the lady and stepped back outside. She pulled her phone from her pocket. Four missed text messages.

Maggie! Did you leave yet? Never mind!
Stop! Someone helped her. Car unlocked.
Maggie??!! Abort mission!!
Maggie? Crap. Sorry.

Maggie didn't respond to Jillian's texts. Let her wallow in guilt for a while. She wasn't Jillian's assistant and she certainly wasn't Louise's. It burned her that she drove all the way to Potsdam for no reason. Just because she didn't have a job it didn't mean she was at everyone else's beck and call.

If she found Louise standing in the rain right now she'd circle her a few times and she wouldn't slow down for the puddles either. But it wasn't raining. And there was no Louise to find. She was pulling another one of her infamous stunts trying to prove to Jillian that she needed her to move back.

As long as she was here she might as well be productive. Her fridge and cupboards were close to empty and the grocery store was just down the road to the right.

Maggie pulled out of the parking space and turned left toward FastTech. So much for productive.

What would it be like to wake up each morning with an actual agenda? Wake up, feed the boys breakfast, scurry them off to school, get herself showered and jump in the car to get to work with a pile of files under one arm and a brown bagged lunch under the other?

She passed FastTech imagining herself sitting at the desk typing some document or report, answering the phone and scheduling appointments, sipping her coffee from a ceramic cup that said something witty like 'It's not morning until I've had my coffee'. It was a long way from her original dream of high heels and briefcases and business trips overseas but the years had ratcheted her dreams down a few notches. She would be ecstatic now with a pair of flats, carrying a brown bag lunch and crossing the bridge in Hannawa Falls instead of the Atlantic Ocean. Sweet success.

She slowed enough to look in the big picture window of the office but couldn't see anyone and continued on. A block later she turned around and drove by again. This time she saw Mandy standing behind the counter and then she disappeared. She was surprised to see Mandy but she was glad. It was both good and bad, good the position was probably still open and bad the position was probably still open.

She drove to the grocery store and ended up spending twice what she usually did. She couldn't focus. The aisles were too narrow, the carts all had one wheel that thumped, the people were, well, stupid. When she got home she put her groceries away and pulled her phone out of her purse.

Jillian I'm really mad at you but we'll talk about that later. I'm going crazy! You have to help me. I need a life. I'm becoming a miserable person.

I'm really really sorry I sent you chasing after Louise. Seriously sorry. Why are you going crazy? Why are you miserable?

I need something to do! I need a job! I'm thinking about accepting Mike's offer.

No! That would be marital disaster! We'll figure it out, let me think.

Think fast, I'm about to jump off a bridge, or push someone, yeah probably push someone.

Make a list.

What?! That's your idea of help? I'm pushing someone off a bridge. I am.

Make a list of things you want to do.

We tried that before. It's a pathetic idea. I'm pushing YOU off a bridge.

At three thirty the boys tromped in the door and immediately headed to the kitchen. Maggie listened to the fighting begin. They hadn't noticed her sitting on the couch folding laundry as they bee lined to the kitchen but she knew the minute they needed something they would remember her and seek her out.

"Mooooommm!"

So soon?

Derek materialized first but Dylan was so close behind that he stepped on the back of Derek's foot and sent him tumbling to the floor and then Dylan tripped over him and landed half on top of him and half on the floor. She waited to see what would happen, either they would jump up and continue rushing to wherever they were rushing to or they would start wrestling which would turn into an all out fight before she could separate them. Neither happened. D.J. came next and was so focused on his texting that he tripped over both of them and landed on top of Dylan. Todd walked in next with Daniel right behind him. He would have ended up falling over the whole mess but Daniel reached out and grabbed his shoulders and stopped him. Unfortunately Todd didn't share Daniel's insight and shook out of his hands and dove on top of the other boys.

This would not turn out good.

Maggie dropped the towel she was folding and jumped to the pile of boys. She pulled Todd off and then with her hands on her hips she yelled, "D.J. up! Everyone stand up! Don't touch anyone! Don't say a word! Just get up!" Surprisingly they did. She never knew if it would work, there was always that fear, and recurring nightmare, that she would start yelling and they would completely ignore her and she wouldn't have a clue what to do.

Everyone was standing. They were all looking at her. What were they waiting for? Wasn't saving them from each other enough? No one spoke and then everyone spoke.

"He's an idiot!" "Not my fault." "There's nothing to eat." "I hate my life!" "Why were you even born?" "Mom hates you." "I hate you!" And on and on. Todd curled up at the end of the couch and settled in for after school cartoons while the rest of the boys fought their way to other parts of the house where they weren't seen but could still be heard. She sat back down and picked up the towel she'd been folding. It was impossible to be happy in this house.

She turned her mind back to the job and decided she was going to tell Donnie. Tonight. The minute he walked in the door.

But the minute he walked in the door she knew she wouldn't go through with it.

"Donnie? What's wrong?"

He went straight to the kitchen and grabbed a bottle of beer from the fridge.

She followed him as far as the doorway. He opened the beer, took a long swig and then turned around and saw her standing in the doorway watching him. She knew better than to try to pry it out of him. Whatever caused that look on his face was something he would tell her about or he wouldn't, but he definitely wouldn't if she nagged him.

"You want me to fix you something to eat?"

"I'm not that hungry, just a sandwich."

They had been married long enough that Maggie was able to read everything in the intonations of Donnie's voice, even in one short sentence, as long as he wasn't drunk. And he wasn't drunk. He wasn't angry. He was worried.

She fixed his sandwich and brought it to the table. D.J. was in his room, surprise surprise, Dylan was in the basement working out, surprise surprise, Derek, Daniel and Todd were in the garage working on a project together, which really was a surprise. For the moment they were alone and the house was quiet, it would have been a perfect time to spring her plan on him but she couldn't. He may not notice or show sensitivity to her moods but she was wired differently. She would have to 'fix' his problem first.

"They laid off four guys today."

"Did you…"

"No, but there's no more over time and who knows if they'll lay off more guys." He looked straight at her for a second and then went back to eating his dinner.

"So what's that mean? I mean, we're okay right? Why are you so worried?"

"It means that we're going to have to cut back. They could lay me off tomorrow for all I know." He let his fork drop on his plate and sat back. "It means, Maggie, that we need to stop wasting money we don't need to be wasting, okay? But we'll be fine. Just cut back where you can okay?"

Maggie nodded. "Okay. But, you know I could still get…"

"Don't!" Donnie held his hand up between them. "Don't start. Just do your thing with the boys and don't spend where you don't have to."

"My thing with the boys?"

"Moooom?!"

Right on cue, thanks Todd.

"That." Donnie waved his hand toward the living room, "Just keep doing what you do and I'll keep doing what I do."

Don't start?! Keep doing what you do?!

"How about this Donnie? How about you keep doing what you do and I'll do *something* because I don't do *anything* now."

Donnie sighed. "Is this where I'm supposed to tell you that you're irreplaceable? That we couldn't live without you? What are you fishing for? You're great? You do everything?"

"I applied for a job."

"You're not getting a job."

"I already got the job." True.

"You're not taking it."

"I did. I took it." False. But a minor detail.

Donnie jumped out of his chair. "Undo it!"

"No." Maggie stood up to face him. "No. I won't undo it. It's always all about you. I've put my life on hold for you and the boys and all I get in return is…is nothing. I AM TAKING THIS JOB!"

Maggie took a step back. Donnie had never physically touched her before but she'd never seen this much anger in his face either. He turned and stomped out of the kitchen.

She followed him, saw him putting his jacket on. "Where are you going?!"

He turned around and shook his finger at her. "Maggie you are NOT taking this job and you better be ready to let it go by the time I come home or I swear to God Maggie, it's over! I will fight you for this house and the boys and you will be no where!. NO WHERE! Then you can have your stupid life you keep crying about!"

The door slammed so hard a picture fell off the wall.

Maggie stood frozen in place.

"Mom?"

She turned around.

"Mom? Are you still taking the job?"

She let out a long exhale and looked up the stairs and straight into D.J.'s eyes, "Can you come down here? We'll talk."

"Are you taking the job?"

"Yes. I am."

CHAPTER THREE

Maggie's desk was old, scrapped and scratched, missing two drawer handles and was covered with a trace of a black substance she guessed was a long ago spill. She loved it. Every inch of it. The desk had been a part of her life for three days and she already cherished it more than any piece of furniture in her own house, possibly even more than anything she owned. The minute she slipped into the chair each morning she felt herself surface, like she had been held underwater and now she was coming up for air.

The job itself was taking a little longer to get used to. The morning she called to ask if the job was still available Mandy answered and told her it was. Not only that it was but that she could start that day. She asked to talk to Mike but Mandy told her to just come in as soon as she could. Two hours later Maggie walked into FastTech expecting to be greeted by Mandy and trained by Mike. She was wrong on both counts.

The desk had been cleared and was completely empty other than an old stained tattered eight page list of instructions and a sticky note attached to the top that said, 'Just wing it and do your best. Thanks. Mandy. Below that, as if an afterthought it said, 'Mike's out of town. I'll let him know. Please don't quit'.

Her first instinct was to turn around and walk out the door.

But she didn't. She glanced at the instruction packet, walked around the office, glanced at the instruction packet again, pulled out the chair and sat at the desk. Her desk. That was when she knew she wouldn't walk out. She stood up to take her coat off and hung it on the coat rack in the back room and came back to the desk, her desk.

By eleven o'clock that first morning Maggie had made coffee and made peace with the absurdity of being left alone on her first day of work, if it could even be called that. She had answered the phone twice and discovered her professional phone voice. By the third call at eleven thirty she already had perfected the greeting that came out as smoothly as if she'd been reciting it for years. At noon she ate the smashed crackers she found at the bottom of her purse and thought about what she would do with the office if it were hers. By the time she finished the crackers and popped a piece of gum for dessert she decided to do it.

As she walked around the office pulling out file drawers and snooping in cabinets she thought about the insanity of it all. Donnie hadn't spoken to her in three days, he hadn't served her with divorce papers either though so she couldn't grasp a down side to that, she started her first job ever at thirty two years old, was abandoned on her first day, and was happier than she could remember being in a long time. So be it.

By the time she left that day all three filing cabinets in her office had new files folders and new labels. She hadn't heard a word from Mike and when she left at three she hoped he would still be out of town the next day, she had a plan for rearranging the office furniture. She turned the lights off and locked the door with a key she'd found when she was snooping.

The door was still locked when she got there the next day. There were no messages from Mike and it didn't look like anyone had been there since she left the day before. She began rearranging and cleaning. She found a stash of things in a storage room in the back and brought them out and back to life. She hung pictures on the walls, placed a desk organizer on her desk and filled it with office supplies, brought an old phone message pad back to life and centered it on her desk with neatly written messages from the calls she'd taken. By the time she left at three the front office looked like a completely different office. The only thing she hadn't touched was the computer on a corner desk next to hers. She didn't even turn it on. What was the point?

On her third day and when she came in nothing had changed. She was beginning to wonder if Mike had abandoned the business altogether but at a little after ten the phone rang and it was him.

"Good Morning! Thank you for calling FastTech. How may I direct your call?"

"Maggie! Oh thank God! Thank you! I am so so so sorry, I had no idea Mandy would pull this stunt and leave you there alone. I tried to call a million times but the cell service sucked. I'm on my way back. Thank you thank you for staying! Are you okay?"

"I need a raise."

"Seriously are you okay? Is everything okay?"

"Yes and no. I think so but how the hell would I know? I haven't even turned the computer on. I don't have a clue what I'm supposed to be doing. I've taken messages and made excuses for you but for all I know your clients have all gone elsewhere. If you even have clients. Not one single person has come in the door."

"I'm sorry Maggie, really. It's all good though, that office is a satellite office for the main office in Austin Texas and it's...I'll explain everything when I get there. Don't worry. Will you be there when I get there?"

"When will you get here?"

"About four, four thirty?"

She snickered. "I work nine to three so no, I won't be here."

"Oh. Right. You'll be in Monday though right?"

"This is the weirdest job. Is showing up optional?"

"I'll see you Monday. I'll explain the whole company and

the process and everything then okay?"

"See you Monday. At nine." She hung up and glanced around the newly decorated office. She might have some explaining to do too.

Nine o'clock Monday morning Mike wasn't there. She let herself in and made herself comfortable. She had to wonder, had she won the lottery or the booby prize of jobs? Time would tell.

At ten after ten Mike walked in the door. He strolled in acting like he owned the place, which apparently he did. He was wearing jeans and sneakers (or running shoes or jogging shoes? She'd never understand the difference). He had on a long sleeve L.L. Bean polo shirt. So the dress attire was casual woodsy. Good to know, she'd have to go shopping.

"Hey Maggie!" He tossed his jacket on the counter and did a double take. "Oh. You decorated."

She grimaced, not the reaction she had hoped for. "Yeah a little. I didn't know what to do with myself so I decorated."

"About that, I'm really sorry. This business is so random sometimes."

"Mike, what business is this exactly?"

"Let me just grab a cup of coffee, make a couple phone calls and we'll talk."

"Sure, and in the meantime I will...?"

Mike rubbed his hand over the lower part of his face as if smoothing his beard, if he had one, which he didn't. "Hmm, the counter and desk look great. The pictures on the wall though, maybe you could find something not so flowery?"

Maggie looked at the pictures, they were nice. "Really?"

The phone rang and Maggie answered it, asked the person to hold, and turned to Mike, "Mark Schillinger?"

"I'll take it in my office, put him on hold." He started toward his office, from around the corner she heard, "Thanks. And get rid of the flowers."

Her first task, put the call on hold, she aced it. Second task, remove the flowery pictures. She looked at each one, there were six all together, other than being slightly out dated and slightly cheap they were nice. She left them where they were.

A few minutes later Mike hollered "Come on back." She really needed to talk to him about an intercom system or something.

She walked into his office and took a seat. "Should I have brought paper and a pen?"

"For what?"

"For taking notes."

Mike laughed. "Maggie I think this job is a lot more laid back and easy going than you're thinking. Don't get me wrong, I'm thrilled, ecstatically thrilled, to have someone responsible manning the front out there but I hope you weren't expecting a Wall Street type pace."

Mike leaned back in his chair, put his feet on the desk and cupped his hands behind his head. Maggie sat back and relaxed.

"Better." He smirked. "Seriously, the office staff here consists of me. And you. That's it. If anyone walks through the door it's probably going to be a Jehovah's Witness or a kid selling something. We're a satellite office, our clients are all over the world and I'm willing to bet not a single one of them has ever even heard of Potsdam."

"Okay. So what do we do? What is FastTech?"

"We're a computer programming company. The main office is in Austin Texas but there are satellite offices all over. The office in Austin is really more of an IT type place, there are about twenty, twenty-five people that work there and all but two are techies, the other two are receptionists."

"Techies?"

"People that keep the servers up and running, computer geeks, you know."

No she didn't know but she nodded anyway. "Okay, so these satellite offices, what do we do?"

"Okay, there are people that write computer programs, like me, we can do pretty much everything we have to do from anywhere so we set up office wherever we want, some guys even work from home. Once in a while we meet up in Austin for a meeting or some kind of training or something but that's pretty rare, maybe three or four times a year. Okay, how do I explain this?" He rubbed his non-beard again. "Okay, FastTech is a company some computer wizard created, he's the owner. There are sales people and programmers, the sales people travel around get contracts then they hand out the contracts to a programmer. The programmer writes the computer program and then goes to the client's place of business and sets the program up and trains them how to use it. If they ever have a problem with it they call the programmer and we have to fix it. That's why I was out of town, fixing a problem I couldn't fix from here. That's what we do, over and over again. That's it really."

"So what do I do?"

"Lots, first you answer the phone. Most of my clients have my cell number and call me directly but it's extremely distracting and I want the receptionist to be the go between, couldn't do that with Mandy though. So that's what you'll do , it's just a matter of taking messages and then either I'll call them back myself or I'll tell you what to tell them and you'll call them back. If I can stop spending so much time on the phone I could probably write twice as many programs."

She could do that, so far so good. "What else? That's not it I hope."

"Billing, you'll need to invoice the clients, keep track of invoices, payments, all the accounts payable and receivable."

Uh oh. "Okay, I'll get some training on that?"

"Yeah, I'll show you, it's simple. We use Excel, I'd like to write my own program for it but who has time?" He snickered. Computer humor? "When I get a new client I travel to wherever they are to meet with them and spend a little time with the employees. I like to find out exactly what they're looking for and what they need. I like to know as much as I can about the company before I go so that's something else you'll do, research companies. It's simple, really Maggie, a monkey could do the job. Don't worry, I'll show you everything you need to know."

"Okay." She didn't feel okay about it yet but she'd have to trust him. "So do you actually work for FastTech or are you like a contractor or something? Do I work for FastTech or do I work for you?"

"I work for FastTech. You work for me. I get paid by FastTech, each contract is different, bigger contracts are bigger pay, smaller contracts are smaller pay. I can accept or refuse a contract. There's a lot of leeway and freedom of choice in it but still I work for FastTech, push comes to shove I answer to them. There's a lot of time consuming administrative stuff, that's why I need someone, a lot of bullshit too, another reason I need someone. You'll do all the things that I don't want to do so I can focus on writing programs and making money." Mike took his feet off the desk and leaned against it. "Seriously Maggie don't worry, it's an easy job, it's no different than taking care of a home with the finances and decisions and all that stuff you already do. It's just for a company instead of a family."

That simile didn't make her feel any more comfortable but she got the point. "Okay so what else do I need to know?"

"What else do you want to know?"

What else did she want to know? What happened between him and Donnie years ago for one thing but she probably better stick with business for now. "Why would you pay for an office and all the overhead if working from home is an option?"

"Let's not do that."

Do that? "Excuse me?"

"Personal life. Let's not go down that road yet," Mike clarified.

What was she supposed to say? She glanced at the wall, the floor, finally back at Mike but her mind hadn't figured out what he was talking about so she glanced back at the floor.

"Look, we were friends a long time ago," Mike said.

No we weren't.

"I've got a hundred questions to ask you and I guess you have a hundred for me too," he continued.

No she didn't.

"We've got a ton of catching up to do and I would love to spend the rest of the day doing just that but I have a program to work on and a trip overseas in a few days. So how about we table our personal lives for now and start some training?"

What just happened?

"Sure. Whatever. You're the boss."

She followed him out to the front office where he pulled a chair up to the desk next to hers and turned the computer on. As it was booting up he glanced at the walls and grunted at the flower pictures.

By noon Maggie had an entirely new perspective on the job. She couldn't wait to learn more. She was going to love it. She was almost disappointed when he suggested they break for lunch and order sandwiches to be delivered.

"So, guess it's time to start catching up. Tell me what's been happening in the life of Maggie for the last fourteen or so years."

In the excitement of training on the computer she had forgotten the moment of awkwardness with psycho Mike and his personal life rules. Her first reaction was to change the subject but after she thought about it for a second it really was an innocent question. They had attended the same school from kindergarten through graduation and hadn't seen each other in fourteen years, it was just common curiosity to wonder. In fact, she planned on finding out a bit about his life during those fourteen years as well.

"Oh you know, pregnant at graduation, had a kid, then another and another…"

Mike's eyes widened. "Three kids? Really?"

"And another…"

"Whoa! Four kids?"

"And another." Why was she feeling embarrassed? What difference did it make what Mike thought?

"Five?!" Mike laughed. "Wow Maggie! I mean that's really cool. I'm happy for you. I guess. Five? Wow! And Donnie…" He dragged Donnie's name out asking the question without having to ask it.

"Is the father of all five yes," she answered.

"So how many boys and how many girls?"

"Five and zero."

Mike grinned and nodded his head up and down. "That's awesome. Five boys! Who would have thought it way back then right? Maggie Kennedy head cheerleader and Don Conners star athlete with five kids! Everyone thought you'd climb the Wall Street ladder straight to the top. But here you are, still in Colton and with almost enough kids for a baseball team."

Maggie smiled weakly, was he mocking her? "Donnie," she said.

"Hmm?"

"Donnie not Don."

"Oh right, sorry."

Maggie didn't get the impression he really was. He held eye contact a couple seconds too long but maybe it was just her imagination, maybe she was projecting something that wasn't there. After fourteen years of knowing how much Donnie hated him but not knowing why it was only natural to be suspicious of him. She would have to be careful of her overactive imagination, she loved the job, it wasn't Wall Street but it was a job.

"So what about you?" she asked. "Do you have any kids?"

Mike took a deep breath and let it out. "Well, that's kind of a complicated story but yeah I do. I have a daughter. Actually you've met her."

Maggie's eyebrows crinkled and met in the middle of her nose. "I have?"

"Mandy."

"Mandy?" she thought for a second. "I don't think I know anyone named Mandy."

"My receptionist." Mike rolled his eyes.

"What?! No! The receptionist? Here? The one that, the, the girl that…"

Mike laughed and nodded his head.

"But she called you Mike."

"Yeah, that's part of the long complicated story. I just found out about her a few months ago, that's why I moved back and decided to open a satellite office here. We're just getting to know each other. Actually it would be safe to say we really don't know each other at all yet, but I'm working on that. Her mother's not, how should I say it, mother of the year material. From what I understand from the social worker Mandy has been basically without parental guidance for a while. Her mother's an addict. She pretty much started letting Mandy do whatever she wanted a few years ago and Mandy got in with the wrong crowd. She's been kicked out of school, went to a GED program and got kicked out of that. That's about the point I was notified, last spring I guess it was. I came back, social services agreed to let her stay at her mother's if her mother went through a drug rehab thing and Mandy enrolled in an evening GED program. She's under a pretty tight watch with social services, they both are. I'm still figuring out my part."

Maggie drew in a long breath and exhaled. "Wow."

"Yeah, that about says it all."

"So she knows you're her father?"

"Knows it but hasn't decided if she's going to accept it yet. Time will tell." He shook his head back and forth. "I don't know the first thing about raising a teenage girl."

"Neither do I," Maggie said.

Jillian? He's so nice! After he told me that about his kid it broke the ice. We felt like old friends.

Please tell me you don't have a crush on him.

NO! It's not like that, I SWEAR!

Okay, I believe you but still, promise me you will not have an affair.

SHIT JILLIAN! What's wrong with you?! I am NOT going to have an affair.

Okay okay, sorry. I can hardly remember him from hs.

Me either. He was invisible till whatever happened with him and

Donnie.
Anything new on that front?
Still not talking to me.
That sucks.
Says who?

Maggie wouldn't admit it but Jillian was right, it did suck. As much as Donnie annoyed her most of the time he did have a good side. In a perfect world he would remember to give her the silent treatment when he was about to say something stupid and forget to give it the rest of the time. But obviously it wasn't a perfect world because his silent treatment was working. It wasn't working the way Donnie undoubtedly hoped it would, she was holding firm and keeping her job even if he didn't speak to her for the rest of his life. But still it was working. She felt guilty and well, it sucked. It was time to break the silence and talk to Donnie.

Of all days the boys were in rare form, not good rare form either. The sounds of fighting preceded them. Maggie looked out the kitchen window and sure enough before they were all even off the bus D.J. and Dylan were in a tangle of swinging arms and kicking feet. The next thing Maggie saw Todd scurried off the bus and jumped right on top of them and that's when Maggie stopped watching and reacted. She ran to the door, ran down the driveway and pulled Todd off and placed him safely aside. Then she grabbed Dylan by the ear and lifted him up. She would have lifted D.J. up the same way but his hood managed to stay up during the entire brawl and she couldn't get to his ears. She reached out and got a death grip on his sleeve before he had a chance to roll away.

"WHAT IS WRONG WITH YOU TWO?" She screamed as she looked from one to the other. Out of the corner of her eye she saw the other three boys make a beeline for the house. She dragged Dylan and D.J. up the driveway and into the house. Neither of them spoke or tried to get out of her grip. "YOU ACT LIKE ANIMALS! I SWEAR TO GOD I'M

GOING TO SEND YOU TO JUVINILE BOOT CAMP!"
She pulled them into the living room and dropped them to the couch. Derek, Daniel and Todd escaped to the kitchen.

"WHY?!" She screamed at them. "WHY?!"

Neither spoke.

She yanked D.J.'s hood down, backed up a step and put her hands on her hips, her eyes slid from one to the other. "WHY?"

D.J. sat with his head down, she had a better chance of getting an answer out of Dylan. She slid her eyes and focused in on him. "WHY?"

Dylan held eye contact with her, shrugged his shoulders and said, "Cause we're boys?"

"No you're not! You're animals!" She broke eye contact and sat in the recliner. The fight dropped out of her. She felt a lump form in her throat and the threat of tears. This was too hard. Having kids was too hard. She was so sick of their fighting. Of everyone's fighting. It had to be her fault, other kids didn't act like this. Other couples didn't act like this. She dropped her eyes to the floor and blinked multiple times. When she looked back up both boys were watching her. She just shook her head.

D.J.'s normally vacant expression showed a hint of concern and Dylan began fidgeting. She swallowed and tried to get her throat to open up but she didn't think her voice would get around the lump that was there. So she said nothing. She thought of Donnie. Such power in the silent treatment.

She decided to let the boys stew in discomfort and start dinner. She would deal with them later. Right now she would just focus on dinner and try to calm down. She fixed a pot roast with potatoes and carrots. And chicken nuggets with sweet potato fries and lima beans. Two dinners. Donnie's most and least favorite meals. Talk about being conflicted.

When everything was finished and cooling on the top of the stove she went back in the living room to check on the boys. Dylan and D.J. were still sitting on the couch. They were watching television but they both looked uncomfortable when she walked in and despite knowing it was wrong to feel this way it lifted her spirits.

But that was about to change.

Daniel, Derek and Todd were building something with Legos on the living room floor. As soon as she walked in the room a discussion turned into an argument. Before she had a chance to decide if she cared the argument turned into a fight. The next thing she knew they were throwing Lego pieces and the swinging began. She decided she cared. She was about to intervene when Derek jumped up and the other two immediately followed suit and then they were chasing each other toward the kitchen.

"Stop!"

A second later she heard a bang followed by a very large crash.

"Mom?" Daniel called out. "Umm, Mom? Mom!"

"I'll go." Dylan stood up from the couch and walked toward the kitchen before her mind could process what was happening. Even D.J. had a shocked expression on his face as his non-hooded head ping ponged back and forth from Maggie to Dylan's back as Dylan walked toward the kitchen. Dylan? Helpful?

"Oh. As in uh oh." Dylan stood in the doorway between the kitchen and living room. "Mom? You know how you keep telling Dad you want him to take this wall out so you can have an open floor plan? This might be a good time to bring it up again."

She was pretty sure she didn't want to know but pretty sure she had no choice.

"Do I want to come in there?"

"Ummmm," Dylan pretended to be thinking about it.

"Do I have to come in there?"

"Ummmm, yeah."

She stood. Took a deep cleansing breath. Walked to the kitchen. Dylan stepped back to let her pass through the doorway. She stepped in. Stopped. Took another deep cleansing breath. There are some things a person thinks they need to know, like why D.J. and Dylan were fighting. But then there are some things a person doesn't want to know, like how an entire roasting pan worth of pot roast with potatoes and carrots ends up splattered across a twelve foot wall.

Maggie didn't necessarily believe in signs but the only thing that crossed the shock in her mind was that the most favorite dinner was smeared across the wall which left the least favorite dinner. There had to be some cosmic meaning behind that.

Maggie rested on the couch recovering from the kitchen clean up and her subsequent decision at seven o'clock to send all the boys to their rooms without parole for the rest of the night. The three younger ones couldn't decide whose fault the pot roast debacle was, each one could only confirm that it wasn't their fault. As long as she was sending them to their rooms she decided to pick up the Dylan/D.J. fight where she left off, except this time she didn't care why, she just sent them to their room too.

Donnie strolled through the door at a little after eight. Based on the hour and the no overtime rule three hours were unaccounted for. Maggie glanced his way just long enough to gauge his sobriety, for three hours unaccounted for he was moving extremely steady and purposefully, not drunk then. If she really wanted to talk to Donnie and break the silence the stage was clear for it.

She got up quietly and tip toed to the kitchen, peeking in before she made her final decision to tear down The Great Wall of Donnie. He was sitting at the table with his back to her eating his meal. She watched the ripple of his shirt as his arm raised to his mouth and back down to the plate again. She watched as he sat nearly perfectly still while he chewed, and then the ripple again as his arm raised more food to his mouth. She felt sad, a house full of people and she was lonely and he was alone.

"Hey." Her voice was barely louder than a whisper but the kitchen was so quiet he heard it and turned around. She held her breath waiting for a reaction.

She couldn't read any expression in his face but she broke

the silence and now she needed him to decide where to go with it, she waited him out.

Finally he took a deeper breath and she knew whichever way he decided to play it there was no backing down now.

"Lima beans?"

He said it so seriously and without any expression that it took Maggie a second to comprehend. A smile slowly crept across her face.

"And sweet potato fries. And chicken nuggets."

"Is this my final meal?"

"I guess that depends. Can we talk?"

Donnie nodded slowly. "We can try."

"Do you want to finish eating first?"

"Nah." He pushed his plate to the center of the table. "Come in, sit down."

Maggie took the seat kiddie corner to him, her usual seat was across the table but instinct told her to sit closer, bridge the distance a little. He wouldn't get it but maybe on a deeper level somewhere the symbolism of it would sink in.

"The boys are…"

"In their rooms being punished," Donnie smirked. "I know."

"How?"

"Dylan." Donnie picked up his phone from the table and opened it to a picture of the kitchen wall. "I'm actually surprised they're still alive."

Maggie smiled but at the same time she was feeling conflicted about Dylan sending the picture to Donnie. What was that about? She'd have to table that thought for later.

"I figured it would be too much work to hide the bodies."

Donnie snickered.

"Did he tell you why he and D.J. were sentenced to their room?"

"Yeah, the fight."

Maggie knew they were filling the space with talk of the boys because it was relevant but also because neither of them knew how to transition to what they really needed to talk about.

"Did he tell you what they were fighting about?"

Donnie nodded. "Us."

"What?" Her stomach rolled. "They were fighting about us?"

"I don't know exactly how it started or how it went but the gist of it was that Dylan told Derek that we're getting divorced and D.J. told him that in confidence and, I don't know, they got fighting and it got out of hand."

"Shit. Donnie? We are so screwing our kids up," Maggie's voice hitched. "We have to stop."

Donnie nodded. "Yeah, we do." He got up and put his plate on the counter. "Come in the living room, we've got a lot to talk about and the Clorox smell in this room is killing me."

An almost snicker rolled to Maggie's throat but died out before completion. The boys thought they were getting a divorce, shit.

Maggie noticed that Donnie didn't grab a beer from the fridge like he usually did when he left the dinner table, which was a good sign. It also occurred to her that she hadn't smelled any alcohol on his breath when they were talking. Another thought to table for later.

Donnie sat in the recliner and she sat on the couch. Again, both waited out the other, neither quite sure where to start, Maggie cleared her throat. "Well, it's probably my fault, the boys and the divorce thing. The night you threatened it and walked out D.J. was standing on the stairs. I asked him to come down and talk about it but he wouldn't. It didn't even occur to me to talk to him again after, guess I was kind of self absorbed with my own problems. And he's D.J., I don't know, he's D.J., he doesn't talk, but, this kind of proves that he just doesn't talk to *us*."

Donnie looked toward the stairs as if he expected to see D.J. standing there now and then he looked back to Maggie. "So what do we do? I'm not good at this Maggie you know that."

"What do you mean? Not good at what?"

"This," Donnie swooped his hand through the air, "All of it, but let's start with D.J., what do we do?"

Maggie grunted. "I don't know. He's a teenager, he hates us but all teenagers hate their parents' right?"

"I guess."

"Well, I guess we start by trying to make him like us. We still have to be parents but maybe we need to reach out to him more."

"What's that mean? Reach out to him?"

Maggie rolled her eyes. This wasn't going to be easy if she had to explain everything she said. "Come on, you know what I mean. Be around more, talk to him more, act interested in the things he's interested in. Both of us, we both have to make more effort."

"But what's he interested in?"

Maggie sighed in frustration. Sshe wanted to be patient but he could help out a little, did she have to guide him through everything? "I don't know! That's what I'm saying. Find out. Talk to him."

Donnie sunk further into the recliner.

"Donnie?"

"Yeah. Got it. Talk to him. I will. So, what about the other boys? Should we tell them we're not getting divorced?"

"Who says we're not? Wait, wait, sorry." She held her hands up in the 'stop' 'freeze' motion. "Sorry, it just came out, what I mean is before we talk to them we should probably talk about it ourselves."

He relaxed slightly.

"Donnie, please try to listen and talk and not get mad and walk out okay?"

"Okay."

"So where do you want to start? We have to talk about my working."

"Maggie, I don't really see what there is to talk about, I don't want you to work. You want to work. You went to work. What's left to talk about? Seems like a done deal to me."

Hmm, he was right, sort of. "Is it?"

"Are you going to quit?"

"No. Are you going to divorce me?"

"No. So I guess it's a done deal." He turned and reached for the remote.

Guess it is. There was so much more Maggie wanted to talk about. What was the real reason he didn't he want her to work? And he still didn't even know that her boss is his old high school enemy but she really didn't want to go down that road yet. She would take what she could get. At least they were talking again. She decided to be thankful that the issue of her working was finally out of the way even if the real issue behind it wasn't completely solved. The next battle could wait.

"Donnie, wait. What about the boys? We should tell them we're not getting divorced."

"We don't have to."

"Why not? We can't just let them think we are, remember how we're screwing them up?"

"We don't have to Maggie. D.J.'s been lurking at the top of the stairs since we started talking and apparently he talks to Dylan. And apparently Dylan talks to Derek. Problem solved."

Maggie's mouth dropped open but no words came out. That was so wrong on so many levels. She stared at Donnie but he was already pointing the remote at the television. She shook her head. He didn't notice. He hit the on button and The Outdoor Channel came to life.

She cleared her throat and he hit the volume button on the remote. Up.

"You'll have to check emails throughout the day, most of them you can respond to yourself once you get the hang of how things work, others you can forward to me and I'll take care of them." Mike showed Maggie how to find her way around the company's email account. He had tried to introduce her to Excel but at one point she got so confused that he thought it smart they take a break from it.

She thought she was picking it up pretty quickly, minus certain parts of the excel spreadsheet, and Mike seemed to think so too. He complimented her many times already and told her she was a natural. She thought so too, but she knew he was partly blowing smoke just to make her feel good, didn't matter, a compliment is a compliment.

"So," Mike sat back. "Time for a break, I'm going to order a sandwich, Reuben for you again?"

"Sure." As long as he was paying. "Fries too? They soak up the acid of the dressing, less chance of indigestion, if not that's fine I'll pass on the sandwich. I'll just eat the apple I brought."

"That's pathetic." Mike shook his head. "Seriously Maggie that was the best you could do?"

"Are you getting me fries?"

"Fine."

"Then I didn't need to do any better did I?"

"If you're self-training for a job in sales forget it. You can't guilt people into buying things. Doesn't work that way."

"Oh Mike, you have no idea do you? I guess that's why you're a programmer and not in sales."

"You know," Mike leaned forward in his chair. "Not to jump the gun here but if sales is an area you're interested in there are openings in our sales department, its pre-sales actually. FastTech sends their pre-sales people all over the world. Once I get you trained here I wouldn't want you to leave but if you were thinking of this as a stepping stone to something else, and I wouldn't blame you for that, this is a great company to work for."

"I'm not really that great with sales, if I were you would be ordering now and I'd be getting a slice of peanut butter pie too."

Mike shook his head, picked up his phone and ordered.

When he hung up she was smiling from ear to ear. "Nice, fries and a piece of pie. I guess you better tell me more about that sales job!"

While they waited for the food Mike told her a little about the sales job and then changed the subject and asked all about the boys and what it was like raising them and what they wanted to do with their lives. By the time the food arrived she felt like the topic of the boys had run dry and decided to take a stab at a topic she was curious to know more about.

"Tell me about your daughter, Mandy."

Mike shrugged his shoulders. "There's not a whole lot to tell. I don't even really know her yet."

Stike. But that was okay, she couldn't get the sales job out of her mind. "Then tell me more about that sales job, you were just kidding right?"

"Stick around here a while, you'll know all the programs FastTech uses and all about the company and how things work. It will be an advantage but even more importantly, you'll have an in…me."

"You really think if I worked as your receptionist for what? A year? Two? That you could get me a job in sales?"

"Yeah, I do. I know I could. In a year or two you could be flying all over the country, world actually, on FastTech's dime and making six figures."

"SIX FIGURES?!!" Maggie grinned. "Wait, you're not talking like a thousand-dot-change-change?"

"Huh?"

"Six real figures?? And free travel??"

"And bonuses."

"Where do I sign?"

Mike laughed. "Let's get excel spreadsheets under your belt first."

"Eh, I couldn't anyway, kids and all, you know. Back to that, tell me about Mandy."

Mike leaned back in the chair and put his feet up on her desk. She gave him the evil eye but he just rolled his eyes. She kept giving him the evil eye anyway.

"I'm going to take my feet off your desk now because I just decided to make a fresh pot of coffee but before I do I want you to understand I'm taking them off because I want to not because you want me to."

She'd been dealing with man/boy mentality for too long to fall for it but she let him have this round anyway. "Understood."

Mike returned with two cups of coffee and sat back down, both feet planted firmly on the floor. "So where were we?"

"Your daughter."

"Oh right. Mandy." He said her name like it was a clue to a puzzle he hadn't yet figured out. "Well, you remember what a stud I was in high school?"

Maggie choked on her coffee spraying what was in her mouth. Mike jumped back nearly knocking his chair over in the process.

"What the hell?"

"Sorry." Maggie grabbed Kleenex and began wiping the front of her shirt, it took every ounce of self-control to keep from laughing out loud. Mike a stud in high school? Hardly. Mike was the opposite of stud, Mike wasn't even Mike, he was some invisible entity that had a reputation as an idiot savant computer nerd. She would bet that at any given time if a survey had been done to find out what Mike even looked like, the majority of the survey's would have been turned back in blank. It astonished her how much he'd changed, not a stud then and not a stud now, but still quite a transformation.

"I'm not sure of the meaning behind that but I'll let it go for now. So, anyway, I didn't know this until a few months ago but apparently one wild night in high school resulted in Mandy."

"You didn't know? At all? Not even suspect? Ever?"

Mike shook his head, "No. I didn't even know her mother until that night, never heard from her again until a few months ago. Me and a few friends wound up at a party in Potsdam and," he shrugged, "fast forward and I find out I have an almost fifteen year old daughter."

"Wow!" He had friends? "That's crazy." He had friends? "So how did you find out about her?"

Mike leaned back and put his feet on the desk, glanced at Maggie, took his feet off the desk. "Well, starting back a little earlier; right after high school I went to Texas for a job, not this one a different one then, and I settled in there. I think I came home for a visit a total of maybe ten times since we graduated. I had never heard from her, and I left like a week after we graduated so I guess by the time she found out she was pregnant I was already gone."

"Wait, that doesn't make sense, your parents were still alive then, it's not like you just disappeared off the face of the earth. She could have found you if she wanted."

"Yeah probably, if she really wanted to. We didn't have social media then though. It would have been harder than it would be now. And honestly Maggie, I don't even know if she knew my name."

"Well obviously she did, she found you now."

"Well social services did but I guess she must have given it to them, I don't know, it's just how it worked out. One drunken high school night and, a few months ago I get a phone call and I find out I have a daughter named Mandy who is almost fifteen and quite possibly headed to foster care unless I was willing to move back and save her from herself."

"And you did."

"What else could I do? Once I knew she existed I couldn't pretend she didn't."

"So how did she react to you waltzing into her life like that?"

"Well, honestly, she still hasn't reacted. It's a little weird. Well, a lot weird, but Mandy, she's different. I haven't figured her out yet."

"Different how? Besides the obvious."

"Her mother told her the truth, that she was the result of one night with a stranger back in high school. I probably wouldn't have handled it that way but... but anyway, Mandy never asked for more than that. There wasn't more than that to tell anyway. When social services tracked me down and told me the situation I came back and met Mandy and her social worker at a restaurant for dinner and that was where the social worker told her who I was. Mandy didn't even seem to care. It was like she told her I was the waiter or the maitre de. That's how she's been ever since. It's like she lacks comprehension or something. She's not stupid, she's not rude, I can't figure out what she is."

"Weird."

"That's what I'm saying, she's weird. She lives in her own little world. She doesn't show any interest in me but she doesn't avoid me either. She doesn't hate me but she doesn't like me. It's so frigging weird. She lives in some whole different place in her mind where nothing exists but what she wants to exist. Like working here, it seemed to fit in for her at first but when it didn't anymore she just decided not to. It's not just me, she's like that in everything, she lives in Mandy's world. If all teenagers are like that the future is in for a world of hurt." Mike looked up at Maggie like he just realized she was there. "What about your teenagers? Are they like that?"

She was thinking about it but Mike must have thought she wasn't going to answer and continued.

"I know we were a little like that when we were teens, I know some of it's probably normal. I don't think I spoke more than a dozen words to my parents a day. My world was my computer, I spent pretty much every waking moment on my computer, I guess maybe my parents might have thought the same about me. I don't know, is it really different now? Different interests maybe but is the teenage behavior really any different than it was when we were teens?"

"I think it is. I think it's way different, they have a lot less respect and society's expectations seem to be a lot lower for kids now than they were when we were kids. Failure is an option now. Just watch the news one night, our world is a mess Mike. The bar is so low they don't even have to stretch."

"That's pathetic."

"It is pathetic," she agreed. It was also pathetic that this was the first time in longer than she could remember that she felt completely at ease and free to voice an opinion. For once, finally, Maggie felt like Maggie.

In the weeks that followed Mike and Maggie developed a comfortable working relationship. They rarely spoke about their personal lives but they got into long discussions about the world and their places in it. It sustained her. That, coupled with the fact that Jillian was moving home was enough to balance the fact that Donnie had done nothing to reach out to D.J. or to improve things at home. At work she was Maggie Kennedy. At home she was Maggie Conners.

On the surface she felt happy enough but on those long nights when she lay awake in bed she knew deep down that it couldn't sustain her forever. On those occasions she imagined herself traveling to exotic places and meeting with worldly people as a future FastTech Sales Representative. In those half awake half asleep dreams there were no meals to be made or children to take care of, the monotony of her real life didn't exist.

It did though, the monotony of her life was a very real part of her days. She taught herself, without trying, to pretend. She pretended when she had a birthday party for D.J. when he turned fifteen and again for Dylan when he turned fourteen. She pretended when she took the boys trick or treating on Halloween. She pretended when she fixed meals and did laundry, when she attended parent-teacher conferences and Cub Scout meetings and asked Donnie how his day was and when she filled the cart at the grocery store after work.

She pretended through the rest of September and October and by the middle of November it occurred to her that she wasn't pretending anymore, it was her new way of life.

CHAPTER FOUR

To every Mother that has school age children the term Thanksgiving Vacation is a cruel slap in the face. There is no thanks. There is no giving. It is no vacation. And, if you can't find somewhere to go where the matriarch of the family loves to cook, you'll spend the day cooking and cleaning up from cooking. That's it. That's the definition of Thanksgiving to every Mother that has the courage to be honest.

Fortunately Maggie knew someone that loved to cook and clean and she had one week to weasel an invitation.

Jillian was the key. She had to get to Jillian to get to Louise. Piece of cake.

What's happening in N.J.?
Not much, same old. You?
Dreading Tday vacation, office closed for week, will be home with boys. Dreadful.
Don't be pretentious. Come home, you need a little N.Y. before you're ruined completely.
Thought about it. Maybe.
Nice. Louise cooking?
If we come, probably even if we don't, you know her.

You're overdue. You should come.

Maybe. Will talk to George tonight, let you know. Hey, if we do, you want to come to Tday dinner?

Maggie paused with the phone in her hand her thumbs poised to type. Play it smart!

Nah, thanks though.
Why not? Why cook if Louise will?
True. Think she would mind?
Louise? She'll cook enough for an army anyway, she always does.
Right. I forgot. Okay, let me know, if it's on we'll come.
K. Let you know tonight. Yay!
Maybe Yay, you gotta convince the city boy first.
Shouldn't be a problem.

It turned out convincing George wasn't the problem, convincing Donnie was.

"For the last, however many years, I've spent Thanksgiving day cooking all morning and half the afternoon and cleaning the rest of the afternoon and evening while you watched the parade, ate, then watched football and ate some more. Jillian and George are coming home and I'm spending every single minute I can with Jillian and that includes Thanksgiving Day so either you're going with us or you're staying home by yourself. No! Wait! Either you're going or you *and* the boys are staying home by yourselves."

"You're bluffing."

"Am I?"

Donnie hung his head in resignation, whether he believed she was or not didn't matter, he wasn't willing to risk the consequences if she wasn't.

"So we're going, all of us?"

"Fine."

Maggie pumped her fist in the air, she was really starting to like standing up for what she wanted. Maybe the future didn't have to be more of the same. Somewhere along the way she had heard the expression 'if you always do what you've always done you'll always get what you always got', it sounded like a lot of mumble jumble and a dire prediction of the future, then. Was she really able to change things now, at this late stage in the game? For so long the life around her had squeezed her in place but now, now she felt the space around her. She wasn't suffocating anymore. She was breathing fresh air and with the fresh air came fresh hope.

Maggie had no trouble falling asleep for a change. The worries and thoughts that locked themselves in the back of her mind all day, but always slid to the front of her mind demanding to be listened to when she laid down at night, were nowhere around tonight. She drifted off to sleep before her head hit the pillow.

"What the hell?!"

Maggie startled awake, her eyes opened.

"Damn it Maggie! You poked me right in the frigging eye!"

Donnie was sitting up holding one hand over his left eye. Maggie blinked to clear her sleepy vision. It took a second or two before sleep and wake separated. And when it did she started laughing, first a giggle and then a laugh and then uncontrollable laughter.

"It's not funny! I think you scratched my frigging eye!"

Maggie rolled and shoved her face into her pillow to muffle her laughter, when she got some control of herself she looked back at Donnie. "I'm sorry. Were you awake?"

"What do you mean was I awake?! Not until you scratched my eyeball with your fingernail!"

Maggie felt the laughter bubbling up. "Why were your eyes open?" But she couldn't hold it in, she couldn't understand how she scratched his eyeball when he was sleeping but it didn't matter, all she could do was laugh.

"There is something seriously wrong with you!" Donnie slammed his feet on the floor and left Maggie lying in bed uncontrollably laughing into her pillow.

"Things are finally starting to feel right." Maggie told Jillian after they snuck outside to steal a few minutes to themselves Thanksgiving morning. "I love my job and Donnie hasn't said a word about it since we talked. D.J. hasn't gotten in any trouble and the other boys are status quo. Everything is finally going right!"

"That's wonderful Maggie."

"Whoa, did you just say wonderful? Grandma Jillian from 1948?"

Jillian rolled her eyes, reached out and shoved Maggie.

"Seriously Jillian I think you need to move back, you're not Jillian Francis Harper Emerson anymore, you're turning into just Jillian Emerson."

"That was kind of mean, even for you."

"Aw come on, Jill I'm not trying to be mean, just honest. Friends are supposed to be able to be honest with each other right?"

"I think there's a correlation between time spent together and levels of honesty. If we were together every day you could be completely honest but since we're only together a few hours every couple months you have to filter the honesty now. You're supposed to just say what I want to hear."

"Or you move back here and we can spend time together every day."

"Speaking of that, do NOT tell Louise yet but George had a meeting the other day, they are talking spring."

"WHAT? WAIT? You are moving home in the spring?!"

"Hold on, maybe, probably, fingers crossed!"

"YEEEESSS!!"

Jillian grabbed Maggie, put her hand over her mouth and held it there. But it was too late. George was first but the entire household emptied right behind him as they ran onto the front stoop in reaction to the scream.

"What's wrong?!" George gasped. He had stopped a little too short and before anyone had a chance to respond Donnie flew into his back knocking him down the stoop and to the ground. Donnie fumbled to catch his balance and lost, falling on George's legs. Dylan was next in line but with his athletic ability and younger quicker response he managed to jump over them and landed on his feet on the other side. Everyone else had slowed enough to stop themselves on, near, or around the stoop. Louise, last out the door and carrying Shea, was the first to speak.

"Oh, my." She glanced from the men to the ladies to the children. "Oh, my. Is everyone okay?"

"Ow."

Everyone's heads turned toward George.

"Really ow or get off me fat pig ow?" Maggie asked.

"Maggie!" Louise grimaced.

"Get off me fat pig ow." George answered.

Frank stepped to Donnie and reached his hand out pulling him off of George. He then reached his hand out to George and helped him up.

"What just happened?" George asked as he brushed himself off.

"Jillian and George are moving home in the spring!"

"Maggie!" Jillian yelled.

Maggie held her hands out in front of her feigning innocence. "What? Why does everyone keep yelling at me?"

Louise had already handed Shea to Frank and bounced to Jillian. She had her trapped in a big bear hug and still managed to bounce up and down. Over Louise's shoulder Jillian saw Frank and George pull their wallets out of their back pockets and each hand a twenty to Donnie.

Maggie had seen it too and simultaneously they asked, "What's going on?"

Frank shook his head. "I really thought it wouldn't be until after dinner."

George grunted. "I was absolutely certain it would be during dinner."

Donnie grinned from ear to ear. He made a big production of folding the twenties and slipping them in his pocket. "You obviously don't know them as well as I do. I'm surprised it took this long."

"What are you guys...hey! You bet on if I would tell

Maggie?" Jillian still spoke over Louise's shoulder.

"Not if, when." Frank corrected, then added, "Louise, you should probably let go of Jillian now."

Louise reluctantly let go, but only because the timer in the kitchen dinged and if there was one thing that could get Louise's attention it was that ridiculous egg shaped timer.

"Dinner is served." Louise proclaimed a few minutes later.

"My three favorite words." Frank led the way to the kitchen. Frank and Louise lived in an older farm house and though there wasn't a formal dining room the kitchen was huge and had plenty of room for their normal kitchen table and two additional tables Frank had set up earlier in the day.

"Wow!" Maggie exclaimed. "This looks great Louise."

The table was covered, the additional tables were covered, the counter was covered. Louise had prepared every traditional Thanksgiving dish and then some. Everyone's mouth was watering as their eyes were traveling from dish to dish to dish.

"Sit!" Louise commanded.

Finding where they were to sit was not a problem, Louise had made turkey shaped name tags and attached them to turkey shaped chocolates. Maggie watched as the boys settled in their seats and quickly stopped the younger two from opening their candies. Jillian helped Pete find his place next to Todd and then put Shea in a high chair next to her own chair.

Once Shea was settled in her high chair all the adults dove for their seats, a prayer was said and Thanksgiving dinner officially began. In traditional Thanksgiving style, it was devoured with numerous 'oohs' and 'aahs' and in record time everyone was sitting back and holding their overfull stomachs, except Shea who had fallen asleep sitting up and was slumped over a bowl of something purple and pureed.

"Jillian I'll take Shea to her crib if it's okay? Everyone else feel free to move to the living room. I'll clean up in here in a few minutes."

The men and boys quickly obeyed but Jillian and Maggie lingered at the table a little longer.

"Maggie, I'm happy that your life is filling in the way you want. I have to tell you though I'm still a little concerned about, "she lowered her voice to a whisper, "about Donnie not knowing about Mike."

Maggie got up and helped herself to a cup of coffee from the carafe on the counter. She brought it to the table and sat back down. "I know."

Jillian waited her out but when she didn't elaborate Jillian put her hand on Maggie's arm. "Listen, I'm not trying to tell you what to do but I think you should tell him. It seems like it would be better to tell him instead of him finding out some other way. And it seems like the sooner the better, the longer you wait, well, it's like living a lie isn't it? Just my opinion, that's all I'll say okay?"

"I am living in a lie but it also feels like I'm being true to myself for the first time ever. Kinda sucks that to be true to myself I have to lie to my husband."

"Do you think there's any way he would let you stay there if he knew about Mike?"

"I don't know what would happen but I'm pretty sure the answer is no, he wouldn't."

"That really does suck. I'm sorry Maggie. What are you going to do?"

Louise came back in the kitchen just then. "The little princess is sound asleep! Jillian she's adorable! I can't get enough of her! Are you really, *really* going to move back in the spring?"

"I hope so Louise, I can't promise anything yet but the pieces are falling into place so hopefully."

Louise's eyes gleamed, she stepped behind Jillian and hugged her shoulders. "I'm so happy, so *so* happy. I can't wait to babysit the kids. If you move back you'll let me watch them some won't you?"

"Of course!" Jillian laughed.

"In the meantime I have..." Maggie pointed over her shoulder toward the living room and the sound of boys and more boys and more boys, "I have..."

"So. Anyway, I'll just pick up here and then we'll start thinking about dessert. Why don't you two steal a few minutes to yourselves and take a walk?" Louise began gathering dishes from the tables.

Maggie frowned at Jillian who laughed and shrugged her shoulders.

"Go on ladies, I'll get this, go! Go!"

"You look like you're enjoying yourself." Mike swept through the door at Fast Tech, unexpected, to catch Maggie doing a happy dance to the copier.

"Geez Mike!" She dropped the stack of papers which fanned across the floor near her feet, completely out of order now. "Shit!"

"Nice way to welcome back the boss." He tossed his jacket in the general direction of the coat tree where it managed to snag on a peg and hung perfectly like he purposefully meticulously placed it there.

"Nice way to scare the crap out of the Administrative Assistant."

"Administrative Assistant? When you left for Thanksgiving vacation you were a receptionist. What happened in the week I was gone?"

"I needed a title that sounded more impressive so I gave myself one. What are you doing here? You're supposed to be in California for another week."

"Finished early. They wanted everything up and running before everyone started taking off for Christmas. Worked a little overtime, the weekend, and voila, here I am."

"Well voila you could have called."

"Why? Is there something you do here that you need to hide, besides the crazy person dance?"

"No, but I could have adjusted your schedule so you wouldn't be sitting around all week. I might still be able to get you a few appointments but a little notice would have been nice."

"Don't bother, I have plenty of programming to do, and Christmas shopping. Hate Christmas shopping. Hey, you're my assistant? Isn't that what you called yourself?"

"No! Administrative Assistant, I only assist in admin...i...strate..." Maggie crinkled her nose, she hated when words didn't work out the way they were supposed to, "Work stuff."

"Fine." Mike stepped through the doorway heading to his office, once out of sight he yelled back over his shoulder, "And about that appointment schedule thing, we need to talk."

Maggie put the papers she had gathered from the floor onto her desk and followed Mike into his office. "What do you mean we need to talk?"

"Oh geez. Don't give me that look. Would it be too much to ask for a few minutes to acclimate myself after being away for eight days?"

Maggie rolled her eyes. "Acclimate yourself?! Here, let me help you acclimate," She pointed to his desk, "Your desk." She pointed to his coffee maker, "Your coffee maker." She pointed to the tables of computer parts and pieces, "Your mess." She pointed to herself, "Your Administrative Assistant who kept everything running smoothly *and* negotiated two new contracts with sales."

"How long have you been married?"

"What? Fifteen years."

"Frigging miracle. That guy's got to be a saint." Mike shook his head. "Now get out of my office and go read Administrative Assistant for Dummies...or something...office etiquette...something."

Maggie rolled her eyes and left him to acclimate, in their own offices they were both smiling, rolling their eyes and shaking their heads, but both smiling.

At noon Mike finally emerged from his office and announced that he had ordered sandwiches. He pulled a chair from the back room and sat at the corner desk next to Maggie's. "So, fill me in on what happened while I was gone."

She did. She had prepared for that very question since it

was his first lengthy trip out of town leaving her in charge and she wanted to prove to him how capable she was. She ticked off every report, correspondence and accounts receivable or payable that she thought he needed to know about. To further impress she had hard copies of the important correspondences and reports in manila folders and handed them to him at the appropriate times.

"Wow. Impressive. Okay, you can keep the A.A. title."

"The…"

"Administrative Assistant."

"Oh. Right."

"Now, about negotiating contracts with the sales guys," Mike tapped the folders on his knee, "that's not exactly in your job duties."

"I'm an overachiever." Maggie was getting a little nervous, he was uncharacteristically in serious mode, she mentally ran through the contract deals, she still thought she nailed it, both of them. He should be thanking her, why wasn't he thanking her?

"You're gung ho that's for sure. Listen, I don't know how you even knew to negotiate a contract, forget about having the confidence or nerve to do it, but you did good, you negotiated the contracts probably better than I would have been able to."

"So what's the problem?"

Mike sighed, fidgeted, tapped the folders. "Well, the problem is you're a receptionist, my receptionist, you're not in the sales department, that's their job."

"I don't get it. I negotiated better deals for you, better scheduling and more money. Why is that bad?"

"First, tell me how you even knew what to negotiate."

"I have to refer to your contracts remember? For the menial receptionist tasks? I read them. I could see what was weak and needed to be negotiated to your advantage. So I did. So Mike, I'm not trying to be stupid, or arrogant, but I don't get why it's a bad thing."

"John wants you to join sales."

"Sales?! As in six figure sales?"

"Sales as in travel and leave your kids to their own demise sales."

"Damn, you have an evil streak."

"It doesn't matter though, listen, John's not going to recruit you unless I give the okay and Maggie, nothing personal but you're not ready. You did great with those two contracts, thank you, but you don't have enough knowledge of how things work yet." He held his hand up to prevent an interruption. "I think you are perfectly capable of a job in sales but you've only been here, a few months? Take your time, slow down, learn the company. If you jumped into sales now you'd be starting from scratch in their skimpy training program, if you wait and learn the company you'll have a huge advantage, seriously Maggie you'll be way more equipped for success if you wait. When the time is right I'll give John a call and you'll be in, simple as that. Just trust me on this Maggie, okay?"

Maggie's heart pounded and her mind swirled in ten different directions. Six figures?! Travel?! A fleeting image of Christian Dior clothing flew past her mind's eye. "Wait, let me get this straight. John wants to hire me now. For sure? Six figures, travel, all that? But you think I should wait and learn more about the company? You think I should pass on all that so I can keep being your recepti….administrative assistant?"

Mike nodded his head.

"I repeat. And you think I should wait? Are you crazy?"

"I can't guarantee anything but the company is solid, I don't see anything crumbling there. Even if John left the company I could still get you into sales, he's just a sales guy his recommendation skips a step or two that I would take but a recommendation from either of us holds the same weight. And Maggie, six figures is possible, a lot of the sales people are making that but they didn't in the beginning. Well, some did but the income depends on ambition and how much time you're willing to devote to the job. A nine to three schedule isn't going to make you six figures. As a matter of fact, that wouldn't fly, you'd have to commit to full time plus, are you really willing to do that?"

Yes! "No. You're right. I have the ambition and the drive and I really think I could make it happen, the job I mean, I know I could be successful, but you're right about the time. Kids. It's never going to happen."

"Never say never. Just be patient Maggie. It doesn't matter how much you plan and plan, things that are meant to be will be, and things that aren't won't. It's good to have goals and it's good to be working toward those goals but sometimes you just have to let life unfold how it's going to, and then you have to accept what it is."

"Do you have low testosterone?"

"WHAT??"

"I just never thought I'd hear a guy say something like that."

Mike puffed his chest out, ran his hand over the stubble on his face. "Don't worry about my testosterone."

Maggie tilted her head toward his legs, his legs crossed at the knee. "Yeah okay but just man up a little would you?"

Mike glanced down at this crossed legs, uncrossed them and jumped up. "I'm going to get the sandwiches." He turned, grabbed his jacket off the coat rack and started out the door.

"I thought they were being delivered!" Maggie yelled.

Just before the door shut behind Mike she heard him mumble something about the gym.

Three days after Christmas Maggie served dinner and the usual conversations ensued, who was a dork, who broke what toy, the end of Christmas vacation, George and Jillian moving back in the spring. During most of the meal everyone was talking above everyone else and no one was actually listening.

After dinner she cleaned the kitchen, checked on the boys and found the three younger ones in Derek's room building a massive Lego town. Dylan was back in the basement with his weights. She went in the living room but it was empty, and quiet. She was just about to fall into the couch when she heard a noise that sounded like the garage door banging. She should ignore it and fall into the couch. It was just a garage door banging. But D.J. wasn't in his room. And Donnie wasn't in the living room in his recliner like usual. It wasn't much but it was enough to set off an alarm of concern for a household of people that were, however dysfunctional, ritualistic. But there was also a free couch and a quiet room.

She heard another sound coming from the garage but this time it was voices. D.J. and Donnie?? Was it possible? She went to the door that led to the garage and opened it. It took a moment for her to comprehend what she was seeing but when it did anger soared through her brain and every molecule of her body.

Donnie and D.J. were sitting in lawn chairs. They each had a beer in their hands.

"D.J.! Go to your room! NOW!"

D.J. jumped at the sound of her voice. He dropped his can of beer and didn't bother to pick it up, he was past her and headed to his room before Donnie was even out of his lawn chair.

"Hold on!" He held his hands up to stop her. "Wait! Just listen."

She didn't want to listen but she was so angry she could barely breathe forget about speak.

"It isn't what you think. Don't freak out. You told me to talk to him, remember? Remember when you told me to try to get closer to him? That's what I was doing. I was doing what you told me."

The stupidity of his defense jarred her speech free. "I didn't tell you to serve alcohol to a fifteen year old!! YOU IDIOT!!"

"Wait!"

"NO! You listen to me…"

"Maggie you told me to talk to him! Okay maybe I shouldn't have given him a beer but it was just one beer, he didn't even drink it."

"Donnie YOU IDIOT! What is wrong with you?!"

"You told me to talk to him!" Donnie's voice cracked and he stopped yelling and started talking, "I'm not you Maggie. You can't tell me to do something and then tell me how to do it. Okay, giving him a beer was maybe wrong but..."

"Don't. Go Donnie. I don't care where you go, just go."

"Maggie..."

"Go." She looked him in the eye and it took every ounce of control she had not to punch him. "Give me two hours to calm down. Two hours, and then you better come home because you better believe we are going to talk about this, and the rest of our lives. And you better come home sober. If you can't come home sober then don't come home. At all."

Donnie didn't come home in two hours. And he didn't come home sober. She lay in her bed after getting the boys to bed and warning D.J. that in the morning when her temper was back in control they were going to discuss what happened. When two hours had passed and Donnie hadn't come home she entertained a period of pure anger and then pure sadness. She fell asleep with tears drying on her face as she wondered how she could be mourning the end of a marriage she wasn't happy in.

Maggie dreamt the song "Crazy" by Gnarls Barkley, but only one verse, kept playing over and over. She was somewhere in that space between dreaming and awake where she couldn't determine the spot where the dream ends and wakefulness begins. She rolled to her side and the sound became slightly louder, she rolled to her other side and the sound became softer. She was too groggy to make sense of it but not groggy enough to ignore it. Fortunately it stopped. She pulled the blanket up tighter and tucked it under her chin and curled into herself. Sleep.

*I think you're craaaaazy...*Auughh!

She didn't have the energy to open her eyes but she did, barely, have the awareness to realize she wasn't dreaming and suddenly it made sense. Her ring tone! She threw the blankets off and in one second consecutively noticed Donnie was not in bed, it was 1:14 a.m., her pounding heart was dangerously close to breaking out the front of her chest and her phone was just out of reach. She sat up and leaned over and grabbed the phone.

"Hello?!"

"Mom?!"

Her heart slammed against her chest. "D.J.?!"

"Mom don't yell don't scream don't freak. I'm okay but I need your help."

Tangents of every possible thought and reaction slammed together and fought for the forefront space in her mind. D.J.? Help? In his room? 1:14 a.m.? He speaks complete sentences? Where is Donnie? What's going on? Don't freak?

"D.J.?! Where are you?!"

"Okay, this is the part I need you to not freak about, I'm out by the cemetery, on Wildwood Road. I need you to come get me."

Huh? "D.J.! Why? How? What…"

"Mom PLEASE! Just come get me. And take Dad's car, I kind of have yours here."

WHAT??? "WHAT?"

"Just come get me. PLEASE!" He hung up.

Maggie jumped out of bed and ran down the stairs. She saw Donnie on the couch and began shaking him.

"Donnie?! DONNIE!" He didn't stir, didn't blink, didn't move. He's dead! she thought, then she smelled the liquor on his breath and was both relieved and pissed. She shook him harder but he still didn't stir. She ran to the hallway and grabbed his keys and her purse off the stand, her jacket from the closet, and shoved her feet into someone's boots.

Donnie's car was covered with about two inches of new snow, she brushed it off the front windshield and took off. It wasn't until she was out the driveway that her mind resumed thinking and again all the possible thoughts started scrambling and fighting to be heard. She had left her kids home alone with an unconscious drunk, what if one of them woke up? What if they needed something? What was D.J. doing out at this hour? He stole the car! Where was he? What happened? Should she call the police? Should she kill him? Was he hurt? What would she do? What should she do?

The fortunate part about being called out at 1:14 a.m. was that there was no one else on the road, the unfortunate part, besides everything that was encompassed by being called out at 1:14 a.m., was that the plows weren't out yet either, or at least not on the roads she was taking. She drove as fast as she could while still trying to stay safe. She had to get to D.J. Who would if she didn't?

She turned onto Wildwood Road and within seconds she saw her car, in the ditch, really really in the ditch. Damn. She pulled behind it being sure not to get too far off the road and end up in the ditch with him. In one swift movement she put Donnie's car in park, jumped out and began running to her car. D.J. opened the driver's side door of her car and began climbing the ditch heading toward her.

"D.J.??!! Are you okay?" She yelled. She was running toward him now, ready to grab him and pull him into the safety of her arms.

"I'm fine I told you don't freak out!"

"WHAT HAPPENED? Are you okay? Why were you even out? Are you okay? D.J.! You STOLE my car?!"

"You're freaking out. I was going to a party. I went in the ditch."

Maggie stared at him as he walked right past her. Who is this person? She stood behind him now, her eyes directly on him willing him to look at her. She was about to make an angry accusation that she knew she would never be able to take back and she wanted, needed, him to look at her so she could see the D.J. she gave birth to. She needed to see the little boy that she thought she'd glimpsed just a matter of hours ago. She needed to put that person over this person in order to stop the words that were dripping in her mind.

"D.J.?"

He stopped and turned and she saw what she needed to see. He was still there, hidden, but still there.

"Get in the car and don't say a single word."

When they pulled into the driveway Maggie stopped the car and put it in park. She hit the child safety lock. All he had to do was hit the button on his door and he could escape but she hoped the sound of the lock engaging would make the point that he wasn't to move. They had ridden home in total silence with one exception. When they first got in the car Maggie, with her eyes facing forward and her hands stiff and straight on the steering wheel said, "DO. NOT. SPEAK." He had obliged. He probably hadn't planned on speaking anyway.

Maggie took a deep breath and let it out. She had a feeling she was more nervous than he was. On a deeper level it made sense, his actions and behaviors were inexcusable but he was fifteen and whatever punishment he received would most likely be long forgotten in time. Her actions and behaviors, on the other hand, would play a part in molding *who* he was to become.

"D.J." She took another deep breath and let it out slowly so he would hear the anguish she felt. "Before I say anything else I want you to understand that I love you and that I believe that you love me too. I mean what I'm going to say but I want you to understand the whole picture. I loved you from the beginning and I'll love you to the end. This is one incident and as serious as it is, no matter what I say, my love for you doesn't change. Okay?"

She looked at him but he only offered her a slouched profile.

"D.J.?"

He nodded. Or at least his hood bobbed up and down, slightly.

"Okay. Now. I love you but you are an asshole."

His head snapped up and he looked straight at her.

"You are, D.J. I know that deep down you're not but you've been acting like an asshole for some time now and I've let it go. I'm done with it now. You crossed the line tonight.

I know you're smart enough to understand this so listen. IT'S OVER. DONE. I want you to think about everything, your entire life, from the very first moment you can remember to the very last moment you can imagine. And I want you to think very long and hard about where you are right now and where you'll be if you keep going in this direction. I want you to THINK." She paused a second to let it sink in and though she had no intention of letting him speak she waited to see if he would. He didn't.

"Now go in the house, go to your room, get some sleep and we WILL talk about this tomorrow. You will be punished and you will pay the consequences. Do you understand?"

His hood bobbed.

"Go."

They both got out of the car and went into the house. Not another word was spoken between them. She went to the kitchen and he went up the stairs to his room. When she heard his door close she took off her jacket and the boots, brought them to the hall closet and then went to the living room to deal with Donnie.

By now he must have slept off enough of his drunk because he stirred after the third hard shove, of her foot, against his ribs.

"Maggie?" He rubbed his eyes and blinked hard and repeatedly like she might disappear one of the times he opened them.

"Get up. And wake up. Do whatever you have to do to wake up because in one minute you and I are going to talk and I need you to understand exactly what I say." She sat down in the recliner across from him and stared at him.

Donnie shook his head a little to clear the cob webs, fat chance, and stretched. He made an effort to see the clock but she doubted that even with the exaggerated super squint he could see it. He sat up and put his feet on the floor, shook his head again and then looked at her, "Okay." He said.

Far from it but he'd find that out momentarily.

"While you slept off another stupid immature drinking

spree your fifteen year old son stole my car, drove off in the middle of the night to go to a party and put my car in the ditch. He called me to rescue him and I tried to wake you up. I couldn't. I took your car and rescued him, brought him home, my car is still in a ditch out on Wildwood Road. Now listen closely. Those are the facts of tonight. These are the facts of the rest of your life…"

Maggie paused just long enough to take a deep breath. Her eyes never left his though his eyes left hers long enough to try another attempt at reading the clock.

"…Donnie, I'm going to tell you the same thing I told our son. I love you but you are an asshole. That's part of what I told him but here's where the rest differs. You told me when I took my job that you would divorce me if I took it. Well guess what Donnie? Do it. Divorce me. If you don't I'll divorce you. Either way, I don't care, your choice. You will NOT fight me for these boys or this house. It's over. You're an immature drunk and an asshole and you're about to be a single one. I will not spend the rest of my life, not even one more day, married to a drunk. IT'S OVER. DONE."

She stood up and walked out of the room. He didn't try to stop her or say anything. She imagined him squinting at the clock again and then laying back down and falling asleep. She just hoped he would remember this conversation because she meant it with every fiber of her being.

"How was your holiday?" Mike strolled in the office at ten after ten carrying two cups of coffee and a box from a bakery. Apparently being on time wasn't one of his New Year's Resolutions.

"You don't even want to know." Maggie shook her head and rolled her eyes. "I hope you're not planning on writing that off as a company expense?"

"Oh, yeah, the receipts in the box." Mike handed the box to Maggie which she immediately opened and helped herself to a cheese danish the size of a dinner plate, the receipt she pulled out and threw in the garbage.

"I've got a couple calls to make then we can talk." He placed one of the cups of coffee in front of her and helped himself to a cheese danish and then started talking as he went to his office. "I'm leaving for Australia day after tomorrow, you'll need to hold down the fort for a week or so, ten days maybe…" There was more but she didn't catch it, she'd ask him about it when he came back into her office and his mouth wasn't full of danish.

Maggie took the lid off the coffee, mocha with whipped cream that hadn't completely melted yet and a drizzle of chocolate syrup. Her mood was still pretty horrible and a cup of mocha wasn't going to cure her life but it was one of the little things in life that gave her pleasure. And Mike knew that. He knew she loved Mocha Cafe's. Why didn't Donnie?

Ah well, did it really matter now anyway?

She meant every word she said and every word she didn't say. What she didn't say was that she didn't really want a divorce, that she would have preferred a scenario where Donnie cleaned up his act on his own and became the stand up man she wished he was. But how many times can you ask a person to do that before you finally give up on it and ask for a divorce instead?

"Time difference, forgot about that, I'll have to make those calls later." Mike pulled a chair up to Maggie's desk. "So what don't I want to know about your holiday? Didn't get everything you wanted?"

Maggie laughed at his choice of wording.

"What?"

"Well. I asked for a divorce and as of the moment I'm still married so I guess you could say I didn't get everything I wanted."

"Whoa! What?" Mike's head jutted forward as if understanding was an inch in front of him. "What? What are you talking about?"

"Long story. I seriously don't think you want to hear it, I'm not even sure I want to tell it." But she did, she felt the words lining up and fighting to be heard.

"I'm the last person in the world that you should be talking to, I suck at giving advice. Not to mention that I have no doubt Don would despise you talking to me of all people, frankly I'm shocked he's even allowing you to work for me, but if you want to tell it I want to hear it."

Maggie took a sip of her mocha, its magical powers weren't working. "About that," she took a deep breath, "Donnie doesn't exactly know you're my boss."

Mike blinked several times. "Maggie?"

"I haven't exactly told him. But…it's only partially my fault. He refuses to even discuss my job, he didn't want me to work and he has never, not one time, asked about my job." She raised her shoulders in a what-else-could-I-do shrug.

"So you never told him anything? Nothing? Not where you work, not what you do, not who you work for?"

Maggie shook her head.

Mike started shaking his head back and forth, back and forth, "Shit Maggie, that's not good. No wonder you have marriage problems, even I know communication is a big deal in a marriage."

"That's not the problem, well, communication maybe but not this, well, okay probably this would be a problem if we got to it but we never have because he won't talk to me about it. The problem is that Donnie drinks too much. He's not an alcoholic, well, maybe he is but he's not always an alcoholic."

"Either you are or you're not."

"I don't think so. Sometimes he doesn't drink, or he only has a few and he's a whole different person. Other times he gets so drunk I can't wake him up when our kid steals my car and puts it in a ditch."

Mike shook his head again, rapidly from side to side. "Stop, let me catch up. So, Don is a sometimes alcoholic? He doesn't want you to work? You're working anyway and keeping it a secret? Your kid stole your car? Don was too drunk to wake up to help? And you told him you want a divorce?"

"Donnie, not Don. But that's about right. Except I'm not keeping my work a secret. He knows I'm working he just doesn't want to know about it."

"And he doesn't know I'm your boss?"

Maggie shook her head.

"Wow. This puts me in an awkward position."

"Really Mike? Really? This is about you?"

"What do you think he would do if he found out you worked for me?"

"I don't know." Maggie felt frustration and annoyance begin to fray the edges of the conversation, "How the hell would I know? I don't even know what happened between you two and even if I did what difference does it make now? You said yourself that was a long time ago and you were just boys being boys, or something like that."

"Are you really getting divorced?"

"I don't know."

"What do you mean you don't know?! You asked him for a divorce what did he say? Is he still home? Are you still living together? How can you not know if you're getting divorced or not?!"

Maggie felt a tightening in her stomach. She should never have brought it up. But now that she did she couldn't stop, "The night that D.J. stole the car and put it in the ditch I tried to wake Donnie up but couldn't so I went and rescued D.J. myself. When I got home I was sick of it all, sick of D.J. and his black hoodies and his dark goth attitude, and sick of Donnie and his random drunkenness and his irresponsibility as a parent. So I told him to divorce me. I told him if he didn't divorce me I would divorce him." She couldn't believe she felt like she was stabbing Donnie with a knife of betrayal with every word she spoke.

"And?"

"And we haven't spoken since."

"Maggie?!"

"WHAT? Mike you don't get it. Donnie and I are, we've always been on again off again, we've never been apart but we always have," she looked up at the ceiling searching for the right words, "we always have periods of incompatibility. It works itself out."

"So you don't want a divorce? You just want to wait it out until it works itself out?"

She didn't think so, she thought this time she meant it. Was she really just waiting it out again or was she waiting Donnie out? When the ice broke would they be back to normal or would they be making separation arrangements?

Mike shook his head slowly. "I don't know what to tell you Maggie. There's a lot at stake here you know? Well, yeah of course you know. You've got a crap load of kids to think about too. If I can suggest something? I wouldn't mention the part about my being your boss just yet, maybe just concentrate on the drinking and the rest of it for now. Man, Happy New Year huh? So other than that did you get everything you wanted?"

Maggie almost laughed at his attempt at a joke. "No, I didn't. You can give me one more gift to make up for it. Tell me what happened between you two."

Mike looked away from her and stared at the wall for so long she was about to turn away and get to work when he said, "I pulled a little prank that maybe went too far, well, okay, it did go too far."

"A prank?"

"A computer prank."

"What's that mean? A computer prank?"

"I'm not going there Maggie. I pulled a prank, it got out of hand. End of story. It's been a long time, everyone just needs to forget it. It doesn't matter, high school stuff."

"Donnie hasn't forgotten it. Every time your name has ever come up his face turns beat red and he gets so mad he practically spits. I don't think he'll ever forget it."

Mike stared at the floor. "Maybe you shouldn't work here Maggie. When he finds out I'm your boss that's obviously not going to go well. I really just assumed the past was the past and you were working for me because Don let it go, like it should be, but you can't keep who you work for a secret forever. He's going to find out eventually."

"Should he hate you? Whatever he hates you for, do you deserve to be hated?"

Mike stared at the floor a while longer before looking up at Maggie. "Probably. When you're a kid you're naïve, you don't think things through, the consequences, you know? You just do what you do, what fixes that moment. That's all you think about when you're a kid, that moment." Mike looked away and took a deep breath before looking back at Maggie, "Yes, I deserve to be hated."

"Will you tell me what you did?"

"No."

"Why not?"

"Because I still believe, in this case, that not knowing is better than knowing."

"Better for who Mike? Better for you? For Donnie?"

"For you."

How could it be better for you?

I don't know. That's what he said though.

This is getting totally out of hand. Maggie I'm worried about you.

Yeah, I'm a little worried myself. Jillian? Where do I even start? Donnie? D.J.? Work?

Start with yourself for once. What do you REALLY want?

I wish I knew. I guess I REALLY want to stay married but to the good Donnie.

Then tell him that. But don't back down this time. But don't make ultimatums you won't stick to. But talk to him. But don't back down.

That's a lot of buts.

BUT you always back down.

Move home and help me. Help me be strong. Help me figure it all out. Fix me.

Maggie you are strong. Just be true to yourself.

You sound like a country song. You belong in Colton not N.J. Move home!

Three months, they meet again next week and it will be official.
Come now! George can live without you for three months. I can't!
Stop being dramatic. It will be here before you know it.
But I could be divorced by then, or dead.
Way to stop being dramatic.

Depending on how you looked at it, January first seemed an appropriate day to get rid of the kids, fix a nice dinner, and tell your husband to either step up or step out. Depending on how you looked at it. The pressure of being thankful was over weeks ago when the turkey was digested. The pressure of peace and joy were boxed away and put back in the attic for another year.

To Maggie it seemed an appropriate day considering she'd run in to Frank and Louise earlier in the day at the grocery store and out of the blue they'd asked if they could take all five boys for the evening. She thought she was hearing things at first but it seemed they'd enjoyed the boys at Thanksgiving and had been talking about having them over. They even offered to pick them up after school, feed them dinner and bring them back home by nine.

She sent a simple text to Donnie, *Can you come home? We need to talk.* He replied with a simple answer, *K.* She didn't know how he would reply, if he would even reply at all. She looked back down at the text, *K.* There was no sense wasting time trying to interpret that.

As she prepared a pot roast she thought back to the last pot roast she had made and wondered briefly if she should have chicken nuggets, sweet potato fries and lima beans as backup. She decided to stay positive, nix the backup dinner.

She finished in the kitchen and walked around the house, unsure what to do with herself now.

Jillian? Advice?
None. Just be honest. Let fate take care of the rest.
FYI that's advice.

She heard Donnie drive up just as she was about to nudge

Jillian for some more advice. She didn't expect him home so soon.

She hurried to the couch and quickly grabbed the remote and turned the television on to look like she hadn't heard him drive up. So much for just being honest.

Donnie walked in and hung his coat up. He glanced at Maggie sitting on the couch and put his finger up in a 'wait' motion and went into the kitchen. He came back with a bottle of water, sat in the recliner and nodded the go-ahead nod.

Something about cave men flittered past Maggie's brain but was gone before she could grasp it.

"Thanks for coming straight home."

"Where are the boys?"

"Believe it or not I ran into Frank and Louise at the grocery store and they offered to take them for the evening."

Donnie's eyebrows furrowed. "They offered, just like that, just out of the blue?"

"Yeah, weird huh?"

"All five of them?"

Maggie nodded. "I think they're just lonely. It will be good for them when Jillian and George move back."

"When is that?"

"Six weeks, one day, twenty hours, give or take."

Donnie actually half smiled. He was trying, she had to give him that.

"So Donnie, I wanted to talk about, you know, us."

"Okay. Did you make pot roast or chicken nuggets?"

This time she half smiled. "Pot roast."

"Good."

"Okay so, here's the thing. I'm just going to put it out there. I don't want to live like this anymore."

"So you still want a divorce?"

"I don't think I do but I want you to stop drinking and I want to live like normal people. I want to work without feeling guilty for it. I want you to step up and be a part of the boy's lives, take some responsibility, be involved with them. But I meant what I said the other night Donnie. I'm done. I don't really want a divorce but I'm done living with you the way things were, are. If you're not willing to change then we need to talk about divorce."

He didn't respond. His expression was void of any hint of what he was thinking.

She didn't take her eyes off him. The longer he didn't speak, the more determined she became. "Donnie. I'm serious."

He put his water on the end table and stood up. "Come with me." He got his coat, took hers from the closet and held it out for her.

"Where?"

He didn't answer. She got up and took her coat, put it on and followed him out to his truck. Neither spoke as he drove. He drove into town and turned north on Route 56 and then drove through Hannawa Falls and into Potsdam. Still neither said a word. He drove a little further, turned. Maggie's heart began beating faster. He was heading toward FastTech. He slowed and put his blinker on. Her heart began to thump against her rib cage, what was he doing?

He pulled into the empty parking lot at FastTech and put the truck in park. "Tell me about your job."

She couldn't say anything for a moment. Her mind was spinning and she felt dizzy. "I didn't think you even knew where I worked, you never asked me."

"Do you like it?"

"My job? Yeah, I do. But Donnie how did you know where I worked? You never asked me anything about it. Why did you bring us here?"

"Tell me about it. Tell me about what you do, the people you work with, tell me what you like and what you don't like."

Maggie shifted in her seat, she was suddenly freezing, and incredibly uncomfortable. "Let's just go. I have a pot roast at home, let's go eat and we'll talk at home."

Donnie didn't budge. "Tell me about it Maggie. What kind of company is it? What's your job?"

"Donnie I'm…"

"Tell me."

"It's a computer company. I'm a receptionist. I answer the phone. The company writes computer software programs. I do the billing, stuff like that."

"Do you like it?"

"I told you I did. What's going on?"

"Tell me about your co-workers."

"There aren't any. I work by myself. The owner is always gone, installing programs and training the companies and stuff." What was he up to? Why was he doing this?

"Do you like your boss?"

She felt like she was in a trap and there was no way out. He knew. Somehow he knew. There was no other explanation. She had to tell him the truth. She took a breath and opened her mouth but it wasn't the truth that rolled off her tongue.

"I don't really know him. He's gone out of state a lot, out of the country even. A lot."

Donnie put the car back in gear and drove them back the way they came. He didn't say another word. She didn't dare either. In the ten minute drive her heart rate slowed but was still twice as fast as normal. Her mind was spinning in circles. It spun even faster when he didn't turn to go home, he turned onto Higley Road and then onto Cottage Road. He pulled to the side of the road next to the spring. He put the truck in park.

She knew this spot well. Every kid in Colton that ever road their bike on Higley Road knew this spot well. Every summer resident knew this spot well. It was just a rusted old pipe sticking out of the edge of a hill with a continuous stream of spring water pouring out of it. There was barely room for one car to pull over and park. It was nothing special but it was a place to stop and get a drink or fill a jug. And it was as good of a place as any to steal a first kiss. They knew this spot well.

"This is where I come after work, sure once in a while I stop at a bar but most of the time I come here. I park just like this and I try to figure things out. Usually I have a six pack with me, and usually I drink all six before I come home. So far, I haven't figured anything out yet. I just sit here. And drink."

Why? Why would he do that? Why here? And why was he telling her now? She had to say something, the silence was deafening.

"What are you trying to figure out?"

"Different things. Sometimes the kids, sometimes you, sometimes things at work. You want to know what I've been trying to figure out lately?"

Maggie's stomach turned. "What?"

"Lately I've been trying to figure out why you would take a job working for Mike Jensen and not tell me."

She grabbed the door handle, she was sure she was going to throw up. She swallowed hard. She stared out the window, away from Donnie, her hand still on the door handle.

"That's what I've been trying to figure out lately. Trying to figure out why you would criticize everything I do, everything I say, why you would make yourself come across as the perfect one and me the loser that keeps messing up our marriage and our family when we're both guilty of that Maggie. And not only that, I've been trying to figure out why you would work for Mike Jensen. That's what I've been trying to figure out Maggie, why you would work for Mike Jensen and not tell me. And, I guess, how that makes you any better than me."

Maggie couldn't speak, and even if she could what could she say? He would never believe how it happened. She knew it looked bad but looking at it from his point of view she saw how bad it looked. Damn it. She should have told him right from the start. No, she should never have taken the job at all. He was right. She was just as guilty as he was, in a different way, but she was still just as guilty. Why hadn't she seen it before? Because she only saw what she wanted to see, that everything was his fault.

Donnie put the car in gear and did a three point turn. They headed back down Cottage Road and back down Higley Road and back to their home and back to the same unsolved problems with one huge new one piled on top.

He knows.

???

That I'm working for Mike.

WHAT?! HOW?!

Don't know. Doesn't matter. I'm worse than him. I've been lying to him all along. I'm scum.

Not scum, maybe just a little scum, pond scum.

JILLIAN!

Sorry, what are you going to do?

What can I do? I think we're broken. So good question what am I going to do? Quit to try to redeem myself or stay to try to support myself?

You think this is it? For real this time?

I don't see how we can fix us. It was so much easier when he was the only one to blame.

Maggie he's been an on and off drunk since you married him, he's still to blame, but maybe you can still fix it. I seriously believe, truly believe, that you both love each other.

You're a romantic, I'm a realist.

You going to work tomorrow?

No! How could I? I just want to bury myself in my blankets and never come out.

Is he there? Maybe you better finish this.

It's already eight thirty, the kids will be home soon, no time to finish it.

I'll call Louise, she can keep them overnight.

They have school tomorrow.

Maggie, trust me, all five Conner boys absent in one day, they'll make it an official holiday.

Right. Okay. Do it. And thanks, I think.

Maggie left the eerie quiet sanctuary of her bedroom in search of Donnie and found him sitting in his recliner, no drink in hand, no television on, no lights, just sitting in his recliner in the dark.

"Donnie?" She approached quietly, spoke softly. "I think it's time to get everything out in the open, whatever happens we need to get past all this, one way or another."

Donnie didn't move but she heard him take a jagged deep breath and then heard it escape in a long exhale. She turned the light on and in that instant Maggie felt her life jump tracks.

Donnie was crying.

Not once in all the years they dated or were married, not once, had she ever seen him cry. She froze, her body, her breath, even her mind. If time ever stopped, if time ever stood still, this is what it would feel like. Nothing existed. There was no past, there was no future, there was no present.

Her mind clawed to resurface. Her eyes caught a glimpse of Donnie's arm dangling off the side of the recliner, his hand loosely clasping his cell phone. Maggie's mind grasped one sense that wasn't a word or a thought but the most terrifying fear a million times worse than any fear she'd ever felt before. Each of the boy's names traveled with lightening speed past her cognizance.

Her heart slammed against her rib cage. "DONNIE!!!"

Donnie turned to Maggie, behind his tear streaked face and red water filled eyes she saw his expression flicker from sheer angst to understanding, "My Mom!" he shook his head furiously. "Not the boys! Not the boys!"

Maggie collapsed on the couch. She closed her eyes and when she opened them again her own tears flowed. Her body shook. She tried to speak, to apologize, to ask about his Mother but no sound came out. Her mind overflowed with a combination of relief and apprehension.

"My Mom." Donnie sniffled and wiped his eyes with his sleeve. "Heart attack."

"Is she..."

"No, hospital. She's recovering. From surgery."

Donnie's parents, Don and Ann Conners, retired to Naples Florida four years ago. They sold their home in Colton and made Naples their permanent residence. Don, a retired carpenter, had his mind set on moving south the day he turned sixty two and would have been perfectly content never stepping foot back in New York State. It was a tough sell trying to convince Ann but she ultimately agreed with the promise of a minimum of two return trips a year to visit the boys.

"I should have visited. I just kept putting it off, there's lots of time, we'll get there eventually." Donnie shook his head, "I didn't want to take the time. You know? I always thought it would be more convenient later."

"You didn't know this would happen. She's going to be okay isn't she?"

"The doctor won't lean one way or the other but it doesn't look good, he says it could be a few days before they know. Dad said he wanted to call earlier but everything happened so fast."

Maggie wiped a tear away. "Donnie, you should go."

"We should go. All of us. I want her to see you and the boys again too."

"We will. We'll go. All of us."

Around two in the morning Maggie left the couch to make a pot of coffee. Donnie followed her in the kitchen and sat at the table. They talked until the early morning. At seven thirty, instead of Donnie being long gone to work and Maggie putting the boys on the bus like any other day, Donnie was calling his father and Maggie was calling Louise. By eight o'clock they had both called in to work for a week off, Donnie talked directly to his supervisor and Maggie left a message for Mike and contacted the school to get the boys work for the next week. By eight fifteen they were in bed trying to quiet their minds and fall asleep so they would be alert enough to begin the drive to Naples at four when Frank and Louise brought the boys home. Both wondered what would happen to the conversation they left unfinished. Neither asked.

.

CHAPTER FIVE

The van was crammed full with suitcases, toys, and people. Donnie drove, Maggie rode in front, D.J. and Dylan had the two back bucket seats and Derek, Daniel and Todd shared the bench seat behind them. Suitcases and duffle bags were piled to the roof in the back and at the boy's feet and smaller tote bags were wedged in the seats between the boys. No one complained.

"Mom? Is Grandma going to die?" Todd asked her the same question when she sat him down and explained that his Grandma Ann was sick and they were going to take a trip to visit her. He asked her again as they packed the van. He asked her again when they first began the trip. She suspected he wasn't going to stop asking until she told him that no, his Grandmother wasn't going to die, but she couldn't tell him that. She couldn't tell him she was and she prayed like crazy that she wouldn't have to, but she couldn't tell him she wasn't either.

Donnie glanced in his rearview mirror. "Boys, it's a long trip and we're all worried about Grandma. Let's just try to think of ways to make her happy okay?"

"Dad? I think it would make Grandma happy if you stopped at McDonalds."

"You're a dork Todd."

"Dylan…"

"What? He is. You shouldn't lie to him. It's better to tell him the truth so he knows."

Maggie and Donnie shared a glance and Maggie turned in her seat and looked at Dylan. He shrugged. "Just sayin."

She knew what he was saying. If nothing else, Dylan was perceptive but was he right? Should she tell him the truth? The part about his Grandmother not the part about being a dork, that part she would leave to fate with the hope that he would grow out of it eventually. She debated the merits of telling a five year old that it was a *possibility* that his Grandmother might die when Derek interrupted her thoughts with another unpleasant topic.

"Are we going to see Grandma and Grandpa Kennedy too?"

Like there wasn't enough to worry about.

The boys had never met Grandma and Grandpa Kennedy but they asked about them from time to time. The day Maggie moved in with Donnie's parents her own parents cut all ties with her, in reality they cut the ties the day she and Donnie told them she was pregnant but the day she moved out was the last day they ever spoke to her. She told each of the boys this when they asked, in varying versions depending on what was appropriate for their age when they asked. They knew as much about the reasons why as she did, Grandma and Grandpa Kennedy didn't approve of choices Maggie made and they stopped talking to her because of it. She never told them more than that, not necessarily because she didn't want to but because there was nothing more to tell. How could she explain something she didn't understand herself? She tried to reach out to them over and over through the beginning of her marriage and after each of the boys was born but after Todd she stopped. They never responded to any of her attempts. Over time the pain of being rejected stopped burning and became a dull ache she could live with and eventually it became nothing more than a scar that she picked at now and then.

Even that transformation was so long ago and the feelings buried so deep that mention of them brought the same emotional response as discussing the compositional make up of sedimentary rock.

"They live in Florida too right?" Derek persisted.

They did. They moved to Florida after D.J. was born which was a blessing and a curse. Living in a town as small as Colton they wouldn't have been able to avoid each other. A blessing *or* a curse.

Donnie answered for her. "Florida is a big state Derek. I think we're going to just concentrate on Grandma Conners this time okay?"

"Okay."

Maggie gave Donnie a thank you glance and then turned to look out the window. It was going to be a long trip, a lot of time to think. If it weren't for the boys she would take a sleeping pill to avoid having to deal with all the thoughts that were fighting for attention. She probably still could, other than the boys' random questions they were being exceptionally quiet. She expected an initial period of quiet while they each processed the news in their own way but she would never have guessed it would last this long. By now she thought they'd be clawing at each other. She pulled the seatbelt loose and turned to check on them.

D.J. was plugged in to his ipod, his eyes closed, his knee bouncing to the music, if that's what it could be called. Dylan was looking out the window, felt her eyes on him and turned, "What?" She shook her head and looked behind him. Derek and Daniel were working together making a card for their Grandmother. Todd was picking his nose.

Her boys. A feeling took hold in her chest that reminded her of a description she read once in a magazine, a description so cheesy it made her close the magazine and toss it in the garbage. 'A mother's heart swells with love.' She felt it now. How embarrassing. But, it was true. She used to catch her heart doing something weird all the time when the boys were babies and toddlers but once they turned into people it was much more of a rare oddity than a regular event. She supposed that feeling was, dare she think it, a swelling of the heart. And here it was again. She had an uncharacteristic urge to verbally let them know how much she really did love them.

"Boys?" Everyone looked up but D.J., "I love you."

"Dad? Make her turn around."

She smiled at Dylan. "Does that bother you? Dyyyyylannnn, I loooove youuuu."

The three younger boys laughed. Donnie even chuckled. Dylan scowled. She turned her attention to D.J., reached back and tapped his knee. He opened his eyes, looked at her for a second and then took his earpieces out. She grinned at him. He turned and looked at Dylan, then turned around further and looked at the boys in the back seat, he turned forward again and looked at Maggie, "What?"

"Boys? Let's tell D.J. what I said. Ready? One, two, three."

Everyone except Dylan sang, "I loooove youuuuu." The backseat boys giggled, Dylan rolled his eyes and Donnie chuckled quietly. Maggie grinned at D.J.

He shoved his earpieces back in his ears, laid his head back against the seat and closed his eyes.

The trip was consistently erratic. There were spaces of time when the boys were animated and active but not once did they ever complain or fight. There were spaces of time when the van was exceptionally quiet and Maggie heard the thoughts floating in her head. Not that there was a good time for anyone to have a heart attack but Ann's timing couldn't have been worse.

By the time they crossed the Pennsylvania state line the boys were drifting off. The quiet stretched for miles. Maggie knew that Donnie was as conflicted as she was. First and foremost they were worried about Ann, but neither one could pretend, even in the hidden recesses behind that worry, that there was a very big question waiting to be answered. Where did they stand and who would they be in the days after?

Maggie fidgeted as the silence grew too loud to ignore, she

turned to look out her side window, turned back to look out the front window, turned and studied Donnie's profile. "Donnie…"

"Do you remember the crocodile tooth my parents gave Derek when they came home that one time?" He interrupted, "Remember how he put it under his pillow thinking the tooth fairy would give him a fortune for it?!"

Maggie read the meaning loud and clear, he didn't want to discuss it yet and, although she didn't know how he knew she was going to, she was relieved. "Yeah I do, and I remember how mad he was when he woke up and the tooth was still there. He took it outside and threw it as far as he could and then he cried for two days because he couldn't find it again."

They looked at each other briefly and in the look that passed between them they agreed not to talk about it for now. A comfortable silence settled around them, broken only miles later when Maggie commented on a restaurant sign and then a comfortable conversation pattern developed.

"Do you realize we just spent twenty minutes talking about orange juice?"

Donnie chuckled.

"I miss those mindless no purpose kinds of conversations."

"Really?"

"Donnie remember a million years ago when we remodeled the kitchen and you were teaching me about load bearing walls and that stuff that I thought was so incredibly boring, and useless?"

Donnie turned and gave her a quick confused glance. "Not really but make the connection for me."

"Those are the only kinds of conversations we have anymore, the load bearing kind like the load bearing walls, we talk about what we have to, to hold everything together but we never have the orange juice conversations. Those are the other walls. The ones that bring it all together and make it… complete."

"Did you really just make a marriage analogy out of carpentry and orange juice?!"

"Did you really just use the word analogy?"

"What? What's wrong with the word analogy? Wait, I did use it right didn't I?"

"Donnie? Every now and then I forget about why we're on this trip and for a minute I think we're on a real vacation. Why haven't we ever gone on a real vacation? The boys probably think a vacation is going to the Higley Flow State Park with a bucket of Kentucky Fried Chicken."

"That IS a vacation. I LOVE those days."

"You do? Why didn't I know that?"

"I don't know, it's not load bearing?"

Maggie smiled but behind her smile she felt sad. You don't miss what you don't have. Until you do. "I miss small talk. I miss all the nonsense conversations. Donnie I know now isn't the time to get into it but, do you think we have a chance? Do you think we can rebuild us?"

"I think we have a lot to talk about. A lot of decisions to make. A lot to work through if we decide to go that route. Honestly Maggie I don't even know what I think, or want and I'm willing to bet you don't either. On the bright side we don't have a deadline or anything right?"

"No. No deadline. And Donnie? I'm sorry about your Mom."

"Me too. Let's get off the next exit, stop for the night okay?"

"Fine with me. You do realize thought that we'll be waking the boys up so they can go to sleep?"

Donnie nodded. "Seems so very wrong and so very right at the same time."

It was the first time in a long time they'd laughed together.

Colton to Naples was a twenty five hour trip, without stops. They made it in fifty five hours; twenty five hours of driving, two ten hour hotel stops and ten hours worth of food and bathroom stops. Due to the circumstances they had hoped to get there faster but it just didn't work out that way. It was midnight when they pulled in to Don and Ann's driveway.

"I still feel bad about getting here so late." Maggie would

have voted for another hotel stop but when she called to tell Don they were staying another night so they wouldn't get in so late he insisted they drive through the rest of the way no matter how late they arrived.

"You talked to him. You're the one that said he insisted."

"I know. He did. I still feel bad about it though." She did feel bad. She felt bad for arriving so late but she also felt a little secretly sad that she couldn't pretend they were on vacation anymore.

"Looks nice." Donnie turned the ignition off but made no effort to get out of the van. "It looks just like the pictures so why do I feel, hesitant? Awkward?"

"Because you've never been here? Because it's your parents home but you've never shared it with them? Because the minute we get out of this van we have to face the real reason we're here? Because you've just driven for days and you're exhausted?"

"Mom?" Daniel was the first of the boys to wake. "Are we here?"

"We're here."

The rest of the boys slowly started stirring and showing signs of comprehension. They were as conflicted as she and Donnie were. Glad to be there and done with the drive but apprehensive about what was to come mixed with a bit of exhaustion and a stock of unspent bad behavior. She was incredibly grateful for their behavior and thought she should probably acknowledge that. "Guys, before we go in I just want to tell you that I'm proud of you all. I know it wasn't easy being in the van for so long. Dad and I really appreciate you guys getting along and not fighting."

They looked at her like she was crazy, or annoying, or both.

"Hey! There's Grandpa!"

Everyone scurried to get out of the van to begin the week no one wanted to have to begin.

Don stood in the doorway while Maggie, Donnie and the boys climbed out of the van. He hugged each one of them as they passed him on their way through the door. The boys were perfect little gentlemen hugging their Grandfather and uttering little reassuring words until Todd spotted the pool out of the sliding glass doors at the back of the house and screamed "Pool!" He sped off before anyone could stop him and ran smack into the sliding glass door. The boys instantly broke into a fit of laughter. Maggie and Donnie rushed to Todd to assess the damage and when they turned back they saw Don doubled over laughing along with the boys. Even D.J. was audibly laughing. The ice was broken. Todd's head and the door were not.

Don unlocked the sliding glass doors and they all went outside to admire the pool area. The boys were in awe. They'd never seen anything like it. A UV screen covered the entire pool area which spanned the width of the house and ran thirty feet out. There was a large twelve by eighteen covered patio with a ceiling fan, outdoor dining set and a barbeque grill. The screened area encompassed a huge hot tub that spilled via waterfall into the pool. The ground was completely hardscaped with beautiful paver stones and there were multiple lounge chairs along the circumference of the pool. Although it was dark they could see a glimpse of the yard behind the screened area that led to a pond.

"Like it?" Don asked proudly.

"Like it? I love it! Can we swim?" Todd bounced from one foot to the other, "Can we swim Grandpa? Can we?"

"Sure."

"Tomorrow." Maggie amended before any of the boys got the bright idea to jump in now.

"Aww Mom! Come on!"

"Todd, no. We haven't even brought the suitcases in, it's one o'clock in the morning and Grandpa's tired, we're all tired. Tomorrow."

"I'm not tired." Todd retorted.

"Me either." Derek chimed in.

Before she could open her mouth to stop them Don stepped to the side of the pool and jumped in. Everyone was so shocked the only sound that could be heard was the splatter of the water as the drops rained down on the pavers. Everyone was wide eyed and staring at the water waiting for Don to break the surface and pop up. When he did the boys laughed and cheered.

"Grandpa you have your clothes on!"

"I do?" He pretended to look down in shock.

Donnie snuck behind Dylan and pushed him in. By the time Dylan surfaced all the boys, including D.J. were in the pool laughing and splashing, all their anxiety instantly washed off in the water.

Maggie sided up to Donnie and whispered, "Holy crap, even D.J. is laughing! In all the ways I was envisioning tonight would go this sure never crossed my mind!"

Donnie rested his arm on Maggie's shoulders, "Circumstances not included, I think this trip is going to be good for all of us." He took his arm from her shoulder and stepped closer to the pool and she followed, "Hell, Maggie, who knows," he whispered, "maybe some night you and I will even find ourselves out here skinny dipping under the stars."

Maggie's mouth dropped open for the second time in a matter of minutes, and then she reached behind him and shoved as hard as she could and laughed like she hadn't in years when he screamed right before he hit the surface of the water.

Maggie couldn't get over how beautiful the house was. Even though she went to bed at two she was awake at six and couldn't wait to begin exploring the house and the property. She snuck quietly out of bed and went to the kitchen to make a pot of coffee and was pleasantly surprised to find the carafe was full and there were two mugs and a display of condiments on the counter. She could get used to this! She poured a cup and walked quietly to the sliding glass door that led to the pool. After seeing the area last night all she could think about was sitting at the table in the early morning hours sipping a cup of coffee.

She opened the curtain just enough to be able to open the door and sneak out. She had one foot and half her body out when she spotted Don at the table. If she were being honest with herself she would have to say she was a tiny bit disappointed but she instantly squashed her selfishness and as soon as she closed the door behind her and put her coffee on the table she went right to him and gave him a huge hug. When she pulled back Don squinted and said accusingly, "Was that a sympathy hug?"

"Not at all. It was a thank you so much for having the coffee made hug. Now stop squinting at me while I give you the sympathy hug." She squeezed him again, tightly.

They sat together comfortably and leisurely enjoying their coffee. For a man that was living the nightmare of not knowing if his wife was going to live or die he gave the appearance of being fairly relaxed but she suspected that just below the surface he was a mess. She made no effort to try to hide the fact that she was assessing him. His close cut thinning hair was more silver than gray, his face showed signs of aging but other than the puffy areas around his eyes Maggie thought it was more of a natural aging than a result of worrying over Ann's condition. He looked tired but relaxed. He was dressed sharply, as he usually was, in a white polo shirt and navy colored shorts. His legs, as was the rest of him, were a deep bronze from the sun. He wore boat shoes that were a perfect match to his shorts. He dressed himself this morning but Ann obviously had him trained.

"Don your house is beautiful, well, what I saw of it so far. I can't wait to see the rest."

"It is isn't it?! You'll see the rest soon enough but this is the best part right here, especially in the mornings. Ann and I always have our morning coffee out here although I'm usually on my second cup by the time Sleeping Beauty wakes up. I'm always out here early, always sitting here with my coffee when the day opens."

Maggie smiled at his reference to Ann. "When the day opens? That's an odd way to put it."

"It's the only way to describe it. Something you'd have to see to understand, wake up at five tomorrow and you can watch it open with me."

"Five? A.M.? Uh, no promises."

"I can sweeten the offer, there's an Italian bakery just down the street and…"

"Okay. Definitely. But there better be something with chocolate waiting for me. "

Don chuckled. "So tell me, was it an awful trip down? I love the boys but I know them. How awful was it?"

"Actually it wasn't. They didn't fight at all, believe it or not but there was not one single argument the whole time."

"No kidding? Oh," he tipped his head back and then began nodding, "Oh that makes sense, I would have done it too probably."

Maggie tilted her head. "Done what?"

"You drugged them didn't you?"

Maggie laughed. "No I didn't drug them. But only because I didn't need to. We told them Ann was sick, D.J. and Dylan know about the heart attack and prognosis, the other three only know that she's sick. I think they're all a little nervous and trying to process it in their own way. I'm sure they didn't make the conscious decision to behave, we all know better than that! So how is she? Really?"

Don sighed and leaned back in his chair. "Not good. The damn doctors and nurses won't tell me anything more than fifty-fifty. I hated to leave last night but I hated to stay too, if you know what I mean. It tears me up seeing her lying there like that, tubes and machines everywhere. I have to tell you Maggie I am more grateful that you guys came down than I can ever ever tell you. I'm a big boy and I can handle whatever I have to but," he swallowed his emotions, "but the distraction of having you here is, well, a relief. When Ann wakes up I know it will speed her recovery too, she'll fight a hundred times harder just knowing you are all here."

Maggie wiped at the corner of her eye.

Don stiffened and put his macho on. "You're not going to

be a big teary mess the whole time though are you?"

"Oh Don you know me, tough as nails, it's just hearing you say what a fantastic daughter-in-law I am that made me spring a leak."

"I didn't say that."

"Believe what you want but what I heard was 'I'm glad Donnie and the boys came but Maggie it was really you I wanted here. You're the answer to all my prayers. You're the one that I can lean on, the one that's strong, intelligent and you're…"

"Oh for the love of Pete."

"Hey! Don! Wait! Where are you going?"

The minute the boys were awake enough to open their eyes they remembered the pool and were out of bed and in their swim suits in record time. Don agreed to go out with them while he waited for Donnie to take a shower, in one of the three bathrooms. Maggie couldn't get over the size of the house and took advantage of the opportunity to show herself around. It wasn't even the size of the house, although it was a good size, definitely a good sized home, but it was more the flow of the lay out that made it seem enormous. Open floor plan. She was taking a sledge hammer to that kitchen wall when she got home.

It was a single story home and from what she could see last night it had a lot of character. Cookie cutter for sure, all the houses she could see on the street last night looked much the same but instead of taking away from its appeal it added to it somehow. She planned to go outside and take a look around as soon as she had a chance.

The kitchen was super spacious with all stainless top of the line appliances, tons of cabinets and counter space that wrapped around the inner side of the kitchen with stools on the outside of the counter, an island with matching stools on the outer side, and there was a cute little den area at the end of the kitchen that was and wasn't a part of the kitchen.

The dining room was large enough for a solid walnut table with seating for eight. She wondered if Don and Ann ever used it or if it was strictly aesthetic. Probably just aesthetic, thus the perfectly clean and pressed cloth placemats. The dining room was directly across from the kitchen and the space between the two was and wasn't a part of the living room. For a house that appeared to be so large there was actually a lot of space that was and wasn't, a consequence of an open floor plan perhaps but it worked, it didn't add to or take away from and no one could deny that there was plenty of room even with the was and wasn't spaces.

To her left was an entrance that led to the only room at the south end of the house with its own bathroom. To her right was the living room which was wide and spacious and ended at the north end of the house at the sliding glass doors. There was a doorway to the right that led to Don and Ann's master suite with of course it's own bathroom, and to the left was an entry that led to a small hallway off of which were two rather large bedrooms which were divided by a very large bathroom.

It was amazing really, from that one spot in the was and wasn't area between the kitchen and dining room Maggie could see the entire house, not inside the bedrooms or bathrooms of course but the layout of where each room was. It was so simple and yet so elegant.

And, of course, through the sliding glass doors was the lanai, which was a new word she just learned this morning for what she previously called a patio.

It was stunning. Every bit of it was stunning. According to Don, the houses in Naples ranged anywhere from a hundred thousand to a few million, theirs was at the lower average range of two hundred and fifty thousand, give or take. Maggie couldn't imagine ever being able to afford a home like this and wondered how they could. Ann never worked outside of the home a day in her life and Don was a retired union carpenter. They must have struggled and saved every penny he ever made. Now that she was seeing the home she thought it was absolutely worth the struggle.

She wandered to the bedrooms to look around. Ann had chosen a Floridian type theme for each of them. The theme was shells for their master bedroom, palm trees for the other room with the queen bed, and nautical for the other two rooms which were adjoined by the bathroom. The rooms were airy and spacious and the minute she stepped into any one of them she felt like she might have been in a tropical resort. The two rooms that shared the bathroom each had a single and a bunk bed.

Every room was tastefully decorated to make a person feel completely at home and comfortable. She loved it. She left the bedrooms and went to the front of the house and walked to the end of the driveway to get a good look at the house. Cookie cutter or not it was absolutely beautiful and inviting. She loved everything about it even the pale yellow painted traditional stucco siding.

Jillian! I want to live here!

It's about time you talked to me I've been going crazy wondering what's going on!

Sorry, long trip, lot's going on. I LOVE this house, I wish you could see it.

Send pictures. Now what about Ann? And you and Donnie? Scoop please.

Ann- no change yet. Donnie-Haven't resumed 'the talk' but we've been getting along good, better than normal. And get this, the boys are actually getting along, even D.J. is smiling and having fun.

Wow. Did you drug them?

Why does everybody keep asking me that?

?? When are you coming home?

Never.

She slipped the phone in her pocket and moseyed to the back of the house observing and enjoying everything her eyes could take in at once. She'd have to make sure she found time for a good long walk and as much as she would have loved to have begun investigating the neighborhood right now it wasn't the time for it, Donnie would be done with his shower any minute and he and Don had to get to the hospital to see Ann.

She entered the lanai from the outside and just the little different perspective made it seem like she were seeing it for the first time and it was even more beautiful than it was just a few minutes ago. The boys were swimming and laughing and playing together and she was certain, right then and there, there was something magical about this place.

As soon as she reappeared Don gathered his things to take inside.

"Do we have to get out? Where's Grandpa going? Where are we going Mom?"

"We're not going anywhere. Dad and Grandpa are going to see Grandma at the hospital."

Maggie pulled a chair poolside, close enough to feel like a part of the boy's fun but far enough to stay dry.

"Can we keep swimming?"

"For a little longer then I want you to come out and get a bite to eat."

"Speaking of bites, watch out for the alligators, occasionally the little ones get lost and find their way into the pools."

"Grandpa! He's kidding right Mom?"

"Of course he's kidding." She turned around, "You are kidding right Don?" But he was gone.

She didn't see any alligators but she thought again about magic and based on the way the boys were getting along she believed the water might have magical powers too. They swam for almost two more hours without an argument or a fight and they actually played together. All of them. If she didn't know them she would have thought they were five friends instead of five brothers. Seeing D.J. in a swim suit instead of black pants and a black hoodie was almost the best part of it for her, seeing him smiling and laughing and playing like a boy *was* the best part.

The boys swam for another half hour before Maggie

insisted they take a break and have something to eat. She hated to do it but they had to eat.

"I love it here Mom." Daniel turned to D.J. "Do you love it here too?"

D.J. nodded. He was toweling his hair and she couldn't see for sure but she thought he was smiling behind the towel.

"I love it here too," Dylan added, "But don't forget about Grandma. That's why we're here Daniel."

"Are we going to see her?"

Dylan shrugged. "Probably. Do you want to?"

"I do." D.J. said.

Maggie stopped putting the plates around the table and turned to the boys, she had to look to make sure her ears were accurately communicating that the boys were having an actual conversation just a few feet away from her.

"I've never been to a hospital. I'm scared." Todd stepped next to Derek. "If I go will you go with me?"

"You might be too young anyway, sometimes they don't let little kids in." Dylan threw his towel on a lounge chair and laid down in it. "If they do let you in Mom or Dad or D.J. or I'll go with you, don't worry."

D.J. stepped to the side of the pool and sat on the edge letting his feet dangle into the water. Derek and Daniel watched and then did the same. Todd pulled a chair up next to Dylan and sat in it. "Can we live here? Do we have to go back home?"

Dylan answered from his lounge chair. "Of course we have to go home. Mom and Dad have jobs and we have to go back to school."

"I would go to school here if we didn't have to go back. Can't they get new jobs here?" Todd asked Dylan but he didn't answer.

"I would too." Derek said.

"So would I." Daniel.

"Me too." D.J.

D.J.?? Maggie stared at the back of his head, his too long stringy dark hair made him look like the D.J. of home but his voice, calm and strong, sounded young and innocent. Did she dare hope?

"The doctor says there's hope!" Donnie returned later in the afternoon but Don decided to stay by Ann's side. "He said she took a huge turn for the better during the night and he upgraded her from fifty-fifty to eighty-twenty!"

The boys all shouted and began high fives. Donnie joined in and Maggie couldn't help but to stand back and smile.

Donnie came to Maggie and hugged her. "He says she should wake up anytime and if she keeps going at this rate she might even be able to come home in a couple weeks."

"A couple weeks? That's insane!"

"I know but I guess now days they don't keep them in the hospital very long."

"Dad! I'm happy!" Todd ran to his side and hugged his legs. Everyone laughed.

"I'm happy too Todd." Donnie picked him up and squeezed him and then put him down. "Now let's eat I'm starving!" He turned to Maggie and whispered, "Who are these kids and what did you do with our boys?"

She thought to say, 'who are you and what did you do with Donnie' but she didn't want to jinx a good thing. If she could freeze this moment she would.

Donnie went back to the hospital after having something to eat and Maggie and the boys took a walk through the neighborhood. The boys were in culture shock seeing the palm trees and the hard thick southern grass and the stucco buildings and the pools behind every house. She tried to answer their questions but she was in just as much of a cultural shock as they were.

"Where are all the kids Mom?"

They had passed a few seniors in their walk but hadn't seen a single person under the age of sixty. She assumed this was a retirement villa and explained 'snow birds' to the boys.

"Can you live in Florida if you're not old?" Todd and

Daniel couldn't contain themselves and kept bouncing off ahead and then circling back to join the rest of them. "Can you Mom?" Todd asked as he circled back and then literally circled them.

"You can but you have to live in the Everglades with the alligators." Dylan told him and began chasing him with alligator arms. After he caught him and rolled him on the ground a bit he stepped back in line with Maggie and D.J., "I know we're not here for a vacation but do you think we could go to the Everglades?"

Maggie thought for a minute, she would love if they could take the boys somewhere like that while they were here but the Everglades? Not in a million years. Couldn't they want to see something less, Everglade-e? She didn't get a chance to answer because Todd asked what the Everglades were and Dylan began explaining and the next thing she knew they were all off running and chasing each other, Everglade style apparently.

Except D.J. He stayed by Maggie's side as they walked. She tried to think of something to say but she didn't want to spook him. What a weird way to feel about her own child. She looked at him out of the corner of her eye. He was wearing shorts, black, and a t-shirt, also black, but that was probably all he packed, probably all he owned for that matter. He'd taken a huge step forward in just the couple days of the trip and especially this morning. She decided to take a chance.

"Deej, you don't have to but would you like to go on a little shopping trip with me after Dad gets back? You can wear the clothes you brought but black gets really hot in this sun. You don't have to, it's up to you."

D.J. didn't say anything for a minute and she was just about to give up hope when he said, "Yeah, okay."

Her heart swelled. She wasn't at all embarrassed this time but she wasn't going to say anything about it either, she wanted to turn and hug him but she just said, "Okay, cool."

"Cool." He replied.

Donnie came home in the late afternoon and could barely contain himself, Ann was awake. Don stayed at the hospital and planned to stay by her side through the night. Maggie told him about her plan to take D.J. shopping and he insisted they all go for dinner and then on a shopping spree.

"It's Florida. Ya'll look like Yankees. Look at Todd his shirt even *says* Yankees! I say pizza and plaid shorts for all."

Dylan shook his head. "No way, I'm not wearing plaid shorts, next you'll be wanting to put us all in Sperry's."

"Yes! Sperry's for all! Now let's go! Get out of those clothes and into something presentable. Go! Go!"

When they scattered to their rooms and he was alone with Maggie he whispered, "What are Sperry's?"

She laughed and shook her head. "You'll find out. And I'm getting two pairs."

"Pairs?"

The boys ended up getting Crocs. Way cooler. Apparently. After the shoe store they went for pizza and then embarked on an all out shopping excursion. Maggie was in her glory, Donnie and the boys not so much but by eight thirty they all had a bag of what Maggie referred to as 'Florida approved clothing'.

"So can we Dad?" Derek was insistent on getting an answer for the boys' idea of a trip to the Everglades.

Donnie and Maggie answered at the same time but not with the same answer

"No."

"Maybe."

"You don't have to go Mom, if you're too scared of alligators and snakes and stuff. Maybe Grandpa will go with us, you can stay with Grandma."

"I'm not scared Daniel." I'm terrified. "I just think it's too far."

"How far is it?"

She didn't want to admit she didn't even know the Everglades were in Florida. "Too far."

"Mom, it's only like two hours from here."

Thanks Dylan. "Since when did you become Mr. Geography? And why do you want to go anyway? Alligator wrestling isn't exactly one of your sports."

Todd jumped all over that. "Alligator wrestling?! Can you really wrestle with them?! Mom I want to go!!"

"Oh good Lord Todd your skinny little body would be an appetizer for a baby alligator. One bite and it would be goodbye Todd."

"Boys? Did you really want to spend hours shopping tonight?"

"No!"

"What I'm thinking is since we did what Mom wanted that, I don't know, that maybe she should do what we want. Let's take a vote, who thinks Mom should have to go to the Everglades if we go?"

"Donnie!"

By the time they pulled in to Ann and Don's driveway Donnie had promised a trip to the Everglades as soon as Grandma was out of the woods.

"Why is Grandma in the woods? I thought she was in the hospital?" Todd questioned.

"Dork!" Dylan reached over the seat and started roughing up Todd's hair.

"Stop! Mom! Make him stop!"

Daniel pushed Dylan's hand off Todd's head and then Derek grabbed Daniels hand and of course Dylan couldn't stop himself from joining in. And they're back.

Before Donnie turned the van off all but D.J. were out of their seatbelts and in a tangled mess of arms and legs flying in every direction. D.J. was crouched a bit with his hands over his head and then he dropped them and started pushing and shoving and disappeared into the mass of flying Conner boys.

Maggie and Donnie looked at each other to see who was going to take lead and break it up. Neither did, Donnie yelled, "Last one out has to carry all the bags in!" and they both opened their doors and high tailed it for the house.

CHAPTER SIX

"I knew it was too good to be true." Maggie told Donnie later that night when the boys were all in bed and they were sitting outside by the pool. "The boys I mean. I was hoping they left their fights back in New York."

Donnie tipped his glass of lemonade back and finished it off. He hadn't had a drink since they'd been there. "Still, you have to admit they've been abnormally normal."

"True."

Donnie got up and pulled his shirt off. He wandered around the pool but ended up slipping into the hot tub instead. "Join me?"

Maggie hesitated, she would prefer slipping into bed, it was a long day and she was tired but there would be plenty of time to catch up on sleep when they returned home in a week. "I'll get my suit on, back in minute."

They sat across from each other, closed their eyes and relaxed. He relaxed, Maggie kept opening one eye and peeking at him. It was the first time they were alone since the night Donnie revealed his secret of knowing about Mike and then receiving the phone call about his mother. She debated bringing it up. It loomed over them no matter how veiled it was by the circumstances. They had to talk. Sometime.

"Everyone seems so much happier here. Even you. Even with your Mom and the circumstances you seem like a different person. Have you noticed it? I feel like we're all the same but better versions of ourselves."

Donnie opened his eyes and sat up straighter. "Yeah, definitely, I agree. What do you think it is? The scare with my Mom? Getting away from home? I mean even with Mom in the hospital and not being completely out of the woods yet it still feels like we're on vacation. Think that's it?"

"Yeah, partly." She thought about it a minute. "But we could have been at each other's throats too, I mean all that time in the van on the way down, it could have gone the opposite way. I think it's getting away from normal. I know you have to have normal but I think being yanked out of it so suddenly gave everyone a fresh burst of, I don't know, different."

"A fresh burst of different?" Donnie smiled.

"If you make fun of me I will drown you."

Donnie stopped smiling. "Okay, go on."

"Well, I have an issue with normal..." Donnie opened his mouth to speak but Maggie held her finger up, that finger, and he closed his mouth. She continued, "Everyone's normal is so different. How do we know our normal *is* normal?"

"Don't follow."

"I mean, think about it Donnie, we've always followed the days the way they laid out, one after another, we never stepped outside of what was laid out in front of us. It's like our life was already drawn out and we just stayed between the lines."

"Don't follow."

"Okay, when we were kids we did what kids do, no choice. And then we got pregnant and we got married, we did what we were supposed to do. We always took the obvious path, you know, the next step, we just did it and never questioned it. You've been at the same job since you were eighteen, we've been in the same house in the same town. Donnie look around, there's a whole world and a million different ways of life we have access to but we've never even thought about anything other than what we wake up to. Do you get what I'm saying?"

"Starting to. Keep going."

"I don't know if I can."

Donnie raised an accusing eyebrow. "I'm pretty sure you can."

"Right. Let me think a minute." She closed her eyes and thought a minute then opened them again. "Okay, follow my thoughts a minute, we're in the car on the highway, we're in the slow lane all the way to the right, we keep going, and going, and going, we never get off an exit and we never see anything other than the same kind of scenery. We never even veer in the left lane to pass anyone, we just go and go and go. What happens?"

"Really? I was hoping we'd have sex tonight not play fourth grade word games."

"I am so close to drowning you…"

"Okay okay. It sounds boring, but we eventually get where we're going."

"Right! Or we run out of gas."

"So, then we call Triple A and they rescue us. So was Mom's heart attack the AAA rescue?"

"Hmm, maybe. Maybe your Mom's heart attack was the fuel that gets us going again. So we have a choice now, do we stay on the highway until we run out of gas again or do we take a new route, where there's gas stations along the way?"

"Remember when we used to smoke pot? In high school? This is one of those conversations."

Maggie chuckled. "Yeah, maybe I missed the mark but I'll find the right way to explain it eventually. I miss those days, not so much the pot smoking, well maybe a little, but I miss the future."

Donnie scratched his head. "I don't get it. We have a future, everyone has a future."

"Do they? Even if we do we don't have the one we thought we had."

"No one has the future they thought they'd have. When

you're a kid you're stupid, you don't know anything, you don't imagine the days ahead with bills and stomach aches and kids fighting over drink boxes and cars needing new brakes and people having heart attacks."

"But that's exactly what I mean. I miss that. I miss that naive tunnel vision of the future being only good possibilities."

"You want to always live in a high school state of mind? We've grown up Maggie, we live in the real world now, you can't go back to that kind of naïve thinking."

Maggie swept her hand back and forth across the top of the water.

Donnie watched her hand, watched the rippling of water. "What are you thinking Maggie?"

She stopped sweeping the water and looked at him. "I'm thinking that, speaking of high school, I need to know what happened between you and Mike."

Donnie sighed. "I know you do and I will tell you. I'll tell you now if you insist but Maggie I'm begging you to wait until after this week, until we're home. We're having a…I don't want to say good time, that feels wrong considering my Mom but it's the only thing I can think to say. We're having a good time. Can you wait until we're home?"

Not fair. That was like putting a piece of triple chocolate cake in front of you when you just finished a huge meal. She wanted it now and she could have it now but she was pretty sure if she gave in and took it she would regret it. "Do you promise to tell me when we get home?"

"I promise."

"Okay." Maggie began sweeping the surface of the water again.

"Maggie don't think about it, please, don't let it ruin our week, you're deep in thought I can see it on your face."

"Actually this time I was thinking about triple chocolate cake."

"Can we go to the Everglades today Mom? Can we?

Please? Pleeeaaaase?"

"Not today. Dad's at the hospital with Grandpa and you guys are going to get started on your school work right after breakfast."

Maggie ignored the chorus of groans and continued putting sliced fruit on each of the boy's plates. D.J. climbed onto a stool and began eating but the other boys stayed rooted in place.

"Come on Mom we're on vacation! People don't do homework on vacation!"

She poured glasses of milk and brought one to D.J. "You're not on vacation, you're on a medical leave of absence. Now eat! Dylan counter. Derek, Daniel, Todd table. Now!"

They sat as ordered. Dylan shoved half a banana in his mouth and didn't bother chewing before speaking. "I have gym class first period. Swimming."

"No you don't. This is what we're going to do, we'll work on homework until eleven o'clock and then I'll give you all a two hour break and you can swim."

"Then what? The Everglades?"

"No Todd, no Everglades today, get it out of your mind. One o'clock back to homework."

"What if we're done by eleven can we swim all afternoon?"

"You won't be done by eleven. I'm checking your work so don't think you can speed through it, if it's not done right you'll do it again."

The boys ate breakfast and scattered to their rooms to get their school work. They slowly returned one by one to the kitchen and sat at their appointed places, except Derek.

"Where's Derek?"

No one answered.

"Derek?!"

"Where's my science book? I can't find it, didn't you get it at school? It's not here!"

"You didn't have any science homework. Get your other books and get out here." Actually, he did have science homework but both Maggie and his teacher agreed it would be best if he waited and stayed after school to make it up, in a well supervised safe environment.

The boys did homework until eleven and then swam as promised. At one o'clock they were back at the table resigned to the fact that Maggie wasn't going to give in. By three o'clock she felt sorry for them and furloughed them for the day. They were back in the pool within three minutes. They were still swimming at four when Don and Donnie returned.

"How is she?" Maggie asked.

"She's weak and tired and still has a long way to go but she's doing great. She wants to see you and the boys." Don shook his head, "The boys are not allowed in the unit but she's determined, she'll talk them into it."

"Should I go tomorrow then?"

"Should I check her schedule?" Don said to Donnie and they both laughed. "The woman has it all planned out. She made a schedule for the whole week. She wants us to take the boys to the Everglades tomorrow so she can spend time with ..."

The boys heard Everglades and tomorrow and suddenly tidal waves began crashing over the sides of the pool. All three adults stopped talking and watched, partly in amazement that humans could act that way but mostly to make sure no one got hurt. Kids were flying everywhere.

They were only marginally calmer the next morning at eight a.m. when Maggie and Donnie put their breakfast on the table and they were fully amped again by nine a.m. when they left. Maggie stood in the driveway waving and thanking her lucky stars she didn't have to go with them. She didn't know which would have scared her more, the boys or the alligators.

She took her time over a cup of coffee sitting by the pool and then showered and got ready to spend the day with Ann. Before she left she peeked into Don and Ann's room, chances are Don hadn't thought to bring anything personal and if she knew Ann she would appreciate something of her own.

Ann was five seven and not thin and not thick. She probably weighed a few pounds more than the current BMI charts called for but she wore it well. She and Donnie referred to her as New York Ann or Florida Ann but not to pinpoint geography or time in life but to identify which Ann they were talking about. The first time they saw her after she'd moved south they couldn't believe the transformation. The Florida weather or lifestyle or something agreed with her. She looked like a completely different person.

Her hair was grey and in New York her extent of hair care consisted of washing and occasionally cutting. Period. Her hair was thin and fell where it wanted to and she never challenged it with a comb. In Florida she found a hairdresser that talked her into a style and since then she was a fanatic about her hair. It was always styled and classy. She had an entire cabinet in her bathroom devoted to hair care products.

She also left her jeans and sweats in New York and dressed every day in skirts and sundresses. And colors. Lots of colors.

Maggie felt a little guilty looking through her closet but she didn't think Ann would mind, especially if she could change her hospital gown for something brighter. She pulled a white gown and robe set with bright orange bold circles off a hanger. Not something she would have bought herself but it suited Florida Ann just right.

Ann also acquired a fondness for accessories and there were totes and boxes lining the entire shelf in her closet. Maggie knew there had to be a one filled with just accessories. She was wrong there wasn't one. There were three. She found two with scarves and one with jewelry and she pulled a couple brightly patterned scarves out and on impulse grabbed a couple colorful bracelets. She could always bring them back home if she didn't want them or couldn't have them.

The GPS in Don's Camry guided her directly to the hospital without incident. The visitor desk volunteer guided her directly to room 226 without incident. The nurses' station was empty and so was room 226.

"Wait!"

Maggie turned around to a short plump nurse scurrying toward her.

"Are you a relative?" The nurse caught up to Maggie who was standing with one foot in the room.

"Her daughter-in-law." Was she supposed to sign in? Get permission? Don hadn't mentioned anything. "This is Ann Conner's room isn't it?"

"Come with me please." The nurse had a strong chubby hand on Maggie's arm and was already walking away from the door making it impossible not to 'come with me please'.

"Is there a problem? Don didn't mention signing in or anything. He's taking a break this morning..."

"Have a seat please." The nurse had escorted her to a small room that housed a table and five chairs. She pulled a chair out for Maggie and nodded her head toward it. "Someone will be with you in a minute."

"Is there..."

Nurse Chubby was gone and before Maggie had a chance to have a seat as directed, a middle aged man with a face covered with stubble stepped into the room. He pulled out a chair and sat before motioning to Maggie to do the same.

"You're Ann's daughter-in-law? Don couldn't make it today?"

"He'll be here later. We're visiting, my husband Donnie and our boys, Don took the morning off to take them to the Everglades. Is there a problem?"

"We've been trying to get a hold of Don for the last hour. He hasn't answered his phone. Ms. Conners, it's Conners?"

"Yes."

"I'm sorry. Ann passed away just about an hour ago."

"WHAT??" When she could coordinate her mind and her voice she said, "No, that can't be. Don said she was doing better. He said it was eighty-twenty."

"I'm sorry Ms. Conners. She had a massive heart attack. There was nothing we could do."

"But...Don..."

"Do you have another number or another way to get in touch with him? Ms. Conners I realize it's no consolation but you should know that Ann didn't suffer. It was very fast.

Would you like me to call your husband for you?"

"Donnie. Oh God." The tears started streaming down Maggie's face. "Don. He'll be devastated. And Donnie..." Except Donnie came out mingled with a sob and she couldn't put another thought in place. She let go of the bag she'd been holding for Ann and laid her head in her arms on the table and cried.

Maggie heard the doctor ask if there was anything he could do, heard him ask if she would be okay if he stepped out, felt him gently place his hand on her shoulder, but she had no concept of the space of time between each of those occurrences. She might have been crying for a minute or she might have been crying for hours, she didn't know. She didn't know if she answered him, she wasn't sure when he took his hand off her shoulder, she didn't remember him leaving the room but when she finally lifted her head again he was gone. She was alone.

Maggie sucked in a series of short sharp breaths and on the tail of each breath there seemed to be an awareness of each of the grief's she had yet to deal with. With each breath rose an image of telling Don, of telling Donnie, of telling each of the boys. She was both thankful and resentful that it was her that came today and not Don and Donnie. But did it matter? Did the all consuming pain of the shock of death that emptied the heart, mind and soul, did the strength shift in intensity no matter who broke the news? Of course it didn't.

She laid her head down and sobbed some more. She knew she was both over reacting to the death of a person she loved and under reacting. She couldn't stop sobbing no matter how hard she tried and she couldn't move from the little room where time stood still, where as long as she didn't leave the parameters of these four walls she didn't have to leave the parameters of her own grief.

Maggie still had her head buried in the crook of her elbow on the table when the doctor came back in. She didn't know how long it had been but she felt like she shouldn't have still been there. She felt ashamed and then she felt angry that she felt ashamed and then she felt ashamed that she was angry. The emotions volleyed back and forth so fast she couldn't grasp either one to hold on to and so when the doctor said, "Can I get you anything?" she burst out sobbing again.

Why weren't there words invented for times like this? There were no words reserved for death. The one event when a person most needed to rely on rote, those in their deepest grief and those wanting desperately to convey their condolences, and both reached in their endless well of vocabulary and came up empty.

"No, thank you."

The doctor took a step inside the doorway and placed his hand on her shoulder. "Take all the time you need." He disappeared again.

All the time she needed would be the rest of her life didn't he know that? Just like words there was no time frame for the steps after the loss of a loved one or for preparing to break the news to others. How much time did she need to leave this room and drive back to the house and wait for Don and Donnie and the boys to come home and walk in with sun tanned skin and stories of alligators and swamps and then for them to see the wrongness in her eyes and on her face and to stop in mid sentence and know, and know that by the time the other end of the breath they just took in was back out their own eyes and faces would catch up to hers? How much time doc? How much time?

How much time did she need to process the news of Ann's death? How much time did she need to prepare herself to tell Ann's husband, her son, her grandsons? How much time did she need to grieve the loss of a wonderful person? How much time doc? Forever.

Maggie picked up the bag with Ann's things and slowly pulled herself from the chair. She walked out of the room and past the nurses' station and down the elevator and through the hall and past the visitors' desk and out the front door without looking at anyone. She unlocked the Camry and threw the bag in the passenger seat and started the car. She turned on the

GPS and let the voice guide her back to the house and when she pulled in the driveway and put the car in park she thanked the voice. The voice that had no inflection, the voice that didn't ask her if she needed anything, the voice that guided her to where she had to be when she would never have been able to do it herself. The voice that she trusted for the last half hour and when she didn't do what it told her at that one confusing mess of ramps, it simply continued to tell her what to do next.

But now she was on her own. She turned the car off and took the bag from the passenger seat and took the keys out and walked to the house and unlocked the door and stepped inside. Of Ann's house. The house Ann loved and would never step inside of again. She was racked with another round of heart stabbing grief and had to slide into the nearest stool and when she felt she could move again she took the bag to her room and placed it on the dresser and fell into the bed and cried some more.

She cried and wondered if she were crying for Ann or for herself or for Don or for Donnie or for the boys. She thought maybe she was crying for them all and for all the people that were experiencing the loss of a loved one and ever had and ever would. Because in the end, as individual as everyone was, wasn't it the same for everyone?

She cried herself to sleep and when she woke she remembered and it was just as paralyzing as it was the first time. She hadn't ever thought about that. That grief isn't something that happens once to a person but that it happens over and over and over every time they wake up and every time they remember. She knew in her mind that it would ease, not just for her but for Don and all of them, that Ann would never be forgotten and her life would never be any less meaningful but that the grief would abate and that the day would come when Don could wake up and not feel the stabbing emptiness and sorrow. But that day was sure to be a long way off. He hadn't even experienced the initial attack yet. Don was somewhere thinking she and Ann were sitting together in a hospital room making plans and chatting and giggling while he wrestled alligators and unruly boys.

Just as she thought, after hours of alternately sitting and lying down and waiting for the future to catch up to the present, the front door opened and Don and Donnie and the boys barged in all talking at once and all stopping at once when they saw her face. And just as she thought, in a matter of the blink of an eye, the knowledge came without the need for words and Don stumbled to the couch and all the blood drained from his face. Donnie leaned against the wall and slunk to the floor.

"Mom?" Dylan knew and yet he didn't know. He and the other boys needed to hear it and she was surprised to find she needed to say it.

"Grandma passed away. This morning. Before I got there." It was all she could say under the weight of the boy's eyes and the men's shallow breaths but it was all she needed to say for the moment.

Todd ran into her arms and Daniel came to her side and tucked himself as close to her as he could. Derek took a step toward his father and Donnie reached his arms out and Derek fell into them. D.J. and Dylan went to the couch and sat on either side of Don and Maggie burst into a new wave of sobs when she saw D.J. put his hand out and Don take it.

Of all of them, Don was the first to speak. "Ann wouldn't like this." His voice was soft and the words were pocketed with air but he cleared his throat and spoke again. "She wouldn't want us to be this way. She'd probably allow us a few minutes and then she'd clap her hands and tell us to get busy with the arrangements." His voice cracked on the word arrangements and he sniffed and wiped his eyes with the back of his hand. "Maggie? What happened?"

Maggie told them in bits and pieces between her own sniffing and sobbing. Dylan got up and went to the bathroom and returned with a box of Kleenex and handed them out, taking one himself and wiping his own red swollen eyes. When he got to Maggie and Todd and Daniel, Todd took a Kleenex and then put his arms out to Dylan and Dylan lifted him into his own arms and hugged him. Maggie nearly choked and Daniel scurried into her lap and she put her head in the nook of his shoulder and held him tightly.

Daniel fell asleep in Maggie's arms and Todd fell asleep in Dylan's. They carried them to their beds and Donnie carried Derek to the couch where he curled into the corner and fell asleep.

"I better call the hospital." Don stood from the couch and Donnie put his hand on his shoulder and Don pulled him into a hug and then let him go and went to his room to make the call.

"Do you want us to go to our rooms?" D.J. asked his father and Donnie looked to Maggie. She shrugged and he told them that no, if they wanted to stay they could but if they wanted to go to their rooms they could do that too. They stayed.

When Don returned the five of them began planning Ann's memorial service.

Don opted for a private memorial service with just the family. The next day he asked each of the boys to write a letter or draw a picture to send her to heaven with. Todd drew a picture of himself in the pool. Daniel drew a picture of the house with all of them standing in front of it, including Ann. Derek created a three dimensional card with a pop up likeness of each of them. All that remained of the brightest colored crayons were tiny stubs. Dylan and D.J. each gave Don a sealed envelope.

The memorial service took place three days later. Maggie and Donnie cried from beginning to end but Don hadn't cried since the day he walked in and saw Maggie's face. The boys alternately wiped away tears and leaned against each other and when they returned home Don sat the boys down and he explained to them that it was okay to cry but that he had so many good memories with their Grandmother that whenever he felt like crying he just thought about one of those memories. He told them it didn't mean anything one way or the other, to cry or not, that everyone had their own way to deal with death and no one's way was right and no one's way was wrong.

The eight of them were sitting in the living room still in the clothes they wore to the memorial service. Todd sat in Don' lap with his head against his chest, D.J. and Dylan flanked him on either side. Don's protective army. The three of them hadn't left his side in three days.

"Donnie?" Don's voice was strong and full of intent. "Do you remember what your Mother said she wanted us to do? Remember when she was making a schedule and she said to make sure we took the boys with us?"

"No, can't say as I do."

"Well good thing I do then. Boys, Grandma had a task for us to do and we're going to do it."

"What was it Grandpa?" Daniel scooted to the edge of his seat ready to spring into action to accomplish whatever task Ann had scheduled for them.

"She wanted us to go to the beach and search for shells. She said to pick only the very best ones, bring them back and scatter them around in the flower bed behind the pool. She always said she was going to do that and for some reason we just never did." Don looked over at Donnie. "Remember yet? Do you remember what she said about scattering the shells?"

"She said she was glad she never got around to it. She said having shells that the boys picked out would be so much nicer than having shells she picked out."

Don smiled. "So that's what we're going to do. I can't think of a better way to spend the day than honoring your Grandmother's wish. Boys, go change your clothes and put on some beach attire."

The boys didn't need to be told twice. Donnie got up from the chair and went to the couch and sat down next to his father. "You sure about this Dad? I can take them if you're not up to it."

"I'm up to it." Don reassured him. "There will be no moping around. New York Ann might have allowed a day or two more but Florida Ann would never hear of it."

Donnie and Maggie exchanged a startled glance. "You knew we called her that?" Donnie asked.

"Of course I knew. She knew too." He stood and began walking to his room. "I'm going to miss them both."

The sand was white, warm and refreshing. The boys were shoeless and shirtless as they filled bags with shells and other skeletal remains of creatures Maggie hoped never to see in their entirety. Don and Donnie were walking off alone to the north and the boys knew instinctively to give them their time alone together. She shook out one of the boys shirts and laid it on the sand to sit on. She yelled out, "Boys don't go too far, stay where I can see you." But they must have heard, "Come sit next to me and ask me a thousand questions."

"Mom can we swim in the ocean?"

"Why did Mom even name you Todd? She should have named you dork. This isn't the ocean it's the Gulf. We're on the west side of Florida, the ocean is on the east side. Dork."

"Dylan," Maggie tilted her head, "I know Grandpa said he wanted us to be as normal as we could be but seriously tone it down. And where's all this geography knowledge coming from anyway?"

"Obviously I'm just smart."

"I wish I was." D.J. mumbled.

"So does everyone else." Dylan shoved him and the next second the two were chasing each other across the beach. Maggie smiled. How incredibly indescribable she felt. Every emotional tag came to mind, happy, sad, stressed, calm, frustrated, scared, tense, relaxed. She felt them all and more. She watched the boys as they ran out of steam and began walking side by side. The emotion that teetered above the rest was happy. She never dreamed she'd see Dylan and D.J. walking side by side. Like brothers. She wiped away a tear that formed in the corner of her eye.

"Mom? Are you crying again?" Daniel scooted across the sand bridging the gap of space between them.

"No, sand in my eye this time."

"You look like you're crying."

"Well I'm not. But I will be if you three don't stop blocking my sun. How's a girl supposed to get a tan with you three muscled hunks blocking my sun? Now scoot. Go get shells."

The sun felt amazing on her skin and she could feel the paths on her face where it dried her tears nearly as quickly as they fell. She was crying for Ann, but it felt like something more. It felt like she was shedding.

"Maggie?"

She turned to see Don and Donnie standing just a few feet away, how had they snuck up on her like that?

"Maggie?" Donnie whispered, "Look!" He pointed toward Dylan and D.J. who were sitting together on a rock at the edge of the parking lot.

She looked and then looked back at Donnie. "Why are you whispering?"

He squinted and thought. "Dunno, guess I didn't want to jinx it. What's the deal? They look like, like they're talking."

Maggie smiled. "I'm telling you this place is full of magic." She heard the joy in her voice and immediately felt remorseful for it, "I'm sorry Don. That sounded awful."

"Listen Maggie, and you too Donnie, Ann was a great woman and I loved her with every ounce of my being but she's gone and you know her as well as anyone, she wouldn't want us grieving for more than five minutes and I intend to honor that for her. You might find that awful but it's how it's going to be. I love Ann, I always will, but I love you guys and the boys and you're here and I intend to make the best of every moment that you are here. If you need to mourn and watch everything you say so be it. I don't." He straightened his head and walked off toward the younger boys.

"Is that healthy?" Maggie asked Donnie.

Donnie reached a hand out to Maggie. "If it's what he has to do then I guess so. Walk with me?"

They walked without talking until they were far from everyone else. Donnie kicked his sandals off and waded in the water. The water temperature was sixty six. They knew that because Encyclopedia Dylan informed them on the way there. Maggie stuck her toe in and immediately pulled it back out. After the eighty degree heated pool back at the house sixty six felt like thirty six. Donnie turned around and smiled. "You've been here six days and you're already acclimated to the southern temps.'"

Acclimated? Was he secretly studying dictionary.com or something? Maybe it downloaded as a package deal with Dylan's encyclopedia.com. "I love it here. I mean, I'm sorry," she reddened. "Oh geez Donnie I don't know what to say. I don't want to disrespect Ann or you or Don but I can't seem to get the words right."

"You can be sad about my Mom and still love it here Maggie. But, that brings up something we need to talk about." He walked to her side, "Can we sit and talk a minute?"

They both glanced back and spotted all the boys and Don. "They haven't even noticed we're gone." They sat side by side on the sand, "What's on your mind?"

"I'm worried about Dad when we leave. He's putting on a good show now but what's going to happen once we're gone? We're supposed to leave day after tomorrow, Maggie, hear me out okay?"

Nothing good ever came from a sentence that started out with 'hear me out okay' but what choice did she have? "Okay."

"I have six weeks' vacation, well, five left. It's slow at work and I know they would approve it. I want to stay here with Dad for a while."

Her thoughts derailed. Stay? Him? Twenty five hours drive alone with the boys? "Wait. What do you mean? You? Alone?"

"I was thinking about him coming back with us but he won't even discuss it. So I mentioned my staying here a while but he's the one that actually came up with an idea, we don't know how it would work though. Or if you'd want to."

"What? What are you talking about?"

"Do you think we could enroll the boys in school here for the five weeks? Is that even possible? I mean, if it is we can all stay. I don't want to leave my Dad yet and just look at the boys, they're so different here. They're happy."

Maggie held her hand up. "Process."

"What?"

"I have to process, I feel like screaming Yes! No! I feel like laughing and I feel like crying. Just give me a minute okay?" She closed her eyes and thought. Could they enroll the boys in school here for five weeks? How would they feel about that? She thought they would love the idea of staying but she had no idea what they would think about going to school here and having to meet new people and new teachers. She'd have to find out. First, was it even possible, then would the boys want to. Did she want to? The processing came fast and furious, snow/sun, heat/cold, shoveling/beachcombing, fighting/getting along, black hoodie/plaid shorts. "Processed."

"What?"

"Donnie I think it's a great idea. But there's a lot to figure out first. I think we should find out first if it's even possible to enroll the kids for five weeks then I think we need to ask them how they feel about it. That's a big deal Donnie, they should have a say in it. If they want to then I say let's do it!"

Donnie grinned. "I haven't told you this for a long long time. I love you."

Maggie couldn't hide the shock. "Is…is that the emotion of the day speaking?"

"No. Yes. But I do love you. I know we still have a bucket load of things to talk about and work out but I want to work them out Maggie. I do."

"You do?"

"Of course."

"Donnie I do too. But, I'm not sure we can really work it out unless you stop drinking, for good."

Donnie nodded slowly. "I'll try. I promise I'll try." He looked away a minute and then looked back, "Do you think I should get help like AA or something?"

"Probably. Yeah, I do think you should."

"Will you, do whatever wives do, like go with me?"

"I don't think I go with you but they'll tell us. Let's start with getting through today for your Dad and tomorrow we'll deal with the school issue. Once we figure out where we'll be we can make some calls and find out how to start, or where to start."

"Sounds like a plan. Maggie do you realize if we put this plan in motion there'll be a ton of calls we'll need to make? We'll have to have someone check on the house and, what about the mail? Should we have it forwarded? I'll have to call my work probably first thing right? Should I call them anyway or wait until we find out about the school first? My head's spinning. "

"Slow down cowboy. What happened to sounds like a plan? Today just focus on your Dad. Tomorrow we'll call the school. If it will work then we'll talk to the boys. There are a lot of steps before we even think about contacting your work. Or my work." Maggie added and watched Donnie cringe. "Donnie I'd have to let Mike know too."

"Okay okay."

"Remember you said you'd tell me what went down with you two when we got home? If we stay here for five weeks I don't want to wait until we get home, you'll have to tell me here, soon."

Donnie nodded and they sat silently sorting their own thoughts.

The boys went to bed early and voluntarily. When Maggie finished showering the sun, sand and lotion off she took a quick peek in the boy's rooms and then wandered outside to find Don and Donnie stretched out in lounge chairs by the pool although the sun had set long ago. She closed the sliding glass door behind her and proceeded to dramatically lower herself to one knee and sweepingly bowed her head.

"What's wrong with your wife?"

"Not sure."

Maggie slowly raised her head. "I'm paying my respect and gratitude to the Gods of the South for fixing our kids." She bowed her head again.

"Quit being ridiculous and come over here, there's something I want to talk about."

Maggie stood and raised her hands to the sky, which was actually a yoga pose she learned from a demonstration on a Today show episode, and then crossed herself Catholic style before joining the men by the pool. Instead of pulling up a chair or lounge she scooted next to Don on his lounge and leaned over and hugged him. "You doing okay?"

"Didn't we talk about this?"

"Don I respect your wishes not to dwell in mourning but I can still ask about you. Are you doing okay?"

"Inside or out?"

"Either. Both."

"Outside I think I'm doing okay, it helps having you guys here, and by the way the boys aren't fixed Maggie, they're still quite broken but I like them just the way they are. To answer your question to your satisfaction, there were times today that I was thinking about Ann and I'd see one of the boys shoving sand in another one's shirt or chasing each other with something slimy and I'd catch myself smiling, and I'd realize that for just one second I wasn't thinking about Ann." Don took a breath and let it out slowly. "So I guess inside's a different story. Inside I feel hallowed out. I feel like without Ann I'm just one of those useless shells we picked up on the beach. Without Ann I'm empty, my purpose is gone."

The toll of Ann's death clearly showed on his face.

"You're staring at me."

Maggie smiled and took one of his hands in hers. "Yeah. Because I don't know what to say, I want to say you'll be okay or take one day at a time, something like that but we both know those words are just filler words people say when they don't know what to say."

"I always thought I'd go first. It should have been that way, Ann's much stronger than I am, she would have been okay."

Maggie heard Donnie sniffle and then clear his throat to try to cover it.

"Florida Ann maybe but Florida Ann was just New York Ann in disguise. I bet she would have been exactly like you are now. I bet she would have felt the same way. You're right Don, she was strong but I don't think she was any stronger than you are. Why do people think when the person they love most in the world dies that they have to be strong anyway? You're entitled to feel what you feel."

Don squeezed her hand. "You're a good kid."

They sat quietly, Don and Maggie hand in hand and Donnie stifling sniffles in the chair next to them. Don rested his head against the back of the lounge chair and stared at the top of the palm trees, or further beyond at the sky. After a space of time he spoke again. "I'm not sure what to do with Ann's things. It feels wrong to get rid of everything, especially so soon, but the truth is, I can't stand seeing it all. Every time I walk into our room I see her clothes or her shoes or her jewelry and it feels like a knife twisting in my heart."

"I'll do it. I'll box everything up and store it or donate it. You just tell me what you want me to do."

"I'd appreciate that. I don't think I can do it. I don't even want to go in our room anymore."

"Dad?" Donnie sat up and wiped his tears with the back of his hand. "Take our room, we'll bunk with the boys for now. You can move in there or we can even remodel your room if you want. Whatever you want Dad, just tell us."

"I don't want to erase her but I don't think I can live with her things…in our room. I've been sneaking into the boys room you know, after everyone's asleep I've been going into the room with D.J. and Dylan and sleeping in the spare bed."

"It's okay Don, it's not erasing her, Ann will always be a part of you. And you haven't been sneaking, we all knew you were, we just were giving you time to figure out what you needed."

"Dad? Take our room okay? Maggie will pack up Mom's things and we'll do whatever you want to your room, or you can make our room your new room."

"I'll start tomorrow Don. Is there anything special you want me to keep out?"

"I feel like I should say yes. I feel like I should keep everything but the truth is," he looked directly at Maggie, "I can't. It hurts too much to see any of it."

"There's no rules, whatever feels right to you is right. I'll pack everything. I'll donate everything except what I think you might want someday. Is that alright?"

"Perfect. Thank you."

Jillian, lots of news, you better sit down for this, ready?

Yeah, what's going on?

We're staying here for five weeks. Donnie's using his vacation time.

WHAT????

I know. It's complicated but not. We didn't want to leave Don alone yet and he wouldn't come back to NY. The boys love it here, we love it here, Donnie's work is slow now anyway.

I don't even know what to say! What about school? What about your job?

We called school and they suggested home schooling for the five weeks but I'm not that crazy, called the school here and they were awesome, they called Colton and worked everything out between them, the boys start tomorrow!

And they're okay with that?

Believe it or not! They're all a little apprehensive except Todd. We took them in to see the school and meet their teachers. D.J.'s the most apprehensive but he really wants to stay here too so he was willing to give it a try. You wouldn't believe the change in him, he's not even the same kid, I think I even like him now.

Lol. What about your work?

Called. He said he would get his daughter to come back until I get back.

It's all unbelievable! But awesome! How's Don? How are you and

Donnie?

Don's struggling, keeps a lot inside but he's making progress every day. Donnie's still struggling too about his Mom but he and I are doing good, great actually, he's starting AA on Thursday.

WHAT??!! WOW!! I'm speechless.

Lol that's a first! So how are the move home plans going? Will you be there when we get back?

On schedule for April, so not when you get back but soon after.
YAYAYAYAYAYAY!!!

Haha! Gotta go, Pete just flushed a ? sock? yikes…overflow…

Donnie and Maggie debated driving the boys to school for their first day but decided it would be best if they started out taking the bus. There were already enough changes going on in their lives and the sooner they could establish some consistency the better. Don had five paper bag lunches lined up on the counter and Donnie was putting them in the new backpacks they'd picked up when they went shopping for new school clothes and supplies. Maggie sat at the table sipping a cup of coffee, listening to the sounds of the boys getting ready in their rooms and nervously switching her attention between the men packing the backpacks and the clock on the microwave.

"Maybe I should have home schooled them."

Don and Donnie stopped and turned to Maggie.

"Are you crazy?" Donnie whispered.

"I know but I feel so, nervous." Maggie admitted. "What if they don't fit in? What if they don't like it? What if I don't like it? It's going to be too quiet here without them. I've gotten used to having them around."

"They'll be fine. You saw them yesterday, they loved the school."

Maggie blotted at the corners of her eyes with her sleeve.

"Are you…" Donnie smirked. "Are you crying?!"

"No! Don just needs to take a shower, the stench in here is awful."

"Don't blame me you big softy." He turned away but lifted his arm and gave a quick sniff anyway.

Donnie shook his head and ignored them both. "Come on boys!"

Todd came running into the kitchen followed immediately by Daniel and then Derek. All three wore plaid shorts with color coordinated t-shirts and Crocs. They looked classic Florida. They're faces were flush with a combination of sun and excitement and their hair was already beginning to look a little bleached out.

"You guys look like you need a surf board more than a backpack,." Maggie teased. "You look great boys." She stood up and hugged each one of them.

Dylan emerged from his room wearing navy blue cargo shorts and a light blue polo shirt. He walked up to Todd and spit on his hand and tried to tame Todd's cowlick.

"Dylan! Gross! Even I wouldn't do that!" Maggie cringed.

"Ma? He's a hot little dude, all the Florida girls are gonna be standing in line to become Mrs. Todd Conners, I'm just making sure he's up to par. Plus I had a snot ball I had to get rid of."

"Ewww Mom!!" Todd turned around and punched Dylan in the stomach.

Donnie stepped toward the boys prepared to break up a fight but D.J. walked into the room and everyone stopped and stared.

He was wearing jeans and sneakers and black t-shirt and a black hoodie, hood over his head. He stopped and stood by the counter waiting for someone to say something.

"Deej?" Maggie stood from her chair.

"Ma," Dylan turned to face D.J. "I got this. D.J. let's talk." He nodded toward the bedroom and began walking. D.J. hesitated but then turned and followed.

Don busied the other boys handing out backpacks and walking with them toward the door to wait with them outside for the bus. Donnie and Maggie looked at each other and tried to read the other's thoughts and decide what to do. Donnie broke eye contact and looked at the clock. "Five minutes," he whispered. "The bus should be here in five minutes."

"Give Dylan two. If they don't come out in two I'll go in," Maggie whispered back.

They watched the clock until one minute passed. And then another. They looked at each other and just as Maggie stood up to go the boys reappeared. Dylan acted as if he were walking out for the first time that morning, as if the last few minutes hadn't happened. D.J. walked next to him wearing jeans and sneakers and a solid royal blue t-shirt and a New York Mets baseball cap.

"Deej…"

Dylan interrupted her. "Ma? Todd needs you outside, he's got snot in his hair."

Donnie grabbed the backpacks and handed them to the boys. "Let's go, outside, two minutes until the bus comes!"

Maggie felt the second wave of emotion of the day hit her an hour later when she stood facing Ann's closet. Far be it from her to criticize God but at that moment she couldn't help it. He made a mistake. People's belongings should not outlive them. If He could create the whole world in six days He should have taken the seventh day and spent some time working on a better transition for the whole departing part.

Maggie stepped back and sat on the end of the bed while still staring into the closet. Polyester, cotton, silk, purple, green, orange, v-neck, crewneck, it was all there. But Ann wasn't.

How long had Ann stood at the clothing rack debating whether or not to buy that lime green sleeveless v-neck shell? Had she thought about what she would wear it with when she bought it? Had it been full price or had she found it on sale? Had she bought accessories to wear with it when she bought it? Did she like it as much when she brought it home or did it stay on the hanger in her closet?

Maggie stood back up and gently pulled the lime green shell from its hanger. She rubbed the shiny shimmery material between her fingers. Had Ann done the same when she pulled it from its hanger in the clothing store? If she showed it to Don would he instantly visualize Ann in it? Remember a specific dinner when she wore this shell? Smell the food they ate? Hear the sound of her laughter at some silly thing he'd said?

How could this top and all of the memories associated with it still be here when Ann wasn't? God made a mistake.

Maggie folded the shell and placed it in a box on the bed. She stepped to the closet and took each item, one by one, from its hanger. She gently and respectfully folded each of Ann's possessions but she closed her mind to the memories they might represent. She placed them in the boxes, one after another until the empty hangers hung without purpose.

She turned her focus to the shoes at the bottom of the closet. Open toe, closed toe, pumps, flats, Maggie picked up pair after pair and carried them to a box on the bed and gently placed them inside. Next she pulled a small step stool that was tucked neatly under the dresser and began pulling small totes from the closet shelf. She carried them to the bed until the bed was covered and the closet was empty.

That's how Ann's closet should have looked. The minute Ann's soul departed her body this was how her closet should have been.

Maggie slid the closet doors closed and returned to the bed to begin sorting the totes. Three were large clear totes, the same ones she'd peeked in the day she picked out things to bring to Ann at the hospital. Three were dark woven material with snug fitting lids. She placed the three dark woven totes aside and began with the clear totes. She sorted through scarves and bracelets and various accessories pulling out things and putting them back until she was satisfied that there was nothing that might be of sentimental value to Don. She put the totes in cardboard boxes.

"Need anything? Want some help?" She wondered how long Donnie had been standing in the doorway.

"Closet's done. Well, except for those." She waved her hand at the three woven totes.

"That's a lot of boxes. Mom sure did like to shop."

"Yeah, that's just the closet. I still have to do the dresser. Her coats and things are in the entryway closet. I think she has some things in totes in the garage too. It bugs me how when a person dies all their stuff is still fine. They're dead but their stuff is fine. Doesn't it seem like when a person dies their stuff should disappear or something?"

Donnie stepped into the room and glanced in one of the boxes. "I get what you're saying but sometimes it's nice to have something that belonged to the person that died. You know? Like a remembrance or something. Maybe you should keep something out for the boys, they might want to have something of Mom's." He folded the flaps and secured it closed. "Anything in here they'd want?

"It's all just clothes and stuff. Do you really think they'd want something? Do you want anything?"

"I don't know. Maybe. If you come across something you think I'd want let me know, it might be nice to take something home of hers, you know? I'll take these out to the van. Why don't you take a break and we'll take them to the donation place, pick up some lunch maybe?"

"What about your Dad?"

"He wants to stay here and make some phone calls, wants to call a couple of Mom's friends. I think that's good, it's kind of a step in healing don't you think?"

"Probably. It's just so sad. All of it. Donnie? Promise me I get to go first."

Donnie snickered and shook his head. "Sure, you first, but let's go," he took her hand and pulled her to her feet. "I can't talk about your demise on an empty stomach."

Demise? "Seriously Donnie, are you and Dylan studying together?"

"Huh?"

It slipped Maggie's mind how hungry the boys were when they got home from school and she had failed to prepare for it, or to warn Don. The three adults watched out the window as the bus stopped. As the boys got off one by one. As they charged into the house and went directly to the fridge pushing and shoving and grabbing whatever they could before someone else grabbed it.

"Oh yeah." Maggie mumbled from a safe distance. Donnie stood a little closer but just out of physical danger range. Don, however, tried to be helpful.

Maggie whispered to Donnie, "It's like driving by an accident scene, I want to look away but I can't."

Don had been standing the closest to the counter and when the boys charged the fridge he got pinned against the cupboards. He looked at Maggie and then Donnie and then spun around at lightning speed, opened a top cabinet pulled out a bag of chips and held it above his head. "I have chips!" He yelled.

The boy's bodies froze and their heads spun toward Don.

"Don't move!" Don yelled. "Everyone stay still and no one gets hurt." He gingerly tiptoed out and away from the counter. The boy's eyes were trained on the bag of chips as it moved slowly above Don's head and away from them. "Follow the chips!" He led them into the living room, once all five were lined behind him and in front of the couch he turned and pointed at the couch. "Sit!" They sat.

Maggie and Donnie stood watching from just outside the kitchen but well out of the pathway should the boys dart back in.

Don turned to them. "The kids aren't broken. Their parents are. What is wrong with you two? You allow this kind of animalistic behavior? Who is in charge here?"

Maggie looked at Donnie but he cowered so she stepped forward. "Uh, you are, right now. But," she pointed at the couch where Dylan and Derek were inching their way off the couch and eyeing the kitchen "you're going to lose the battle any second."

Don turned and saw what she was warning him about. "Sit!" They scooted back. "Let's get something straight right now boys," he paced in front of them military style still holding the bag of chips above his head. "This kind of behavior will NOT be accepted in this house. No, this kind of behavior will NOT be accepted anywhere from any of you ever again! Is that understood?"

Apparently not, Dylan looked at D.J. who looked at Derek who looked at Daniel who looked at Todd who was picking his nose.

"IS THAT UNDERSTOOD?"

All five boys jumped and Todd yelled "Ow!" took his finger out of his nose and started rubbing the outside where his finger dug in when he jumped.

"Grandpa we're hungry." Daniel tried to reason.

"You may be hungry but you are NOT animals! From now on when you walk in this house after school you will WALK. Then you will take care of your backpacks. Then you will go to the kitchen like civilized human beings and you will calmly and orderly find a snack, A snack, ONE snack, and you will sit at the table like civilized human beings and use manners while you eat your snack. You will NOT push, shove, fight, run, grab, or anything else like what I just witnessed in there today. Is that clear?"

"Yes." All five in unison.

"Now I'm going to go to the kitchen and put these chips in a bowl in the center of the table. You will follow me in single file and sit at the table. Your mother will pour you each a glass of milk and your father will get you napkins to put your chips on. You will pass the chips, eat like humans and tell us about your day. Are we clear?"

"Yes." All five in unison.

The boys followed as directed. Maggie poured as directed. Donnie handed out napkins as directed.

"Grandpa?" Todd took some chips as the bowl came to him and passed it on. "Did you make Grandma behave too?"

"No I didn't make Grandma behave, she knew how to behave all by herself. Now how was your first day at school Todd?"

"Cool. Did you know they have a pool there? I have to bring a swimsuit and in gym we get to swim sometimes. They don't let you eat the glue but the food is really good. And I have three new friends, Jim, Brandon and Alicia."

"That's great! I think. Remind me after snack and we'll make sure you get a swimsuit in your backpack so we don't forget okay?"

"Okay."

"Daniel? How about you? How was your first day?"

And around they went, Don asking each boy how his day was, the boys taking turns answering and politely eating and drinking and Donnie and Maggie both secretly thinking they should sign over custody and get out of Dodge while they could. When it was D.J.'s turn both Donnie and Maggie paid extra close attention.

"It was okay. It's different. Everybody dresses up more here."

Dylan broke the rule and piped up out of turn. "He sat with a girl at lunch."

D.J. blushed. "She sat with me. I was there first." He tilted his head down and looked toward the floor but Maggie could see a grin at the corners of his mouth.

"Think you'll adjust, to the school I mean not the girl?" Don asked him.

"Maybe," he turned to Maggie, "Mom, do you think we can get some different school clothes for me?"

Don spoke up. "If it's alright with your Mom I could take you tonight."

Alright? "Sure!"

Don looked around the table at the boys. "Anyone else need anything?"

They all looked at each other but no one spoke until Dylan finally cleared his throat and spoke up. "Umm, maybe some more snacks. Grandpa we're growing boys, chips are good but," he shrugged, "maybe something more?"

"Understood. Maggie I think there's some apples and oranges in the fridge if you want to grab them for the boys.

D.J. we'll head out after dinner. "

"Grandpa?" Todd struggled with an orange. "Can you help me peel this and what do we do until dinner? Can we swim?"

Don took the orange from Todd and began peeling it, "Homework. We do homework after snack and then if there is time we swim. That's the way it is in this house boys, every school day, got that?"

"Got it." They all said, including Maggie and Donnie who both blushed when they realized he wasn't talking to them.

The next morning the boys were up and ready before anyone had to call them. Don had their lunches made and Donnie had their backpacks ready for them. Maggie watched the boys as they ate their breakfast. Sergeant Don had made an impression. She could get used to this.

The boys were dressed in shorts and t-shirts, D.J. included. Don had taken him for a haircut last night while they were out shopping, Maggie wasn't sure whose idea it was but the stringy long hair was gone. He looked like every other Florida teenager. Her heart swelled.

"D.J. you look…"

"Don't." He warned.

"Okay, but you do, you look…"

"Mom?!"

"Okay, sorry. Handsome."

D.J. rolled his eyes.

After the boys left, which wasn't soon enough for D.J., Maggie, Don and Donnie enjoyed a cup of coffee outside by the pool.

"Dad?" Donnie had put his coffee down and was sitting on the edge of the pool letting his feet dangle in the water. "Thanks for everything. I mean it. I don't know what you did to D.J. last night but he's a different kid today. He really likes it here. He seems to have really taken to you too."

"We talked a bit. It's not me though, the clothes, the haircut, it's a girl. Lindsey. But you didn't hear it from me."

Donnie grinned from ear to ear. "Ah that explains it. His

first crush. Boy oh boy am I ever thankful to be out of that phase of life!"

"You and me both," Don added. "Do you two have any plans for today? I was thinking maybe we could visit Ann's grave and then maybe take a ride down the coast. It's just something she and I always like to do and it seems, I don't know, I just thought it would be nice but it would be a lot more enjoyable if you two came along."

"Would you two mind going without me?" Maggie stood and stretched. "It sounds nice and I'd love to go another day but I thought I'd keep working on Ann's things today."

Once the men were out of the house Maggie slid into her swimsuit and into the pool. She did plan on working on Ann's things and she would but she'd been itching for a chance to have the pool all to herself. She pulled herself onto a float, closed her eyes and let the sun warm every cell in her body. When she felt completely relaxed and at peace she slid off the float, showered and dressed. She would spend the entire day going through Ann's things, the sooner they put that behind them the sooner she felt they would be able to heal a little easier.

She'd been in Ann's room for only a few minutes when she'd opened the first of the dark woven totes and found it filled with letters postmarked all the way back to fifteen years ago. She picked up one after another after another. She opened the second and the third dark woven totes and found more of the same. There were different color inks and different sized envelopes but other than that they were all identical in that they were all addressed to Ann. And they all had a return address label from the same person. Maggie's mother.

CHAPTER SEVEN

What the hell is this? Maggie dropped the letters from her shaking hands and stared at the boxes. There had to be well over a hundred letters. To Ms. Ann Conners. From Ms. Sophia Kennedy. From Mrs. Thomas Kennedy. From Mr. & Mrs. Thomas Kennedy.

Maggie scooted back a few inches. If she reached out and picked up an envelope she would open it. If she opened an envelope she would read the letter. If she read one letter she would read them all.

How dare she do this to her! Her mother sealed their relationship the day D.J. was born when she cut off all ties to her. How dare she unseal the relationship through Ann all those years ago and all those years since and never, not even once, have the decency to include her!

Every one of those letters represented a slap in the face. Every time Sophia Kennedy sat down and wrote a letter to Ann Conners and not to Maggie she slapped her in the face. If she'd written them to her instead... but she didn't, she chose to write to Ann. All these letters, a hundred or more, a hundred or more slaps in the face all at once.

Maggie grabbed an envelope and held it by the top with both of her hands, her two pointer fingers and her two thumbs posed to rip it.

Why didn't Ann tell her? Why did she keep them? Did she intend to give them to her someday? Did she keep them because she thought Maggie should read them? Why hadn't she given them to her?

Maggie dropped the envelope back in the tote. What could her mother say that would make it okay to write to Ann but not to her own daughter? Did Ann write back or was this a one way correspondence?

Were all the answers to her mother's choice to shun her in these letters? Were all the answers to all the questions Maggie ever wondered about in front of her in these totes? Or did her mother just suck the information about them from Ann without reciprocating?

There was only one way to find out.

But she couldn't do it. Not yet anyway. Maggie put the lids on the totes and put the totes back on the top shelf of Ann's closet. Maybe opening and reading the letters would change everything or change nothing but either way Maggie couldn't bring herself to make that decision yet. The letters had sat on Ann's shelf for fourteen years, they could sit for a few more minutes.

Maggie closed the closet door and closed the bedroom door. She walked around the house trying to ignore the pull back to the bedroom. She stood at the sliding glass door and stared at the pool seeing nothing but the totes filled with letters. She walked to the front of the house and looked out the window and stared at the van seeing nothing but the totes filled with letters. She walked to the counter and grabbed her purse and went to the van. It didn't occur to her to lock the door, it didn't occur to her to check to make sure she had her cell phone or her keys or her wallet, she just got in the van and fished the keys from her purse and drove.

She knew how to get to three places. She had no desire to go to the boy's school or the strip with all the stores so she went to the beach. She parked the van and walked to the same spot she and Donnie sat and talked the day they decided to stay for five more weeks. What would have happened if they had not decided to stay? They would be home already. She wouldn't know about the letters. Would Don have found them and told her about them?

Maggie sat up straighter, did Don know about the letters? Of course he would know, how could they have come in the mail month after month for years and Don not know? She thought about the two of them sitting at the kitchen table reading the letters, maybe even discussing if they should share them with her and then she closed her eyes to that vision. No, she didn't think Don knew. She was pretty sure she would be able to keep something like that from Donnie and she was pretty sure Ann kept them from Don. Maybe in the real world husbands and wives shared secrets like this but in Maggie's world it was something women did. Which was why other than Jillian most of her friends had always been men, women had too many layers.

Jillian. Maggie opened her purse and looked for her cell phone. Full charge. Perfect. She pressed the text icon and opened the string with Jillian. She started typing.

Hey.

And then she hit delete.

If she told Jillian she would have to tell Donnie. No she wouldn't. But she would have to do something about the letters. Maggie sighed and threw her cell phone back in her purse and stretched her legs out, leaned back and supported herself with her arms.

The water was rough and the waves crashed against the shore matching her mood perfectly. She watched them angrily crashing in and submissively retreating back. Water *had* to be female. She almost laughed out loud. Here we go again, she thought, it doesn't matter where you are, Colton, Naples, anywhere in the world, you are still who you are and you will still wonder who that is.

Maggie looked around her at the sand and debated the consequences of lying in the sand without a towel or blanket and decided she didn't care. After a few attempts at molding the sand beneath her head she settled in and relaxed. The sky was brilliant blue and completely void of any clouds. An occasional bird flew overhead and Maggie made sure to keep her mouth closed until it passed but other than that her body remained as still as a statue.

But her mind was as stirred up as the sand in the water. Her mind traveled to the clear sky and zeroed in on Ann. She tried to imagine what she would have done if she were in Ann's place, would she have torn the letters as they came in the mailbox? Would she have refused to accept them and had them returned to sender? She thought she probably would have opened the first, curiosity, back when there was hope. Once the first was opened the decision was made, the rest would be opened as they came. She ultimately decided she probably would have done the same. She had to assume they were requests for updates on her and the boys, maybe even requests for pictures. She had to assume Ann honored those requests, probably sent pictures, probably toyed relentlessly with the decision whether or not to tell her about them.

Knowing Ann she probably felt it wasn't her place to interfere in the relationship of a mother and daughter however dysfunctional or defunct it was. And knowing Ann she probably sympathized with her mother's longing to know about her grandsons even if she didn't want to know them. Maybe if Ann were alive Maggie would feel different but she didn't think so, she couldn't be angry with Ann. Ann stood by her from the day they told her she was pregnant. She never asked Maggie to be anyone other than who she was and she always accepted her and the boys unconditionally. She could forgive Ann.

Her mother was a different story. A mother's love was supposed to be unconditional not based on popular opinion or egregious mistakes. She didn't forgive her when she disowned her the day D.J. was born. She didn't forgive her at any time over the years when she needed her and she wasn't there. She didn't forgive her, she forgot her. Sophia Rose Logan Kennedy did not exist.

Sophia Rose Logan Kennedy could not exist. Maggie would not be Maggie if her mother came back into her life even if only in the form of old correspondence. She knew what she had to do. Maggie sat up and shook the sand from her hair. She stood and brushed it from the back of her arms and legs. The rest of the sand on her clothes and in her hair came off in the van and in the house and what didn't she would shower off when she was done.

The first letter caught immediately and Maggie held it in her hand until she felt the heat of the flame on her fingers and then she dropped it in the sink. She watched it finish burning until there was nothing left but a piece of ash. She picked up another and lit it, held it, dropped it. Two pieces of ash. As each burning envelope turned to ash she wondered if she would ever regret what she was doing. She wondered if there were pictures inside any of the envelopes. If there were secrets she would now never know. If there were words of apology or explanation.

As the last of the envelopes burned Maggie packaged her thoughts and packed them away. It was done. She would clean the sink. She would clean the sand from the van and from the house. She would shower. And she would go back to this morning before she discovered the letters.

While she was vacuuming the van the mailman walked past the driveway and put a handful of mail in the box, Maggie caught a glimpse of him and looked up from the van and it hit her, she wasn't done. More letters would come. Don would check the mail someday and sort through the junk, the advertisements, the bills, and a hand written envelope would fall out addressed to Ann. He would look at the return label. He would wonder why Sophia was writing after all this time. He would open the envelope. He would learn of Sophia and Ann's secret.

She had to make sure that wouldn't happen. Maggie dropped the vacuum hose and hit the off switch and ran into the house. She searched through Don's desk and found a piece of paper, a pen, an envelope and a stamp. She quickly scrawled a letter:

Dear Sophia,

You don't know me but my name is Alice Bailey, I'm a friend of Ann Conners and I wanted to write you to let you know that Ann passed away recently. She shared the secret of your letters with me and I can assure you that she never shared the secret with anyone else nor have I. I thought you would want to know about Ann as well as to be sure not to mail any further letters due to her recent passing.

Alice Bailey

There. The words had come fast and natural, no qualms, no regrets. Maggie folded the letter and slid it in the envelope. She sealed the envelope and wrote her mother's name. She read the address enough times on the envelopes she'd found that it was engraved in her memory and she wrote it down, added the stamp and ran out of the house and in the direction she'd seen the mailman walking. She slowed at an intersection six houses down and spotted the mailman on the road to the right. She was completely out of breath when she reached him.

On her walk back to the house she didn't think about her mother or the letters or the sink or even vacuuming the van. She thought about how good it felt to have made a decision and to have acted on it. She thought about how liberating it felt to take control, whether it was the right decision or the wrong decision she'd made a decision, she'd taken action. No regrets.

"Mom? Mom?!" Todd skidded to a stop when Don's hand grabbed hold of the sleeve of his t-shirt.

"Didn't we have a talk about this?" Don spun Todd around and pointed at the other boys walking in the door single file. "Look at your brothers. See how they're not running in the house yelling like wild animals?"

"Oh yeah. Sorry Grandpa. But I have to tell Mom something it's very important."

Don let go of his sleeve. "Walk back to the door, walk in the house like you're supposed to, take care of your backpack and if what you have to tell your mother is of life or death importance than walk to her and tell her. If it's not of life or death importance than go to the kitchen and get your snack and sit at the table and we'll join you there and then you can tell her."

"Okay, it's important. Be right back." Todd walked back to the door, walked through the house to his bedroom doorway where Don, Maggie and Donnie watched him toss his backpack and then speed walk back to his mother. "Mom! Guess what! This is a-m-a-z-i-n-g. Guess what!!"

Maggie put her hands on his shoulders to stop him from bouncing. "I give up. What?"

"My friend Jim? You know my friend Jim? He's never seen snow!!"

Don shook his head and turned to follow the other boys in the kitchen but Maggie saw the beginning of a grin before he turned away.

"That is a-m-a-z-i-n-g!"

"I know!! I'm the coolest kid in my class cause I'm the only one that lives in snow!!" Todd bounced through Maggie's hold and ran in the kitchen.

Don's voice boomed from the kitchen. "Todd!"

He ran back to Maggie, turned around and walked to the kitchen under Don's watchful eye.

Maggie got off the couch and tiptoed into Ann's room to put the empty totes back in the closet. She had fallen asleep by the pool after she vacuumed the van and showered and the next thing she knew the men were home and before she had a chance to wipe the sleep from her eyes the boys were home.

She just put the last tote in and closed the closet door when Donnie walked in. "Dad needs you in the kitchen. Dylan has a question and Dad says he needs to ask the second in command, apparently I'm the third."

Maggie smiled. "What's Dylan want?"

"You'll see. You okay? You know, I mean with doing this?

Mom's stuff?"

"I really don't mind. This might sound strange to you but I'm getting to know your Mom even more by going through her things. It's weird I know, it's just, I think when you go through someone's personal things you, I don't know, connect with them more."

"Do you want me to help you?"

"Not unless you really want to. It's the last thing I can do for her you know? I kind of feel, I kind of like doing it."

"Okay, I'd rather not help to be honest but Maggie, it means a lot to me and Dad that you're willing to do it."

"That was a compliment. It's like an enchanted kingdom here!"

Donnie rolled his eyes and led her to the kitchen.

The boys were sitting at the table eating bowls of Lucky Charms. Don saw the look on Maggie's face and shrugged, "It's all we had left. How do they eat so much? We probably should go shopping soon."

"I'm on it. I'll go tomorrow morning. So what's up?"

Derek, Daniel and Todd ignored her, D.J. looked down and Dylan looked up. She zeroed in on Dylan and waited. And waited.

"Dylan?"

He put his spoon down. "Okay. So Grandpa has all these new rules which are good for the dorks but me and D.J. are older and we're already set in our ways." Maggie laughed before she realized Dylan was serious and almost choked trying to stop the laugh. Dylan gave her a dirty look and continued. "We think some of the rules should be different for us like we want to do our homework after dinner so we can…so we can go for a walk after we get home. Grandpa said to ask you."

Maggie glanced at Don who challenged her with raised eyebrows. Donnie stood against the counter with his hand over his mouth unsuccessfully hiding a smirk. Derek, Daniel and Todd shoveled Lucky Charms in their mouths like no one had just called them dorks. Something was up.

"What do you mean walk? Where do you want to walk?"

D.J. dropped his head even more, his chin couldn't have tucked into his neck any further without surgery. Dylan looked at D.J. out of the corner of his eye and then stood up. "Mom?! This isn't about where we want to walk it's about the right to have privileges appropriate to our age. It's not fair to treat us all the same we're…"

"D.J. has a girlfriend!!!" Todd jumped out of his chair and ran behind Maggie.

Derek and Daniel froze with spoonfuls of Lucky Charms halfway to their mouths. D.J.'s chin tucked further into his neck, without surgery. Dylan leaped back knocking his chair over and lunged behind Maggie's legs at Todd but Donnie acted a second quicker than Dylan and snatched Todd up and whisked him out of the room for his own safety. Dylan belly flopped on the floor.

Don and Maggie stood with their mouths dropped opened.

A sound drifted up from the floor, it sounded like "ow".

D.J. untucked his chin and the top half of his body slowly slid to the left until he was leaning half way out of his chair and able to see around Maggie. "Dylan?"

"I'm okay." Dylan's voice floated to everyone's ears but his body remained flattened on the floor.

D.J. stood up and hesitantly stepped to where Dylan lay. He poked the toe of his shoe into Dylan's side. "You sure you're okay?"

"I'm good." He rolled over to his back. D.J. offered his hand and pulled Dylan up.

Maggie was dumbfounded, D.J. and Dylan? Acting like buddies? She had no recollection of them ever acting like they so much as acknowledged the other's existence before they'd come to Florida. Now they were not only acknowledging the other but conniving for and caring about each other? If her heart swelled anymore… she softly breathed out the words, "In Naples they'd say, that Maggie's small heart grew three sizes that day."

"Mom??" D.J. eyed her skeptically. "Are *you* okay?"

"I'm okay,." she put her arm around D.J. "Come sit next to

the pool and talk with me." And then she added, "privately" when Dylan started to follow.

Maggie, Donnie and D.J. sat down poolside and discussed some ground rules for after school, walks, and girlfriends. D.J. wasn't willing to voluntarily give up any information other than to say that Ava lived in Palm Breezes, the subdivision of homes to the north of theirs, that she was fourteen and that she rode the same bus and that they were in all of the same classes. With a little prying she and Donnie were able to ascertain that no meet up was planned between the two of them but that there were more kids in Palm Breezes and they often got together after school to 'shoot hoops or whatever' and that Ava told him he 'should come over'.

"And Dylan?" Maggie asked.

D.J. shrugged. "He wants to show off his foul shot. Plus, he's been kinda nice to me and we've been talking a lot. I kinda wanted him to go with me."

"I'm kinda happy to hear that." Maggie looked to Donnie, "What do you think?"

Donnie pumped his fist in the air, "Go get her!"

"Donnie!!" Maggie turned back to D.J. "Be home by five." D.J. bee lined away from his parents as quickly as he could. "Donnie! Seriously? Go get her?"

"What? I'm proud of him, little D.J. has a chick in the coop!"

Maggie shook her head. "Just when I start thinking there's hope for you…"

"What? What? Where are you going?"

"Where are you going?"

Donnie was leaving for his first AA meeting. It had been three weeks since the day on the beach when they decided to stay and although they only had two weeks left they decided it would be good to have a couple meetings under his belt before returning to normal.

"I have a meeting." Donnie answered Dylan.

"What meeting? How long is it? Can you drop me off at Micah's house and pick me up after?"

"Wait for me! I'm going too, drop me off at Ava's though." D.J. sped from his room and skidded to a stop just before running into his father.

"Who are you?" Donnie teased. D.J. was wearing plaid shorts and a matching bright orange polo shirt and orange crocs.

He looked down at himself and blushed. "Ava picked it out."

"Boys," Maggie was sitting at the kitchen table working on a puzzle with Todd and Daniel. "Let Dad go, he can't be late. You'll have to walk and make sure you're home by nine."

They both groaned but they beat Donnie out the door.

Derek came in the door as Dylan and D.J. went out. "Where you going Dad? Hey, can you take me to…"

"Maggie? Why do we have so many kids? I have to go!"

"Why *do* you have so many kids?!" Don pulled out a chair and started fitting puzzle pieces together. "Boys, you think I could borrow your Mom a few minutes? Think you can handle this puzzle without her?"

"We got it." Daniel said. "But where are you taking her?"

"Just outside by the pool, you'll be able to see us through the door which, by the way, means we'll be able to see you too, just remember that Todd."

"Can we come? Can we swim?"

"Not this time, we need a little grown up time to talk about boring things."

Maggie watched Don get up and nod toward the back of the house. So that's where Donnie got it from. The longer they were there the more Maggie saw habits of Donnie's in Don which she thought was a little odd since they hadn't spent more than a few days together every year. She wondered what habits the boys had already picked up from them that would stay with them forever. She shuddered.

"What's up?" Maggie sat where she could keep an eye on the boys.

"I wanted to talk to you before I talked to Donnie. This is something I just felt that you should have the right to shoot down before I bring it up to him."

"Shoot down?"

"Yeah, I already expect you to so don't be afraid to, I've been thinking about something and it's kind of out in left field if you know what I'm talking about. It's way out in left field. Left field. Way out."

"I get that part. What's on your mind?"

Don fidgeted. "Well," he paused. "Alright. I'm just going to throw it out there."

"In left field?"

"Don't speak. Just listen. This house is too big for me now without Ann and truth be told I don't really want to stay here after you, Donnie and the boys leave. There's a house for sale across the pond," he pointed, "That one. It's a two bedroom one bath. No memories. Of course I don't want to forget Ann but I don't really want to live here alone, without her. I know it's only right there, I'll see this house every time I look out the back windows, but I can live with that. I just don't think I can live here. So, anyway, I put an offer on it and they accepted it."

"Wow! Don that's...that's great..."

"Wait, ssh, and I want you guys to stay here. In this house."

"What??!!"

"I mean I don't want you to, no I do want you to, I mean I want to offer it to you," he said. "Let me start over, Maggie, I'm moving across the pond and I'd like to know if you and Donnie and the boys would consider staying in Florida and living here?"

"Holy f'ing left field!!"

"Watch your language! But I know, its way out there. But what do you think?"

"Holy f'ing left field!!"

"I get that part," he smiled conspiratorially. "Listen, I know it's crazy but the boys love it here, they love it Maggie.

D.J.'s a totally different kid and you and Donnie keep saying how much you love it here. I would love to be a part of the boys' lives like we've been these last few weeks. And Donnie could get a job here, I even know some guys in the union, I'm betting if I talk to them I could get him in, and you could get a job here too if you wanted, the boys could just come to my house after school until you got home." He put his hand up, "I know I'm being pushy, I know it's not fair to spring this on you when you're just about ready to pack up and head back and I'm sorry but I would kick myself if I let you go home and didn't try. And there's one more thing, the house is yours either way, I already signed it over to you and Donnie, it's just a matter of a quick trip to the lawyer's office to finalize everything."

"Holy…"

"I know, f'ing left field." He stood up and leaned over and kissed the top of her head. "Just think about it okay, no hard feelings if you decide not to stay. You could always rent the house out for a little extra income, half of the houses in here are vacation rentals."

Jillian abort move to Colton. Move to Naples instead.

Maggie? What's going on and DO NOT tell me you're not coming home.

Don dropped a bombshell on us. He bought a smaller house across the pond, he's giving us this house! Whether we stay or not.

WHAT???

F'ing left field right??

Left field? Maggie?? You're not coming home?????

I don't know. We haven't decided yet, we're too shocked! It's tempting though. We do love it here and the boys do too. And no mortgage!

Maggie noooooooooo. Okay, that said, I understand. It would be awful tempting. Hey! Can we have your house if you stay??!!

Haha! Wait, really??

I don't know. I just thought it, maybe. We do need a place to live!

Wow. My head is spinning.
Now mine is too! Oh but Maggie, I would miss you sooooo much.
Missing me didn't stop you from moving to N.J.
Touché. You're right. We're grownups now, we make decisions based on things besides just us. Gawd I hate being a grownup.
Gawd? Ugg I hate N.J.
Lol. Maggie? I love you. Bff's no matter where we each end up.
Bff's.

Donnie paced the bedroom floor until Maggie thought he was going to put a hole in the carpet. She had to grab his hand and pull him to the living room and sit him down on the couch. "You're making me crazy. Plus that's our carpet you're wearing out."

"I can't believe it. It's been, what?" He looked at his watch, "six hours since you told me and I still can't wrap my head around it. What did Jillian say? Maybe an outside opinion would help."

That was exactly how Maggie felt too. It was three o'clock in the morning and she still hadn't processed it anymore than she had three minutes after Don told her. Everything she looked at she thought 'this is ours' but it still didn't register. "She said she didn't like it but she would understand, that it would be tempting."

"It is tempting. Crazy tempting. What are we going to do? How do we decide something like this?" Donnie stood back up and began pacing again.

"The smart thing to do would be to go to bed and talk about it tomorrow but I know I won't be able to sleep."

"Me either. I can't even sit down. Tell me what you're thinking."

Maggie fluffed a pillow and stretched out on the couch. What was she thinking? The first thing that filled her mind was an image of D.J. in his colorful shirts and plaid shorts. He had changed so much in the few weeks they'd been there. If they went back to New York would D.J. go back to his dark clothing and his dark attitude? She thought he might and that thought worried her. And then the image of D.J. was covered with an image of her kitchen at home and then she thought about her job and then Donnie's job and then the sand on the beach and then Jillian and then the Colton library and then Ava and then Ann and then...

"There are too many splintered thoughts, I can't even separate them all to think them through. I try to think about one thing and something else pushes it out before I have a chance to think about the first thing."

Donnie stopped pacing. "Come on, kitchen, I need a drink." When he saw the look on Maggie's face he amended his sentence. "An ice tea. I need an ice tea." They poured two glasses of ice tea and hopped up on bar stools. Donnie spun his around to face Maggie, "The splintered thought thing? I know, me too. One second I'm thinking that we should call a rental agent and the next I'm thinking that we should call and reserve a U-Haul. Wait," he hopped off the stool and started pacing again. "Dad said his new house is furnished, we don't need a U-Haul, we don't need our stuff. Wait, we need our clothes and stuff. Wait, how much do vacation homes even rent for?"

Maggie put her hands over her ears. "Think inside your head please."

Maggie watched him jump down from his bar stool and begin pacing again. She watched him pace while thoughts traveled in and out of her mind and she knew his was the same but when he came to an abrupt stop she saw the deer in the headlight look on his face and had no idea what he was thinking.

"What?!" She sat up.

"I just thought of something, the most important thing, are we good?"

Maggie tilted her head, they really should go to bed, neither one of them was making sense anymore. "What do you mean?"

"Are we…happy? Like…happily married again?"

Maggie got off the stool and went to the couch and fell into it. "Crap." With all the thoughts fighting to be heard in her mind how did that one get missed? They were in vacation mode and then grief mode, and then a mix of the two and they hadn't resolved any issues yet. Or had they?

Something had changed between them. It started the night Don called about Ann. The minute she'd walked into their living room and saw Donnie crying in the dark she felt something that she hadn't taken the time to decipher. Before she even knew what was wrong she hurt, because he hurt. Even before her mind alerted her to the possibility that something might be wrong with one of the boys it alerted her to the pain Donnie was feeling and it matched it. For him.

That was something. That wasn't ordinary compassion. It was the kind of shared pain that only occurs between two people that love each other, not like, not tolerate, love.

Okay, so she loved him. But love didn't sustain all things, obviously. But, that night she also wanted to, no, needed to be with him. She didn't think twice about staying up all night and talking to him, she didn't even think once about it, she needed to be with him through his worries and fears and sadness because there was nowhere else. Her own feelings slid away, temporarily for sure, but they slid away to make room for his. She didn't plan that. She didn't make it happen, it just did. She didn't have to pull the kids out of school, she didn't have to go with him to Florida, she wanted to because there was nowhere else. If Donnie needed her there was nowhere else she wanted to be.

"Maggie? Does crap mean no?"

"Hmm? Oh, no, I'm thinking."

"About if we're happily married?"

"Have we ever been happily married? No, I'm thinking about if I love you. I think I do. Okay, I do. Now I'm going to think about if you love me. Go away."

"You're going to think about if I love you? Why don't you just ask me. Or better yet I'll just tell you, Maggie, I love you."

"Shh."

"Alright whatever, just tell me if I love you and if we're happily married."

"Will do."

Did he love her? How could he not right? She rolled to her side and wondered briefly if they would get the couch too or if Don would take it to his new house. She had to stop, she had to focus, she had to either give it serious thought or get some sleep and try again tomorrow. Did Donnie love her? How was she supposed to know? Men were a mysterious species. They didn't think so they didn't think to do things to show their love and words are useless without actions. So how was she supposed to know if he really loved her or not?

When he drank he treated her horribly, well, that wasn't quite accurate, he didn't treat her horribly as much as not treating her at all. Indifference. Indifference was worse than hate, at least hate was an emotion. Indifference was no emotion. Uh oh. But when he wasn't drinking he wasn't indifferent, he was… sweet, he was, oh forget it. She stood up and went to the bedroom, leaned against the door jam. Donnie was stretched out on top of the bed still dressed except for his shoes.

"Donnie do you love me?"

"Yes."

"Okay, done. The love part is good. I'll think about the happily married part tomorrow," she stepped to the bed and laid down next to him. "We should get under the covers and try to get some sleep."

"No point. I'm not going to be able to sleep."

"I know. Me either." But she closed her eyes anyway.

Maggie rolled to her side, opened her eyes and glanced at the clock. Nine twenty two a.m. they must have dozed off! Nine twenty two? "Donnie!! Get up! We slept! The boys! School!"

She leapt off the bed and ran toward the boys rooms. D.J. and Dylan's room was empty. The beds were made. She darted from their room to the room Derek, Daniel and Todd shared, empty, beds made. She spun around to search the house and caught a glimpse of movement on the patio behind the sliding glass door. She skidded to a stop. Don and the boys were in the pool.

"Maggie?" Donnie emerged from their bedroom rubbing the sleep from his eyes. "It's Saturday."

It took a second for that fact to register and another second for the panic bubble to pop and a third second for yesterday's revelations to re-emerge. She turned back around toward the patio. Don was standing in the center of the pool holding Todd who was lying horizontally on his stomach across the surface of the water kicking his legs and alternately slicing the surface with one hand and then the other. Don let go and Todd moved about a foot and a half before beginning to sink. Don reached out and supported him and Todd began moving again this time with Don's arms guiding him.

Daniel and Derek were swimming back and forth across the short end and Dylan and D.J. were sitting on the edge furthest from the others with their feet dangling in the water, talking.

"Maggie? What do you think they would be doing right now if we were home?"

Maggie didn't think she'd been standing there long but she must have been because Donnie came up next to her with two cups of coffee and handed her one. She gratefully took a cup and held it as she thought about his question.

"D.J. would be in his room. Dylan would be in the basement working out or still in bed sleeping maybe. The other boys would be zoned out watching cartoons. Or they would all be fighting, somewhere, about something."

Donnie smiled. "Do you think this could last? If we stayed here?"

Maggie took a sip of her coffee. "Or is it a vacation phenomenon? Would they fall back into themselves eventually? Would we? I bet we've talked more in the last four weeks than we have in the last four years."

"We all needed a shake up. I think I know what would have happened if we never came but I don't know what will happen if we go back now."

"Or if we stay."

"Right, or if we stay. If you think about though, what have we got to lose? What's holding us back from trying for a new life here?"

"Is that what you want to do then Donnie? You want to stay?"

"It's intriguing for sure. Tempting as Jillian said. But I don't know. How do we make a decision this big Maggie?"

"I almost wish someone would just tell us what we have to do, take the choice out of our hands. The only thing I know for sure right now is that I'm not going to be able to think about anything else."

"I think you and I need more time to talk, alone. How about if I ask Dad to keep the kids for the day, we can go somewhere, talk, think, maybe try to make some sense of our thoughts and see if we can get things to lean one way or the other. What do you think?"

She turned and gave him a shove. "Go, ask. What are you waiting for?!"

"Donnie if you don't turn soon I swear I will call 911. I can see the signs you idiot. Everglades. Everglades. Everglades. Turn this van around!"

"Will you stop? I told you I'm not taking you to the Everglades. Exactly. Trust me, please?"

"No! I don't trust you. If this is a test we failed. You said we were going to go somewhere and talk! Turn around! I can hear the alligators snapping! I'm not kidding Donnie I want to go back!"

"What is wrong with you? There's a place Dad was telling me about down here that I want to take you to, it's the oldest standing trading store or something like that, Indians used to bring their stuff there by canoe. He said there's even an original handmade canoe or kayak or something like that there, it's like a little museum now. It's up on stilts right on the edge of the water. I thought you would like to see it."

"Oh my God! Donnie! Stop! Now!"

He glanced at Maggie and saw she was visibly shaking and about to burst into tears. He pulled to the side of the road, "What?!"

"That truck! Donnie please, I'm begging you, please turn around and get me back to civilization."

Just up ahead the swamp widened to the side of the road and there was an SUV stopped and parked. The top three quarters of the SUV was visible, the rest was hidden in the tall swampy grass. The SUV was green, or black, or brown. It was impossible to tell because of all the graphics of snakes and alligators and crocodiles.

Donnie read the banner on the side. "Alligator sightings guaranteed. Fifteen dollars per person."

"Turn around NOW!"

He turned around. "I wasn't taking you to the Everglades. I was taking you to a museum."

"That was the Everglades!"

"No it wasn't, it was the edge of the Everglades, like the Everglade suburbs."

She gave him a look that kept him quiet for the next thirty five minutes as they backtracked the way they'd come. The silence remained another thirty five minutes as he drove further north and back through Naples. When he pulled into a shopping plaza and parked the van and told her to 'wait here' she still refused to talk to him.

While she waited she replayed her reaction to the Everglades and toyed with the idea that she may have overreacted. She had a tendency to do that. But when she saw the side of the SUV in her mind again she decided it didn't matter if she overreacted or not. She was just glad she was back in the civilized world. When Donnie returned almost fifteen minutes later with a beach blanket, a cooler, drinks, food and two fold up chairs and said, "The beach?" she thought about saying she was sorry but she wasn't, really.

He drove to the beach. They walked to the same place where they sat and talked the day of the memorial and where

Maggie sat and thought when she went alone. She mused that they already had a beach habit but didn't share the thought. Donnie laid the blanket out and then reached into the bag and pulled out a notebook and a pen. "We'll make a list? Write down our pros and cons? Things to do, either way?"

She nodded.

He reached further into the bag and pulled out a box of Godiva chocolates and held them out to her.

"Fine. You're forgiven." She took the chocolates and opened them and didn't offer him any.

The beach was barely inhabited, a few fisherman fished from the pier and a few sets of couples and groups of families were scattered along the beach on blankets but for the most part it was very quiet. They each grabbed a bottle of water from the cooler and Donnie handed her the notebook and pen. They watched the waves for a while.

"Look!" Donnie pointed out toward the pier. "Halfway out, can you see it?"

"What?"

"Dolphins. They're jumping next to the pier, see them?"

"That? That little splash?"

"Yeah, that's a dolphin jumping. Come on!" He grabbed her hand and pulled her up. They walked out onto the pier and stopped about halfway out and leaned over the edge of the railing. "Just wait."

A minute later a dolphin jumped about twenty feet out and swam back toward the pier right in front of them.

"That's awesome!" Maggie took out her cell phone and tried getting a picture but the dolphin swam under the pier. She hurried to the other side but ended up with a dozen pictures of water. She put the phone away and a dolphin swam right in front of her, jumped and disappeared. She laughed. "They're beautiful! I can't believe I'm seeing dolphins right here! How far are we from home?"

"Ten minutes."

"Seriously?"

"Seriously. Come on, let's go start our list. Start with

Florida pro...dolphins ten minutes from home."

Maggie held the notebook in her lap and the pen in her hand. The sun was warm and with so little sleep last night it would have been so easy to lie down and nap. But her mind wouldn't allow it. They left the house almost three hours ago and none of the thoughts that rattled in her head were any closer to sorting themselves out.

"How do we start?" She asked Donnie.

"Maybe we need a list for that."

She expected Donnie to laugh at her but he said, "Start a list. House. Boys. School. Jobs."

"Us." She said as she added it to the list.

"Or we could just decide. Maybe we're making this too hard. Maggie do you want to live in Florida in a house that's paid off and mortgage free where it's warm all year and the boys are happy. Or. Do you want to live in New York in the little house we bought when we thought we were only having two kids and where we have to shovel snow and the boys are miserable and most of our friends and family have already moved away?"

"When you put it like that it's a no brainer."

"Maybe it is a no brainer."

Maggie put the notebook and pen aside. She stretched out on the blanket and closed her eyes. "It probably is a no brainer, really. But every time I think about actually moving down here, permanently moving here, I get, I don't know, sad. That's not right, I don't know how to explain it Donnie. I think I actually want to and it's exciting to think about it but I feel...tied."

"To Colton?"

"I guess. Maybe not Colton itself, well, yeah I guess Colton. It's the only place we know. It's home. If we leave Colton we will have left, us. That's who we are right? Augh, I can't explain it. I like the Florida us better but I don't know if it's real. I feel like if we leave Colton we will be amputating something. Donnie, we grew up there, we had our kids there, our house, all of our memories have a Colton backdrop, our entire lives have a Colton backdrop. If we leave we'll be severing something, I don't even know what but it scares me."

"Roots."

"Huh?

"We'll be severing our roots. Roots are what give you that security that no matter how bad or how good things are you always feel secure. Or comfortable. They're like the old shoe that you never ever want to get rid of because it's so comfortable, you can't even wear it anymore but you won't get rid of it. That. Roots."

Maggie sighed. "The old lady had it all figured out didn't she? Here everyone thought she was crazy but she wasn't', she just put the two together."

"What old lady?"

"The one that lived in the shoe."

Donnie lifted his bottle of water and held it over Maggie and poured. Her eyes popped open, she jumped up and off the blanket and screamed all at the same time. She stood dumbfounded, water dripping down her face, staring at Donnie.

"Maggie. Let's stay here."

"I'm scared."

"And wet." Donnie smiled. "So what if you're scared? Take the chance. If it doesn't work out we'll go home. We can you know Maggie. We can keep the house and we can go back home anytime we want."

Maggie wiped her face off on her sleeve and sat back down on the blanket.

"What if we make a deal? How about if we say we'll stay the rest of the school year and then we'll still have the whole summer. If things don't work out we'll move back home before the boys next school year. If things do work out we can talk about selling the house in the summer."

Maggie thought about it. It made sense. It wouldn't feel quite so…severed. "If we went back in the summer that's a lot of job quitting and getting."

"People do it all the time. Come on Maggie, let's give it a

chance, let's give the boys a chance here, let's take this chance at a new life for us, all of us."

Maggie leaned back and looked out at the water. "Okay. Let's do it."

CHAPTER EIGHT

Don and the boys were outside weeding flower beds when they arrived back home tanned, excited, and with a van full of groceries. Donnie, Dylan and Derek carried the groceries in while Don and the younger two finished weeding.

"Where's D.J.?" Maggie asked Don when she finished putting the groceries away and went outside to look at the weeding progress.

"Ava's," he said. "Ava called, D.J. had those puppy eyes, I'm a softie what can I say? He should be back soon."

"I thought you had a landscape company that mows and does all this stuff?" Donnie had put on a pair of gloves and was filling a bag with the pile of discarded weeds and browned palm fronds.

"I do. It's good for the boys to do a little manual labor though. Maybe learning something they might need to know in the future?" Don raised his eyebrows.

"Boys? Finish up here and then take your showers and get cleaned up for dinner. We need to talk to Grandpa a minute."

Don, Donnie and Maggie poured glasses of ice tea and took them to the table by the pool. Maggie still couldn't believe that either way, live here till summer or live here forever, either way this house was theirs. This kind of fortune happened to other people, not to people like her and Donnie, people who thought they would spend their entire lives making the bills with just enough left over to afford the small extras that made life comfortable. She never imagined luxury. And that's what this house represented. It might be considered on the low end of average to Floridians but it was on the high end of luxury to them.

"Well? Did you get any closer to a decision?" Don leaned back and put his hands behind his head trying desperately to look nonchalant. He was failing terribly.

Donnie told him their plan and Don leaned forward and slapped him on the back. "Welcome to the neighborhood!" He leaned toward Maggie and kissed her on the cheek. "You don't know how happy this makes me, Ann would approve too I know she would."

Maggie opened her mouth to speak but Don held his hand up. "I get it. It's just for now. Future decisions will be made in the future. Isn't that the best way to live anyway? A little bit at a time?" He held his ice tea glass up and Donnie and Maggie followed suit and they toasted to 'a little bit at a time'.

"What's going on?" D.J., clad in plaid shorts, a matching polo shirt, matching crocs and a never ending grin opened the gate and joined them at the table. "Why does everyone look like the cat that ate the canary?"

Maggie nearly spit her ice tea out. "The cat that ate the canary?!"

"Ava's Grandma says that a lot. It's kind of stupid isn't it? Hey, since you're all here there's something I want to talk about."

D.J. Wants to talk. There it was again, her heart swelled. She studied D.J.'s face, whatever it was he wanted to talk about took the grin away but she could still see the joy in his eyes, the happiness that couldn't leave. She was happy for him, not because of Ava or his new friends or his healthier self-esteem but because of his peace of mind in who he was. Whether he knew it or not D.J. had discovered D.J.

D.J. realized they were all waiting for him to begin. "Uh,

please don't jump all over me when I say this. Just hear me out okay? We're supposed to go home in thirteen days. Don't just say no okay? Here's the thing, I wish we could stay here. I was thinking maybe I can. Maybe I can stay here and live with Grandpa."

Maggie felt a kick under the table, she glanced at Donnie and then Don to see who kicked her but neither of them acknowledged her.

"Okay," Donnie shrugged. "If that's what you want."

D.J.'s head snapped up and his eyes grew twice as big. He stared at Donnie and then snapped his head to Maggie and then Don.

"Well, not you living with Grandpa but I guess we could all live here." Maggie shrugged at Don "What do you think?"

"Oh, I don't know. Yeah I suppose. You know, I just had this idea, why don't you live here? Literally I mean, just take the house, half the houses in this complex are for sale I'll just buy another one."

D.J.'s eyes narrowed and he sank into his chair. "Come on. I'm serious. I don't want to go home."

He looked so close to tears that Maggie couldn't continue. "D.J.?" She got out of her chair and stood behind him. She leaned down and put her arms around his shoulders and then kissed the top of his neatly trimmed hair. "We were waiting for you to come home and for the other boys to come outside to tell you. You and Grandpa seem to be of the same mind. Grandpa bought a house across the pond, he's asked us to stay and live here, in this house."

D.J. jumped out of Maggie's arms and out of the chair, "What?! Seriously?! We're staying here?! For real? Is this for real?!"

"We're going to stay until the end of the school year and then we'll decide but D.J. calm down a minute and sit down." Donnie waited for him to sit. "We are staying until the end of the school year but after that it's your mothers and my decision. If we decide to move back to New York you go with us, got it? There will be no staying and living with Grandpa, either we all stay or we all go."

D.J. nodded. "But we're staying for now, definitely right? And we might stay forever? Might?"

"Might."

D.J. pumped his fist in the air. "Yes! I'll take it. Can I please go call Ava?"

The other boys wandered out one by one and when they were all around the table they told them the news too. In hindsight Maggie thought she and Donnie should have talked to the boys first and saved themselves the trouble of making the decision. It was the most excited she'd ever seen the boys. No one wanted to go back to New York.

"Maggie?" Donnie slammed the front door behind him. "Maggie?!"

Maggie came out of the bedroom carrying the last of the boxes of Ann's things. "What are you doing home so soon? I thought you were going job hunting?"

Donnie took the box from her and placed it at the floor. "You are looking at the newest employee of Williamson Construction! I got a job! I don't know why everyone's crying that there's no jobs out there, I filled out an application and talked to the owner and he hired me right then and there! I start on Monday, a week from today! He wanted me to start tomorrow, can you believe it? But I told him we had a lot of transition things to take care of still, he was okay with it." Donnie grabbed Maggie's hands, "Maggie! I got a job!"

Maggie bounced up and down with him. "Yay!" She laughed but even she heard the forced effort in her voice.

"What's wrong?"

"Nothing's wrong. I'm happy, really, and I'm proud of you Donnie. It's just, it's real. We're really staying."

"Are you having second thoughts?"

"Not second thoughts, I don't know what I'm feeling, I'm excited and I really do want to stay I just feel, umm, misplaced. It's the transition from temporary to permanent. I just need time to adjust and I will. Donnie I'm really happy and I will adjust I promise." She let go of his hands and stepped in to hug him, she felt the tears beginning to form and she couldn't even decide herself if they were tears of joy or sorrow, "It's not that I miss home but we just left in such a hurry and everything happened so fast, I didn't even water the plants before we left, I didn't say goodbye and they're probably dead now."

Donnie laughed. "Maggie? Do you need to go back home before you can settle in here? If you do its okay, I understand. We can use the vacation buy out money and you can fly home to water the plants."

Maggie stepped back from Donnie and took his hand again and walked him to the couch. "I always thought it was cool how people just stepped out of their lives in movies. When we were fighting or the boys had me at my wits end I'd secretly fantasize about it. But it was just a fantasy, not even one I deep down really wanted. It was just a mental escape. But we did it. We walked out of our lives. I really don't have second thoughts about it Donnie I swear and I really am excited. I want to be here. I'm just, adjusting. But yeah, I might need to say goodbye to the plants. And Colton."

"I could go with you if you want. Maybe we could fly home tomorrow and have a moving company come later in the week? Fly back by the weekend? I'm sure Dad would be okay with the boys for a few days."

She'd never flown before. She and Donnie had never been anywhere without the boys for more than a day. Maggie let her mind wrap itself around the possibilities. As much as she wanted to be independent she liked the idea of them going together rather than her by herself. She didn't like the idea of walking around home and deciding what to bring and what to leave behind. She didn't like the idea of packing up a home she might have to unpack in a few months. She didn't like the idea of saying goodbye and not knowing if it really was goodbye or not.

"Is there anything we have to go home for?" she asked. "Besides closure?"

Donnie thought about it a minute. "Did you clean out the fridge before we left?"

"Yes, idiot."

"Then probably not. I'm paying the bills online and the mail is already being forwarded here. We have clothes, furniture, everything we need is already here. We'd have to go home sometime if we decide to stay here but I don't think there's anything we need right now. Have the boys asked for anything?"

"Surprisingly no. I'm sure they'd like their bikes and toys and Dylan's chomping at the bit for some weights but they haven't asked for any of it yet. We could definitely pack a moving truck if we went home but honestly Donnie I don't think there's anything we *need*. That's weird. And scary. We've accumulated fifteen years worth of stuff and we don't need any of it? Is that possible?"

They both sat on the couch mentally walking through their rooms, opening drawers, looking at everything they own. The furniture could stay, the dishes could stay, the towels and linens, the shovels and tools, the shoes and clothes, the wall hangings and knick knacks, the pillows, the books, the nail polish and jewelry and laundry baskets and throw rugs. They didn't *need* anything.

"I can't think of a thing we need. It would be different if we had to get everything out of the house, I wouldn't want to get rid of any of it but since it can all stay right where it is… Donnie? Do you realize what this means? We have a house full of stuff we don't need! That can't be possible, do you have any idea how much time I've spent standing in stores debating over a certain towel or wall art or candle or, or everything! There must be something we can't live without!"

"Pictures. And important papers. When you had the McKenna's overnight the birth certificates to get the boys enrolled in school did they send everything from the lockbox? We need that stuff."

"Pictures. Right. We don't want to get rid of them for sure but we don't *need* them. And yes, they sent everything that was in the lockbox."

"Then Maggie, I think we have an entire house full of stuff we don't want to get rid of but we don't need. It's kind of cleansing if you think about it. But if you need to go home to feel better about being here we can. We can still get the stuff we want even if we don't need it. Or if you want me to put the vacation buy out money aside and hold it in case you ever decide you need to go home I will. I'll do whatever you want."

She didn't know what she wanted but she thought that was actually a pretty good idea. The idea of an envelope of money earmarked for a trip home at any time was comforting. Knowing she could go home was needed more than going home.

They had some lunch and moved on to the process of setting up another life of things they didn't need. They went to the bank and opened an account and transferred half of their savings into their new account. They took out enough cash for the trip home envelope and a shopping spree to get the boys some new bikes and toys and weights and to pick up some things for the house. Donnie bought clothes for work and Maggie picked out some new clothes for the boys and herself. By the time they unpacked the van and took care of all the things they'd bought Don's house already was beginning to feel like their house.

Jillian? Are you speaking to me yet?

No. I'm still mad at you. Traitor. I can't believe you actually decided to stay.

What happened to bff's forever?

I lied.

You'll forgive me once you see this place!

I won't forgive you. But I'm happy for you.

I can live with that. At least you'll have a place to stay when you move back. Can you throw away my dead plants?

Have you thought about how weird this is? We're storing our stuff so we can live in your house so you can live in Don's house. That's weird.

It's just till you get a house of your own. Or the end of May if we don't stay, then you're out on the street.

George can start working from home in a few weeks, that means we might move back sooner. I'm thinking of heading up next week to start getting the house ready, you okay with that?

Sure, the McKenna's have the key just get it from them whenever you want, you remember them right? They live in the green house past the big oak tree. Do whatever you need to do with our stuff, use whatever you want, there might still be some milk in the fridge, help yourself.

That's disgusting. You sure you don't mind if I pack up all your stuff and store it?

Not at all, saves me the trouble if we decide to stay here.

Geez Maggie, glad to be able to help. Anything else I can do for you?

Yeah, why don't you rent a U-Haul and bring me the stuff, that way you can see the house? And throw away the dead plants, they're probably crawling with bugs by now.

Speaking of bugs, how are things with you and Donnie?

Missed the correlation, what's that got to do with bugs?

I don't know, seemed like a good segue.

You're weird. Actually things are good. I think I like him again.

Nice! I told you! I knew you still loved him you just needed a fresh start.

I said I liked him I didn't say I loved him.

But you do. And the boys?

Great. D.J. has a girlfriend! And short hair! And colorful clothes! They've all made new friends and act like they've lived here forever.

And they lived happily ever after?

And they lived happily for now. Good enough. Don says to live life a little bit at a time.

Good advice. You going to get a job down there?

Thinking about it. Haven't talked to Donnie about it yet, not sure I want to start that all over again. Plus there's a pool here and a hot tub, I'm kinda busy.

Living the life! Good for you! I miss you Maggie.

I miss you too Jillian.

Don signed the papers on the house across the pond the same day Donnie started his new job. Maggie couldn't help but to wonder if he was moving too fast and too soon after Ann's death but he was determined to get on with life on his own, without the constant memories surrounding him.

He encouraged them to make changes to the house and was thrilled when they changed a wall print or a bedspread or a set of curtains. He said the more changes they made the more comfortable he was there. They decided that when Don moved into his new house they would move back into the bedroom at the south side of the house, away from the other bedrooms. They planned to give D.J. Don and Ann's room and have Dylan and Derek bunk together. But D.J. surprised them by deciding to stay with Dylan. The boys were all happy as things were, for now, so Maggie decided to make Don and Ann's room into a guest room.

She had no idea if she would ever have any guests but it was fun to decorate it with guests in mind. She chose the linens and knick knacks thinking of Jillian and George and the kids.

There wasn't anything else they wanted to change, they loved the house just as it was, and apparently so did the boys. D.J. and Dylan didn't want to change a thing in their room. Derek, Daniel and Todd added some posters and a set of shelves to hold their things but they were happy with everything else just as it was.

When Don returned home from the attorney's office he insisted on packing his things and moving into his new house but Maggie insisted he let them help him move in the evenings and wait until the weekend to move. She won.

Every evening during dinner Don and Maggie would begin discussing what to bring to the new house that evening and they would inevitably end up in an argument. He insisted he buy new pots and pans for his new house and Maggie insisted he take his with him and they would buy their own. He won. She insisted he take enough linens and comforters and pillows for the two bedrooms and he insisted he buy his own. She won. They went back and forth each evening until dinner was done and someone had won and then they all helped pack some things in the van and took them to his new house across the pond.

On Saturday morning Donnie slept in and Maggie tip toed out of the bedroom to grab a cup of coffee and a few quiet minutes by the pool. She slowly pushed the sliding glass door opened and covertly stepped out onto the patio. She sipped from her mug while her eyes scanned the pool and the landscaped backdrop and palm trees behind the screen. She didn't think she'd ever take this for granted. It was beautiful, peaceful, tropical.

She glanced across the pond at the back side of Don's new house, a smaller but nearly identical house. She wondered how he felt, how he really felt. Would he be lonely there? Wouldn't it be difficult looking across the pond and seeing the home he and Ann lived in? The home where they had once planned to live out the remainder of their retirement years? Surely they thought they'd be there another ten or even twenty years.

A movement in the corner of Maggie's eye caught her attention and her eyes swept back to her own poolside area. Before her mind registered what it was seeing the foot at the edge of a lounge chair twitched and Maggie jumped and dropped her coffee mug. The sound of the shattering mug woke the body attached to the foot and D.J. sprang up in the lounge chair.

Maggie's hand flew to her heart at the same time as D.J's flew to his heart.

"Geez Ma! Crap! You scared me!"

Maggie opened her mouth to respond but she could only suck in air. She closed her eyes and waited for her lungs to process the air and her breathing to resume. She opened her eyes and took a deep breath and let it out.

"D.J.!"

The sliding glass door flew opened and Don stepped out onto the patio and stopped short when he saw Maggie standing over the shattered coffee mug, her hand still over her chest.

"Maggie?"

His eyes scanned the area and stopped when he saw D.J. sitting in the lounge chair with his hand over his chest.

"What the hell? What happened? What's going on?"

Maggie dropped her hand and slid into a chair. "Nothing. It's okay. D.J. just scared me to death, that's all, we're okay."

D.J. dropped his hand from his chest. "*She* scared *me* to death!"

Don's eyes traveled from Maggie to the shattered mug to D.J. and back to Maggie. He turned and went in the house and returned a second later with a roll of paper towels and a bag and began picking up the shattered pieces of the mug.

"Sorry Don," Maggie got out of the chair and began helping him pick up the pieces of the mug. "I didn't know D.J. was out here. He moved and I just…"

"It's just a mug Maggie, don't worry about it."

When they cleaned it up Don went back in the house and returned a minute later with two new mugs of coffee and sat at the table with Maggie. D.J. joined them.

"Sorry Ma."

"Don't be sorry it's not your fault. What were you doing out here anyway?"

D.J. looked at Don and then at the ground. "I couldn't sleep so I came out here, I guess I fell asleep."

Don stretched and leaned back, folded his hands behind his head. "It's been a long time, refresh my memory D.J., what kind of stuff keeps a kid your age awake at night?"

D.J. leaned back and folded his hands behind his head. Maggie wondered if he did it on purpose or if it was a coincidence but either way she couldn't help but notice how much they had in common. Granted, Don was much older and although he wore his age well he still had the weathered look of someone that worked his way to who he was now. D.J. still wore the taunt skin of a young boy with all that work ahead of him but in their eyes, their expressions, their gestures, Don and D.J. shared a lot of the same characteristics.

"It's stupid." D.J. unfolded his hands and laid them in his lap and then on the table.

Don did the same and Maggie had the feeling she was watching a carefully choreographed scene unfold in front of her. She sat back and watched.

"If you feel it's not stupid D.J. What's on your mind?"

D.J. stared at the ground. "What if I get it wrong?"

Maggie felt the urge to sit up and put her hand on D.J.'s shoulder or to jump in and tell him he wouldn't, whatever it was, but something kept her from acting. Something told her this was a conversation between D.J. and Don. She breathed in and out waiting for what seemed like forever before he spoke again.

"What if I get it wrong like they did?" D.J. kept his eyes on the ground but jerked his head in Maggie's direction. "They've been fighting for as long as I can remember and Dad was drinking and Mom was unhappy, and, and I was a jerk. Then we came here and everything got better. What if I pick the wrong place? What if Grandma didn't get sick and we never came here? We would have been in the wrong place forever. What if I pick the wrong place and nothing ever happens to get me in the right place?"

Maggie felt her heart lurch and tears form in her eyes.

"D.J.? Listen to me pal," Don said. " I understand why you think it's a matter of place. I do. It seems obvious but it's not. It's not a matter of place it's a matter of time."

D.J. lifted his head just long enough to steal a quick questioning glance at Don and then looked back at the ground.

"It's easier to see when you look back at it from my age so you're going to have to trust me a little bit here. It's not about New York or Florida or Timbuktu. It's not about a place on the map it's about a place in time."

D.J. was quiet for a minute and then began shaking his head. "I don't think so. I think you're wrong Grandpa. I think if we stayed in New York we would all be the same. I don't think anything would change. And if we go back will everything go back the way it was?"

"Well, I've been wrong before. But I do know this, you could have chosen to wear your dark clothes and be a jerk here too, there's no law against dark clothes or jerks in Florida. And guess what D.J.? They sell beer here. I don't think it's about where you are, I think it's about being the time to change and you and your Dad were smart enough to recognize it…and you changed."

They remained in their own minds thinking about that for a while. Maggie could see both sides, she had to agree with Don that the changes were choices and it didn't really matter where you were but she had to agree with D.J. that nothing would have changed if they hadn't come to Florida. But they were both wrong. There wasn't a right or a wrong place. It wasn't a matter of time. It was getting out of normal.

"One more thing D.J., who we were is connected to who we'll be. Don't waste too much time thinking about what's behind you and don't waste too much time worrying about what's in front of you, if you just get today right it all connects the way it's supposed to."

"Good advice Don, live life a little bit at a time, right?"

"Right." Don reached across the table and patted D.J.'s shoulder. "So did we help or make it worse?"

D.J. yawned. "I don't know. But if I have trouble falling asleep again tonight I think I'll have you two carry on a conversation, I'm suddenly exhausted."

Don's pat on the shoulder turned into a slap on the back of the head.

Don was completely settled in his new house by mid afternoon. He insisted on leaving behind everything he didn't need. Maggie and Donnie offered to move pictures and knick knacks and all the things he and Ann had accumulated over the years but he wouldn't hear of it. He wanted the new house to be free of constant memories that would make him live in the past. When he added that life had tossed him a lemon and he wanted to make lemonade everyone groaned except Todd who fell on the floor laughing.

"What now?" Derek asked when the last box was emptied and Don's things were all put away.

"Now we go home and let Grandpa begin to enjoy some

peace and quiet in his new house," Donnie answered.

"Actually I'm thinking about testing out my new pool." Don walked through the patio door and onto the patio outside, everyone followed. "Anyone interested in swimming with me?"

Five shirts and nine shoes flew through the air. The tenth shoe was still on Todd's foot when Derek flew past Dylan who bumped into Todd who lost his balance and fell into the pool with one navy blue croc still attached.

Maggie screamed at Donnie to check Todd who popped out of the water laughing while she flew after Derek. She grabbed him by the ear and sat him in a chair. Her hands flew to her hips. She waited for her brain to produce the words that she needed but instead it told her she was tired and overreacting. The best she could come up with was, "Stop! Running!"

As soon as she furloughed Derek from the chair and the boys were all in the pool Don suggested to Maggie that she and Donnie head home and rest a bit and offered to walk the boys over before dinner. She didn't hesitate. She grabbed Donnie's hand and dragged him away from the pool chaos. She was all for relaxing, she was exhausted, but she also needed to talk to Donnie. She hadn't had a chance to tell him about the early morning discussion and D.J.'s fears of living in the wrong place. D.J. seemed to have all but forgotten about it but it pecked at her mind all day. If they go back would everything go back the way it was? It was a question D.J. had asked and it was an answer Maggie didn't know. Would it?

"Maggie I don't think there are any guarantees here or there," Donnie stretched out on his side of the bed. "I thought we came home to rest not to talk. Why aren't you lying down?"

She stood at the window looking out at the palm trees in the front yard and in the yard across the street. "I'm so tired. I think the last few weeks just caught up with me today. I feel like I've been run over."

Donnie patted the bed. "Then come lie down. How often

do you get a chance to take a mid afternoon nap? We'll talk when we wake up. I promise."

When Maggie woke up she stretched and rolled over to glance at the clock. It was eight eighteen. She jumped up and saw that Donnie's side of the bed was empty. She jumped out of bed and went to the kitchen and then the living room and found Donnie sitting on the couch watching television. Alone.

"The boys?"

"Dad called. They're having their first sleep over."

"All of them? Tonight? His first night there?"

"Yeah. They ordered pizza. He said they were watching movies and have bets on who can stay awake the latest."

Maggie squinted her eyes, opened them, squinted them again.

"What are you doing?"

"Waking up. Deciding."

"Deciding what?"

"Deciding whether I should be thrilled or furious. He's going to send them back in the morning you know. They'll be tired and miserable."

"Speaking of tired and miserable..."

Maggie waved at him, one fingered. "If you order a pizza for us I'll forgive you for saying that."

Donnie got off the couch and went to the kitchen. Maggie followed him then stopped and watched as he opened the fridge and brought out two plates.

"What's that?"

"I cooked."

He unwrapped the plastic film and Maggie's mouth started watering. "Is that..."

"Chicken Alfredo and green beans with almond slivers. Did you know you can get recipes online?"

Maggie reached out and grabbed a green bean. "But why would you want to?" She popped the bean in her mouth. "I mean, who does that? Mmm, this is good!" She reached for another bean but Donnie pulled the plates away and took them to the microwave. "I didn't even know we had Alfredo."

Donnie laughed. "You don't have Alfredo you make it. From a recipe. Online, that's what I'm saying there are recipes online for everything!"

"I knew there were recipes for making bombs, I didn't know there were recipes for food too."

"Why would you know…never mind."

Donnie's phone started trilling and he asked Maggie to grab it while he tossed the salad.

"Stop tossing!" she yelled from the living room. "Todd threw up from too much pizza and Daniel threw up from watching Todd throw up. Abort dinner!"

Donnie popped his head in and listened to Maggie telling Don they would be right there and assuring him it was no problem and not to be sorry.

Donnie and Maggie ate cold chicken Alfredo later that evening after the boys were in bed and asleep.

Don didn't ask to have all the boys over again. They spent the night with him quite often but it was usually one or two at a time depending who was available and who hadn't been in a while. Donnie didn't attempt chicken Alfredo again but he did help out with the cooking, occasionally from an online recipe but mostly from a box.

As the weeks went by life in Naples fell into a new normal. Donnie worked during the week and on an occasional Saturday. He was happy, he was sober and to anyone just meeting him he appeared to be Floridian. During the week when the boys were in school Maggie started her days with a long walk in the complex and then a long swim in the pool, she usually finished her routine with a relaxing soak in the hot tub. She picked up a book that must have been Ann's one day and became hooked, after that she started reading and became a regular at the local library where she met some new friends and eventually was talked into joining a weekly book club.

On the weekends she fell into a routine at home with the boys, swimming and taking walks and when they grew bored with that she took them to the beach or to their friend's houses or once in a while just for a drive along the coast. She broke up the occasional fight but they were far more rare than they had been back in New York. Don sometimes went on rides with them but more often than not he was busy meeting his friends for coffee or for a shuffleboard tournament or a fishing derby.

D.J. and Ava spent as much time together as they could, sometimes at her house, sometimes at his but mostly at the spot in her complex where the teens met up and played basketball or swam in the community pool. Dylan joined them more often than not and although D.J. and Dylan were closer than ever Dylan had made quite a few new friends of his own and even joined a community racquetball team.

"Life is good isn't it?" Donnie commented more than asked one night when they were sitting by the pool after the boys had gone to bed.

Maggie had taken to wearing tennis skirts and tank tops when she wasn't in her swimsuit. Tonight she wore a pink tennis skirt and a white tank top. "It is." She agreed.

"Florida agrees with us."

"It does. I've lost fifteen pounds and I've read a million books!" she laughed. "The boys are happy, I'm happy, you're happy and Donnie, I'm proud of you too, eight weeks sober is pretty amazing."

"Thanks."

She wasn't sure but she thought he actually blushed. "I mean it. I'm proud of you."

"Thanks. Maggie, I hate to say anything to curse our good luck lately but I have two questions."

"Hmmm?"

"First, why do we sit out here every night watching an empty pool?"

"I guess it's what you do in Florida. For once our reality is better than watching other people's non-reality reality lives on television."

"Huh?"

"Never mind. What's the second question?"

Donnie didn't answer right away.

"Donnie?"

"What are we going to do?"

"What do you mean?"

"I know we don't have to make a decision yet. We said we'd stay through the school year and we'd have the summer to decide. I'm just wondering if we'll have to decide or if the decision made itself. We haven't talked about it but I think about it a lot. I'm happy just how things are, don't get me wrong, but it's always in the back of my mind, will we stay or will we move back, it's like that one little piece of the puzzle that's always missing."

"I know what you mean," she tried to ignore the question when it itched at the back of her own mind. "I think about it too but the question that keeps plaguing me even more is the one D.J. asked that time. Remember? If we move back will things go back to how they were?"

Donnie thought about it a while. He stood up and walked around the pool, fished out a toy someone had forgotten that floated along the edge. He looked out through the screen across the pond at his father's house.

"I like being around my Dad like this. I'd hate to leave and leave him alone, although I know now that he'd be fine. I guess that's one obstacle that's out of the way. He sure did build a new life quickly didn't he?"

Maggie got up and went to the hot tub, sat on the edge and dangled her feet in. "He did but I think it's good. Your Mom and Dad kept busy all the time doing something, he had to fill the time or he would have gone crazy."

"Right, no I know it's good. I'm glad." Donnie joined her at that hot tub and let his feet dangle in too. "That was one of the main reasons I wanted to stay though, so I'm just saying it's not an issue. He's fine.

"Sometimes I still feel like we're on vacation and other times I forget and everything just feels like this is the new normal. Donnie? Do you miss things from home? Do you miss Colton or our house or anything from home?"

Donnie moved his feet back and forth, held them in front of the jets and then let them dangle again. "I think the answer is supposed to be yes, but honestly Maggie I'd have to say no. I guess I could say I miss the pine trees and the country feel and yeah Colton. Its home, I think I'll always think of it as home. But I can't say I miss it in the sense of feeling homesick or anything. What about you, do you miss anything?"

"I miss Jillian."

"But she's still in New Jersey. When is she moving back anyway?"

"There were a bunch of delays, one thing after another she said. She's hoping everything is good to go now though, she plans to move next week and George is supposed to join her the week after."

"Does it bother you that she's moving home to our house and we're here?"

"Sort of. Not that she's moving in our house but I wanted her to move back so badly and now I'm not there. It feels weird."

"What else do you miss?"

Maggie slid into the hot tub, tennis skirt and tank and all. "I love Colton. I really do, I don't know if I knew that before but I know it now. So, I miss Colton. I miss the roots. I miss seeing a certain tree and remembering climbing it in second grade. I miss driving by the school and remembering sitting by the window during regents exams. Remember how you could hear the janitor mowing the lawn and you could smell the fresh cut grass? I miss the streets, the diner, the library, the people I knew and liked and even the ones I didn't. I love it here but I miss the feeling of belonging. I don't think I'll ever feel that here."

"Do you want to go home?"

"That's the million dollar question isn't it? I wish I knew. I can honestly say I don't know. I want to go home and I want to stay here."

Donnie slipped his shirt off and slid into the hot tub.

"Maggie, I told you I would do whatever you wanted and I meant it."

She slid next to him and put her head in his shoulder. "I like you again."

Donnie snickered. "You love me again."

"I hate it here! I want to go home!" D.J. slammed the door and dropped his backpack and stormed to his room.

The door opened again and Dylan came in followed by the other boys, he grabbed Maggie's arm and led her to the kitchen and practically pushed her into a chair. "Ava broke up with D.J. you have to do something."

Derek, Daniel and Todd traipsed into the kitchen and Dylan screamed at them, "Get out!" They stopped. "Get out!" Dylan stomped a foot in their direction and they turned and ran out.

Dylan stood back and swiped his arm through the air pointing at the door. "Do something! Go fix him!"

Maggie grabbed his hand and pulled him down into the closest chair. "What happened?"

"I told you! Ava broke up with him!"

"Dylan calm down! Just tell me what happened. Why did she break up with him? What did he tell you?"

Dylan stood back up and started pacing. "He didn't tell me anything. Matt told me, in school, in math class. He said Ava and D.J. were standing by the lockers talking between sixth and seventh period and then between seventh and eighth period Ava was standing with Lucas and they were practically all over each other. And then after eighth period we went to the buses and D.J. sat in the back and wouldn't talk to anyone. Tara said Samantha said Ava said she broke up with him. So go talk to him! Fix him!"

Maggie's head was spinning. Who? Said what? "Dylan stop pacing. Seriously. What's going on? Why are you so worried about him?"

"Because he's my brother and I care about him."

Maggie tilted her head and narrowed her eyes, they had gotten close but not close enough to equal this amount of drama. "Dylan?"

"Because I want to ask Tara out and she's Ava's best friend and I can't if D.J. and Ava broke up."

Ah ha.

"Plus he's my brother and I care about him."

Maggie almost laughed. She might have if the reality of slipping into the phase of many years of dealing with teenage broken hearts and drama didn't just rear its ugly face. How did she not see this coming?

"Okay, here's what we're going to do. I'm going to go talk to D.J. if he'll let me in, if he wants to be alone right now he's entitled to it Dylan. And you, you're going to go find your brothers and bring them in here and give them a snack."

"Mom?!"

"Do you want a chance at Tara or not?" Did she actually just say that?!

"Fine! But you better fix him."

Maggie couldn't fix him. D.J. was inconsolable. His door was unlocked and Maggie went in but he was hunkered in the corner of his bed sitting against the wall with his head in his knees. He refused to talk to her. She left him alone. He didn't come out for dinner and after dinner she sent Donnie in to try. He came out a minute later looking as sad and beaten as she imagined D.J. felt.

"This is as bad as when we had to spank him when he was little. It really does hurt us more than him huh?"

Maggie felt deflated. "Well that did but I'm not sure this is the same. It's his first broken heart. There's bound to be a million more nights like this in our future. If he was a girl I'd bring him a quart of Ben and Jerry's but I don't know what to do with boys. What worked for you?"

"I was the heart breaker not the other way around."

"Oh, please!"

"What? Seriously I never had my heart broken as a teenager. I don't know what to do."

Maggie rolled her eyes.

"You guys stink at this. I'm going in."

"Dylan no. If he doesn't want to talk about it you can't make him."

Donnie put his hand up to stop Maggie, "Wait, let him. What do we know, neither of us had a sibling, maybe he's the key."

Dylan threw his arms in the air. "Seriously? Do you want to maybe go to the library and see if you can find a book on how to raise kids? Shouldn't you have done that *before* you had us? You guys suck at this!" he stormed off to his room.

Donnie smirked at Maggie. "We do suck at this."

"We do. It breaks my heart to see him so sad but yeah, we do suck at this."

Twenty minutes later Dylan came out of the room, walked past them, went to the kitchen, and walked back past them carrying a half gallon of mint chocolate chip ice cream and two spoons.

"He's healing," Donnie whispered.

Maggie slumped and gave him a look of indignation. "That's exactly what I would have ended up doing. I should have done it. I want to be the hero."

Donnie patted her shoulder. "But you didn't. Don't worry, you'll have lots of opportunities to get it right."

Twenty minutes later Dylan walked past them carrying the empty ice cream container and the two spoons. On his way back from the kitchen Donnie whispered, "Dylan? How is he?"

Dylan stepped closer and whispered, "He's on the phone with Ashlynn. He's going to ask her out."

Dylan disappeared and Donnie and Maggie looked at each other. Donnie shrugged and grinned.

"Ashlynn? Who is Ashlynn?" Maggie asked.

Donnie shrugged again. "I don't know. If you go to the store tomorrow buy some more ice cream though, we better stay stocked."

Maggie got up to tuck the other boys in. "Ashlynn?"

Donnie and Maggie were just getting ready to head to bed when Dylan burst into the living room.

"Okay so Mom? Tomorrow night's Friday. Tara and Ashlynn are coming over for pizza. Okay? So we need pizza. And ice tea. Girls drink ice tea right? The no calorie kind. Okay?" He spun around and started back to his room and stopped after three steps. He spun around again. "And get rid of the dorks." He disappeared back to his room.

"What just happened?" Maggie asked Donnie.

"Teenagers just happened. I feel like I just had a flashback. Remember our pizza parties?"

"We made our own pizza. And we drank Tab. Remember Tab? We thought life was so complicated then. If we only knew."

"You and Jillian drank Tab. The guys drank real soda. And life was complicated then. It was just a different kind of complicated."

"Why are you making this so complicated?" Don's voice resonated through Donnie's cell phone. Maggie could hear both sides of the conversation from her side of the bed. "I'll come over and help keep the younger boys occupied. There's no need for sending them away just because the older boys want it that way. *Especially* since the older boys want it that way. I'll come over and we'll all have pizza."

"Dad they're teenagers, it's their first double date, can't you take the boys for just a couple of hours?"

"Of course I can take them I just don't think I should. The younger boys being there will keep all hands where they should be. I wish I had an extra set of eyes when you were bringing girls home. Use the boys to your advantage, and I'd make Todd point man if I were you."

"Dad. Four o'clock. Pick them up or I'll bring them over. Which will it be?"

"Fine. Be stubborn about it, you can bring them over but I'll bring them home. I want to meet these girls."

Donnie put his phone on the nightstand and turned the light off.

"Tell him to bring the boys back at nine." Maggie pulled the sheets over herself.

"Nine? The girls will probably be gone by then won't they?"

"That's what I'm hoping."

The following night, just as Maggie hoped, and maybe even pushed a little, the girls were gone by nine and Dylan and D.J. were hidden in their room probably comparing notes or planning their next double date. Don grumbled for a while but Todd insisted he read him a night time story and Maggie sat on the couch with them listening as Don became preoccupied by a Tyrannosaurus Rex named Genius whose mother was being held captive by a Brontosaurus named Bruno and the only way they could communicate was by writing letters that were secretly delivered by a Dinobird named Tuxedo. He stopped reading mid sentence and Maggie saw his face turn white.

"Don?"

He handed her the book and stood up. She watched him walk hesitantly toward his and Ann's old room. Derek took the book from Maggie's lap and continued reading where Don left off. She glanced at Donnie across the room and they both stood and followed Don.

"Dad?"

Don stood at the closet holding an empty tote. Maggie's heart dropped. Everything froze for a second while her mind spun the information her eyes were seeing.

Don knew about the letters. He'd probably forgotten about them. And now he remembered them. And now the totes were empty.

He would ask. She would have to tell him what she did.

It wasn't just Ann's secret. It was Don and Ann's secret.

"Dad?"

And soon Donnie would know too.

Had Don read them or only knew about them? If he'd read them then he knew what they said, and he would tell her. And she didn't want to know.

Maggie felt her body sway and she stepped gingerly to the bed and sat down.

Donnie looked at his father standing at the closet holding the tote. He turned and looked at Maggie sitting on the bed. "What's going on?"

Don slowly turned around and when he looked at Maggie his face was void of color. "I'd forgotten," he whispered.

"Dad?" Donnie took a step toward his father but Don's eyes remained on Maggie.

"With Ann dying, I forgot. I didn't think. I'd just forgotten," Don's eyes searched Maggie's. "I'm sorry. I should never have asked you to...did you..."

"I burned them," she whispered.

Don blinked. He shook the tote and then placed it back in the closet and picked up another, shook it and put it back. He turned back to Maggie. "Did you...did you read them?"

Maggie shook her head. "No."

"None of them?"

She shook her head again. "No. Did you?"

Don turned back to the closet and took each tote out and shook it before putting it back.. When he turned around the color was beginning to come back into his face. He looked at Maggie and then at Donnie and back to Maggie. The only sound in the room was the sound of Derek's voice reading from the living room.

Don went to the bed and sat next to Maggie.

"Yes, I did," he draped his arm around her shoulders. "But I take it you don't want to know?"

She shook her head.

"What's going on?" Donnie tried again but no one answered him.

Don took his arm off her shoulder and picked up her hand and held it. "Then that's the way it will be. If you ever do want to know you just have to ask. Otherwise, that's the end of it." He loosened his fingers and gently patted her hand and then stood up and clapped his hands together. "That's it.

Let's go. Let's find out what happened to Genius and Bruno and Tuxedo." He sent a look at Donnie that left no question as to what he was to do. Donnie turned and led them into the living room just in time to hear Derek say "and no one ever heard from Tuxedo again." And he closed the book.

CHAPTER NINE

Don had long since gone home and the boys were tucked in for the night. The kitchen was clean, the living room picked up and try as she might Maggie couldn't think of anything else to do to postpone going to bed. Her hope was that she put enough time between the end of the evening when everyone went to bed and now, God knew it didn't take long for Donnie to fall asleep once his head hit the pillow but if the question of the totes was weighing heavily on his mind he probably didn't drifted off as quickly as usual.

She folded and refolded the dishtowel. If their roles were reversed she didn't think she could have waited even this long, the curiosity would have eaten away at her. She had to give him credit for his patience. It was *his* mother after all and *her* totes. She could only imagine what scenarios ran through his mind throughout the evening. Add Don's reaction and hers and the little bit they did say and then look at it from Donnie's perspective and it certainly was enough for the imagination to create some wild scenarios. She owed him the truth, if for no reason other than to put an end to the possibilities he was probably imagining, which she was sure none of which involved the actual truth of what was in the totes.

The fact that her mother and Ann corresponded all these

years added to the realization that Don also knew and had read the letters twisted in her gut but it wasn't that, or even the unbelievable and unimaginable concept that her own mother cut her out of her life and then invited herself back in without her knowledge, it was the weight of dealing with it that she wanted to avoid at all costs. Ignorance is bliss. If she could feign ignorance she could slip into a sense of status quo on the emotional topic of her parents. It was just like when she quit smoking so many years ago, it was the *idea* of quitting that ignited every negative emotion and panic button possible, the actual act of quitting, once she did it, was nowhere near as hard as the idea of quitting. Since she had no plan to act she needed the whole letter subject to go away.

She wanted more than anything to avoid the topic, to put it somewhere deep and hidden in the recess of her mind, forever if that was possible. She didn't want to think about it. She didn't want to deal with it. She wanted the easy way out. But that wasn't fair to Donnie. She couldn't just ask him to pretend the little incident with the totes never happened and expose him to a lifetime of wonder and worry knowing that if she just told him the truth it would drive out all the false conclusions that would pass through his imagination and take hold and grow out of proportion.

She put the dishcloth down and went to the bedroom with reluctant determination to get this over with. Unless he was asleep. She crossed her fingers and shuffled to the bedroom. Wide awake, Donnie sat against his pillow propped against the headboard and watched her as she walked into the room and changed and climbed into bed next to him.

If she slid down into the sheets and rolled to her side she was pretty sure he would respectfully follow her lead and that would be the end of it. For now. But it wouldn't go away just like her knowledge of the letters wouldn't go away no matter how much she tried to fool herself that they would.

"Thank you for not asking." She took a deep breath, sighed, and began. She told him the whole story of finding the letters, of driving to the beach, of deciding not to read them, of how she burned them one by one. She told him about cleaning the van and seeing the mailman, of the letter she wrote, the letter written by the fictitious Alice Bailey.

He listened to every word she spoke. He didn't interrupt her or ask any questions. He didn't gasp or sigh or shake his head. He didn't say a word.

"Do you think I'm crazy?" She finally asked him when there was nothing left to tell.

"Yes. But not for any of that," he reached his hand out and offered it to her and she slid her hand in his. "It's what you felt you had to do. I have to say though, I'm glad Dad read them in case you ever do decide you want to know what was in them."

"I can't imagine that day will ever come. But maybe. Who knows."

"Are you okay?"

"I think so. I don't blame your Mom or your Dad, they were put in the middle of it and they had to make a choice. I do understand where they were coming from, I think, I imagine, knowing them, they probably didn't ask or give opinions, they probably just kept to the facts and kept her apprised of the boys and our lives. I tried to put myself in your Mom's shoes and I'm guessing she just didn't want my mother to go to the grave not knowing anything about the boys. At least that's how I want to think it went down."

"Sounds about right. I really can't imagine my mother getting involved in the emotional side of it other than to feel some compassion for a grandmother that wants to know about her grandchildren."

"That's what I'm thinking. Your parents are pretty great you know, were, are." Maggie flinched at her choice of words, she would never get used to them being just him. She looked at Donnie but he didn't get caught in her fumble, he was still a step behind in the conversation.

"It was a pretty final act, burning the letters, do you regret it at all?"

"No, not yet anyway. The only thing I regret is that she

never trusted me to forgive her. Why else would she make contact with your mother but not me? Unless it was just the easy way out and she never wanted my forgiveness, maybe she never thought she needed it, maybe forgiveness wasn't even a part of the whole equation. She might have always believed she was right to do what she did."

"Would you have forgiven her if she asked?"

Maggie was shocked that he even had to ask her. "There is nothing she could have said, or done, that couldn't be forgiven. Except for not trusting me to forgive her. That didn't make sense did it? I know what I feel but I can't explain it." Maggie thought for a moment and Donnie waited her out, "All she had to do was talk to me. Whatever she said, whatever her reasons, I would have eventually forgiven her. I might have been mad or hurt initially but eventually…she was my mother…I would have forgiven her. Eventually."

"Are you sure?"

"What do you mean am I sure? Of course I'm sure."

Donnie slipped his hand out of hers. "Maggie, don't get mad at me but I'm not so sure," he watched her for a reaction but there was none so he continued. "I'm not sure you would forgive her if she asked. I believe you think you would have, you look back and create a hindsight you want. You think if she had come to you ten or twelve or even five years ago you think you would have forgiven her but she didn't so you can create it that way. I'm not so sure. You can say you would have forgiven her in the past because it's the past but Maggie, what if she comes to you tomorrow, will you forgive her?" He paused long enough to know she wasn't answering because she couldn't know she would. "What's the difference?"

This was exactly, *exactly* why she didn't want to talk about it. "It doesn't matter, she won't."

"How do you know that? Maybe now that she doesn't have my mom to go through, maybe now she will."

"She still has your dad."

"Maggie?" Donnie reached up and pushed a piece of hair off her face. "Could you put the past behind you and forgive her, no matter what the reasons were for doing what she did, if she asked you to?"

Maggie felt her eyes filling with tears and didn't bother trying to blink them away. She let them slide down her cheeks and half expected Donnie to wipe them away and tell her it didn't matter, not to think about it, he was sorry, they should get some sleep. But he didn't. He gently laid his hand on top of hers and waited for an answer.

"I don't know," her voice was quiet and airy. "I don't know what I would do tomorrow, I only know that as of today she hasn't asked. And by not asking she is telling me she doesn't trust me enough… or care enough…to ask. I want to believe that anything can be forgiven but *she didn't ask*. How do I know if she doesn't ask?"

Donnie closed his eyes and when he opened them there was sorrow in his eyes. He took his hand from the top of hers and picked up the edge of the sheet and fidgeted with it then let it go. "What about us?"

Tears still trickled from Maggie's eyes and without knowing why she knew they weren't going to stop anytime soon. She knew these were tears of hurt from the years of rejection from her mother. But somehow she knew the tears that were still forming behind her eyes would soon follow the others down her cheeks and they would be tears for something else. It was concealed from her understanding for the moment but she could see it in Donnie's eyes.

"Don't," she whispered. She didn't try to guess where the look in Donnie's eyes originated, she just knew it was something she didn't want to hear.

"I have to," Donnie whispered. He took a breath and when he spoke his voice was somehow both strong and weak.. "Maggie, I love you and I care and I trust you. And I need to give you the chance to forgive me."

She shook her head and the tears that were for something she didn't yet know fell from her eyes.

"It's a long story. What I'm going to tell you Maggie is not anything you're imagining. Please let me tell it all before you say anything. Promise you'll let me finish before you react, please?"

She didn't want to know. What if she was wrong? What if not asking for forgiveness was better than asking? What if whatever Donnie needed to give her a chance to forgive couldn't be forgiven?

"I'm going to tell you about Mike."

He was right, it was not anything she was imagining. Hope slid back in where it was just a second ago missing, there was nothing he could tell her about Mike or high school or what happened between them that she couldn't forgive. They were just kids being kids. She breathed again.

"We were seniors, you, me, Jillian, and whoever she was dating at the time. We were on top of the world, remember? Hell, we *owned* the world."

Maggie smiled in spite of herself and Donnie smiled back, it was a genuine smile but bulleted with holes of regret, the kind of smile that's made up from the thin wisps of the memory of a different time.

"Then you were pregnant and our whole lives changed. We went from being on top of the world to having to carry it on our shoulders. We were too young Maggie, it was too much responsibility for two kids that never imagined a life beyond perfect, beyond adventure and fun and freedom. Anyway, the pregnancy was awful, you were so sick all the time and I felt so bad for you. God it was awful, all the other kids, all our friends were going to ball games and concerts and parties and drinking till they puked and you were waking up puking, every day. I couldn't do anything to make it better for you, I would have, God, I wanted to but I couldn't. I felt so responsible. I felt…"

"Donnie it wasn't just your fault it was…"

"Don't Maggie. Let me tell you everything. Please. You're not going to feel that way when I'm done, just wait."

Maggie felt her throat hitch, no, they were kids being kids.

"You were missing school like crazy, you were lucky if you made it one day out of a week. Even half the time when you went you left early. You tried. Remember? You were determined to finish school and get your diploma and put that phase of life behind you neatly the way it was supposed to be. Remember? We talked about if you had to stop and get your GED instead and you refused, you were determined to finish, even though two phases of life collided and combined you were determined to finish the one so you could move into the other with that one behind you, remember? So I tried to help. Jillian and I both did. We started helping you with your homework and then we started just doing it for you."

Maggie's heart raced, this trip down memory lane was not fun and every sentence he uttered made her wish it was over. "What does this have to do with Mike? Donnie don't drag it out, just tell me."

Donnie pulled into himself and Maggie felt the distance between them opening. "I have to tell you my way, it's been fifteen years Maggie, sixteen really, when I'm done you can say anything you want but just let me tell it."

Maggie closed her eyes and when she opened them again Donnie continued.

"I knew I wasn't as smart as you and when you got your papers back your grades were okay, not as good as if you did it yourself but you were passing. That's all we cared about at that point, remember? You didn't care what your final grade was, you just wanted to pass, you just wanted to get your diploma and be done. It was going okay. You did some of the work, the classes you had that I didn't, I usually let Jillian do, and the ones we had together I did. Between the grades you got when you did the homework and the grades Jillian got you were doing okay. Even the grades I was getting for you were okay. You were passing. You were going to graduate. All I could do for you then was to make sure your homework was done and turned in and that you passed. And graduated. And I thought I was doing that. I thought everything was going fine."

"And it was, Donnie, please…"

"And then about a month before graduation Mike Jensen came to me. I don't think I ever spoke to the loser before in my life and he just comes up to me at my locker at the end of the school one day out of the blue and tells me he has information I need to know. I asked him what and he said it was too sensitive to talk about there. God Maggie he said sensitive I remember it as clear as if it were yesterday. I thought he was such a dweeb I just turned away from him but he said to meet him in front of the library, on the steps, in a half hour. I wasn't going to. What the hell kind of information could he have that I would care about? The kid was practically invisible, no one paid any attention to him, all he ever did was play on computers and carry around computer pieces that he fiddled with all the time. So what was he going to tell me? That he cracked some big federal top secret file and the government was spying on us?! Who cares!"

He paused and Maggie could tell he was trying to calm himself down, trying to come back emotionally to the present. When he started speaking again his voice was calmer and slightly quieter.

"I met him. I guess my curiosity just got the best of me."

Maggie felt her heart quicken, whatever it was, whatever was between them from so long ago was within reach of her for the first time and she found herself more curious than scared. She wanted him to hurry up and finish. "What happened?"

"He told me he broke into the school's computer files. He said you were failing and you weren't going to graduate."

What? "But that's impossible!"

"I thought so too and I said so too. But he said it was English. And you needed English to graduate."

Maggie shook her head. "Well it's not true, it wasn't true, I graduated."

"He told me he could fix it, he could change your grades in the computer. Said it would be a piece of cake for him."

Maggie's thoughts slammed together and fell apart.

"I panicked. If you were failing English it was my fault, if you failed English you wouldn't have graduated with the rest of us, you would have had to get a GED and...Maggie you swore you weren't going to let that happen. I couldn't tell you."

"Wait! What? Wait!"

"So Mike changed your grades."

No, that wasn't possible. "Donnie I wasn't failing! You saw my grades, my teachers would have contacted me, they would have told me. They wouldn't have just let me fail and not told me! I wasn't failing!"

"Maggie I'm not done, there's more, but about that, sometimes I wonder if they did contact you, if your mother got to it first, if it was just another nail in our collective coffin so to speak. I'm not trying to spread the blame here but she was out of control pissed at us. I have wondered about it."

Her mother? Would she do that? Was she so angry at her for getting pregnant that she would have kept something that important from her and let her fail? Her own daughter? Maggie couldn't handle that on top of everything else and pushed the thought aside for the moment. "So what more is there? You said there's more? What happened?"

She tried to merge the Mike Jensen from high school with the Mike Jensen she'd worked with. He couldn't have. He would have let it slip somewhere, somehow, wouldn't he?

"There was a price. He told me he got a girl from Potsdam pregnant but that he was drunk and he didn't even know her and he wasn't going to let it ruin his life, that he was going to make her have an abortion. But he needed money for it. He told me he would change your grades for five hundred dollars."

Maggie shook her head, it was coming too fast. It wasn't making sense.

"I paid him. Maggie I'm so frigging sorry I can't even ever *ever* tell you how sorry."

"Wait. Stop. Wait." Maggie needed it to make sense, it wasn't making any sense. Failing English? Mike? Abortion?

"There's more. He came to me again a couple days after I paid him and told me he needed another five hundred. I didn't have it, I took the first five hundred out of my savings account from the money I got for birthdays and stuff, but I didn't have any more. So I stole it. From my mother's purse. From my father's wallet. I even stole some from your parents. I took money from your Mom's mad money jar. I sold some stuff to friends to make up the difference and then I paid him another five hundred dollars."

"This doesn't make any sense! Donnie..." She shook her head and opened her mouth to protest again but Donnie didn't give her a chance.

"After graduation I thought it would all be over. But it wasn't. Maggie that bastard, your new boss, kept calling me for months and telling me if I didn't send him more money he would tell you what I did. I sent it. Every time. If he told you I was afraid you would leave me."

"No. This isn't making any sense. None of it. My diploma..."

"Is fake Maggie. I didn't want you to work because I thought someone would find out. I'm stupid I know. I was afraid someone would get your high school manuscript or something. I didn't know what to do and it just kept snowballing. When you were home with the boys I thought maybe everything would be okay that you would be happy being home with them, but you kept talking about working and I didn't know what to do. So I just fought you on it. I just tried to keep you from trying to get a job."

"DONNIE! DAMN IT! What does this mean? I don't even have a high school diploma?!"

"Yes. You do. But it's...fake."

Maggie closed her eyes. She couldn't breathe.

"Mike moved to Texas that summer, I thought it was over, I was so sure we could just go on and you'd have the baby and he'd disappear, but you kept wanting to work and he kept calling me. I started drinking more and more. I sent him money for a few years, every time he told me to, and then it just stopped. But I didn't stop drinking. For a long time, every time the phone rang I thought it might be him. Eventually I started to believe it was finally over. I know now that I was deceiving myself, it would never be over because I did it and I couldn't undo it and I just made everything worse by drinking so much. But I never, ever, imagined that he would come back and you would wind up working for him."

Maggie's thoughts were strung further than she could think. He needed to stop talking, but he didn't.

"He called me. He told me you were there looking for a job. He told me he would hire you. He said he felt bad about everything and that it was kid stuff and that he wanted to make it up to us. I told him if he gave you the job I would go to the police and tell them about what he did and blackmailing me all that time. But he gave you the job anyway. He knew I wouldn't."

It was too much, Maggie couldn't sort it fast enough, she was drowning.

"Maggie?" He reached to take her hand. "I had to tell you, to…"

"Don't! I have to think!" She heard her voice escalating but she couldn't stop herself. "Everything is a lie? My diploma? That job? Us? It's all a lie? It's all a lie?! My mother? The letters? Now this? How could you tell me this *now*?!"

"It's not all a lie. Not us. I know you're going to leave me, damn it Maggie it's what I've always been afraid of. I knew you would never forgive me. Maggie don't you understand? I never wanted to tell you because I knew you would leave me the minute I told you. I knew you would never forgive me. But after you said that about your Mom I had to tell you. I had to give you the chance to forgive me. Maggie you have to believe me, I love you, that is not a lie, our kids are not a lie." He paused and tried to clear some of the emotion from his throat. "Even if you can't forgive me, please tell me you know I love you."

Maggie shook her head. "I don't know anything right now." But as quickly as the words were out she did know. She knew with such clarity that she didn't need to think about it. The words came out as if they had been waiting in the back

of her throat for just the right moment.
 "Donnie, I want to go home. Alone."

CHAPTER TEN

Maggie's flight left Fort Myers Florida at nine twenty in the morning and after an almost two hour delay at Douglas Airport in Charlotte North Carolina she walked through the main terminal at the Syracuse Hancock International Airport at three forty five. She spotted Jillian, Pete and Shea almost immediately and burst into tears.

"It's a nightmare," she sobbed against Jillian's shoulder. "I can't believe everything hit at once like that, I should have known it was going too good to be true."

"Shh, it's okay. We'll figure it out." Jillian patted her shoulder. "Come on, let's get your bags and get to the car. We have lots of time to talk."

Maggie sniffled and pulled away from Jillian and turned her attention to the kids.

"They know you're sad about grown up stuff, " Jillian whispered. "I told them you wouldn't be regular fun Maggie for a few days."

"I hate grown up stuff," Maggie whispered back and they shared their first smile together in way too long.

Last night when she told Donnie she wanted to come home alone she was absolutely certain it was what she wanted. But as they made the arrangements and this morning when he took her to the airport she started second guessing herself. By the time the plane touched down in Charlotte she was already regretting acting so compulsive. But now as conflicted as she had made herself about leaving home to come home, she knew she made the right decision. There was no one she would rather be with.

"Do you really think I'll be fun Maggie again that soon?"

"Sure you will. Let's get your luggage and get this party started."

Maggie shook her head at Jillian's choice of words and wiped eyes. She put on her best fake happy face and bent down to greet Pete. "You got so big! What kind of stuff are they feeding you down there in New Jersey?"

He shrugged and looked away. Maybe he needed a few days too.

While they waited for the empty luggage carousel to come alive they chatted about the weather and their trips and all things non-invasive. Even walking to the car and for the first few miles until they were on their way north on Route 81 Maggie managed to follow Jillian's lead but once she turned around and saw that Shea was asleep and Pete was occupied with a coloring book and crayons and she blurted out, "Jillian what am I going to do? Everything was great and now it's gone to shit."

Jillian startled at the abrupt change and glanced in the rearview mirror. "No swearing. It's only two hours to Frank and Louise's. Once we drop the kids off there and head back to your house you can swear up a storm if you have to."

"Louise is keeping the kids?"

Jillian looked at Maggie like she was dense. "Of course. This is serious stuff, I'm here for you for as long as you need me, we'll talk all night, all week, however long it takes until we figure it out and get you back to fun Maggie. George even said to take my time, he told me if I had to I could just stay here and get things ready for him to move up."

"God Bless Louise! And George! I love Louise and George."

"No you don't." Jillian rolled her eyes and whispered, "Louise annoys you. And George ticks you off."

"That's true," Maggie whispered back. "But right now I love them. And you." She stopped whispering. "Seriously Jillian, I don't know what I would have done if I didn't have you to turn to. I'm so confused. And mad. And sad."

"I know. And I know you're dying to talk but I promise, just a couple hours and we will. For now, tell me more about the house."

"It will just make me sad. It's beautiful. I miss it already."

"Okay. Tell me about the boys. How are they doing?"

"It will just make me sad. They're awesome. I miss them already."

"Okay. Tell me about Naples. What's it like there?"

"It will just make me sad. It's beautiful. I miss it already."

"Maggie? Take a nap."

"I'm not tired." But she closed her eyes anyway and she and Shea slept all the way to Potsdam. She pretended to still be asleep when Jillian stopped the car at Frank and Louise's. Jillian whispered to the kids as she got them out of the Suburban and when Frank came out to get the kid's luggage Maggie heard Jillian explaining how wiped out she was and that she didn't have the heart to wake her. Maggie felt a tinge of guilt until Jillian got back in the Suburban and pulled out of the driveway and told her it was safe to open her eyes.

"Holy crap its cold here." Maggie bounced from one foot to the other while Jillian struggled with the key in the door. "Hurry up!"

"It's sixty eight degrees out and I'm trying! What's wrong with this key?"

"Nothing and I'm used to eighty eight. Here give it to me. You just have to wiggle it right."

Jillian gave Maggie the key and she opened the door and hurried inside against the frigid sixty eight degree weather but three steps in she stopped short and froze.

"What?"

"Nothing. It just feels weird. Like home but not home. I

think I'm going to cry now. You okay with that?"

Jillian put the bags down and put her arms around Maggie. Once they hugged it out, not the airport kind of hug but the 'we've been best friends since preschool' kind of hug, they pulled apart and Jillian brought the luggage to the bedrooms and turned the heat up and began doing all the things a person does to a house after being vacant so long. Maggie walked from room to room turning on lights and letting her eyes adjust to the light and her mind adjust to the sights. She touched the tops of dressers and ran her hands across the couch and opened the cupboards. Everything looked just as she expected it to, just as they'd left it.

"Everything feels so…foreign,." she said when she caught Jillian out of the corner of her eye watching her. "I expected it to feel more, I don't know, comfortable."

"Give it time. You have been away a while."

"Not that long, I thought it would feel like…an old shoe."

"An old shoe?"

"Yeah, but it doesn't. It feels like the very same shoe but brand new, it looks right but it doesn't feel the same."

"I bet it will. You've never been away before, that's how I feel when we go to the Cape every year but by the second day there its old shoe again."

Maggie turned around and faced Jillian full on, "I hate that you go to the Cape every year. I hate that I've been away. I hate that you moved to New Jersey. I hate when everything stays the same and I hate when something changes."

"Anything else?" Jillian smiled.

"Yes, I hate this feeling."

"Come on, let's get unpacked, it might help. And then we'll go pick up a pizza, put our pajamas on and talk all night. You can tell me everything you hate."

"I hate you telling me what to do."

They unpacked, picked up a pizza, put on their pajamas and talked all night. Maggie cried off and on and laughed just as much. She cried hardest when she told Jillian that she had lied to the boys telling them she had to make an unexpected trip home to take care of house things and she would be gone a week or two.

"I can't believe they just bought it. D.J. and Dylan were too preoccupied with girls and the younger ones didn't question it. I didn't want them to question me but they just let me walk out like I was going to the post office."

"What about Donnie, what was he like this morning?"

Last night, after Donnie purged himself of his big deceitful secret they spoke only what had to be spoken, money, flight arrangements, turns on the way to the airport. He carried her bags to the luggage check in and walked her to the security checkpoint line. He didn't try to hug her or kiss her. He didn't even ask her about her plans. He simply said, 'Call me, please' and touched her hand before he walked away.

"He was probably exactly how he should have been. He gave me my space. He told me to call him."

"What about Don? What do you think he'll tell him?"

Don would know something was up and he would probably hound Donnie until he told him. She wondered if he would tell him everything, probably. "I don't know, I think he'll beat around the bush a while but Don will get it out of him. You know, that whole mess bothers me but you know what's really bothering me right now?" she and Jillian lay side by side the wrong way on the bed, feet against the wall like they did when they were young. "I told Donnie I was afraid I wouldn't ever feel like I really belonged there, you know, I thought it would never feel like home, like it does here. Except now I don't know if I'll ever feel like I really belong here anymore either. Or anywhere."

"It's too soon Maggie, don't borrow tomorrow's worries. You need to just let it all sink in. I still can't believe the whole story about the grades. It just doesn't add up. Wouldn't the teachers or the school or somebody have told you that you were failing?"

"You would think." She told her about Donnie's theory that maybe they did and her mother chose not to tell her.

"No way! Your mother was snooty and she was super

crazy ticked at you guys but I can't believe she would do that. All she cared about was appearances, she would never have let her daughter fail if she could help it, it wouldn't have reflected well on her. You don't think Donnie's lying do you?"

"No, I think everything happened like he said. Why would he lie about it? I don't think my mother would have done that either, but I still can't believe the school wouldn't have told me. I don't know Jillian, none of it makes sense."

"We need to think about it more. I guess the first thing to think about is if it's all true and you would have failed but he changed the grades so you wouldn't, does it matter? I mean, you let us do your homework for you, does it matter how you got the diploma? It isn't like you had squeaky clean standards. I guess what I'm asking is, is the issue at hand more about the diploma or more about Donnie lying to you all this time? And actually, either way, does it even matter? Don't get me wrong I understand why it upset you but I'm just saying in the scheme of things now, fifteen years later, does it matter?"

"Of course it matters. Either way. Both ways. My diploma is a fake. That matters! Donnie lied to me for fifteen years. That matters!"

"But does it? Maggie it's fifteen years later, you have a diploma and technically it would be a fake even if you passed and Mike didn't change your grades because *you* didn't do the homework. And Donnie lied about it but if you look at it from his point of view you have to give him some credit, he didn't really have any choice, at least not looking at it from his point of view at that age with those circumstances. So, does it matter now, a whole lifetime later? Really? Does it matter?"

Does it matter? Maggie didn't know anymore. She was so tired it all seemed like a dream she'd just woken to that was quickly disappearing. She couldn't grasp enough of it to make sense. "I can't think anymore. I have to sleep. If I weren't so tired I would be mad at you but I'm even too tired for that. Sleep. I need sleep."

Jillian snickered. "Okay, I'm sorry Mags, I don't want you to be mad at me I just want to help you figure out where to go from here. Which bed do I get?"

"This one. With me. We only made up the one bed and I'm too tired to help make up another, unless you want to do it its sleepover time. Like old times. And I'm not mad at you, I'm not even sure I'm really mad at Donnie either but I need to be mad at someone." She barely finished saying it and she curled to her side and fell asleep.

"So Maggie?" Jillian poured coffee while Maggie sat at the table trying not to think about her spacious high end kitchen in Naples and taking her morning coffee out by the pool. "Why did you come home? I mean, when Donnie told you what he did your first instinct was to book a flight and leave. That seems a little drastic."

Maggie groaned. "Already? I just woke up."

Jillian carried the mugs to the table. "If you didn't kick me all night you'd probably feel more rested. Talk."

"Off the top of my very groggy head I'd guess it's one of two things. One, Donnie said 'I know you're going to leave me when I tell you, which I thought seemed dramatic at the time but he kind of planted a seed, like he gave me permission to leave. Or two, I was more homesick than I thought I was and I subconsciously jumped at any excuse to come home. Or is that just one thing?"

"Are you mad at him? You said last night you weren't even sure if you were."

"Of course I am, I was delusional last night. But I'm not sure if I'm mad at him for doing what he did or for keeping it a secret all this time, or for making my life miserable because he did what he did. Did I tell you that's the only reason he didn't want me to get a job? All this time I could have been building a career like I wanted to but instead I stayed home and cleaned toilets and wiped noses because he thought if I applied somewhere they would uncover his big secret. He actually thought they look at your high school grades. Which doesn't make sense anyway, Mike changed my grades, it would show me passing. I guess he thought it would come out somehow. Plus," Maggie took a long sip of her coffee, "plus my diploma is a fake. It's like knowing there's a big hole under the wallpaper, no one else knows it but I do. And it bugs me."

Jillian looked at the painted walls.

"It's a metaphor or a simile or something, I don't know, I failed English."

"I think we have to get to the root of the problem. I'm not trying to make light of it, it would bug me too, but when you put the grade changing part in perspective I think he did what he thought he had to do, and he did it for you, I mean I think his intentions were good at the time. He was a, uh, well let's tell the truth, he was kind of a dumb jock, but he took the only way out he could see, at the time. I'm not saying it was right but in his mind at that time Maggie he saw it as the only choice he had. Either that or let you fail and not graduate. You would have been devastated. Which brings me back to the big question, does it even matter now? I'm not sure that I wouldn't have done it too Maggie, to be honest."

"If you did do it would you have told me?"

"I don't know, probably, eventually. Well, I guess I might have told you then and let you decide whether to pay him to change the grades or not. But then again, I would have been embarrassed and felt guilty that I made you fail in the first place so maybe I wouldn't have told you. I think keeping it a secret put a lot of major pressure on Donnie all this time."

"Oh please! Let's not make him the victim here okay?"

"It's not like he purposely set out to have this big secret between you your whole lives. One thing led to another. It probably tormented him all this time. Mike tormented him too for a while. Just saying."

Maggie's skin prickled and she shivered. "Do not defend him. But that's another issue. Why would Mike hire me? I liked him Jillian. I actually thought we were friends."

"Maybe he really did feel bad and thought he was making amends by giving you the job? Fifteen years ago was a long time ago. People change. It's a big deal Maggie, I get that, but maybe he thought you knew and it was all behind you? And actually, didn't you kind of fall into the job when his secretary quit? He didn't actually hire you, things just fell into place there too. Maggie, I'll stand behind you no matter what, you know that, but here's my honest opinion. I don't think there are any bad guys here. I think in high school Donnie was dumb and Mike was a jerk. Fast forward fifteen years and I think Donnie was a jerk and Mike was dumb. Men don't think beyond the moment. The grade changing was an easy way out for Donnie, it served a purpose that made his life easier. And, fast forward again, hiring you to be his secretary was an easy way out for Mike, it served a purpose that made his life easier. I don't think either guy either time was malicious I think they just grabbed an opportunity that presented itself, with the sole purpose of making their own lives easier."

Maggie shook her head. "I don't want to talk about it anymore, I'm confused, I can't think."

"Isn't that why I'm here? So we can talk about it and figure it out? But fine, I'll give you some space to think but just a little."

Jillian went upstairs and Maggie stood in front of the refrigerator with the door wide open. She could actually feel the jet stream as the cold air met the warm heated air. It was exactly the type of thing she yelled at the boys for. She'd opened the door twice already this morning and it was still as empty as it was both of those times. She was staring at a ketchup bottle when out of nowhere Amazing Grace started blasting through the house. She jumped back and slammed the refrigerator door.

"Jillian! What the hell is that?!"

From somewhere upstairs she heard the muffled sound of Jillian's voice yelling back at her. "It's the new door bell, do you like it?"

New doorbell?! When did she put in a doorbell? And why? "No!"

"Get the door! Someone's here, that's what a doorbell means!"

Maggie took a step toward the hallway. Amazing Grace? "Is it God?"

It wasn't God. It was the McKenna's. She was thankful for having neighbors that kept an eye on the place while they were gone but she didn't want to deal with them. She ran upstairs and begged Jillian to get rid of them.

"What did they want? When did you put in a new doorbell? *How* did you put in a new doorbell?"

"They were driving by and saw the Suburban and wanted to check and make sure everything was okay, that someone hadn't claimed squatter's rights. Is that really a thing? And I put the doorbell in this morning. It's just one of those sticky kinds, no screwdriver needed! Pretty cool huh?"

"No. It's not. Unstick it. Did they bring breakfast?"

"No and I'm starving. Want me to run to the Mini Mart and pick up some yogurt?"

Maggie threw a shoe at her. "If you're not going to be a true friend then just tell me now because I'll find someone else."

After they showered and dressed they called and checked on the Pete and Shea. They were fine and Pete was having the time of his life and didn't want Jillian to come get them yet. They went to the diner for breakfast and then decided to get some groceries but Jillian didn't stop at the grocery store, she drove straight through Potsdam and on to Massena to the mall.

"Maggie come on! It will cheer you up, buying clothes always cheers you up."

Against her better judgment Maggie got out of the Suburban but her mind wasn't on clothes, it was on the boys, and Donnie, and Mike and Naples and Colton. It was split everywhere and she felt miserable and clothes shopping wasn't going to help. She even felt a little angry with Jillian for thinking she would enjoy shopping when she should have been pampering her at home with bowls of ice cream and telling her the things she wanted to hear.

"It's ugly. You look like a clown." Maggie walked away from the dressing room and sat on the bench to wait for Jillian to change out of the hideous outfit. She was miserable. She missed the boys and she felt guilty for leaving. She didn't feel happy to be home and she didn't feel like she could go back to Naples yet. She wanted to be at two days ago. She crossed her arms over her chest and gave death stares to everyone that passed her.

"What is wrong with you? Besides the obvious." Jillian sat on the bench next to her.

Maggie slammed the back of her head against the wall. "This was a stupid idea. I hate this! All I want is peace of mind. That's all I ever wanted. But I don't get that. All I ever get is my mind in pieces! I'm always thinking about this and thinking about that and worrying about this and worrying about that! I feel like I shouldn't have come home but I feel like I had to come home. Nothing makes sense, least of all this, shopping, what were you thinking?"

A mother and daughter coming in the doorway of the dressing room stopped, turned around and walked away. Maggie burst into tears.

"Aww, Maggie, we'll figure it out. I'm sorry I took you shopping. I should have been more sensitive. Let's go. It was a stupid idea, besides, you're scaring people." Jillian put her arm around Maggie's shoulders and pulled her in close.

"I used to love scaring people, now it makes me cry." Maggie laughed between sobs.

"If it's any consolation you still scare me. Come on. Let's go home."

"Can we stop and see the kids? I don't know why but I feel like I want to see them."

"Now you're really scaring me."

Pulling into Frank and Louise's driveway proved to be another validation for Maggie that everything looked right but nothing felt right. She'd heard the saying 'once you leave you can never go back home' and she was beginning to understand what it meant.

Louise ran outside and hugged Maggie as she was still getting out of the car.

"Oh. Okay. Hugs are...okay."

Louise laughed and hugged her tighter. "The kids and I have been cooking all day for you. I was going to send Frank over with the food but this is even better. We've made all the comfort foods; macaroni and cheese, meat loaf and mashed potatoes and gravy, chicken pot pie, chocolate chip cookies and what else? Hmm, oh, Rice Krispy Treats."

"Louise? I can't breathe."

Louise let go and stepped back so Maggie could get out of the car and then she grabbed her again and hugged her even tighter.

"Louise! Stop! I feel violated!"

"Oh Maggie you're such a teaser! Heavens I've forgotten how much I miss seeing you two together, remember when..."

"Yes. Can we go inside? It's cold out here."

Louise playfully tapped Maggie's shoulder. "Such a teaser." She let go of her and shuffled in her pink slippers to Jillian and pulled her into a bone crushing hug. "I hope you're not here to pick up the kids yet, we've barely scratched the surface of all the things we wanted to do. We're having such fun! Tell me you're not taking them yet."

"I...can't...breathe..."

Louise loosened her grip on Jillian and snickered. "Oh Jillian! You two are so comical! Come on in now, I'll make you some tea."

The living room floor was gone. Six chairs were strategically placed and covered with the biggest blanket they'd ever seen. The 'fort' covered three quarters of the living room and tractors, trucks, dolls, and multiple Lincoln Log buildings covered the other quarter.

"Oh! You added on?" Jillian stepped over the toys and buildings making her way to the fort. "What a unique place to add another room! I have to peek and see what you've done with the inside. So where are the kids Louise? Pete?! Shea?! Frank?! Are they napping maybe?"

"We're in here!" Pete giggled from inside the fort. "And we're not kids we're cowboys! And Grandpa's not a kid he's old!"

"Hey!" Frank stuck his head out just as Jillian reached for the edge of the blanket and her hand slapped his head.

"Frank! Oh my God! I'm sorry!"

"Let's hope you knocked some sense into him." Louise mumbled and disappeared in the kitchen.

Jillian climbed into the fort and twisted herself pretzel tight to fit into the tiny bit of free space left. Maggie tip-toed away and joined Louise in the kitchen.

"Oh perfect! Maggie I wanted to talk to you. Is Jillian…?" Louise tilted her head toward the living room and raised her eyebrows.

"Locked up in Fort Knox? Yes." Maggie pulled a chair out from the nineteen fifties retro style metal and marbled Formica table, except it wasn't retro it was original. She helped herself to a Rice Krispy Treat from an overflowing platter in the center of the table.

"Good!" Louise clasped her hands together. "I want to ask you how you are but first I have to ask you a favor."

She'd always suspected Louise was more than just a bumbling old fashioned country senior and she had an eerie feeling she was about to become a victim of Louise's other personality.

Louise slid into the chair opposite Maggie and reached across the table grasping Maggie's hand in hers. "I hope you're okay, sincerely and truly Maggie I hope you and Donnie are okay but what I need is…" Louise peered toward the doorway to the living room and lowered her voice. "I need you to stretch it out until George gets here. I know that sounds awful but for months now Frank has been dragging me from one thing to another trying to make me happy and all I want is to be here with my Grandkids. I can't take another single square dancing lesson or bird watching expedition. Please Maggie, please keep Jillian here with your troubles for a couple weeks!"

"Louise!" Maggie didn't know whether to laugh or be appalled. "You want me to use my problems to keep Jillian hostage here so you can play with her kids?!"

"No! Lord no! I want you to be okay, but I want you to pretend you're not, just for a little while, just until George comes."

Maggie laughed. And she was appalled.

"Ssh!" Louise scolded. "You are okay right? You do realize it wasn't such a bad thing your husband did don't you?"

Maggie pulled her hand out of Louise's and resumed eating her Rise Krispy Treat. "You don't think it was such a bad thing?"

"Maggie it *wasn't* such a bad thing. He made a mistake. They all do. He's a man! They're all flawed. If you throw him away now and try to find another man it's just going to be trading one set of flaws for another. The only difference is the degree of flaw. Is what Donnie did really that bad? He didn't do it for himself. He did it for you. Good Lord if I left Frank for every scatterbrained thing he did I would have enough frequent flyer points to travel around the world twice. So you'll do it? You'll keep Jillian occupied with your non-problems?"

"Ouch. That hurt!" Maggie put her hand over her heart. "Geez Louise you could at least be a little sympathetic!"

"Toughen up young lady, life is full of surprises and disappointments, you can't dramatize them all. You have to take the good and the bad."

"Good and bad what?" Jillian came through the kitchen doorway with Shea in her arms and Pete and Frank following closely behind.

Louise answered without skipping a beat. "The cookies, some aren't quite perfect but I told Maggie to keep them anyway. Just because they look bad doesn't mean they are bad."

Maggie stuffed the rest of the Rice Krispy treat in her mouth and chewed furiously. Someday someone else was going to expose the real Louise behind the floured apron and the innocent Granny act but she had too much on her plate to think about right now, that would have to be someone else's problem.

"I miss my kids so much more than I thought I could." Maggie told Jillian after spending an hour on the phone while eating perfect chocolate chip cookies. "D.J. and Dylan have a double date this weekend, Donnie's driving them to the movies. Derek got an award in science class. Donnie signed Daniel up for little league and Todd for t-ball. I've been gone two days and he's turned into Mr. Mom. I should be there. What am I doing here?"

"Did you talk to Donnie?"

Maggie shook her head.

Jillian put the plate of meatloaf and mashed potatoes and gravy on the table. They sat and began to eat. Maggie shoveled in food like there was no tomorrow and Jillian picked at the mashed potatoes while staring at Maggie waiting for her to continue.

Maggie felt her staring and looked up. "What?"

"I miss this so much. I love being us again, it's been too long, and I know it's only been two days since you left but Maggie you have to start thinking about what you really want to do."

"Why are you pushing me? You want me to move out so you can start getting the house ready for you and George don't you?"

Jillian rolled her eyes. "Of course not." She picked up her plate and reached for Maggie's.

"What are you doing?!" Maggie protested. "I'm not done."

"This isn't a meatloaf and potatoes moment, it's a mac n cheese moment."

"Seriously? We can't eat all the food Louise sent in one night!"

"Why not?" Jillian answered as she began scooping mac n cheese into bowls. "It's Louise, we'll be getting comfort foods like this every day, enough to feed the whole town, trust me."

Maggie and Jillian brought their bowls of mac n cheese to the living room. They ate for a few minutes in silence and then

Jillian broke it, "If you decide to, do you think you can forgive him?

"Forgive is a stupid word, I don't understand what it means. What's it mean?"

Jillian thought for a minute, opened her mouth a few times to answer but closed it again, finally she opened it and said, "Huh. I don't know. It doesn't mean forget. Live with it, I guess, but not hold it against him?"

"I can't quite decide what to do with it, I can't file it under things that piss me off because really you're right, he was trying to do what he thought was best for me, I think I'm starting to get that, I'm not there yet but I admit I'm starting to see it. His intentions were honorable even if it was a stupid thing to do. But I can't file it under forgiven and forgotten because I don't know what forgive means and you can't just make yourself forget something, how do you do that?"

"You can't. It's always going to be between you then won't it?"

"Yeah I mean if I just pretend it never happened it doesn't make it true that it never happened. I'm always going to know my diploma is a fake and I'm always going to know Donnie lied and deceived me. So what do I do with it? What would you do?"

Jillian stirred her mac and cheese around in the bowl, every few seconds she would stop and look off and then she would begin stirring again. "I don't know, it's a tough one. I'm trying to separate the issues and find the beginning."

"That would be the night I got pregnant."

Jillian looked up, surprised at first and then she laughed. "Idiot. I mean the beginning point for us, do we try to figure out how you and Donnie can move forward or do we try to figure out how to fix the diploma issue or how to live with knowing it's a fake, or do we start by figuring out how to deal with Mike? Or something else I'm not thinking about yet? I'm trying to think if someone else were telling me this story what I would tell them. Maybe you should get your GED. Then your diploma will be legit."

"But I already have a diploma. If I apply for to take the GED they'll see I already have a diploma and I would have to tell someone what happened. I don't even know exactly what happened."

"Then maybe that's where we have to start. We have to find out. If you want."

"How?"

"We go see Mike. You and me. We'll find out exactly what grades he changed, what classes, all that, get every last detail and then we can decide what to do with it."

"I don't know. I don't want to see Mike again. What about Donnie? Could he get in trouble for it?"

"It was too long ago, plus he didn't do anything except pay Mike, I don't know if Mike could still get in trouble but who cares?"

"I don't care if he gets in trouble. It would serve him right."

"So? Yes?"

"Let me think about it."

"We should do it Maggie. You should have all the information, all the facts and then you can decide what you want to do with it. And quite frankly it's now or never. Once you make a decision where to go from here you need to be sincere and be able to put it behind you. I'll do whatever you decide but I say we pay this Mike Jensen a visit."

"Quite frankly? No one talks like that! I don't know about paying Mike a visit but I do know this. You have got to purge yourself of everything N.J. that you've picked up over the last four years? Everything."

"Except George of course."

"Would that be out of the question?"

Jillian rolled her eyes. "So the GED isn't an option? Do we strike that off the to-do list."

"For now. I guess we can talk about it after we know the facts, *if* we find out the facts."

Jillian took a bite of her mac n cheese and stared off at nothing again.

"What?"

"Think about paying Mike a visit, I think we should, but in the meantime, I guess we need to revisit the idea of forgive and or forget."

"There is no forget, remember?" Maggie smirked at herself.

"You're not cute. You think you're cute but you're not."

"I'm pretty sure I am. This isn't getting us anywhere, all its doing is making me more confused and tired. I know it's probably helping at some level but it's just depressing me right now. Can we drop it for tonight? I'm feeling tears starting again."

"But we hardly talked."

"Then maybe it's your company."

"Oh nice. Bite the hand that feeds you," Jillian smiled and put her hand on Maggie's. "Seriously, we'll figure it out."

Maggie wished she hadn't done that. She might have made it up to bed before the tears spilled over but the simple touch of affection, though greatly appreciated, freed the tears. She missed the boys, she missed the house in Naples, Don, her new friends, her new life, and yes, she missed Donnie. If she got on a plane tomorrow she would miss Jillian, she would miss this house, Colton, home. So, what? Wherever you are you miss where you're not?

"Jillian? Do you think a person ever feels like they are where they belong?"

Jillian let go of her hand. "I thought you were too tired to talk."

"I am. But my mind isn't apparently. What do you think?"

"I think…yes. I think the secret is learning to accept. Life isn't easy Maggie, things are constantly changing, it's just the way it is. You can be content one minute but the next minute everything could change. It's the time continuum thing, life can't stay still and so things change. Sometimes it will feel right and sometimes it will feel wrong but it's going to keep changing so you have to either change with it or accept it."

"So you don't belong anywhere forever, you just belong to

the moment."

"Maybe. Isn't that what Don told you? Take life a little bit at a time? Maybe you feel like you don't belong because you're trying to belong to a time in the future or a time in the past. Maybe if you just try to focus on the moment you're in you'll feel like you belong."

"I feel like I belong in bed."

Maggie slept until eleven o'clock. She jumped in the shower and then moseyed downstairs in search of Jillian and a cup of coffee. She found both.

"What are you doing?" Jillian was sitting at the table with a pen and a pad of paper, her cell phone and the phone book.

"I talked to George this morning, he's coming next week and I thought I better start getting things ready."

"Coming next week as in moving here? The official move?"

"Yup! He has a moving company coming and packing our things up in four days and delivering here in five, they're going to take everything to Frank and Louise's to store in one of the barns for now, unless I find a place between now and then."

"My coming back messed everything up didn't it? You were supposed to move in here."

"It didn't mess anything up, it's fine. Maggie this is your house. Oh, um, but there is something I did that I need to tell you about though." She glanced at the clock and back to Maggie but before she had a chance to say anything more they heard the sound of a vehicle in the driveway, a door slamming and almost instantaneously Amazing Grace began playing.

"Who the hell is here?" Maggie jumped up and went to the front door. Jillian dropped her head in her hands.

It was *Quick and Courteous Carpets* or so the embroidery on the man's shirt said.

"No, I'm telling you I'm not getting new carpets, I would know if I ordered new carpets. I didn't order new carpets!"

Jillian ran to Maggie's side. "I did. That's the something I had to tell you. I called yesterday and they had a cancellation and said they could install them today otherwise it would be three weeks before they could do it. I figured why not? I went online and did the sizes and picked the colors. If you stay it's my gift to you and if you leave it's my gift to me."

The man, tall, thin, pony tail, weathered face, ripped jeans, turned his attention and clip board to Jillian. "Could you just sign here and tell me which room to start in and we'll get started."

Jillian took the clip board.

"What in your weird warped mind made you decide to call about new carpets? And when yesterday? We have carpets! What's wrong with these carpets?"

Jillian held the clip board in one hand and the pen poised to sign in the other. "Look at them Maggie. I have a baby. You have kids. No matter which one of us ends up staying here they needed to be replaced. They're…they're…disgusting. No offense."

Maggie looked at the perfectly good carpet behind her and then at Jillian and started giggling. Jillian put her hands on her hips and Maggie's giggle turned into a full out bubbled laughter. Pony tail man's discomfort climbed up a notch and he started juggling his measly weight from one leg to the other which only made Maggie laugh even harder.

"Should we come back? Later?" he asked.

"No!" Jillian signed the paper and shoved the clipboard at him. He took it and turned toward the *Quick and Courteous Carpet* van in the driveway. Jillian eased the door shut to the jamb without latching it so he would come back in without playing Amazing Grace again. "What is wrong with you? What's so funny?!"

"Jillian?! You lived in filth in your apartment! You were a chain smoker! There was nothing clean or sanitary within a five foot radius of anywhere you've ever been. Empty pizza boxes were decorations for you! What is wrong with me?! What is wrong with you?!" Her laughter began to finally subside through the effort of talking.

"I've changed. George likes clean."

"Ah, clean freak George. Of course. But Jillian you can't spend that much money on carpets! What if we do move back?"

"We?"

"Aw hell. I said *we* didn't I?" Maggie leaned against the wall and looked toward the ceiling. "Aw crap."

She slid down the wall and put her head on her knees. "I said we. I can't see the future as me Jill. It's we." Her voice hitched but this time it was tears that were choking her up. "I miss him."

The door opened and the end of a carpet roll appeared, levitated in the hallway and then moved the rest of way into the house. The man with the pony tail and thin girly hands held it mid way while another much more stout man with big beefy hands held it at the far end. Pony tail man stepped into the doorway and saw Maggie sitting on the floor against the wall.

"Oh God," he muttered. "Are you sure we shouldn't come back?"

"No!" Jillian grabbed Maggie's arm and pulled her up. "We're leaving. Wait, you won't steal anything will you? No of course you won't, sorry, okay, we'll be back in a couple hours. Go ahead, carpet away." She pulled their coats from the closet and practically pushed Maggie out the door.

"Where are we going?"

"We. You said we. There's something I have to show you."

Maggie sat back and buckled her seat belt. Jillian drove north on Pleasant Street to where the road split into a Y. If she veered right they would have ended up in Parishville, if she continued left they would have ended up on a dirt road, in the middle of the Y was Whispering Pines Cemetery. Jillian drove the Suburban up the incline and through the gate, pulled to the side, parked and got out. Maggie waited and watched. Jillian walked a bit and then stepped off the driveway and walked purposefully toward a specific grave. She stopped and touched the top of the grave and then looked back to the Suburban and waved for Maggie to come.

Her stomach growled. She debated staying right where she was. Jillian waved to her again, this time forcefully enough to make Maggie unbuckle her seat belt and get out. When she sided up to Jillian at the grave she read the inscription out loud. "Michael William Bentley. Geez, Jillian he was just a baby. Who is he?"

"I don't know. After Peter died I came here every day. I brought Champ with me and that fat old beagle stopped here to rest one time. I read the inscription and it broke my heart." She ran her fingers across the etching of the cradle. "He'd be in his forties now."

"He was three weeks old when he died. Is this what you wanted to show me? Why?"

"No it's not. I don't know why Champ stopped and laid on this grave that day but I haven't been able to come here without stopping and saying a little prayer since. Can't explain it. Come on."

They walked back to the driveway and climbed to the top of the hill and over the peak. Jillian left the driveway again and stepped to another grave. Maggie followed.

Peter W. Harper.

Jillian knelt in front of Peter's grave, kissed her hand and placed it on the gravestone over his name then she sat and motioned for Maggie to sit next to her.

"Jillian I get that you miss him and I don't mind being here with you but I'm not sure I want to sit…on him."

Jillian grabbed her leg and pulled her down. "Look."

Maggie looked. She'd seen Peter's grave many times. She wasn't seeing anything she hadn't seen before. "What?"

Jillian took Maggie's hand. "Look. That's the man I loved with all my heart. The man I will always love forever and ever. The man I was supposed to spend the rest of my life with. The man I *belonged* with. He's Pete's Dad but he should have been Dad to a bunch more kids. He should have, *we* should have had the rest of our lives together, day after day after day.

But we didn't." She squeezed her hand. "Donnie's not dead. If you love him, and we both know you do, forgive him. Forget it." She pointed at the headstone. "You never know when you won't be able to."

They sat hand in hand staring at the inscription on Peter's grave.

"Maggie I know you're going through a hard time I get that, but you have to stop dwelling in it. You said we. You said you couldn't see the future without him. So don't have a future without him. You and Donnie grew together again in Naples, you were happy, your whole family was happy, as much as I want you here…well not here…but here in Colton it just isn't the right place for you right now. You belong with Donnie, in Naples. A fake diploma isn't the end of the world. I know you feel like you need to solve that somehow but there may not be any solving to it. I think you should confront Mike and say what has to be said and then move on. I will respect and support you in whatever you decide but Maggie, you have to decide and if you ask me you belong with Donnie…in Naples."

Maggie let go of Jillian's hand and put her arm around her. "I'm sorry Peter died."

"Me too."

"Do you feel like you belong with George?"

"I do. I never thought I'd ever feel like I belonged anywhere after Peter died. I belonged with Peter. But I belong with George now."

"Do you think I'm stupid making such a big deal about the diploma?"

"No of course not, it's the moment you're in right now but that's what I'm trying to say Maggie, this moment is going to fall into the past but there will be a lot of moments ahead of you. Where do you want to be then? If I could accept this, surely Maggie you can accept a fake diploma can't you?"

Maggie reached out and touched Peter's headstone and traced the letters of his name. "I liked Peter."

"I know you did."

Maggie pulled her hand back and stood up. "Come on, let's go see Mike."

CHAPTER ELEVEN

"So what are you two up to today?" Louise asked while strategically bouncing Shea on one hip and straightening an apparently crooked picture frame with her free hand. She looked every bit the classic Grandmother; skirt, blouse, panty hose that were a shade too dark, flat sensible shoes and a flour dusted apron, the classic Grandmother from 1954.

Maggie and Jillian exchanged a glance before Jillian spoke. "Oh, visiting an old classmate, thought we might just drop in and surprise him, nothing very exciting, maybe a little lunch. Are you sure you don't mind me leaving the kids a bit longer?"

By the looks of the house and the kids lack of enthusiasm when they walked in Maggie was pretty sure Jillian couldn't pull the kids out of there if she'd tried.

"Oh I don't mind at all!" Louise bounced Shea and tweaked her nose. "We've already had our lunch. Shea helped me bake a little bit this morning and Pete has been keeping Frank out of trouble. I was just about to read them a book and put them down for their nap. Frank is taking Pete fishing after his nap."

"I am?" Frank shook his newspaper until it was rigid and completely covering the top half of his body, he hadn't turned a page since they'd been there. Toys were stacked a foot and a half high all around him and spilled from the couch to the floor near his feet.

"Never mind him. Couldn't they stay the day Jillian? Or…the night? One more night? We'll be fine and Maggie needs you more than the kids do right now." She threw Maggie a look that sent shivers down her spine. Jillian was too busy pulling Shea from Louise's arms to notice.

Louise reached out and started tickling Shea's neck. "We'll be fine won't we Shea? Won't we won't we?!"

Shea giggled. Frank shook his newspaper again and turned a page. Pete, dressed in Superman pajamas with a full red cape, Big Bird slippers and a raccoon hat ran past them. He had already run about a dozen circles around the living room, arms out Superman style and cape and raccoon hat tail flying behind him.

"Pete did you have a bowl of sugar for lunch? And what's that thing you're wearing on your head? It's gross." Jillian grabbed him when he passed and planted a kiss on his cheek before letting him free again.

"It was my Daddy's and when he was four he could fly." Pete yelled back to her before disappearing down the hallway.

"He *thought* he could fly." Louise corrected.

"Aww." Maggie and Jillian said simultaneously.

"Did Peter really think he could fly?" Jillian held her hand over her heart, a gesture Maggie still caught her doing when she talked about Peter and the good memories.

"He did, until he tried to prove it to some of the boys in his kindergarten class." Louise shook her head.

Jillian smiled. "What happened?"

"Oh he flew," Frank answered from behind his newspaper which Maggie was pretty sure he was only holding to avoid having to run after Pete. "He flew straight from the desk to the floor."

"Nearly broke his nose." Louise shook her head. "It was swollen for a week. Maggie, could you come to the kitchen with me? I have some treats to send home with you."

No! Not the kitchen alone with Louise, not another 'put

your big girl panties on talk', Maggie glanced at Jillian who was too preoccupied with making sure Pete didn't try flying.

"Sure. Umm, Jillian isn't there something else you wanted to tell Frank and Louise though?"

"Oh! Right!" Jillian's eyes followed Pete but she glanced at Louise. "Guess what? George is moving up next week!"

Maggie saw the look on Louise's face and thanked her lucky stars, crisis averted. Louise clapped her hands together and grinned from ear to ear. "That's wonderful! So you're staying here? You're not going back to New Jersey?"

"We're staying here! He's having the moving people come in a few days. Pete slow down!"

Louise grabbed Jillian and pulled her into a bear hug practically squeezing Shea flat. "That's wonderful!" Jillian tried to pull away but she couldn't break free. "That's so wonderful!" When she finally did break free she rearranged Shea and made sure she was okay and then brushed the flour dust from their clothes.

Louise turned to Maggie. "So you'll be going back to Florida then?"

Shoot. Think. "Frank what's the weather forecast? Feels like snow if you ask me. Is there snow forecasted today?"

They all looked at her like she was crazy. Even Frank dropped the paper and looked at her over his reading glasses. She looked from Frank to Jillian and shrugged her shoulders. "It's cold, just saying."

"We haven't worked everything out quite yet," Jillian said. "We'll let you know as soon as we figure out the details."

Louise looked from Jillian to Maggie. "Maggie let's get those treats from the kitchen shall we?"

Maggie felt perspiration popping out around her hairline, "Um…"

Frank put his newspaper down and stood from the couch, "I'll get them, Maggie why don't you give me a hand?"

Louise took a step toward the kitchen but Frank put his hand on Maggie's arm and guided her ahead of Louise. "We've got it Louise." Once they were in the kitchen Frank let go of her arm. "Pay no attention to Louise, she's pushy but she means well. I think." He took a bag from the cupboard and began filling it with baggies of treats, Maggie's mouth watered as she watched him put in bags of cookies and bars and breads. "Let me guess, she tried to get you to keep Jillian and the kids here and now she's trying to get you to leave so they can settle in at your house?"

Maggie didn't know what to say, yes would be the answer but she felt Louise's evil eye burning her through the wall. She watched the smaller baggies of cookies dropping into the bigger bag.

"Pay no attention to her, you do what you have to do, Jillian and George will be fine, there's plenty of places they can find to live without you feeling pressured. Louise is, she's just lonely and wants them here and settled as quickly as possible. I think she's afraid to believe it until it actually happens."

"It's going to happen," Maggie said.

"I know. But she won't rest until it does. Cookie?" He opened one of the baggies and pulled out a mouth watering chocolate chip cookie the size of a plate.

"Oh yeah!"

Frank handed it to her and pulled another out for himself before resealing the baggie and putting it in the big bag. "So what do you think of Florida? Must be getting pretty hot there now isn't it?"

"It is but all the buildings are air conditioned and practically every house has a pool. The boys love it."

Frank nodded and chewed. "And you? And Donnie? Do you love it too?"

"Maggie squinted her eyes at him. "Are you…doing the Louise thing but in a Frank way?"

Frank chewed and took another bite and chewed.

"Okay," Maggie conceded. "I love it. And Donnie loves it."

"Good." Frank shoved the rest of the cookie in his mouth and picked up the bag of treats and left her standing alone in the kitchen.

"Frank and Louise are weird," Maggie told Jillian when they got back in the Suburban and were backing out of the driveway. "I mean trustworthy with your kids and all but when George gets here and you two are starting your life here together, you better watch them close. Especially Louise."

"Maggie you're preaching to the choir. It's me Jillian, remember? I'm the one that drove from New Jersey how many times to help her fix, tend, or solve some non-existent problem?"

"Right. Okay. So what do you think is up with her? You think she's really just lonely? You think after you move up here she'll be normal?"

"I don't know. She was always a little bit unconventional. She's cookie cutter senior citizen Grandma but she has a hidden side to her that comes out now and then. I'm hoping it goes away when we come back, but we have enough to think about right now without solving Louise. So which will it be first? Lunch or Mike?"

"Lunch! Of course!"

"So what's the plan?" Maggie asked Jillian after a quick but filling lunch.

Jillian drove out of the restaurant parking lot. "What do you mean what's the plan? We discussed this already. We go to FastTech, we walk in and we don't leave until we get answers."

Answers. What exactly did they expect Mike to tell them that they didn't already know. Maggie was starting to think this visit to Mike was a bad idea. She believed Donnie and it all made sense, in a warped hard to get your mind around way, even the part about Mandy fit right.

Maggie looked at Jillian who seemed cool and collected while every part of her was starting to sweat or shake, "Yeah but that doesn't really sound like a plan. I'm kind of getting nervous. I think we should come up with a new plan. Like maybe you should go in and I'll stay in the car and be the lookout person."

"The lookout person?! We're not robbing him we're just going to shake him up a bit and get some information. And what do you mean you're nervous? You don't get nervous about stuff like this. You usually love confrontations. You love pinning people to the wall and mentally beating the crap out of them. It's your thing."

"Yeah, I do love to do that. Usually. But that's when it's people that need it, I'm doing them a favor, this feels different. I liked Mike, remember? I hate him now that I know what he did but what if I see him and all I see is the nice guy? He was nice to me Maggie, I liked him. What if that's all I see and I can't beat him up? What if *he* beats *me* up?"

"Oh that will NOT happen! Think diploma. Think about this whole mess and how it's his fault. Regardless of what you feel for Donnie right now think about what he did to him and how that effected him and you and your whole lives because of it, he bribed him, not just once, not just twice…"

Jillian was getting fired up and once she reached a point she would be unstoppable. "Okay, right. Stop. Hate him. Thanks."

"And he lied to you, right to your face, over and over, the whole time you were working there."

"Okay, hate him. Got it."

"He's scum Maggie. Just keep thinking about how different your life might be if he hadn't done what he did. He had no right to interfere in your life like that. He's…"

"Okay!"

It was too late. Jillian was on a roll. If she reciting all the ways her life might have been better Maggie was going to strangle her. "Maggie think about it, what if Donnie hadn't started drinking so much then, maybe he would have been a better father, maybe…"

"Okay I got it!" Maggie yelled. "I wouldn't mind pinning you to a wall right about now."

Jillian turned and shot Maggie a look of surprise. "No need to get testy, but hold that anger, that's good. What do you think he'll do? Or say?"

"The road Jillian! Watch the road!" As soon as Jillian turned back and had her eyes on the road Maggie leaned her head against the headrest and sighed. "I don't know, whenever I asked him what happened he always evaded the question, he just kind of shrugged it away, said it wasn't important anymore. All he ever told me was… Oh My God…wait…he did say he played a computer prank, I'd forgotten all about that, he said he played a prank on Donnie and when I asked him what kind of prank he said a computer prank."

"So why is that Oh My God? We already know what happened. I want to go in there with our fists up, not literally, don't do that okay? But I want to go in there and blindside him. The only thing I'm worried about is that those computer guys are quiet until something triggers them and then they break. Like really break. I don't want him flipping out and having people read our obituaries in the paper tomorrow. He's more the cowering type isn't he?"

Maggie closed her eyes and tried to conjure an image of Mike angry but she couldn't remember one. The Mike she worked for didn't mesh with the Mike that Donnie described. She could only remember him being patient and mellow, even thoughtful bringing her mocha's and always paying for her lunches and making her laugh.

"What are you thinking?" Jillian couldn't keep still, when she wasn't asking Maggie questions she was tapping her thumbs on the steering wheel.

"I'm thinking that I'm not sure what we expect to get out of this. Why are we doing this again?"

"Closure. To find out the facts. To let him know you know. Do NOT tell me you're getting cold feet."

"I'm not getting cold feet."

Jillian pulled into the parking lot and pulled the Suburban into the space next to Mike's truck. Maggie had considered that he might be out of town, had even half hoped it, but there was his truck. This was going to happen.

Jillian put the Suburban in park and took her seat belt off.

"Okay." Maggie took a deep breath. "Go ahead. I've got you covered." She looked out her window toward the road and then scanned the parking lot. "Clear. Go."

Jillian rolled her eyes. "Come on." She climbed out of the Suburban and closed her door, waited for Maggie.

Maggie reluctantly opened her door and joined Jillian. "Are you sure about this? You still think this is a good idea? I may have overreacted you know. It's hard to believe but I tend to do that."

"If we don't do it now we never will. You'll always wonder what would have happened if we had done it. So we do it. Now. Do you want to know the details or not?"

"Fine." Maggie led them to the door but slowed as they got closer and then stepped back to let Jillian lead them inside. Jillian grabbed a hold of her shirt to make sure she didn't try to get away and opened the door and the stepped inside.

The office was empty. No Mandy. No one at the desk. The flower pictures were still arranged on the wall just as she had left them. She stood half next to and half behind Jillian and peered around Jillian at her desk, she had the same feeling she did when she first walked into her house the other day.

"Hello?" Jillian called out and Maggie jumped. "Anyone here? Hello?"

Mike stepped from the hallway and into the office stopping so suddenly when he saw Maggie that half the coffee in his cup spilled over the rim.

"Maggie." He looked past Jillian and stared at her.

Jillian took a step forward and left Maggie feeling exposed. "Mike Jensen." She took another step forward. "Most likely to break into national security. Wasn't that what it said in the yearbook? Yup, that was it, Mike Jensen, most likely to break into national security. What it should have said was Mike Jensen, most likely to break into the guidance counselor's computer. That's what it *should* have said, right Maggie?"

Mike's face visibly paled.

Maggie flinched. The Mike that was standing in front of them was the Mike that brought her Mochas. But that Mike was a liar and a fake. He made believe he was her friend and he was anything but. She felt her nervousness fall aside and Jillian's anger fuel her. No friend is better than a fake friend. She hated him. At this very second she realized how much she hated him.

Mike slowly began to shake his head.

"Don't even try to deny it." Jillian took another step forward. "Do you have any idea, *any idea* what you put Maggie and Donnie through? You conceited selfish stupid…" Jillian stumbled for the word that would define everything she felt about him and what he had done.

"Loser?" Mike finished the sentence.

"No," Maggie finally spoke. "Asshole."

Jillian was too fired up to let Maggie take the reign. "Who do you think you are anyway? How do you think you have the right to screw around with other people's lives like you did? And don't give me that 'we were just kids' crap you told Maggie. Did you really think she would never find out that her diploma is a fake? That you changed her grades?"

Mike side stepped so that he was facing Maggie directly. "Maggie?

Jillian stepped back in front of him. "Don't try to sweet talk her you ass, we didn't come here so you could talk your way out of it we came here to get answers to help Maggie figure out what to do to fix the screw up you created. You're going to talk, you're going to tell us exactly what grades you changed and how many and anything else we need to know and you will NOT try to convince her you're anything but the low life scum you are!"

Mike stared directly in Jillian's eyes and listened to every word she said and when she was done his expression was somber. But there was something else.

He stepped aside again and looked directly at Maggie. "I didn't change your grades."

"Don't lie your way out of this!" Jillian screamed. She actually grabbed his arm but he shook out of her grasp and continued to stare into Maggie's eyes.

"Maggie I did a lot of stupid things I admit it, but I didn't change your grades."

Jillian looked at Maggie and saw the conflicted look on her face, did she believe him?! Jillian shoved Maggie to the side and got in Mike's face. "DO NOT…"

"Stop!" Mike held his hand up. "Stop!" He took a deep breath and sighed, and it seemed to Maggie when he spoke again that all his energy had left with the sigh. "Come in the back. Sit down. We'll talk."

"No!" Jillian screamed just as Maggie said "Okay".

They looked at each other and Jillian backed down.

"Your call," she said.

Maggie led the way to the back.

Mike sat in a chair at the round table in his office and nodded for them to do the same. Once they were seated he rubbed his hands together either buying time while he chose his words or waiting for one of them to speak first, Maggie wasn't sure which. She couldn't collect her own thoughts beyond that he looked like a praying mantis and maybe, just maybe, her diploma was legit, but then Donnie would have been lying. Why? That was absurd, Donnie wasn't lying. So Mike was.

"You have two seconds to start explaining and you better not try to lie your way out of it. I want the truth Mike, the *truth*." She looked to Jillian and received a look of approval.

"Okay," Mike took a deep breath and exhaled slowly, he focused at the center of the table avoiding eye contact with both of them. "Okay, here's what happened. I have to start at the beginning so just…listen. A bunch of us, computer nerds as you cool kids called us, went to a party in Potsdam one night and, and I had a drunken one night thing with a girl I didn't even know, had never even met before…and she got pregnant. I freaked out…"

Jillian slammed her fist on the table. "We're not here to hear about poor Mike…"

"You want to hear what happened or not?" Mike glared at Jillian. "If you want me to tell you the truth you need to let me tell it so shut up and listen." He briefly glanced at Maggie before returning his eyes to the center of the table. "I knew you were pregnant, everyone knew. So I, this sounds so stupid now even to me but it's what happened... I don't think Donnie and I ever spoke two words to each other but I didn't know what else to do. I figured since you were pregnant maybe he would be able to help me out, give me some advice or something. Rumor was you two were keeping your kid and I definitely didn't want to but I thought maybe he looked into abortion stuff, maybe he'd thought about it, knew what to do. I was scared shitless and I couldn't tell my parents and she said she'd do whatever I wanted but if I wanted her to have an abortion I had to pay for it. I looked online, found out what I could but I thought maybe he could fill in the blanks. We were stupid kids, I wasn't thinking clearly and he seemed like the only choice I had."

"So you what? Hacked the school computer and found out Maggie was failing and bribed him?"

"No. I stalked him. I tried talking to him once. All I said was his name and he laughed at me and made some comment to the other jocks about the computer geek. He was a prick. All the jocks were. So I stalked him, I hung around wherever he was, just out of range, just close enough to listen but far enough that he didn't notice me. Not that he would have. I was hoping maybe I would hear something I could use, something that would make him listen to me and it worked. One time I was standing off to the side of where Donnie and a bunch of the jocks were sitting in study hall and I heard him talk about having to do your homework for you because you were always puking and sick and stuff."

Mike leaned against the back of his chair and glanced at Maggie and then briefly at Jillian. He pushed his chair out and stood up. Maggie's and Jillian's eyes followed him but neither spoke. He stood nervously for a few seconds, his eyes shifting around the room and then he sat back down again. He looked directly at Maggie.

"I just wanted to talk to him at first. He was right. I *was* a geek. You guys know that, everyone knew it. Donnie was Mr. Star Athlete but he wasn't all that smart. I might have been a geek but I *was* smart. So when I heard him saying he was doing your homework I got an idea. I decided to tell him you were failing English and that you wouldn't graduate but that I could fix it. It could have backfired on me so easily, all he had to do was go to the English teacher and ask her but I was counting on him being too stupid and paranoid. It shouldn't have worked but it did. I told him to meet me one day after school, that I had information he needed to know and he did. And that's when I told him. I knew he wouldn't want the teachers knowing he was doing your homework and I knew he didn't want you to fail. It was a catch 22 for him." Mike sighed. "So that's what happened."

Maggie stared at the wall behind Mike trying to match his story with Donnie's story, trying to grasp the possibility that she wasn't failing and that her diploma wasn't a fake, but Jillian wasn't about to let a silent second pass.

"You made up the whole thing?! And you were counting on Donnie not checking into it and not telling anyone?! So then you bribed him for the money?"

"I told him I needed money for the abortion and if he paid me I would fix the grades in the computer and no one would ever know."

"And he did and then you bribed him again! And again!"

"I gave the money to Denise. I thought it was done. Done with Donnie, done with Denise, I thought we would just graduate and everyone would go their own way and that would be that, I could put it behind me, pretend it never happened. But then she told me it wasn't enough, she needed more."

Maggie shook her head. "But she never had the abortion."

"No she didn't. But I didn't know that. Honestly Maggie I swear what I told you was true, I didn't know she never had the abortion until just a few months ago."

Jillian leaned forward. "Wait. So you're saying you made the whole thing up about the grades and you counted on Donnie being stupid enough to just believe you and pay you, not once but twice and then you gave the money to the girl for an abortion and you thought it was all over, done. You just graduated and ran away and never thought about it again?"

Mike stood up and pushed his chair out behind him.

"No I thought about it every single freaking day! I thought it would all be over and I could forget about it but no Jillian, I didn't forget about it!"

Jillian jumped out of her seat and leaned across the table. With her face just inches from his she screamed, "No you didn't forget about it you kept bribing him! You kept bribing him from wherever you went you piece of crap!"

They stood face to face, waiting for the other to make a move while Maggie sat with her head cupped in her hands, listening and not listening.

"Stop," she whispered.

"Stop," she whispered again louder although neither had said another word.

Then she yelled, "Just stop and let me think!"

Jillian and Mike straightened and looked at Maggie.

"This is crazy! This whole damn thing started because I didn't do my own homework. That's where it all started. If I just did my own damn homework none of this would have happened!"

"Maggie that doesn't excuse…"

"Jillian, you said you might have paid him too if he came to you! I probably would have too if I were in Donnie's shoes."

"Maggie, that's not…"

"It *is* the point. Jillian I know you want to punch him and he deserves it but I can't ignore the fact that *I* didn't do my homework. *I* went out looking for a job. *I* took this job knowing there was bad history between them. *I* worked for him without even telling Donnie who I was working for!"

Jillian didn't take her eyes off Mike. "But he hired you! He hired you and he even told Donnie you were looking for a job. Maggie he pretended to be your friend. He is *not* your friend. Do not turn this all around now!"

Mike didn't take his eyes off Maggie. "If you remember

Maggie, technically I didn't hire you my daughter did and after she walked out I told you I didn't think it was a good idea. I should have stopped it right then and there. I didn't expect you to actually take the job but *you* called *me* a few weeks later remember? For all I knew Donnie had let the whole thing go. You were good for business. And then we became friends. That's how it went."

"You never changed my grades?" Maggie asked.

"No, I never changed your grades."

"Everything, *everything* is all because you made up one lie when you were seventeen years old and needed money to pay for your girlfriend's abortion that she never had?"

Mike's shoulders slumped.

"I was good for business and *then* we became friends?"

"That's the way it went." Mike's shoulders were still slumped but his voice betrayed his posture.

Maggie stood up. "Jillian, I need a minute with Mike. Wait for me in the car."

"What? No…"

"Please!"

Jillian hesitated but she eventually, reluctantly, turned and left them alone.

CHAPTER TWELVE

Jillian wasn't to the Suburban yet when she heard the door slam behind her and turned around. She stopped. And stared. She couldn't believe her eyes. Maggie was grinning from ear to ear. She was also sprinting toward her with her right arm tucked into herself like she was clutching and protecting the Holy Grail.

"What…"

"Get in the car! Go! Go!" Maggie screamed as she ran passed her and skidded to a stop in front of the passenger door. Reaching out with her left arm she opened it and jumped in. "Come on! Move!"

Jillian darted to the car and jumped in the driver's side.

"Go Go GO!" Maggie yelled.

She started the Suburban and pushed the pedal to the floor, the tires squealed and Maggie burst out laughing. Jillian stole a glance at her arm still tucked into herself so tightly her hand was hidden in the folds of her shirt. "What did you take? What's going on?!"

Maggie tried to catch her breath to answer but a pickup truck coming straight at them laid on its horn and Jillian swerved the Suburban around it and into the southbound lane of traffic. Maggie doubled over laughing and when she finally got control of herself enough she sat up and reached behind her with her left hand and pulled the seatbelt across her shoulder and arm and buckled it.

"What did you take?" Jillian asked as she struggled with her own seatbelt and fastened it.

"Nothing." Maggie began laughing all over again.

"What's in your hand then?"

"Nothing." Maggie managed to squeak out.

Jillian peered in the rearview mirror and cranked the wheel swerving across the right hand southbound lane and pulled to the side in a parking space. "What is going on?!"

Maggie unbuckled her seatbelt and gingerly pulled her right arm away from her body. Her knuckles were red and swollen. "I punched him."

Jillian's eyes opened as wide as saucers and she slowly unbuckled her seatbelt and leaned over to look at Maggie's hand. "You did not," she whispered, but seeing the bruising already turning an ugly shade of purple she added, "Oh my God you did."

"I didn't like his attitude," Maggie said nonchalant and she burst out laughing again. "And it didn't feel finished. But it feels finished now."

"Maggie!" Jillian grinned. "Oh my God!! What if he calls the police?!"

"He's not going to call the police. Trust me. It hurt me more than it hurt him. And he said he supposed he deserved it. He did."

Jillian held her hand out toward Maggie's hand as if to touch it and then pulled it back. "Does it hurt? Is it broken?"

Maggie cringed through her grin. "I'm thinking yes."

"Oh My God! It's broken?! It hurts? Of course it hurts! Should I take you to the hospital? I have to take you to the hospital!"

"I'm thinking yes again. But let's get our story straight first. I punched a wall, at home, I was mad at the…the…carpet color. I was under a lot of stress. I lost my temper."

"Okay, got it. Carpet. Stress. Are you sure you didn't hurt

him?"

"He has a hard head, he'll need some heavy duty aspirin and a band aid or two but not an emergency room."

"Are you sure?"

"I'm sure."

Jillian signed Maggie's cast, 'Nice job Slugger! Let the mending begin' and Maggie knew she meant more than the two fractured bones in her hand.

"I still don't know if I overreacted or not but I've made some decisions," she told Jillian later that night. After they arrived home from the emergency room they admired the new carpets and then sat on the couch eating dinner in the form of a mounded plate of Louise's cookies.

"I don't think you overreacted I think he deserved it, I just wish you hadn't sent me out. I would have loved to see you punch him."

"Oh no I don't mean that, I didn't overreact then, he deserved it. I meant by getting on a plane the very next morning after Donnie told me. I miss the boys, never thought I'd say that but I do. I miss Donnie too. And Don, I feel like he's a part of our family now, I mean you know, our immediate family. I love who we were becoming and I love the possibilities of who we might be, together, without all this mess and his drinking and all the old stuff in the way. So, I've decided I want a fresh start, a new beginning."

Jillian jumped up and practically knocked the plate of cookies off the couch and onto the new carpet, three hands reached out and caught it just before it toppled to the floor. With her two hands and Maggie's one they slid the plate safely toward the back of the couch and then Jillian wrapped her arms around Maggie and hugged her, carefully avoiding her arm. "That's so awesome!"

"But," Maggie said when she pulled away, "I haven't decided if I want home to be here or there."

"You've made the hard decision right? Here or there, that

will come."

Maggie squinted at Jillian. "You sound like a Dr. Seuss book."

Jillian ignored her. "Would Don consider moving back here?"

"I doubt it. Actually I know he wouldn't. His life is there now. He's happy there, but he's happier with us there."

"Would you move back here without him?"

Maggie picked up another cookie and nibbled on it. "The thing is, the boys are so much happier there, Donnie's happier there, and I'm happier there."

Jillian frowned. "So what's the problem? It sounds like there isn't a decision to make. Besides, you might be wanted here now, there's probably a mug shot of you on the wall at the Potsdam Police Station."

"Maggie Kennedy Conners on the lamb! Hey, speaking of lamb do we have any mac n cheese left?"

"Lamb…wait…what? How many pain killers did you take?"

"I thought every eight hours was a suggestion? Never mind, cookies are fine." She took another bite of her cookie and smiled, "So you think I should call Donnie and talk to him? In Naples? Should I tell him what I did?" She held her cast up, "And speaking of that, tell me one more time, why did we get new carpet again?"

"I think you should sleep and decide everything in the morning. On one pain killer."

In the morning Maggie decided to take two pain killers and finish off the rest of the mac n cheese. With one working hand it made more sense to grab a fork and eat it cold and straight from the bowl which was how Jillian found her when she wandered in a few minutes later. "That's gross." She scowled and went to the coffee pot and poured a cup of coffee.

"Wake up. I have something big to tell you." Maggie made a big production of pulling out a chair for Jillian and patting the seat to hurry her along.

Jillian obediently went to the seat and took a long sip of her coffee. "How could you have something big to tell me? We just went to bed. There hasn't been time for anything to happen."

"Nothing happened but we didn't get a chance to talk about it last night and I've been dying to tell you since I woke up this morning. I guess after the showdown with Mike some things cleared in my head. I don't know if I overreacted or not but I've made some decisions. I don't mean about this, I'm glad I slugged him no matter how much it still hurts," she lifted her cast, "I mean about getting on a plane the morning after Donnie told me about Mike. The thing is, I miss the boys, I never thought I'd say that but I do miss them. I miss Donnie too. And Don. Jillian, I think I'm ready for a new beginning and I think I want it to happen in Naples."

Jillian choked on her coffee and put the cup back down on the table before she spilled it. "Oh my God!" She couldn't decide whether to laugh or go along with it.

"I know right?! So you're excited for me? I'm doing the right thing?" Maggie leaned against the back of her chair and waited for Jillian to jump up and hug her or something but she didn't. She sat there staring at her with her mouth half open. "What? Why aren't you excited? I thought you were pushing for this?"

"Maggie? What do you remember from last night? After the emergency room, what do you remember?"

Maggie thought for a minute, "I remember leaving the E.R. and craving mac n cheese, it's gone by the way you think Louise will make us some more? And I remember…hmm, not much. Why?"

Jillian put her hand over her mouth to hide the smirk she couldn't make go away.

"What? What's funny? Why are you acting so weird?"

Jillian's smirk grew wider. "Wait!" she put her hand out to stop Maggie from talking and rolled her eyes to the ceiling. "Wait, let me think!"

"What?!"

Jillian snapped her hand at Maggie to silence her. "Okay," she put her hand down and sat back. "It's just that I had to sort this out in my mind, obviously you don't remember but we talked last night, for a while actually. You already told me your decision, that's why I didn't seem crazy excited for you. But I was last night. I guess you just don't remember. So…I guess you also don't remember telling me I could keep the Kitchen Aid appliances? That's alright." Jillian looked down at that table top and feigned disappointment. "It was probably the meds talking."

Maggie's eyes widened, her glance slid to the Kitchen Aid mixer that sat on the counter. "No! Not my Kitchen Aid stuff! I didn't, did I? Oh, man I *love* those!"

"Yeah, no I know you do, it's okay, I should have known it was the meds talking. Don't worry about it. I always meant to get my own anyway. I'll just have to get my own, it's fine."

"Aww crap! I told you that? I said you could keep them? All of them?"

Jillian waved her hand through the air. "It's fine, take em, I know how much you love them."

Maggie closed her eyes and opened them again. "No," she groaned. "If I said you can have them you can have them. I guess I owe you that much for dropping everything and coming to my rescue."

"Well, if you're sure? But I'm definitely not keeping that original Rothko hanging in your room, that's way too valuable."

Maggie dropped her head on the table and moaned.

"Don't worry there's no way I'd keep it, besides it's ugly even though it still somehow looks great hanging over the bed. But it's yours, I won't keep it, you take it."

Maggie lifted her head an inch off the table and muttered, "Tell me I didn't say you could have it, tell me it's not true…"

"It's not true. You didn't say I could have it. You said you would leave it here and I could enjoy it. But still, that's neither here nor there, it's yours."

"Aughhhh, I hate medication!" She banged her head

against the table. "I'll leave it here."

"Oh, well if you're sure? So, back to you and Donnie, when are you going to tell him?"

Maggie lifted her head. "Tell him? Oh, right. Tonight when he's home from work and the boys are settled in enough that we can really talk." She got up and shuffled to the counter. She paused and looked back at Maggie and then turned around again and picked up the coffee carafe muttering, "My Rothko…my Rothko."

Maggie sat on the bed in her bedroom holding her cell phone in her good hand staring at the Rothko while trying to mentally rehearse what to say to Donnie. She'd started to dial twice already and hit delete both times before she'd finished. Everything she'd practiced in her mind all day long sounded great then but not so great now that it was evening and time to make the call.

First thing this morning, while she and Jillian talked over coffee, the words flew out and everything made sense, it was black and white. She would call Donnie in the evening and tell him that she was sorry she acted so spontaneously but it was such a shock that she needed to get away to clear her head and put everything in perspective. He would understand. She would tell him how she felt when she walked into the house and how she realized that she considered Naples home now. He would agree. She would tell him how she and Jillian went to Mike's to confront him and what he said and then she would tell him that she punched him…and fractured a couple bones in her hand. He would laugh.

But somehow throughout the day of talking and visiting at Frank and Louise's, taking the kids out for lunch, going for a walk and settling back in for the evening, the certainty of how the conversation would go lessened. She practiced saying she was sorry in front of the mirror in the bathroom when she put her make up on. While she sat on Dylan's weight bench in the basement she played with words trying to find the best ones that would convey the sense of their home not feeling like home anymore. She mentally replayed the entire visit with Mike while she and Jillian went for a walk, imagining both parts of the conversation as she told Donnie the story.

As she and Jillian sat on the couch and ate the chicken pot pie that Louise sent home with them she was comfortable with what she would say but the grayness of how Donnie would react began to seep in. What if he didn't forgive her for running away? He hadn't called her either. Was he giving her time to figure things out or had he not called because he didn't want to talk to her?

She glanced at the clock. Eight twenty-four. She glanced at the dresser, it looked almost the same as it did the day she left. The only thing different was that one side was piled with the clothes she'd thought about wearing today and then decided not to. And Donnie's wallet. He'd always put his wallet on the back right corner of the dresser. It was the only spot on the top of the dresser he claimed, one tiny little area for his wallet. She felt a wave of guilt. Was that one little corner all he wanted or had she, over time, simply pushed him into a corner?

She held her phone up and dialed.

On the third ring she heard his voice, he would have seen her name on his phone and known it was her but he still answered as if he didn't. "Hello?" But he had, she heard the apprehension in his voice.

"I'm sorry I only gave you one tiny corner on the top of the dresser."

She watched the clock tick off the seconds as neither spoke, five, six, ten.

"It's..." he cleared his throat. "It's okay, I don't need much."

Maggie felt her whole body relax. She closed her eyes and felt the threat of tears and swallowed them back. She smiled and felt the rush of happiness and relief and excitement at what was to come. "I love you."

The clock ticked one second and then two.

"I love you too." Donnie cleared his throat again. "Are you coming home?"

Home. Home wasn't Colton. Home wasn't Naples. Home was with Donnie and for the first time in her life it was clear. Home was Colton. Home was Naples. Home was wherever she and Donnie decided to make it. "Yes."

"Tomorrow?"

She laughed. "Are the boys that bad?! How about the day after? I'd like to spend one more day with Jillian and say goodbye to the kids and Frank and Louise. Would you mind if I stay one more day?"

She heard the relief in Donnie's voice when he spoke. "Sure. The boys have been pretty good actually, well, Todd's grounded and we had to have a guy come clean the pool and get all the body parts out of the filter but…"

"Body parts?!"

"Just a bird. Forget I mentioned it. So, are you packing things up and sending things here or what's the plan?"

Maggie thought for a second, looked at the Rothko. "I think I'll leave everything, unless there's something you want me to send? I kind of like the freshness of how we were living there, the new start, you know?"

"Works for me."

She smiled. "There's a lot of things I have to tell you. We paid a visit to Mike, Jillian and I. I wish we were together for me to tell you this but I think you should know, are you alone? Are you sitting down?"

Three seconds ticked by. "I'm out by the pool, the boys are in the house, is it bad?"

"Mike didn't change my grades. He lied to you about it. I wasn't failing. I'll tell you everything when I'm home."

Donnie was silent while the second hand ticked halfway around the clock.

"Donnie?"

"I'm here."

"Let it sink in. I know you'll go through a whole range of stuff as it does but I'm putting this whole damn thing behind me, once it sinks in I'm really hoping you can put it behind you too. And there's one more thing. I'm coming home with a cast on my hand."

"What?! What happened?"

"Let's just say Mike's face ran into my hand."

No doubt Donnie would spend the night, and who knew how long after that, sorting his thoughts and emotions about the whole thing but for the moment all he could do was laugh. And laugh. The three times he tried to speak he got one clear word out before the rest were obliviated with laughter. She guessed it was partly that he did find it funny but also that it was a release of all the tension and worry and anger and all the other things that had tied him in knots the last few days, and months, and years. She supposed he deserved a good laugh. She didn't mind, she was glad he reacted this way rather than blowing up in anger but still, how long could a person hold a phone to their ear listening to someone laugh?

"I'll call you tomorrow." She heard an abbreviation in the laughter and a sound that was probably the word 'okay' and then the laughter started again. She took the phone from her ear and put her finger on the end button. And then she had a terrible thought and snapped the phone back to her ear, "Donnie! Don't tell the boys I punched someone!!" but he'd already hung up.

When Maggie woke on her last full day in Colton she laid in bed memorizing everything she could see from where she lay, which was redundant since it was pretty much all well engraved in her memory anyway. Still, it was something she couldn't *not* do. It was bitter sweet, her last full day in the home and the town that defined who she was, had always been, and in many ways always would be.

With the ceiling and every flaw memorized Maggie rolled to her side and stared out the window. Ninety nine point nine nine nine percent of the population probably never heard of the town of Colton, which was kind of what made it so special, it was so very much like every other small town America and yet so very much not like every other small town America. It was Colton. It was *her* Colton. She stared at the limb of a pine tree and zeroed in on one single long pointed green needle. She wondered if anyone else in the world had ever laid eyes on that one particular pine needle. Unlikely. It was hers then, one little piece of the Adirondack Mountains that she would engrave in her memory and take with her tomorrow and everywhere she went, for the rest of her life.

She let her vision slide from the pine needle to the limb and then to the tree in its entirety. When she slid back to the needle she couldn't find it. Her body stiffened and she felt a deep sadness that she had so quickly lost the needle in the midst of the limb but then she saw it in her memory just the way she saw it a moment ago. It was secure in her memory and that would do. That was how Colton would be then. Whether she ever came back or not, whether it changed or stayed the same, it was secure in her memory and that would do.

She pulled the covers off and sat up, letting her feet swing off the side of the bed, half excited to get the day going and half reluctant to get the day going. But the day would go whether she sat and swung her feet for a minute or for hours so she might as well join it. She pulled herself out of bed and tip toed to the room Jillian was using. She quietly turned the door handle hoping to find Jillian lying awake in a contemplative mood. The muffled snore reached her ears before the vision of a lump covered completely in blankets reached her eyes. Maggie smiled and tip toed to the bed and stopped at the side. She wasn't surprised to find Jillian completely tucked in like a mummy, she'd always slept with the blankets tucked tightly around her body and head. It was a wonder she hadn't suffocated herself by now. Maggie felt more melancholy than mischievous but even so, this was an opportunity that couldn't be ignored. Fingertips in warm water? But then they'd have to wash the sheets. Face painting? But she'd probably wake if she tried to move the sheets. She stood for a moment longer debating. In the end she just crawled in bed next to her and whispered, "You're my best friend, always were, always will be." And as an afterthought she added, "I forgive you for lying about the Rothko. No amount of drugs would have made me lose my mind that much, but it's yours, not just to enjoy, to have." And then she rolled over and faced the window and fell back asleep staring at the greenery of thousands of pine needles.

When she woke again it wasn't nearly as peaceful and melancholy due to the elbow that jabbed with pain inflicting force into her ribs.

"Ow!" She grabbed her side and sat up and turned to Jillian. "What the hell?"

"Sorry! How the hell was I supposed to know you crawled in bed with me? You could have been a pervert or something!"

"Yeah because perverts sneak into houses and lie down next to beautiful women and fall asleep! Idiot! I think you broke my rib."

"Well your stupid cast slammed my shoulder and I thought it was…I don't know what I thought it was! Why are you in my bed anyway?"

Maggie shook her head and got out of the bed. "I'm going to make coffee, don't fall back asleep it's my last day and I don't want to spend it by myself."

She shouldn't have worried, Jillian didn't let her out of her sight all day, and if Jillian wasn't by her side then Frank or Louise or Pete or Shea were. Saying good-bye to Louise was harder than Maggie would have guessed. Saying good-bye to Frank was even harder. Saying good-bye to Pete and Shea was the hardest.

"Turns out I guess I do like Louise," she told Jillian on their way home. "Seriously I've always loved Louise, you know that, but the last couple years she's been…"

"Different?" Jillian offered.

"Okay, different. I love her, I do, I didn't think I would get teary saying good-bye but," she shrugged. "If you ever figure her out fill me in."

Jillian laughed. "I will. Fill you in I mean, God knows if I'll ever figure her out. I think she's got a story in there somewhere that none of us has ever heard. Maybe someday we'll hear it."

"Not sure I want to." Maggie teased. "So, Frank's a big old teddy bear huh? Did you see how tight he hugged me? I thought I was going to implode."

Jillian laughed again. "He's always been like that, rough on the outside, soft as a stuffed teddy on the inside. I'll tell you what, if you ever need someone that's the man to call. He'd help anyone in a second without a single question or judgment. Pete's going to miss you. Shea too of course but Pete really will."

"Liar. Pete barely knows me. I'm just the fun 'aunt' that sends him toys, but thanks for saying it. Jill? Do you think you guys will come visit us? I mean soon? Like *soon*?!"

Jillian turned her blinker on and pulled to the side of the road. She fished in her purse and came out with her cell phone and punched some numbers in the whole while ignoring Maggie's 'what are we doing?' 'who are you calling?'.

"Hey baby." She said into the phone and Maggie threw her hands in the air, one hand, one cast. "I miss you too. Listen, I know this is odd calling out of the blue for this but do you think we can plan a trip to visit Maggie and Donnie this fall? Perfect! I love you! Can't wait for you to get your butt up here!" She pressed a button on the phone and turned to Maggie, "Thanksgiving. You're cooking."

Maggie lunged to hug her but was comically, and painfully, stopped by the seatbelt. She reached down and pressed the button and lunged again this time successfully grabbing Jillian in a bear hug that rivaled any Frank could ever give out.

Jillian pulled the car back into traffic and did a U-turn.

"What are you doing? Where are we going?"

"To the mall. I'm buying you a new outfit for tomorrow and new bedding for the kids rooms and maybe a toy or two."

"We have bedding. I have an outfit. You have toys."

"Doesn't matter! It's good-bye eve can you think of any better reason to shop? But while we're driving there are two things I need to know, one, how are we ever going to say goodbye and two, you never told me what Donnie said today when you called him."

Maggie laid her head against the headrest. "One, we don't have to say good-bye we just have to say see you at Thanksgiving and two," she lifted her head back up and smiled, "Donnie said he knows we'll probably talk about it sometime but he is willing, wants to, just start new, tomorrow."

"And you?"

"And me."

They smiled at each other and as sure as anyone could be, they were sure that the topic of Mike Jensen and the grades would never contaminate another minute of Donnie and Maggie's lives. They also were sure, as sure as anyone could be, that they would bring it up from time to time, in private, and relive the punching of the face. It was too important to never talk about again. It was the moment that divided before and after.

NAPLES, FLORIDA

Maggie parallel parked between two other SUV's in the school parking lot, something she'd learned and mastered in drivers ed class during her junior year. If she'd only known then what she knew now she could have saved herself years of worry and grief. But it doesn't work that way, you have to live it out moment by moment and day by day.

She wished she could tell Todd that, today on the day of his kindergarten graduation, 'don't worry too much Todd, life has a way of working out just the way it's supposed to, if you can understand and accept that now you'll be a happier person inside'. She could say it but what would be the point? Todd would have to live his life as it unfolded just like everyone else. If he ever understood this concept it would be at some monumental turning point in his life just like it is for everyone else that finally gets it. And really, is that such a bad thing? If we were meant to understand from the beginning what would be the purpose of the middle?

The sight of the stage and the small chairs centered on the narrow rafters seized her heart. This was her fifth time attending a kindergarten graduation, sixth if she counted her own, and yet the anticipation and nerves knocked at her chest as if it were the very first one. This was history in the making, this was one of those key points in everyone's life that lasts forever, everyone remembers their kindergarten graduation.

Maggie nodded and greeted people she passed as she walked down the aisle toward the front. Early bird parents had already filled the first few rows and staff members were rushing here and there with last minute preparations and fixes. She slid in a seat in the fifth row next to a set of parents dressed as if they were attending a royal wedding, first timers she thought and chuckled to herself. She had a sense wash over her of being both a novice and an accomplished expert.

The first thing she did after settling in her seat and greeting the royal family next to her was to open the program and look for Todd's name. And there is was, listed alphabetically and in the same print and font as all the other twenty six but it stuck out much more vividly than the rest. Todd Michael Conners. Pride swept through every ounce of her. My baby. She ran her finger over his name as if it were printed in raised embossed letters which of course it wasn't, not in the literal sense at least, but to her it was.

There was a sudden loud screech and then Pomp and Circumstance began playing over the sound system. Everyone stood and shuffled to turn toward the back where she could see staff members standing guard at the doors like Buckingham Palace. And then she saw them, a line of kindergarteners with caps and tassels standing at each of the two doors. They began to walk down the aisle, grins from ear to ear, boy girl boy girl, practiced but not perfected as they tapped, pushed and bumped into each other. Tears filled her eyes and she had to blink quickly multiple times to clear her vision.

She tried to remember if she felt this incredible level of pride with the other boys and decided she had but this time was more emotional. It was Todd, her baby, her last kindergarten graduation. And there he was! She spotted him as he entered the auditorium, her eyes filled with just Todd and his little cap and tassel and his white button up shirt and black tie and the cowlick in his hair and her heart swelled and ached with love.

He tripped and fell into the girl in front of him who turned around and placed both open hands on his chest and shoved him back. A ripple of snickers escaped from the parents around them but Todd and the girl both continued on as if nothing had happened, grins still plastered from ear to ear.

The graduates made their way to the stage, climbed the stairs and found their assigned places on the rafters without incident. Maggie could almost hear the collective sigh of relief among the teachers and parents. The graduates were oblivious. They sat and smiled and played with their tassels and waited for the ceremony to begin. The principal made his way to the podium and gave a small speech. Two of the kindergarten teachers gave the same speech they probably gave every year, but every single word was heard for the first time and meant something priceless to each of the parents whether it was their first or their fifth time around.

The names were called one by one and the graduates made their way to the podium to accept their diplomas. When Todd's name was called Maggie slid to the edge of her seat and blinked back tears. Todd walked to the podium, accepted his diploma, she snapped a couple quick pictures and he returned to his seat without flaw. It was over in just a few seconds and the next name was called but it wasn't over for Maggie, not really. She knew this moment would remain in her memory forever.

The diplomas were all handed out and the principal instructed the parents when and where to claim their children and then announced the Poinciana Elementary Naples Florida Class of 2028 and every one of the graduates reached up and removed their caps and tossed them in the air. The audience erupted into cheers and laughter. The music started again and the graduates began their exit from the stage and up the aisle to the back of the auditorium to be ushered to the cafeteria where there would be punch and cookies. The parents would meet them there and take them home for the beginning of summer vacation.

The cafeteria was a zoo. Food and drink was spilled and

haphazard efforts were made to retain a semblance of order. Graduates and their younger siblings ran around wildly hopped up on sugar and excitement. Parents and teachers looked the other way, it was graduation after all.

Gradually parents began gathering their kids and their bags of left over kindergarten existence. Maggie helped Todd carry his things and they said their goodbyes to his friends and teachers. They loaded his things into the car and when they were buckled in she turned to him and smiled.

"What now?" She asked him.

"First grade." He answered without having to think about it.

She laughed. "Right. But I mean what *now*?"

"Ice Cream?"

"You know what? I think that's a good idea. And you know what I think would make it a great idea?"

"Sprinkles."

She laughed again. "Right. But I'm thinking maybe we should get Daddy one too and take it to his work?"

He grinned and nodded his head. "Perfect!"

Perfect. It wouldn't always be, she knew that, but right now it was.

"Mom?"

"What Todd?"

"When Pete and Shea come see our pool that's next year right?"

"It will still be this year but it will be next school year."

"How long will they stay?"

"A week."

"But we're staying forever right?"

"Yes Todd. We're staying. Forever."

ABOUT THE AUTHOR

Pam Covert grew up in Colton, New York. She has lived in Western New York for the past twenty seven years but will always think of Colton as "home".

Maggie's Turn is her second novel. Her first novel *And So This Is Christmas* inspired *Maggie's Turn*. She is already listening to the story Louise wants to tell when it's her turn in the third novel which will complete the trilogy of 'The Colton Books'. Unless it doesn't.

Like 'And So This Is Christmas' on Facebook and feel free to post a message to the author.

Both books are available on Amazon.com.

Printed in Great Britain
by Amazon